FLAME AND FURY

KAYLIN WISE

CONTENTS

1

A NEW BATTLE

Daphne peered with caution from behind a wide oak, straining to perceive the two black blurs that had vanished farther into the woods over a minute ago. *Nothing.*

There was no need to track down the dyszoons herself. While they might flee to regroup, the evil creatures never abandoned a fight for long.

"C'mon..." Daphne muttered, ears still ringing with their shrill screams. She bounced on her cold feet, hoping this would help warm them up. "I know you're coming back."

The woods were awakening with the sunrise. Less than an hour ago, she had been half-asleep in a turbulent dream when she sensed the dyszoons come through the Veil. After a hasty change of clothes, Daphne had stumbled into her car and sped to the familiar woods surrounding Laurel Road.

Doubt increased with each uneventful minute. Was waiting the wrong choice? Should she go after the dyszoons?

Daphne hesitated to move. Banishing dyszoons back to Hell had become routine enough that it almost felt easy, but the two she was facing here were different—just blocking them had winded her.

There was little time to dwell on this new problem. First, she needed to get through the battle.

Daphne was beginning to think she had no choice but to go after the dyszoons when a distant, frigid scream pierced her bones. They were back.

"Okay, you can do this," she muttered with a nod of resolve. Her heart fluttered in response.

Daphne leapt out from behind the tree, a vulnerable move she would have hesitated to make even a month ago.

A shapeless black mass the size of a bowling ball rushed at her face with terrifying speed. Caught off guard, Daphne screamed and clumsily struck out with her mind. The dyszoon veered into the nearest tree and flew away, leaving the bark torn apart.

Winded, Daphne leaned against the oak for balance. The impact had been like two bulls clashing heads, one made of steel. Panic that had crept in at the first exchange of blows was creeping into her lungs. It was Halloween night all over again. She wasn't strong enough.

But the many battles over the more than four months since that night had sharpened her abilities. She couldn't have lost all of that progress overnight, which meant these newly arrived dyszoons were somehow more powerful than the rest.

A brush against Daphne's mind gave a moment's warning as a black blur streaked past her right elbow. She straightened, but the dyszoon had already flown out of sight toward the road.

Another blur passed—the missing second dyszoon. Unlike the other, it circled back to attack. Daphne pushed down her panic. These dyszoons might be stronger, but to defeat them, she would just need to strike hard at the right moment. *Easy.*

A blaze of shadow reached for her, and Daphne met its

blow. The dyszoon bounced away, the teeth-clenching impact making her stagger again. A second presence stroked the back of her mind. Without thought, she turned to deflect the other dyszoon, which had decided to rejoin the fight.

Shaking, Daphne held her balance. The creatures were attacking from different angles, and each blow held them back for only seconds. She spun back and forth to deflect them, gasping with the effort.

Worry sank deeper into her skin like the damp cold. She was weak, so weak, against these dyszoons. How long could she really hope to fend them off?

Even in the midst of battle, Daphne recognized the danger she was in. The dyszoons' evil presence was bringing her worst thoughts to the surface. They would seize on any weakness, heighten any despair.

She yelled and struck harder at each dyszoon, relieved to see them pushed farther into the trees. In the pause, an ignored sound from the road drew her attention.

Voices.

Two middle-aged women walked briskly along the road, visible through the bare trees. Daphne's instinct was to hide, but she was deep enough in the woods to be difficult to spot.

One of the dyszoons rushed her. Distracted, she defended herself too late. It blasted against her weak barrier, pushing her backward onto the dead leaves.

Dazed, she sat up and threw out another defense just in time. The dyszoon shrieked as it flew off, though the sound was chillingly gleeful. It rushed her again, spreading out like dense black smoke against the invisible barrier. Daphne grimaced as she held it in place.

In a corner of her awareness, the women chattered brightly in the early morning as something sped in their direction.

The other dyszoon.

Bright panic blinded her. Her worst fear, that the creatures would harm someone else, was moments away from being realized. If the dyszoon reached the women before she could stop it—

The dyszoon near her pummeled her shield, knocking her backward. On the ground, she held it off, only inches from her face. Daphne squeezed her eyes shut in revulsion. Its evil seeped through the barrier like poison.

There was no time to waste. She sped a phantom hand outward, sensing her way to the dyszoon closing in on the women. The other half of her attention strained to keep up a shield as the creature above crashed into it repeatedly, its scream full of wrath.

The other dyszoon was approaching the road. She struck.

It ran into the ground with a shriek, skidding leaves in its wake. Daphne severed the hand and hit back just as the dyszoon threw itself at her barrier. It soared away with a surprised scream.

Daphne struggled to sit up. The dark mass rushed at her.

"No!" she blocked. It was toying with her, drawing her attention from the other dyszoon as it moved toward the defenseless walkers. Then her worst fear would be realized.

The women would feel pain explode wherever they were struck, the cause unseen. While dyszoons couldn't damage humans the same way as their surroundings, they could still injure. The dyszoon would attack while it had strength, torturing them on every side, perhaps enough to kill them.

The dyszoon near the road swung around. Daphne reached out an invisible hand in desperation, but the creature by her attacked. The hand crumbled.

Panic rose with each blow. After months of keeping the dyszoons from harming others, here was finally a battle she couldn't win. The dyszoon would keep her distracted until it was too late.

No! she screamed silently, pushing it far into the trees. In the pause, Daphne reached through the woods and struck the other one.

The creature veered off course. It would only be delayed only a minute.

The nearest dyszoon pounded her barrier much like bulls charging one after another. As Daphne withstood its attacks, a realization electrified her. The only way to save the women was to defeat this dyszoon first. And there were only seconds to do so.

Daphne pushed outward. The dyszoon billowed like a dark storm cloud, and she attacked it again.

I will never—

Her blows came heavy.

Ever—

Its resistance felt weaker that time.

Let the dyszoons hurt someone—

The other would reach the women any moment.

Again.

Daphne dealt her final blow. The dyszoon shattered into a black cloud.

She whipped a phantom hand through the trees. The creature was just feet from the road—

The hand struck like a lightning bolt, and the last dyszoon dissolved instantly. It was gone.

Daphne's knees wobbled, and she propped herself against the nearest tree, not wanting to lie on the wet ground voluntarily. She ran a hand through her dark hair, startled when dead leaves fell out of it. The oblivious women's voices carried on, fading as they crossed the road and headed in the other direction.

Her eyes closed. *That was too close.* It was the closest call she'd had so far. Usually, there was little traffic on Laurel Road. The women were ambitious walkers.

The battle over, Daphne realized how cold her feet were. She checked the time on her phone—thirty minutes until school started.

A full day ahead. Weariness swept over her. The memory of the dyszoon strikes pounded faintly in her temple. Or, more likely, that was the start of a headache.

Daphne opened her chat with Claire to warn the psychic. They could discuss the battle and why these dyszoons were so much stronger than—

A chill cut through her as if winter had returned with the flick of a switch. Terrible silence encased every leaf, pushed into her veins, stilled her heart—

"No…" Daphne bent over, clutching her frozen head. It couldn't be—

Sound exhaled over the stirring trees. Daphne unstuck her feet and sprinted to her car. The women were distant dots in the rearview mirror. She fumbled with the key. *No, no, no.*

The car started. She drove the last mile toward the Veil, stunned out of all thought except denial.

She reached the hillcrest and parked, staring aghast at the black circle in the sky that was the Veil, the portal that made it possible for dyszoons to travel from Hell. Since its expansion on Halloween, she and Claire had handled the creatures like clockwork as though nothing would change.

Now, the Veil had doubled in size.

2

COMPLICATIONS

Screams rang in Daphne's ears from a great distance, as if from far beneath the earth. Or perhaps that was the sound of blood rushing from her face.

Not today.

The Veil hung out of reach above the center of the stone bridge. A black pupil, staring at her. Unremarkable on the surface, yet terror-inspiring.

The hard battle that morning had been the first sign something was wrong. She hadn't had time to think about it. About what it meant.

Weakened by its journey through the Veil, a dyszoon never arrived at full strength. But today, their path was easier. Daphne pictured the two creatures worming through a long tunnel that had been widened except for the final segment before the Veil, which was the entrance. She hadn't sensed the change taking place until the work was unmistakably complete.

From now on, she and Claire could expect trickier battles and possibly—an echo of the chill returned—more close calls.

But why did the Veil expand today, when it hadn't changed since Halloween? Was Ashley behind it?

Daphne felt the usual sickly unease at the thought of her former classmate, who she hadn't seen since that night. Ashley, who had abilities like her and Claire and was the tool of a powerful demon, had widened the dormant Veil permanently and made it possible for dyszoons to arrive at any time. The latest change proved that the demon hadn't given up on its ambition to reach Earth.

What had it forced Ashley to do these past few months? Daphne imagined her tied to a chair, screaming as a shadowy figure drew blood for some terrible ritual that would connect her further to the Veil.

She shuddered, reminding herself that Ashley had done her work willingly. Even so, Daphne suspected that someone had manipulated her to believe the demon's lies.

Her eyes dropped to the bridge, the last place they'd spoken. *It's going to bring a new order,* Ashley had spat before the demon, its power reaching from Hell, possessed her body. It spoke to Daphne and tried to entice her to join its cause. When it left and Ashley collapsed, a shadowed figure had scooped her into a truck and fled.

No matter, the demon told Daphne at her refusal. *I can still use the girl.*

With a last uneasy look at the Veil, she turned her car around and drove to school.

Daphne dumped her backpack into her locker and shivered out of her dry spare coat. To her disappointment, Claire hadn't yet responded to her text explaining the change in the dyszoons.

Putting her phone away, she twisted the cap off a bottle of vending machine coffee. Coffee worsened her nightmares, but the battle had made the extra caffeine necessary. Daphne took a sip and winced, preferring her usual chai tea. *Necessary.*

A group of seniors moved away from the lockers, granting her an unobstructed view down the hallway. Nathan was pinned against his locker. Veronica, her highlighted blonde hair cascading glamorously down her back, gazed up at him flirtatiously. They were holding hands.

She ignored the expected pang in her chest and looked away. As if she needed to feel any worse…

"Hey, how are you?" Beth, a fellow senior with cropped red hair, interrupted her dark thoughts with a surprise visit. No one usually stopped at her locker for a chat.

Daphne relived the entire morning and decided on the only truthful answer to the question. "Pretty tired, actually. What's up?" Although she considered Beth a friend, or at least friendly, she doubted the visit was without purpose.

"I was wanting to check—are you still interested in joining Stage Crew?"

"Stage—" Daphne cast back in thought and finally recalled chatting about Drama Club at lunch a month ago, in mid-February. Beth was helping to build the set for the next production. "Did the musical start already?"

"Rehearsals have been going on for a while. We started building the sets but could use some more people, if you wanted to join."

Over Beth's shoulder, Daphne saw Veronica lean close to Nathan's face. "Yeah, I do," she decided on the spot. "I don't have a lot of building experience, though."

A memory came to mind. She was a kid, holding screws for her dad as he replaced a rotted porch step.

"That doesn't matter." Beth waved a hand dismissively. "There's something for everyone to do."

Daphne banished the memory. "I'll stop by after school today," she promised.

"Great! See you then," Beth said, and left for class.

As a distraction from looking in Nathan's direction, Daphne checked her phone. There was no message from Claire, just a "Have a good morning, sweetie! Sorry I missed you!" text from her mom.

Daphne wondered how she was doing, the day being what it was. Her eyes flicked to the silver owl bracelet on her wrist, its furrowed brow. If not for the dyszoons, she would have been able to ask.

Her mom luckily never raised questions if her daughter's car was sometimes absent from the driveway in the mornings. On colder days, Daphne liked to go for calming drives after a nightmare instead of walking in the woods. Now the habit was a good cover story for dyszoon battles.

Loneliness pierced Daphne at seeing a nearby group of friends. The minutes until the bell were long. She often tried to arrive as close as possible to the start of class to avoid the pressure of finding someone to talk to. The extra time only made it clear how distant she had become from everyone not worried about dyszoons.

Even Jessica wasn't an option, since she was most likely with her new boyfriend, Zeke. Besides, their friendship had cooled to the point where Daphne could no longer say they were best friends.

At least she invited me to her party, Daphne thought grimly. Jessica's eighteenth birthday party was next Friday, and it would be their first hangout since Christmas break. But it fell on Daphne's mom's birthday, and she kept forgetting to bring it up at home.

Her phone dinged. To her relief, the text was from Claire.

Ok. Meet?

Daphne deflated slightly at the brief message. She was eager for a response that matched her alarm over the new size of the Veil—at least a few exclamation points. However, it was true that Claire's messages were usually brief. The psychic, who was in her sixties, preferred a phone call.

She typed out a suggestion to meet after school, but paused, remembering her promise to attend Stage Crew. But wasn't the Veil more important? The demon she'd spoken to on the bridge had promised her, through Ashley, that its "inferior" would pave its way. What if the latest change meant that the lesser demon was that much closer to being able to travel through the Veil—or that it was on its way?

But honestly, was there anything they could do? The months hadn't brought a solution to the demon problem. At most, they could discuss how to manage the stronger dyszoons.

Her reason for joining Stage Crew was to have something to do besides schoolwork and battling dyszoons, which had taken priority. Uncle Lloyd had given her some advice during his Christmas visit that she hoped to take to heart.

You're always going to have responsibilities, so don't wait for them to end before you can have some fun, he'd told her. *You're not going to see most of your classmates after you graduate. Take advantage of the opportunities you have now while you can, and don't worry so much.*

Daphne revised her text. *I can't after school. Call tonight?*

Not expecting an immediate reply, she put away her phone. The bell rang, and she looked up just in time to see Veronica and Nathan kiss each other goodbye. She sipped more coffee and winced. *You have bigger things to worry about.*

The crowd moved. As if to prove her point, a shade she hadn't seen since before winter break came into view. Heather wore her usual long-sleeved shirt and leggings. Her darkly lined eyes weren't on her younger brother, Nathan, but on Daphne.

Caught off guard, Daphne stared back. Although she was used to shades, Heather unnerved her. Perhaps that was because the shade was the first dead person she'd truly seen. That encounter had led her to seek out Claire, a meeting that changed everything.

She'd hoped that Heather's long absence meant that the shade had moved on and was satisfied that Nathan had found happiness after mourning her death in a car wreck. A wreck that, unknown to anyone but Daphne and Claire, had been caused by dyszoons.

Daphne assumed he was happy, anyway. They only talked on the way to class after lunch, besides messaging now and then. It was too brief a glimpse to know otherwise. But he had his *girlfriend* to make him happy.

Even so, Heather had remained, which meant she was still concerned about her brother. What was more, she had reappeared on the day the Veil expanded, of all days. That couldn't be a coincidence.

"Hey, Daphne."

She yelped, not expecting the subject of her thoughts to appear. "Hi. Sorry. I'm jumpy," she told Nathan, flustered. Heather disappeared behind another group of students.

"Yeah? Any reason?" Nathan grinned, apparently in a good mood. He leaned casually against the locker next to hers, as if they had all the time in the world.

"I don't know," Daphne lied, trying not to imagine him in Veronica's embrace. "I had coffee."

"One of those mornings?"

She met his hazel eyes with a small smile, hoping the thrill that shot through her at the contact hadn't shown on her face. His eyes were twins of Heather's, but otherwise, the two siblings didn't look much alike. Heather's hair was forever in a thick dark bob, while Nathan's was dusty brown and wavy, stuck up at the front in a way that made Daphne want to run a hand through it.

Instead, she self-consciously ran a hand over her own. A small leaf fell to the ground.

"Yeah, definitely," she answered, unable to think of anything normal to say on a morning that had already seen a dyszoon battle, a Veil expansion, and now the reappearance of Heather. "Anyway...I'd better get to class."

"See you after lunch," Nathan said easily, pushing off the locker with a shoulder. "Have a good one."

Heather watched Nathan with a mournful expression as he passed. Shaking her head, Daphne began walking to class and sidestepped her history teacher, Mr. Burnes, who almost bowled her over as he strode around the corner. She muttered an apology.

Daphne arrived at her Advanced Photography class and sat at a computer. Heather had added another complication to her morning, and though her other problem was more important, she couldn't easily cast the shade aside. When the Veil had opened briefly last August and let two dyszoons through, Heather had died. Her continued presence in the realm of the living was a reminder of what would happen if Daphne failed to keep the dyszoons in check.

Perhaps that was why she'd reappeared. The Veil was a threat to her brother as much as anyone else.

The short conversation with Nathan replayed in her mind. Daphne was annoyed by how much she had enjoyed even that brief time. But had she been too distant, afraid of letting her feelings for him slip? The space between her and others was like a wide chasm—one that admittedly had existed before she could see spirits—but the Veil had stretched it beyond any hope of crossing.

It doesn't matter. He's with her, Daphne reminded herself.

That they still talked even after he started going out with Veronica, that he sought her out at all, was a rusted silver lining. If only her thoughts could *stay* at friends...

Thankfully, she would have another opportunity to chat with him later after lunch. Their brief walk, the highlight of her day, was followed by her least favorite hour, with Mr. Burnes.

Her phone lit up with a message from Claire. *Meeting tomorrow is fine.*

Daphne typed back her acceptance just as the second bell rang. If the psychic had insisted, she would have skipped attending Stage Crew. The fact that Claire was in no hurry meant she had reached the same frustrating conclusion as Daphne—there was nothing they could do about the Veil.

Uncle Lloyd was right. She might as well do something *fun*. Since Halloween, her focus had been the Veil at the expense of everything else. She didn't have a job, because what if a dyszoon arrived while she was working? And clubs were out— how could she abruptly leave the meetings? Claire kept watch during school hours for any dyszoons, but the evenings were Daphne's responsibility.

Stage Crew was flexible. She was free to come and go, and it might be a way to fill in the chasm between herself and others. It could be the one part of her life that was normal—as normal as it could be with spirits and demons.

Anyway, it was a start.

3

A PHANTOM OF THE STAGE

After school, Daphne walked one of the hallways that led to the lunchroom, stopping halfway to descend a flight of stairs.

The door at the bottom was open, and she emerged next to a brightly lit stage. Hundreds of cushioned seats took up most of the vast space, sloping upward in neat rows.

She dropped her backpack into a front-row seat and glanced around for Beth. Students were building the framework of a wall on a rolling platform, but there was no sign of her.

A small freshman girl hunched over a clipboard at the edge of the stage. Daphne waited her turn to sign in and then followed the girl as she approached a middle-aged man who was supervising a boy at a saw. He pointed at a wide opening in the back corner of the stage, and the girl moved on.

Daphne hurried forward to introduce herself before he became occupied again.

"Hi, this is my first time," she said nervously over a burst of drilling nearby. "What do I—"

"They're just hauling some wood up. Could probably use a

hand," the man said with a raised voice, adjusting his safety glasses. "Follow that young lady down the ramp and you'll see 'em."

Daphne mimicked the girl's path and discovered it led to a long concrete ramp that was painted from floor to ceiling with show posters signed by the casts. Although tempted to look these over, she continued down the ramp and reached a large room stuffed with old props and set pieces.

The open door at the other end explained the chilly breeze. To her relief, she recognized the person standing in the doorframe.

"You made it!" Beth said cheerfully at her approach.

Daphne smiled. "The guy upstairs said we're hauling up some wood?"

"That's the technical director, Mr. Heigelman. We're grabbing some from the scrap bin out here so we can build the dining room set."

She held open the door for a sophomore boy and the freshman girl Daphne had followed. Between them, they carried a flat piece of wood with strips of floral wallpaper still attached to it.

"That was from *Arsenic and Old Lace*," Beth pointed out. "I helped build the set last year." She kicked a piece of scrap wood into the doorframe to keep it propped open.

Daphne followed her outside. Two chatty sophomore girls stood next to what looked like a dumpster. A senior classmate who was vaguely familiar stood knee-deep inside it, wearing a brown T-shirt that advertised a past show. He slid a piece of wood over the edge.

"Hey! Servants!" he yelled at the sophomores. "Get your butts over here and unload."

"Loosen up, Chad. *Jeez*," one of them shot back.

"Oof, this is heavy," said the other, grabbing an end.

"Hey! No complaining," he said. "This is character-building!" He tucked dark, curly hair behind his ears, revealing a cloud of acne.

"Why are you so *mean?*"

Daphne got out of the way. The two girls kicked open the door, giggling as the wood struck the doorframe. "Hurry up, I'm cold!" one said.

Chad slid the next board out. "Careful," he told Beth, apparently calmer in her presence. He stopped, noticing Daphne. "Hey, is this a newbie? Who are you?"

She shrank a bit at his energy. They were in the same year, but she felt like a tiny freshman.

"I'm Daphne," she said, trying to sound confident. "I just started Stage Crew."

"Oh, good. We need more *sane* people around here."

Daphne smiled awkwardly but said nothing. She saw ghosts, after all. Chad resumed handing over the wood, and she helped Beth carry it to the door, which the returning freshman girl helpfully opened.

"How long have you been on Stage Crew?" Daphne asked, walking backward up the ramp. If the Drama Club was going to be fun, she needed to get to know others. Beth had always struck her as more mature, and she regretted that they weren't better friends.

"Since fall of freshman year," Beth said. "I was in the chorus of the musical that year, but that was the only time I was an actor. I can show you my name on the poster when we go back down."

The lights glared down at them harshly as they reentered the stage area. Daphne strained her eyes against the powerful beams. A catwalk system she hadn't noticed before stretched high across the stage, hidden from audience view by a fringe of gold curtain. The idea of being tasked with climbing up there to adjust the lighting made her shudder inwardly.

Daphne did a double-take. Someone *was* up there—a student, his hands spaced widely apart on the railing, was calmly observing the activity below. He wore an oversize brown suit, and his blonde hair was groomed into waves.

Her grip on the board had gone slack, and she almost dropped it. "Oops, sorry," she said to Beth, readjusting.

She squinted upward again. The student—unmistakably a shade, judging by the curling mist rising from his arms—met her eyes with a hard-to-read expression. If she had to guess, it was disdain.

They set the board down on a nearby pile. Now that Daphne was aware of the shade, his presence was obvious, like a cool touch on the back of her mind that had unconsciously drawn her to look up.

Daphne returned downstairs with Beth. Perhaps she shouldn't be surprised there was another school haunting besides Heather. Thousands of students, plus hundreds of teachers and staff, had passed through the halls over the decades. In a way, it was a wonder there weren't *more* shades— that she had encountered so far, anyway.

But who was he, and why was he haunting the theater? A student wouldn't be wearing a suit, so it was likely a costume. If he was a former actor, when did he die? She couldn't draw him to herself and ask questions while other people were around.

You're not here for shades, Daphne told herself. Yet, her curiosity burned.

"Oh, hang on, I was going to show you my name," Beth said, pivoting. They maneuvered around set furniture and stacks of props until they reached a painted section on the opposite wall. The poster of *Oklahoma!* was much smaller than the older ones inside the ramp.

She pointed to a signature in permanent marker. "There I am."

An idea came to Daphne. As a longtime member of Drama Club, would Beth know about the death of a student actor? If she had a name, confirming his identity would be simple enough—unless the club had a long list of tragic deaths in its history.

"Cool," she said, brainstorming how to get on the topic of tragic actor deaths without being weird. "Was it fun?"

Beth shrugged, unenthusiastic. "It was an okay experience, I guess, but I prefer Stage Crew."

As they returned to the scrap bin outside, Daphne decided on a natural follow-up question that, with any luck, would lead to the topic indirectly. "Did something go wrong? Like, during the performance?"

"No, I don't remember anything happening during *Oklahoma!*, at least nothing the audience would notice. A girl ripped her dress and needed a safety pin at the last minute, which wasn't a big deal."

"Has anything major ever gone wrong?" Daphne continued casually. If Beth could remember something in Drama Club's history that went not only wrong, but tragically so...

"I don't think so. Oh, wait!" Beth added suddenly as they waited for Chad to lift over the next board. "During the play last year, a portrait fell down right in the middle of a scene. It was really embarrassing."

"It just fell off the wall?" Daphne said. The incident wasn't as dramatic as a death, but it was suspicious. "What did the actors do?"

"Everyone froze, and then they just carried on with the scene," Beth said. "The director wasn't happy afterward. She said they should have picked it up and ad-libbed something, so that it wasn't so obvious."

"Why did it fall?" Daphne asked. Was the fall caused by a loose nail, or was the shade making itself known? She hadn't thought that shades could maliciously interfere with their surroundings—though Heather had once knocked over Nathan's books to give Daphne an opening to talk to him.

"*Because*," Chad broke in unexpectedly. He knelt inside the bin, resting an arm on his knee. "We didn't light the freaking *candle* before the performance."

"Candle?" Daphne looked at Beth.

"We always light this special candle before a performance," she explained. "It's tradition."

"What's it for?"

"It's for appeasing the spirit!" Chad said energetically. "You have to acknowledge it and ask for its blessing so it doesn't mess with anything."

"If you forget your lines or a prop goes missing right before you need it, it's the spirit's fault," Beth explained.

"There's a stage spirit?" Daphne wasn't planning to mention that she had seen it.

"Yeah, he's our friendly phantom. His name's Michael."

Daphne raised her eyebrows. "You named it?"

"*I* didn't name it. We just know who it is. Hang on, I'll show you." Chad leapt out of the bin with finesse and marched toward the door. "Follow me, newbie."

"Wait, I need a board!" whined a sophomore girl.

"Get it yourself, minion!" he yelled over his shoulder.

Daphne followed his long strides up the ramp. He stopped before a black section with a painted couple, the poster for *Specter*. The performers and crew had signed their names in white, some more successfully than others.

"We call *this* the Lost Musical. The lead actor died the week before the performance," he said, pointing a finger at a signature. Daphne leaned forward to read the handwriting.

The letters were twice as large as most of the others. *Michael Buza.*

"See? Michael. He's the ghost."

"What happened to him?" Daphne straightened, thankful that Chad had answered her unspoken question about deaths in Drama Club. The shade might be Michael, or else his untimely death served as a convenient story for superstitious actors needing a scapegoat.

"Legend says he fell from the catwalk, or that he hung himself from it."

"That can't be true," Beth protested. "That would *not* happen." Daphne agreed silently.

Chad shrugged. "That's what I heard happened. And now he'll be angry that we're doing this musical again."

"*This* musical?" Daphne said, pointing at the poster.

"Yes, for the first time in thirty years. It got canceled after Michael died."

"No one tried to put on the show until now?"

"No, Miss Rand—"

"—the director—" Beth interjected.

"—said that the writer just gave up on it. It was a total disaster that he died right before opening night," he nodded. "But Miss Rand reached out a few times to her, and she's giving it another chance."

"Is it any good?"

Chad shrugged. "I like it, but I'm biased." His head whipped toward the two sophomore girls, who were carrying up another board. "Hey! You there! Who said you could take my wood?"

As he went to tell them off, Beth explained, "Chad's the lead actor."

"Really?" The news surprised Daphne, though Chad did seem like an actor type. "Shouldn't he be at rehearsal?"

"They meet at four. Chad's involved in pretty much every-thing in Drama Club."

They reached the outside bin. "We might as well wait for him, unless you think you can climb in," Beth said.

"I'm fine with waiting. He'll probably yell at us."

"Oh, he only yells at underclassmen," Beth reassured her.

They hauled a few more loads of wood, and then Chad left for rehearsal. Daphne joined Beth for their next assignment at the growing dining room wall, more or less handing over screws as others who had more experience took over the woodcutting and assembly. Daphne's memory of doing a similar task for her dad came to mind. While busy, she had forgotten what day it was.

The shade's eyes pressed on her neck, but Daphne avoided looking up. Was he Michael Buza, an actor who had died before getting to perform his big part? Maybe it was because of his haughty expression, but Daphne was reluctant to seek him out face-to-face.

Besides, she had enough to worry about. Did she really want to pursue Michael's story when she couldn't even help Heather? After all, Stage Crew was supposed to be a *break* from anything supernatural.

As she signed out an hour later, Daphne glanced once more up at the catwalk. Michael, or whoever he was, was looking down at her. His expression was grim.

Even if she avoided him, he would always be there. A phantom of the stage.

4

———————

HIDEOUT

As she drove home, it occurred to Daphne that there was another benefit to joining Stage Crew.

After-school dyszoon battles were rare, but she could use the club as a handy excuse if she wasn't home before her mom finished work.

At least I don't have to lie tonight, Daphne thought gratefully as the first porch step sagged beneath her feet. The hands that had replaced it years ago were long gone.

She removed her jacket in the entryway and brushed off the sawdust clinging to her shirt.

"Oh good, you're home!" her mom called cheerfully from the kitchen. A fluffy black cat came to greet Daphne and flopped on the floor, her bell collar jingling. Relieved that her mom seemed to be in a good mood, Daphne scratched Mystique behind the ears and then headed to the kitchen.

"You look tired. Long day?" her mom said, removing a pan of black bean burgers from the oven.

Daphne shrugged. "Yeah, I guess so. Stage Crew."

"How was that? Did you like it?"

"I think so. I didn't do any building, but I'll keep going."

"Good," her mom said with a firm nod of approval that Daphne suspected came from worry.

Was her lack of a life outside of school so obvious? True, she hadn't spent time with friends outside of school for a long time, but her mom didn't know that, or anything about her abilities. Jessica's house was a ready excuse whenever Daphne needed to head to the Veil. For that reason, she could no longer vent about their failing friendship.

It's better she doesn't know. Mom would just worry all the time, if she even believed me—which she probably wouldn't.

Even so, she couldn't deny that a distance existed between them because of Daphne's secret. They were technically as close as ever, but being unable to share what felt like a second life had taken its toll.

The thought of Jessica reminded Daphne to bring up the birthday party next Friday as they sat down to eat. She was glad that this time, at least, the invitation was real.

"Would you be offended if I go, since it's your birthday?" Daphne asked. While she was trying to regain some form of a social life, she felt torn about attending the party. A dyszoon could emerge from the Veil, and it would be awkward to excuse herself early.

"I won't be offended," her mom said. "I might cry a little, but I won't be offended."

Daphne knew she was only joking. "I'll let Jessica know I'll be there," she said, rehearsing the party in her head. Maybe if a dyszoon came out, she could tell everyone that she had to leave early because of birthday plans with her mom that she'd forgotten to mention. Or else, pretend to get sick. If a dyszoon arrived, what choice would she have? Claire was working.

"So, how was...how was your visit?" Daphne asked, though she didn't want to hear about it. Guilt gnawed at her for not visiting her dad's grave on the anniversary of his death, but she knew her mom understood and didn't mind.

"It was nice. I laid some flowers and spent a little time," her mom said with a small, reflective smile. The visits had always been good for her. Daphne, however, had avoided her father's grave since they buried him when she was thirteen.

"Oh. Good."

"Did you want to see a picture of it?" Her mom reached for her phone.

"No," Daphne said instantly. Recovering, she added, "I mean, I don't think I really—no. But thanks."

Her mom nodded, unoffended, for which Daphne felt a rush of gratitude. His grave was the key to unlocking memories of that tumultuous time. She wasn't ready to face them. Maybe never would be.

Four years ago, their world had blown apart into shrapnel. They had slowly pieced it back together into some semblance of normalcy, but there was no filling the void her dad had left. It simply existed, and they carried on the best they could.

Daphne changed the subject back to Stage Crew and the return of the canceled musical. After they finished dinner, she left to do homework upstairs, wishing she could have unloaded her worries about the growing Veil and discussed the shade in the theater. There was so much that she couldn't confide in her mom about.

She reached the top step. Phillip, a shade who'd been killed on D-Day, gazed into the mirror at the end of the hallway. Despite being unable to see his reflection, it was his favorite spot, as if the mirror offered a window into years past. Daphne wished she could help him move on, but he had stayed behind for his dying wife, and she was long gone.

She opened her laptop and turned on the desk lamp in her bedroom. She wanted to research everything about Michael

Buza, but doing so would lead her down a rabbit hole from which she might not emerge for hours. Homework had to take priority in case a dyszoon interrupted the evening.

An hour later, Daphne realized she had been staring at the same blank line in her French workbook for some time. She liked the language but had to admit that she was far from fluent even after three years of studying. Maybe she should work on her English essay instead...

Her phone dinged with a message. Daphne expected to see Claire's name, although they had already confirmed their meeting time tomorrow.

It was Nathan. She smiled. His messages were usually a video he had found interesting or a picture of a photo he had developed at home in his darkroom. This time, it was a cat reel and a message.

How's your night going?

She watched the video and replied: *I love that cat. Doing homework atm. You?*

Same. Track practice went late today.

Daphne pictured him at a desk in an imaginary room. Once, he had offered to show her his camera collection at his house. He'd been over to hers only once, to study. Then Veronica had happened.

She glanced at the time; it was past eight. Fatigue settled like fog over her brain, and the soft blanket and pillow on her bed were inviting.

Resigning herself to finish her French homework, Daphne ignored the itch to send Nathan another message. Even when the topic was mundane, she liked talking to him, thinking about each interaction more than necessary and imagining herself by his locker in the morning—

Focus.

The minutes crawled by. Her pen paused, stuck on the

correct answer. A stuffed purple owl perched at the corner of her desk watched her with overlarge eyes. Nathan had won it for her at the Halloween carnival the night she'd been forced to leave to fight dyszoons while Veronica swooped in and sank her claws into him.

Was it pathetic how much she enjoyed spending time—any time—with Nathan? Despite his relationship, she considered him a good friend, though one that came with extra restrictions. Maybe it would have been best if they had remained acquaintances, saying hello in the hallway but nothing more.

It didn't help that after he and Veronica got together, he had acted the same as always. After lunch, they took the same short walk together even though his girlfriend was in the same history class as Daphne. She assumed Veronica hurried ahead in order to have time to chat with her junior friend before the bell rang, and she wasn't going to ask questions.

Her phone dinged. Daphne immediately grabbed it and read the notification on the screen.

This homework thing isn't going well.

She laughed, then set the phone back down. If she didn't finish, she would regret it in the morning.

With sheer force of will, Daphne returned and worked for several more minutes, the desire to respond growing with each line she completed. Finally, when she could resist it no longer, she messaged back.

Need some help?

His response came back right away.

No, I just like to complain.

Daphne laughed. Another message came in.

I miss our study time.

Her heart skipped a beat. What did that mean? That had been months ago. Was he missing *her*?

Daphne reeled her thoughts in. *It doesn't mean what you*

want it to, she told her loneliness sternly. There was no reason to read anything into the comment, especially nothing that hinted at something more than friends. He probably just meant it would be more fun to study with another person. In general.

Good times, Daphne wrote back and set the phone on silent, then upside down. Not, *So do I,* however true it was. She couldn't admit to that, not when he wasn't hers.

The fleeting sense of connection that came with the messages faded away, leaving something unpleasantly empty in its place.

Daphne often repeated to herself that she could be content just being friends. But for many reasons, this wasn't true. Being just friends limited their time together. If he wasn't at track practice, he was no doubt making time for his girlfriend.

She reached the end of the page and turned it over. There was a paragraph to write in French, based on a prompt. Daphne glanced at the clock, the time now past 8:30 p.m. Fatigue pulled her eyelids down. No, she would carry on. There was just this small section left.

Her vision blurred. *Just this small section.*

Daphne's face connected with the paper.

She clutched her books tightly to her chest next to a row of lockers, trying to stay calm as she faced him. School would begin soon, but the hallway was empty. It was the perfect time to tell him.

"I like you, Nathan. More than just a friend."

Nathan rubbed the back of his head. He looked extremely uncomfortable.

"I'm sorry, Daphne, I just don't feel that way."

A black circle slipped into existence behind her like a spinning storm cloud.

"Besides, why would he, when he's got me?" Veronica, glamorous in a short dress and heels, stepped in and slipped an arm around him. He beamed at her.

"I'm sorry. I-I just wanted you to know." Daphne was nauseated as Veronica ran a hand through his wavy hair. "Are you sure?"

"Look, it's really cute that you said something, but we're just not going to work," he said in a very un-Nathan-like tone, as if she were an annoying underclassman who was now getting on his nerves. "I think we should just go our separate ways."

Her stomach squeezed tightly. "I thought we were friends. Good friends." The black void was almost her height.

Pity crossed his face. "Look, we don't even hang out. I think you've read into things a little."

"But—"

"Hey, he's telling you to go away. Don't be weird," Veronica said pointedly. "Bye!" She gave a little wave and kissed him on the cheek.

The hallway was suddenly full of an army of girls like Veronica. They stared Daphne down, full lips curled in disdain. Their heels clicked on the floor in unison as the storm cloud grew across the hallway. How comforting it would be just to vanish into it, to slip away entirely from the stares.

Nathan was gazing into Veronica's eyes. Her worst-case scenario was reality. She had been honest, and now they were no longer even friends. He had always meant more to her than she had to him.

Daphne stepped back into the unfeeling void as the girls closed in. The blackness swallowed her.

She peered into the darkness, searching for something hidden between the wisps of fog without quite knowing what it was.

The smooth ground turned to grass, bone-dry beneath her bare feet. A small world cocooned in the endless dark.

Light came softly as the sky turned a sickly peach color. A scattering of large stones appeared—a graveyard without end.

Every plot was freshly turned. Daphne kept wandering, ignoring the names etched into the stones. There was one, in particular, that she needed to find. She would know it on sight.

The fog parted, revealing a small stone structure with a gently sloped roof. Golden snakes were etched on its shiny black doors. Above them was a name engraved in tall, white letters: *William Cole Jr.*

Bracing herself, Daphne pulled on the handle of the mausoleum and stepped inside.

The graveyard vanished. Instead of a small room of stone, she stood on a tattered woven rug in a one-room cabin. To her left came the sound of a hand brushing over paper.

"Ashley!" she cried, backing up against the closed front door in shock.

Ashley didn't look up. She sat cross-legged on a bed in a corner, face hidden by uncombed and greasy dark hair. Her pencil drew busily over the pad of paper on her lap, redoing lines just erased.

"Ashley?" Daphne said again, taking in her appearance for the first time since Halloween.

She looked much the same and unharmed, to Daphne's relief. A black sweatshirt, the same as the one she'd worn that night, swallowed her frame.

Daphne took in the room and its outdated wood paneling. Judging by the dust and dirt, plus a general air of unkemptness, it had been a long time since the cabin was used.

The light from the grimy windows was dim. No lightbulb was overhead, just a battery-powered lamp on a card table propped next to the bed. A portable gas-powered cooking stove lay on a small counter nearby that overflowed with canned food, boxes of pasta, and granola bars. More stacks of cartons were on the floor.

Daphne approached the window. There was no snow outside. Freshly fallen leaves covered the woods, the spidery tree branches stretching into the sky.

She frowned. There were etchings in the wooden window frame, and she ran a finger over one of the strange symbols—a star inside a circle, crudely carved. Symbols of various sizes filled every inch of the cheap wood, like the hasty vandalism of initials on a park bench.

Daphne backed away from the wall, an unpleasant sensation crawling up her spine. The hint of danger. She looked up. Squiggly symbols covered the ceiling from edge to edge. Had Ashley made them? Daphne glanced at her classmate, doubting this. Surely, Ashley would have carved the markings with more artistic finesse.

Someone sighed behind her. Daphne jumped and turned toward the previously unnoticed figure sitting in a dark corner of the cabin.

A tall man slouched in an uncomfortable-looking wooden chair, arms crossed. He wore an old plaid coat and a baseball hat low over his face. Dejection and frustration moved like waves of stale air across the room.

Though confident that the man couldn't see her, Daphne moved toward him slowly, as if a sudden movement might shatter her invisibility. Familiarity itched at her, but she couldn't place him.

He sighed again.

Ashley threw her pencil down. "*What?*"

The man rubbed a hand over his face and lifted his cap to run it over his hair. Daphne froze at the sight of his unshaven face. A roaring sensation filled her ears, so she almost didn't hear his next words. The room blurred.

"It's been two weeks since we've heard from it. There's been *nothing*."

Ashley picked up her pencil again. "I'm sure it's just busy or something." Her tone was casual, but by its quietness, Daphne thought it was deliberately so. Ashley seemed perfectly fine with the absence of the demon's communications.

The man stood up suddenly. "And you're sure you haven't seen anything? Anything at all?"

"No." Ashley narrowed her eyes when he covered his face and screamed in frustration. "Hey, chill! It's not my fault it doesn't want to talk."

He paced. "We should have heard something. *You* should have heard something." He stopped. "Maybe we need to connect you further..."

Ashley paled.

"I don't think there's any need for that." Her hand tightened around the sharp pencil.

"Then you need to try harder!"

She bristled with anger. Daphne supposed if Ashley could summon lightning bolts, they would have appeared above her head. "Well, it's a little difficult!"

"Then *try!*" He kicked over a stack of food that crashed to the floor. Ashley flinched. "Don't you *understand?* We cannot. Fail. Got it?"

He turned away, rubbing the dark stubble on his face. "If only I could have taken the lead...It would have risen by now."

Ashley's face blotched. "You can't even see spirits, so whatever. *Derek.*"

He turned, assessing her with disdain. "It's right," he murmured. "We would be better off with the other one."

Now Ashley whitened in rage. But their surroundings were

dissolving into smoke, and her reply was lost, distorted in collapsing reality. Daphne had the sensation of falling in all directions, and then—

She awoke at her desk, cheek plastered against her French workbook. Abruptly, Daphne straightened, then regretted it as her stiff neck protested. Her heart was hammering. Claire—she needed to tell her. Would the psychic be up yet? Did she just have the same dream and was puzzling over who the man was?

Daphne checked the time, ignoring a message that had come from Nathan several hours ago. A quarter after one. Likely not, then. She fumbled to open their chat and typed out the essentials, stumbling over her fingers to send each sentence out as fast as possible.

I had a vision.

I know who was in the truck that took Ashley.

She paused, disbelief still thundering in her ears.

It was my history teacher.

Mr. Burnes.

5

AGE OF ANXIETY

Daphne stared at the bedroom ceiling in shock.

It was him. It was Mr. Burnes that night.

While she had listened to her history teacher drone on about Napoleon, he had known where his missing student was. And even worse—her stomach twisted—he was aware Daphne had the same abilities as Ashley. That she was "the other one" the greater demon had preferred to use for its plans.

Was she in danger? Mr. Burnes knew about her but had done nothing with that information. Maybe he didn't consider her a threat as long as she didn't know about *his* involvement with Ashley's disappearance.

Sure, Daphne was stopping dyszoons, but Ashley had told her on the bridge that the creatures were "just a test." They helped prepare the Veil for the demon, but beyond that, they didn't matter to it.

At least Ashley appeared to be okay, or as okay as she could be. But the colorful leaves outside showed that the scene had taken place not long after Halloween. What had the demon made her do in the months since to expand the Veil once more?

Mr. Burnes was clearly more dedicated to the demon's cause than Ashley. Daphne was certain he had carved all those occult symbols. However, his only option to help the demon was to work with someone with their abilities. He was keeping Ashley disconnected, away from anyone who might interrupt her usefulness—or before she changed her mind. In isolation, he and the demon could influence Ashley and keep her in line.

We would be better off with the other one. The way Mr. Burnes had referenced Daphne bothered her. They *would be* better off with her, not *would have been.* That sounded like she was still a backup plan, a tool that could yet be useful if Ashley proved to be a failure.

But Daphne had already resisted the demon's attempt to recruit her to its cause last Halloween. How could it hope to try again and expect a different result? Through Mr. Burnes?

Doubtless he had performed a pivotal role in shaping Ashley for the demon's purpose. But if Mr. Burnes wanted to win Daphne over to the demon's side, he could at *least* be more lenient when grading her assignments. She'd detected no friendliness or any softening of his usual testiness in class.

She checked her phone a few more times, but Claire didn't respond to her message. Had the psychic seen the cabin as well? Daphne didn't know enough about visions to know how they worked. She had only been grateful when Heather stopped visiting her and Claire's nightmares after Halloween and normal nightmares had filled the void.

Her anxious thoughts finally gave in to a restless sleep.

An answer from Claire finally came later that morning, before the first bell. *We can discuss after school,* the brief text said. Daphne read it over with dissatisfaction. She'd have to wait to get another opinion.

The issue was that Mr. Burnes's class would come first. Would he instantly realize Daphne knew he was keeping Ashley? Then it was only a matter of time before questions were raised, questions that would ruin his career and interrupt the demon's plans. To him, those plans needed to be protected —at any cost.

We cannot fail.

It was a struggle to concentrate on the morning's classes as seventh-period history drew closer and dread erased her appetite for anything on her lunch tray. In less than an hour, she would see Mr. Burnes, and her imagination held her in a choke hold.

She stared at her baked potato. He'd find an opportunity to drug her, drag her to the cabin, and offer her unconscious body to the demon as a sacrifice...

At least there was a silver lining to the day: Veronica had chosen to sit at Nathan's table. Sometimes he sat with them, which made lunch a new torture. In his presence, Veronica transformed into someone even more unbearable, laughing at anything he said to the point that Daphne wondered how he stood it.

She snuck a look at his table. Heather was standing near him, but once again her stare was aimed at Daphne instead of her brother.

Not now. She turned her back firmly to the shade and mashed her potato. If Heather was going to make a habit of lurking by Nathan during lunch, Daphne would order her away when he joined their table.

"What about that girl who used to sit here? Amy?" Taylor was saying. Daphne stopped her fork.

"Ashley," Jessica corrected.

"Yeah. Whatever happened to her? Did they find her?"

"No," Jessica said, solemn, as she was whenever Ashley was mentioned. "Olivia's mom told her that Ashley's mom hasn't heard anything. She was hoping Ashley would show up at her dad's, but she didn't. I know it's been really hard on them."

Daphne cringed at this last comment. She often forgot about Ashley's family and how her absence might be affecting them, especially her younger twin brother and sister, who Daphne had met at a football game.

The clock moved unnervingly toward the next period. Could she tell someone? Perhaps if she made an anonymous tip, connecting Mr. Burnes to Ashley's disappearance as a supposed adult runaway, the police could locate her.

But if they questioned him, he'd instantly realize that Daphne was the only person who could have made the accusation. And without evidence, there would be nothing on which to base an investigation. She would still be stuck in his classroom, and he might plot ways to harm or kidnap her and force her to do the demon's bidding...

Daphne shuddered and pierced a broccoli, reeling in her wild thoughts. No, a kidnapping was highly unlikely. Probably.

The conversation moved on. Daphne ate half the potato and gave up. She was nearly silent with the effort of appearing calm, and preoccupied enough not to glance over at Nathan's table for any fresh torture. By the time lunch ended, Daphne was half-convinced it was her last hour.

Stop being irrational, Daphne firmly told the part of her mind that was writing her obituary. She wouldn't *die* in history class. Only of boredom...

Nathan paused by her locker just as she closed it, and they turned in the same direction to go to class. Thankfully, Heather was gone.

Daphne's face warmed. Her confession of her feelings in

the dream had taken place almost in this exact setting. But with real Nathan next to her, the condescending Nathan was laughably unrealistic—just as much as telling him she liked him as more than a friend.

How would he react if she were to confess her feelings? Nathan would likely be nice about it but say he didn't feel the same way. Things between them might be awkward, but maybe not to the degree of needing to avoid each other. Maybe she wouldn't lose his friendship.

It was all pointless. Graduation was two months away, and they would be separated by summer break and different colleges. Daphne, undecided about her career path, had enrolled in the local college to save on boarding costs, but Nathan would be attending a state college over two hours away —the same one as Veronica.

Luckily, Nathan couldn't read her thoughts, for he was talking to her normally. "I developed a few photos last night. I'll show you tomorrow if I don't forget again," he said.

"How did they turn out?" Dread came at full volume and almost blocked out his words. In just a minute, she would be in history class.

"Good. I mean, the shots I took were kind of random," he added, as if wanting to lower her expectations. "I just basically wanted to see how the color would look. I tested out my dad's old compact camera that he used in the eighties. He was happy it still worked."

While she wouldn't trade in her digital camera and its expensive lenses, Daphne's interest in older cameras had grown thanks to Nathan. Their shared love for photography had drawn them closer.

"That sounds fun. You'll have to bring them," Daphne said with what she hoped was proper interest as icy worms wriggled through her veins. The noise of passing students hummed unpleasantly in the background.

"You could borrow my thirty-five millimeter if you want, and I'd develop the film for you." The enthusiasm in his voice grew at the idea. "Or I could show you how to develop them once you take them."

"I'd like that," Daphne said, but she wasn't fooled. She could never go over to his house to see his old cameras, not to mention being closed up in a darkroom together. Not while he was dating someone else.

Unless Nathan had in mind that Veronica would be there with them. In which case, Daphne was far less enthusiastic.

They reached the point where she would turn left to the nearby history classroom while Nathan continued walking straight. She hesitated, staring at the door.

"Don't want to go?" Nathan paused too, his eyes flitting between her and the door curiously.

"Not really."

"Want to go to AP math with me instead? Or you could go *for* me."

Daphne smiled. "When you put it *that* way..."

Nathan grinned back. "See you later, Daphne."

He walked away, taking with him a sense of security. Now there was nothing to keep her from walking through the door. She closed her eyes and braced herself to enter.

To her relief, Mr. Burnes was still in his office in the back corner. She hastily settled into her desk in the middle of the room and avoided all eye contact. Most students had already taken their seats. Ashley's spot was, of course, empty.

Veronica was talking animatedly with her junior friend. Daphne had learned just a few weeks ago that her name was Vivian after overhearing her say she'd been selected as the female lead in the musical and Veronica had congratulated her by name.

The bell rang, and Daphne started, her heart beating a few ticks faster than normal. She opened the day's packet and rested her head casually in one hand, determined not to look at Mr. Burnes more than necessary.

Class began, and she pretended to be hyper-focused on taking notes about early twentieth-century history. Repeatedly, Ashley's empty seat in the front corner drew her eye. *He knows where she is.*

"The aftermath of World War I brought with it an Age of Anxiety, a sense of despair as people struggled to come to grips with the mass casualties and the continued suffering the trauma of war had brought," Mr. Burnes was saying. "It was as if society itself had become shell-shocked."

He paced slowly in the front, a war-torn city on the screen as his backdrop.

"There was a profound sense of cynicism and disillusionment. What had the war brought but great suffering? All the idealism of the past, ideas that humanity was somehow *progressing*, that industry was a great thing and each new invention a sign we were moving toward something much greater than our primitive ancestors...all of this was blown to pieces by the shells of World War I."

A long pause followed. Though it was obvious he didn't enjoy teaching, performance was another matter.

"Paul Valéry, the French poet, captured this attitude of disillusionment with the following." Mr. Burnes cleared his throat and read solemnly from a paper, drawing out each line. Safe from eye contact, Daphne lifted her eyes from her desk.

"The storm has died away, and still we are restless, uneasy, as if the storm were about to break."

She sank further into her chair, the words striking uncomfortably close. Hadn't she felt the same way ever since taking on the responsibility of the Veil?

"...*We do not know what will be born, and we fear the future, not without reason...Doubt and disorder are in us and with us.*"

The future marched forward with terrifying blankness. The only certainty was that someday, whether months or years, a demon would travel the road paved by Ashley to Earth and unleash Hell. She and Claire could only hold back the evil. Not defeat it entirely.

"*There is no thinking man, however shrewd or learned he may be, who can hope to dominate this anxiety.*" Mr. Burnes looked up from his paper at her, deadly serious. "*To escape from this impression of darkness.*"

His dark eyes were like twin Veils ensnaring her in their grip. She sank even lower, a familiar despair pressing over her lungs. A despair that grew each day that passed without a solution to their problem.

Every battle to keep the dyszoons at bay was only like patching a crack in a leaking dam. For now, it was enough. But eventually, the water would explode through. That was a certainty. The Veil had expanded once again. And still there was nothing they could do.

Mr. Burnes broke eye contact, continuing normally. Released, Daphne straightened. "So. In this aftermath of disillusionment, the world no longer believes in humanity. Its faith in man has been shaken to the core."

He paused, perhaps expecting a somber silence. But from what Daphne sensed, the class was simply waiting for his next point. Out of the corner of her eye, she saw Veronica yawn.

Mr. Burnes moved on to review the writers and artists who captured the spirit of the age. Daphne, absorbed in her dark thoughts, struggled to listen. More than ever, she wished to speak with Claire, who was the only other person who could understand their battle. How they were losing it.

Stop it, Daphne told the despairing thoughts clouding her mind again. Only when the girl in front of her half turned around did she realize she had said it aloud.

6

COUNTERATTACK

Daphne paused on the sidewalk before Madam Moon. An old man with mist rising from his shoulders and cane hobbled by, lifting a trembling hand to tip his hat.

Once he had passed, she stepped inside the perfumed studio to the jingle of bells. It had been a month since she had talked to Claire in person, mainly because there was little that was new to discuss. Daphne looked forward to seeing her— their visits reminded her that she wasn't alone in the battle against the Veil.

Voices bled through the dark curtain that separated the shop and the hallway leading to Claire's office and reading room. Daphne bounced on her feet. She had rushed to the studio after school and would have to wait to unload her worries for a while longer.

To distract herself, Daphne browsed the shop's salt lamps, geodes, and porcelain angels for Jessica's birthday present.

The voices down the hall grew louder. A woman with a mop of curly blonde hair came into the shop area, chatting cheerfully with Claire. Daphne preoccupied herself with the glass case full of jewelry and other small items, hoping she came across more like a casual shopper than the type of person who went to see a psychic for life advice. Which, technically, she was doing.

"Thanks for stopping, Sylvia," Claire told the woman, who gave her a hug and a wave goodbye.

When the woman was gone, Claire turned. "Hello, Daphne, it's so good to see you." She wore an elegant black shirt and patterned cardigan. Her necklace featured a gold crescent moon encrusted with black crystal.

Daphne swallowed her desire to launch into the Ashley situation right away. "You too," she said. "Was that Sylvia? The one who does paranormal investigating?"

"Yes, that was her. She dropped by for a visit."

"Oh, she seemed—" *Normal* was the word, unexpected for someone who was good friends with a psychic, one who could see the very ghosts Sylvia sought as a hobby. "—nice...Could I see this blue necklace?"

"Certainly." Claire slid open the glass case and handed it over. The pendant was a polished aquamarine stone paired with a silver crescent moon.

"I'll get it. My friend Jessica is turning eighteen next week," Daphne explained, removing cash from her coat pocket as Claire wrapped the necklace in paper and dropped it in a small bag.

"Here you go. And that's unnecessary," the psychic said, nodding at the cash.

Daphne paused, surprised. "Are you sure?"

"I'm sure," Claire said in a familiar firm tone. "You've covered for me many times these last few months."

Daphne took the bag and thanked her, touched by the generosity. "Not really. You cover the dyszoon attacks when I'm at school."

It was rare that more than two dyszoons emerged at a time. Since each could handle that number alone, they had worked out shifts last November. Claire handled any dyszoons during the first half of the night and school hours. Daphne took watch after school while the shop was open and in the early mornings.

The system worked well, except the dyszoons seemed to prefer arriving during Daphne's time, especially before sunrise.

"I know, but you've had the larger load," said Claire, apparently thinking about this. "I don't know what I'd do without your help."

Daphne smiled awkwardly. She didn't resent having most of the battles. Being unable to respond to a dyszoon during school only made her anxious until Claire confirmed later by text that all was well.

Claire locked the glass case and led the way through the curtain. "I'll make tea," she said, retreating into her cluttered office. Daphne continued along the hallway and ducked through strings of red beads to the room where Claire unveiled clients' futures.

She took her usual seat at the small round table and placed the bag containing the necklace on the floor. There was a new tissue box on the corner shelves and a deep blue tablecloth that glittered with silver thread, but otherwise, little had changed from her first visit last September. Lamps cozily lit the maroon walls, and the electric candles arranged on the table flickered.

In the quiet, worst-case scenarios ran through Daphne's mind, exaggerated by exhaustion. The threat of the expanded Veil paled compared to Mr. Burnes. Sure, she had made it through his class today. But what about tomorrow? The rest of the year? Dyszoons, she could handle. But a human who could try to put her out of the demon's way...

Claire entered with a pair of mismatched mugs and sat

down. Her long nails, a glossy black tipped with aquamarine, interlocked on the tablecloth.

"So. Your history teacher," she said, matter-of-fact. "You saw a vision?"

"Yes," Daphne said, and launched into the details of her dream, tripping over words in her eagerness to explain everything that might be important. The stockpiled food, enough to keep a single person fed for weeks. The November scene through the windows. Mr. Burnes working for the demon, though he didn't have their abilities.

Claire's eyebrows rose in interest at the mention of the occult symbols carved into the wood.

"Do you know what those are?" Daphne asked, catching the expression.

Claire ran a finger over a cloudy moonstone set in one of her rings. "I would say they're an attempt to communicate unwisely with the demonic."

"Which they *would* be trying to. That was the problem—they couldn't contact the demon, and Mr. Burnes was mad about it. He wanted to connect her better somehow. She didn't seem like she wanted to do it, whatever *it* was."

Her stomach squeezed faintly with nausea on Ashley's behalf. "I wish I could have seen where they were. Probably in the middle of nowhere. And she might not even be there anymore," Daphne rambled, staring into her half-empty mug of tea that had become tepid. "He's been teaching this whole time like nothing's happened. He's never even hinted that he knew about me. I was so nervous in class that he would do something to me."

Unexpectedly, Claire laughed. "Why would he do something to you?"

"Because I know he's the one who took Ashley!" Daphne

said defensively, confused that she needed to explain why her teacher was, in all likelihood, plotting to murder her.

"I see," Claire said, her tone pragmatic. "Well, if it's any comfort, if your teacher has been aware all this time that you have abilities like Ashley and done nothing, I don't think you're in any danger."

"But if he suspects *I* know about him, that I'm going to turn him in..."

"I think you're much more valuable to him unharmed, Daphne. He may need you."

Daphne stared, wondering if Claire had also considered that the demon could still use her. "But how am I more valuable? He can't actually think I'd still take Ashley's place, can he?"

"The demon would be foolish not to leave the option open, and your teacher seems loyal to it," Claire explained. "It's not interested in getting rid of you. It may be small comfort, Daphne, but I don't think you are in any physical danger from your teacher."

Her shoulders sagged in relief. Claire's calm words were soothing the worst of her fears from the past day. She *was* worrying too much. After all, if the demon considered her a backup plan, that was all the better. Her supposed usefulness would keep her safe from Mr. Burnes.

"I guess you're right, but I'm hoping he won't find out what I know," Daphne said, resolving to avoid him until graduation, which wouldn't be too difficult. "I'll just keep out of the way."

"That would be wise. He could make things uncomfortable for you." Claire laughed again. "I was going to say that I wouldn't advise you to do anything that would put you in danger, but I *did* ask you to help me with dyszoons."

"Oh. Well, I guess he can hardly murder me in class," Daphne said wryly, moving to take a sip of her tea and then remembering that it was cold. "I wonder if they know about you at all. I mean, Ashley would have seen you on Halloween, but she wouldn't have known who you were."

"And that's a small blessing, I suppose. Though I somehow doubt that they would prefer an old lady like myself to you."

"Lucky for me," Daphne said, not comforted. The greater demon preferred her, most dyszoons came during her watch, and now the vision of Ashley…"Why didn't you get the vision, too, of Ashley? We both had the dream about Heather's car accident, so how does that work?"

Claire pursed her lips in thought. "I couldn't tell you. I've occasionally had visions, but Heather's was the first time I shared one, being that you're the first person I've met like myself. It could be because you know Ashley and I don't."

"But neither of us knew Heather," Daphne pointed out.

"You would have come across Heather at school, and perhaps our paths crossed at some point, too," Claire said. "I don't know for certain, of course. There are things that will always be a mystery."

The shop door chimed.

"I need to check on that. Would you like some more tea?" Claire nodded at the cold mug.

"Oh—sure."

She disappeared through the beaded doorway. With any luck, the customer was interested in merchandise instead of getting a reading.

Daphne rubbed her tired face and yawned. The coziness of the lamplit room was lulling her closer to sleep, and she closed her eyes.

Thanks to Claire, her fears over Mr. Burnes had taken on a more rational focus. Still, it was going to be difficult to learn from a teacher who was hiding a student. If he hadn't brought Ashley under the demon's influence, the most important things on Daphne's mind at this moment would be graduation and preparing for college in the fall.

Mr. Burnes was the reason she was sitting in Claire's studio at all. By helping the demon, he was indirectly responsible for Heather's death. Those last moments in the crashed car wouldn't have visited Daphne's nightmares, and so Claire wouldn't have probed her about them, leading her to notice the unperceived world. Shades might still be glimpses at the corner of her eye, explained away.

And without the Veil to distract, maybe she and Nathan would be together—but if Heather hadn't died, Daphne realized, she wouldn't have met him. He'd remain a face in a yearbook photo, someone she graduated with but had never gotten to know. It was a bleak thought.

The grandfather clock ticked faintly in the other room, and voices rumbled. *It was right. We would be better off with the other one.* Daphne straightened uneasily. While she felt safe to continue attending history class, the reason bothered her. Even now, the demon considered Daphne an alternative to Ashley. Did the demon honestly think, even after she'd refused it on the bridge beneath the Veil, that it could tempt her to join it?

But Ashley fell, came the unwelcome thought. If the demon could twist Ashley from someone normal—even fun, according to Jessica—the possibility was there.

No. She shook her head. It was mistaken. If anything, each dyszoon Daphne fought made her more resolved to continue the battle. She had vowed to herself on Halloween night that no dyszoon would hurt another person again. Every creature she banished was a nail into that promise.

The bells of the shop door rang. A minute later, Claire swept through the strings of red beads and set steaming mugs on the table.

"So. How have you been doing, Daphne?" Claire's gaze

pierced her as she sat. Having expected the psychic to launch first into the pressing problems they faced—the Veil and the threat of the stronger dyszoons—Daphne was caught off guard.

"I'm fine, I'm just tired," she reassured Claire, and sipped the chamomile tea. Her tongue burned.

"Are you sure?" Claire appraised her, and Daphne flushed. Yes, the dyszoons had stretched her these last few months, but she *was* fine. What did it matter? No matter what she felt, the problems were still there. She would deal with them.

"I'm just thinking about the Veil," she said finally, although it was just one of the many problems on her mind. At least it would move the conversation away from her well-being. "The dyszoons I met yesterday were a lot more difficult, and they almost attacked some women on a walk. I almost didn't stop them in time."

"And that was rather frightening, I imagine. I'm sorry that I wasn't there."

"It's fine," Daphne said, brooding into the flickering flames of the electric candles. "Do you think dyszoons will be that strong from now on?" She guessed the answer, resigned. It was hardly a worse situation than they'd been coping with already.

"We should expect it. And it's possible their numbers may change as well, or the frequency."

Some weeks, they were lucky and only one dyszoon emerged from the Veil. The largest group so far had been five dyszoons, capping off a week of daily attacks. Daphne had faced that battle with much more competence than on Halloween.

She'd worried that the dyszoons would keep growing in number, but it had lowered once more to single attacks. There was no pattern.

"I hope it's not more than we usually get," Daphne said.

"But at least I know what to expect. And maybe I'll get better at it again, and it won't be so hard."

"I'm confident you will," Claire reassured her. "And before you worry, I will be fine as well. I am prepared."

Daphne twisted her owl bracelet. Gloom hovered like a darkened cloud. In her imagination, the leaking dam they were holding up exploded. But instead of water, a torrent of dyszoons poured through, followed by a great shadowy figure unlike anything she'd faced before. They would be no match for it.

"I wish there was something we could do about the Veil." The old frustration at her inability to *do* something surged through her. "Like, if we could find out where Ashley was and tip off the police. Then she couldn't expand it any more...But we would still have the Veil." Daphne stared darkly into her mug and mumbled, "It feels like I'm not doing anything."

Though she never shared so with Claire, Daphne had more than once followed several dark threads online for a solution. Her searches provided no useful information and told her much that she would have preferred not knowing. Some posts educated, with a smug air, that demons were not the evil creatures that others presented them as. Others advised what precautions to take when using a Ouija board to communicate with them, like lighting a candle.

There was nothing authoritative about how to close a real portal to Hell.

"I wish there was something we could do about the Veil, but we aren't doing nothing, *you* least of all," Claire said. "What we *can* do is prevent the dyszoons from harming anyone, and we are."

It was an echo of the conversation they'd had last fall. But the situation had worsened.

"But what about the demon? The lower-ranking one, or

whatever. What if it's just one more Veil expansion away from getting through?"

Daphne was having difficulty keeping the frustration out of her voice. All these months, they had managed the dyszoons but done nothing more. While they had the illusion of time as they eliminated the creatures like clockwork, the latest change in the Veil clarified that their time was borrowed.

"We'll deal with it when it comes, and it's possible that only then can we find a way. Think of how much you've improved, Daphne. Each dyszoon makes you stronger. The demon is training you to be more formidable to it."

"But how can we know it's enough? We don't even know if we can *do* anything to a demon like we can a dyszoon. And all this time, we haven't found a way to close the Veil!" Daphne ran her hands through her hair. Her voice was rising in volume as if it had a will of its own.

Although one part of her knew the lack of answers wasn't Claire's fault, the other part, in a sly whisper that felt like it came from outside of her, wondered why the psychic couldn't have searched for a way to close the Veil while it was dormant.

"I know, Daphne," Claire said calmly. "I wish we had better answers. But we have no blood connection to the Veil. Even if you *were* connected to it, the Veil would have the power over *you,* not the other way around."

"But how do you know that for sure?" Daphne challenged.

"Because it's evil and powerful," Claire said, still calm. "Your classmate is now at the mercy of the Veil, even if we brought her back here. You touched the Veil once and came off worse. We can't match this evil, only manage it. I wish it weren't so."

At this last comment, Daphne's frustration leaked away. She might not like it, but the psychic was right.

"I'm sorry," she said, burying her face in her hands and

wishing she could nap at the table. "I'm not mad at you or anything. I'm just exhausted."

"I know," Claire said again. "Which is why I wanted to ask you how you are, Daphne."

"I'm fine. I just need sleep." She unburied her hands and rotated her bracelet underneath the table. "I just wish there was something we could do about the Veil."

The first time she had visited the Veil, she was unprepared. It entranced her, and when she touched it, it threw her back onto the road. Its power wasn't benign.

After that, Daphne had stayed guarded. But she was stronger now, and she had been able to touch it without a special bond like Ashley's.

A new idea came to her, or an old one that was now possible. "You know, the first time didn't work, but maybe I can try again and damage it."

"You already touched it once, and it injured you."

"But that was when I was just starting to perceive things. Both of us have gotten so much better at handling dyszoons," Daphne said, growing more excited despite Claire's lack of enthusiasm.

The psychic set her mug down on the coaster. "No, Daphne. We shouldn't mess with the Veil."

"We've never tried properly, though. Like you said, I've become more formidable, or stronger, or whatever," Daphne said. Being able to *do* something, instead of just waiting for the demon to arrive, was making her feverish.

"I understand your feelings, Daphne." A touch of exasperation had crept into Claire's calm voice. "I sincerely wish we had answers. But we *are* doing something. Protecting others is no small thing. These months have worn on both of us, and especially you."

"I'm fine," said Daphne again. "But if this is how we can do something, we have to *try*, right?"

"It's too dangerous. And also foolish."

"But I *know* what the Veil is like now," she argued, frustrated. Usually she could understand Claire's caution, but the psychic wasn't even considering the plan. "I'd be careful, and we can just see what—"

"No." Claire gripped the table and stood. Daphne stopped talking, startled at how much more authority spilled from the psychic in that small action.

"I—" she said, but let the unknown sentence sputter out. She had seen Claire get stern, even a little angry sometimes, but that anger had never been directed at her.

"You don't know what it would do to you," Claire said, her dark eyes deadly serious. "There is an evil here we cannot match, only manage. It's not about weakness. Or incompetence. Or even a lack of a plan. It's recognition."

Daphne sat back down slowly. Leaning forward, Claire set a lacquered hand on the table between them like a gesture of peace, her gaze softer.

"Daphne. Please promise me you won't attempt to interact with the Veil. There is no room for error in this. I need you, and I can't do this alone."

Fixed by the earnest gaze, Daphne swallowed her desire to argue further. Her excitement was deflating. For a fevered minute, she had thought a counterattack was within their grasp.

"Okay," she said reluctantly. "I won't."

The grandfather clock in the other room chimed five. Its sound highlighted the stretched silence.

Daphne grabbed the bag with the necklace. "I guess I'd better get going. I have homework to catch up on," she said. It was true enough.

"Yes. Good night, Daphne," Claire said, sounding weary. "I hope it's a quiet night for you."

"Yeah. Me too," Daphne said, feeling ashamed as she stood. She hadn't been able to mention Heather's reappearance...

With a last goodbye, she exited the room, somehow feeling worse than she had upon entering it.

7

THE PROMISE

As she might have expected, history class passed without any murder attempts the following day.

A rare good night's sleep helped put the situation into a more rational focus. Getting kidnapped or murdered by Mr. Burnes was unlikely, though she resolved to avoid him as much as possible.

While she felt guilty for arguing with Claire, Daphne regretted her promise to not directly attack the Veil. Doing so was dangerous, yes, but the anticipated demon was even more so. Her abilities were unrecognizable compared to the last time she tried to touch it. Was another attempt so risky if all it did was throw her back?

Friday morning came with a sense of relief. There would be no Stage Crew after school, which hopefully meant a quiet evening. Nathan was at a track meet, so his girlfriend wasn't cozying up to him at his locker. Instead, Veronica was chatting with Jessica, who was absent from her boyfriend for once.

There were ten minutes until the first bell, and two scenarios went to war against each other in Daphne's mind.

She *could* find a corner and scroll through her phone, or even go to class early and start working on her photo project.

The other scenario required more effort. Daphne had promised herself to bridge the gap between herself and others by focusing on her friendships more. Jessica was one of those, but approaching would be tricky with Veronica present.

I'm going to her party, Daphne reassured herself as she approached. Although it had been fading for months, their friendship was still there.

Jessica was explaining something. "It kind of dips down to here, but I think it'll be okay."

"Hey, there's nothing wrong with a little—"

Daphne stepped in. "Did you get your prom dress, then?" she said to Jessica.

"Yeah, it just came yesterday, but I need to get it altered yet. Here it is." Jessica turned her phone to show a picture of herself modeling a silver dress with a high slit and low neckline.

"I like it," Daphne said, though privately thinking the cut pushed the dance dress code to its limit. "What do you need to get altered?"

"It's a little baggy in places." Jessica zoomed in on the photo with a frown. "And I'm going to get the slit a *tad* lower. I didn't expect it to be that high, but I think I'm shorter than the model."

"Did you get a dress yet?" Veronica asked Daphne, to her surprise. However, the question wasn't genuine interest but was likely meant to fish out answers to other, unspoken questions. *Who are you going with? How good will you look? How lame are you?*

"I wasn't that interested in going," she said, with the sensation of stepping willingly into a hole. "But if I did, I'd probably wear the one I did last year."

"Lame," Veronica said, her mascara-rimmed eyes now bored. "That's, like, half the fun."

"Eh, dresses are expensive," Jessica said, still zooming in and out of the photo. "I'm only getting a new one because I borrowed mine last year and my dad's funding me."

Veronica shrugged. No doubt she hadn't hesitated to drop a few hundred dollars on another dress she'd only wear once.

While Daphne had done her best to give off the impression that prom didn't interest her, a lack of plans was the real reason she wasn't attending.

Having no group to get ready with stung. Four years of high school, and was she really ending it so friendless?

Last year, she'd gotten ready for prom with a large group that included Jessica, who was the reason she'd been a part of it. They were much closer last spring, just a few months into their friendship, than now.

"Are you going with Zeke?" Daphne asked, aware that Veronica was probably spinning what she had just said for gossip later.

"Yeah, Zeke. And then V's with Nathan." Jessica tapped on the screen. "We're renting a limo."

Daphne flinched internally at the image of the four of them riding around Long Haven, Nathan handsome in a tux, his hand holding Veronica's.

She couldn't ask to join their limo party. Not as a fifth wheel, and definitely not without a date of her own. And she'd rather skip prom altogether and avoid her phone for a few days, until others stopped posting dance photos, than see Nathan and Veronica posing together.

"What about you? What does your dress look like?" she asked Veronica without interest, to change the subject.

"I love it. It's green—"

Veronica's curly-haired junior friend interrupted them. She held a paper grocery bag.

"I've brought it with me," Vivian said conspiratorially. Veronica took the bag and partly pulled out what looked like a board game. She stuffed it at the bottom of her locker with a grin, but not before Daphne recognized the Ouija board.

"Ooh, is that what I think it is, V?" Jessica said, looking up from her phone with the delighted air of catching someone in doing wrong.

"Nope. You saw nothing," Veronica replied with a laugh and shut the locker.

"Why do you have it?"

"Vivian said she had one, and I wanted to try it."

"Does it work?" Jessica asked. She'd put her phone away, now bright with interest. Daphne was the only one who had eyed the Ouija board with distaste.

"Nothing happened while I used it," Vivian admitted. "But my cousin said it can take a while sometimes before you, like, get any activity."

"Where do you get one? Do they sell them online?"

"Yeah, it's not like they're illegal," Vivian said with an eye roll. Daphne glared in defense of Jessica. "I'm sure you can buy them here too."

"Like that psychic shop downtown?"

She was referencing Madam Moon, Daphne realized. But Claire wouldn't stock a Ouija board. To do so would encourage the very demonic activity they were trying to fight. The shop offered more of a generic blend of mysticism. Customers could purchase a geode and decide for themselves whether it held remarkable healing properties or balanced the energy of a room.

"I don't know. I've never been there," Vivian said, her tone almost rude. Clearly, she disliked Jessica. Daphne's second glare went unnoticed. She didn't have an opinion of Vivian before and had only assumed that, as a friend of Veronica, she couldn't be trusted. Now her dislike was solidifying.

"We can try it sometime," said Veronica.

Jessica bit her bottom lip, though she seemed excited. "Okay. Let's do it."

Daphne shuffled her books to the other arm, hoping for the bell. If any of them had met the demon last year, they'd stay far away from the board.

People mess with things they do not understand...Most of the time, nothing happens, but maybe at some point, something strange and possibly evil can communicate. Claire's warning from months ago came to mind. Even without it, attempting to communicate with the dead made Daphne uneasy. Some types of curiosity were better left unsatisfied. But if she shared her doubts, at least two of the others would sneer at her.

"I'm going to run to the bathroom," she told Jessica, and left the conversation without a second glance from the other girls.

Mr. Burnes could have tried using a Ouija board to get instructions from the demon, she theorized as she entered the bathroom, which was miraculously empty. He had somehow become entangled with the demon without having the same abilities as her and Ashley. A simple curiosity about talking with the dead might have been where it started for him.

A minute later, Daphne opened the stall door. Heather stood right outside, so that they were almost face-to-face.

She swore and tumbled against the side of the stall in shock. "Don't *do* that!"

Lost in thought, she hadn't perceived the shade enter the bathroom. Since spotting Heather a few days ago, she might have guessed that the shade would approach her before the week was over.

"Can you please move out of the way?" Daphne said, more

gently. She hated passing through shades who looked completely solid. Heather hadn't reacted to the outburst, but moved aside.

Daphne turned on the sink and glanced up at the mirror before realizing it wouldn't reflect the shade. She dried her hands and turned, hoping their privacy would hold. Heather was sticking around, and this might be their best chance to speak for a while.

"Why are you still here?" she asked directly. Heather's eyes, hazel-green and striking even in death, were forlorn.

"Nathan. I have to help him."

"Okay, what do you mean?" Daphne said with a frown. She had assumed that Nathan's sister would naturally move on. He was happy in his new relationship, and Heather's disappearance had seemed to confirm that. Wasn't that her sole purpose for staying behind after death? His happiness?

Unless the reason was more complex. A theory she had given little thought to since the other day returned. Since Heather had reappeared the same day as the Veil grew, could she be worried that it put her brother in danger?

"He's alone." Heather's expression was earnest. "My brother. He's alone."

Daphne's stomach sank. The first time she met the shade, those same words had led her to promise to befriend Nathan. Apparently, Heather's reason for staying behind hadn't changed. The shade's timing with the Veil was just a coincidence, and something else had brought her out of the shadows. She might have even reappeared on an earlier day without Daphne noticing.

"He's doing a lot better now. I know he's doing good in his classes. And he's got a girlfriend," Daphne added reluctantly. She hadn't lied—Nathan *was* doing well. But evidently not as much as his sister wished.

"I've watched him. He's alone," Heather insisted, stepping forward. Daphne took a step back. In that small space, the shade towered.

"What do you mean? He's lonely?"

"Yes. You have to help him."

"He has friends." Daphne frowned again. "His track team, and Dom's his best friend. I mean, I don't think Dom's the *greatest* friend, but—"

"I know my brother. He's alone. I've seen him."

"He's doing a lot better, though," Daphne argued. "He seems fine."

"I've watched him," Heather insisted. "I know my brother. He's lonely."

Daphne stilled, realizing what the shade was trying to say. It was difficult to believe that Nathan could be lonely. Not anymore, with Veronica. But she should know that loneliness wasn't about the number of people around or even how many friends one had.

For herself, the isolation of the last few months reminded her of that dark period in middle school after her dad died. That sense of being an island broken away from the mainland, while others continued to carry on their normal lives from afar.

Would she *really* know what was going on in Nathan's life, like Heather might? After all, how much time did she and Nathan spend together in a day?

"Can you help him?" Heather asked.

Daphne hadn't been a good friend to him. After Halloween, she had passed the burden of her promise on to Veronica. Any friendship that remained afterward was a bonus, something good that came out of meddling.

Their limited time together meant there was no chance to fully realize the deeper connection they could have had, if only circumstances had been different. If only the Veil hadn't called her that night.

"I don't know what I can do," she admitted. "We don't see each other a lot."

"Help him." Heather took another step forward. Her tone had intensified, as shades often did when focusing on their reason for remaining behind.

Daphne rubbed her forehead wearily. Helping shades move on wasn't simple, as she had once hoped after her success with Robin at the cemetery last fall.

"I'll do what I can," she said.

Heather nodded. If not for the curling mist that rose from the shade's body, they could be mistaken for two normal girls having a chat in the bathroom. The summer after graduation was approaching, the same period of time when dyszoons had killed Heather. They were, in a way, the same age now. It was a strange thought.

A small group of freshman girls opened the door. "Help him," the shade said solemnly.

Unable to respond, Daphne nudged past the freshmen and emerged into the hallway with her head abuzz, glad to leave Heather behind.

8

———

DRILL

The next Monday at Stage Crew, Daphne asked the technical director for a task and was given a broom.

"We've got all this mess left over yet from last week. If you could sweep it up, that'd be a big help," he said.

At least it's something I know how to do, Daphne thought as she swept sawdust into a pile. She imagined Veronica laughing at her, dressed for some reason in glamorous old-fashioned clothes, her arm hooked through Nathan's.

Despite her promise to Heather, she had talked to him as little as usual. How could she be a better friend to him when they couldn't hang out? Somehow, messaging more didn't seem like the right solution.

Beth hadn't arrived yet. There was also no sign of the shade lurking in the catwalk. Daphne had forgotten to do any research into his identity over the weekend, as two dyszoons arrived separately on Saturday.

She had reluctantly let Claire take on the dyszoon that came in the morning, but paced her bedroom until her cell phone rang. The psychic confirmed it was a tough battle, but thanks to Daphne's warning, the creature's strength hadn't caught her off guard.

The call eased some of her guilt. From Claire's tone, it didn't seem like she held any ill feelings from their last conversation.

A second dyszoon arrived not long after dinner that evening, perhaps confirming their worry that battles would become more frequent. Daphne excused herself to run errands and then rushed to Laurel Road. The dyszoon took longer than usual to banish, but the battle went more smoothly. She didn't fall, anyway.

"How goes it, sweeper?"

Chad, the energetic senior she'd met her first day, held up a hand. Daphne stood on her toes to high-five it. "It goes fine," she answered.

When he didn't move away, she braved conversation. "What's this going to look like?" She nodded toward the set.

"Like a dining room."

"I know, but is there a drawing we go off of, or a picture?"

"If you want, you can see the old set. There's a few photos in the display case."

"Where's that?"

"Just outside the theater entrance." Chad gestured up one set of stairs. "Follow that."

He moved away. Daphne hung on to the broom handle, considering. If there was a picture of the dining room, there was a good chance there'd be another of the former cast. She could confirm whether the stage ghost was Michael Buza, the ill-fated lead of the canceled musical whose leading role Chad was filling.

A break was due. Daphne climbed the steps and reached an enclosed hallway with double doors, which led to a wide carpeted platform at the edge of the lunchroom. A built-in display case she had never paid attention to before was on her right. She peered at the display boards covered in captioned photos and programs, a montage of past performances and sets.

"Trying to find something?" Beth called, climbing up the carpeted steps with her backpack.

"I wanted to see what the set's going to look like," Daphne explained. "I haven't found it yet."

"It's been a while since I've looked at these. Hey! Here's me." Beth pointed to a photo of the *Oklahoma!* performance. Several actors posed in the middle of a dance scene, the scattered colors on the stage giving it a dreamlike quality. Her dark red hair was shoulder-length and curled, and like the other girls, she wore a prairie dress.

"Weird, I wouldn't have recognized you with long hair," Daphne said, hoping that saying so wasn't offensive.

"I know, right?" Beth ran two fingers through her bangs and held them out. "I'm growing it out again. I've had it this short since sophomore year, but I think I'm ready to change it up."

Daphne viewed more photos. In one of them, Veronica stood behind an elegant couch where several actors sat in costume. "*She* was in Drama Club?" Daphne said without thinking, undisguised dislike showing in her voice.

"Who, Veronica?" Beth leaned closer. "Yeah, she was one of the assistant directors last year. Not that she did anything."

It was odd to hear the same dislike echoed in Beth's voice as well, since she seemed to get along with everyone. Daphne's appreciation for her soared.

"She's not helping this year, is she?" she asked.

"Yeah. She's an assistant again."

Daphne grimaced. It was just her luck Veronica was involved in an area of her life that she wanted to be fun. Drama Club was likely how Vivian and Veronica became good friends.

"Here's *Specter*." Beth, who had also become absorbed in

the photos, pointed to a board on the far right. Daphne stooped close to the glass.

The first photo showed the dining room set they were building. In another, a girl with curly brown hair wearing a thirties-style dress carried a pie. Familiarity tugged at her, but then let go.

"I like her dress," Daphne commented.

In a different photo, the girl beamed at the camera next to a taller boy in an overlarge brown suit with one hand tucked in his pocket. In contrast, his expression was subdued, posed. Some of his haughtiness bled through the photo.

It was the shade.

Her heart leaping with excitement, Daphne read the photo caption: *Michael Buza (as Victor Savage) and Rachel Hill (as Ginny Woolworth).*

So the shade *was* Michael, the Drama Club's only known casualty. Daphne had a mad desire to run back to the stage and tell Chad that he was correct about the haunting's identity.

She scanned the few remaining photos from the last performance. The director's name, Carole Finch, caught her attention. Carole was Daphne's middle name, after her maternal grandmother, who had passed away when her mom was in college. By how often her name appeared, Carole had been the director for a long time.

It was enough information to begin her search into Michael's story. Daphne returned to the stage with Beth, who helped hold the dustpan as she swept her first pile into it.

She continued to sweep for the next quarter of an hour, jealous of those assigned more interesting work. Maybe after she'd been part of Stage Crew for a while, the technical director would trust her enough to handle a drill.

Her broom had just made a last pass across the stage when a cool presence crept into her awareness. Daphne turned.

As if the picture in the display had come to life, Michael appeared on the set platform. His attention was on a nearby sophomore girl climbing a short stepladder. Up close, he looked like an ordinary student, albeit one dressed to perform. Curling mist rose from his oversize brown suit. His pants were likewise too long, bunched above rather large leather shoes.

Sweeping forgotten, Daphne slackened her hold on the broom, taking in his features. His chin was sharp, and his nose was upturned just enough to give him an air of superiority. A surprising dislike filled her. She viewed shades with either pity or fear, but this one was different. Even in death, he exuded arrogance as much as mist.

The sophomore girl's screw wobbled in the drill bit and dropped to the floor. She set the drill upright at the top of the ladder and stepped off. A premonition crept into Daphne's mind, like a memory about to repeat itself.

Michael stepped forward and swung an arm across the drill as the girl bent down to retrieve the screw. Daphne gasped, but there was no stopping the inevitable. The drill tipped over and then tumbled off the edge of the stepladder, crashing with a heavy thud mere inches from the girl's back.

The sophomore screamed. Half the stage swung around to look, but the saw was making too much noise for the scene to get full attention.

Chad was the first to move forward. "What happened?"

"It almost *hit* me!" the sophomore said, wide-eyed. Surely, her heart was pounding as much as Daphne's.

Chad picked up the drill and pressed the button. It whirred, none the worse for wear. "Still works. That could've hurt. You good?"

"Yeah," she said, shaking as she accepted his helping hand to stand. "I guess I shouldn't leave it on the top of the ladder."

A few laughed. It was funny now that there was no

grievous injury. The technical director watched a few moments longer, and then apparently decided the incident was a lesson in itself. He turned back to directing the saw.

In the few seconds of distraction, Michael had disappeared. The girl climbed the ladder to attempt the screw once again.

To Daphne, it felt as if the drill had fallen on her own head. Heather knocking over Nathan's books to give Daphne an opening to talk to him was harmless enough for haunted activity, but this was different. A shade, like a dyszoon, had tried to injure someone.

She had always thought shades were harmless once she'd gotten used to them. Or at worst, unnerving. But here was a type of shade she hadn't encountered before—one with the desire to cause the living harm.

It was important now to uncover everything she could about him and why he might be tied to the stage. It was clear she couldn't get those answers from the shade himself. Even if he didn't disappear at random moments, there were too many people around.

From the far edge of the stage, lurking between short curtains, Michael met her stare. The corner of his mouth pulled up in contempt.

Two hours later, Daphne sat cross-legged on top of her bed and logged into a newspaper database. Her mom used the subscription most of the time in service of the historical society or for writing articles on local history.

Armed with several names, she could dig into Michael's story. She paused over the keyboard before typing in the musical name first, narrowing the location to Virginia.

A likely headline appeared from about thirty years ago: "Original Musical to Debut on Long Haven High School

Stage." With a flicker of excitement, Daphne scanned the article, which was accompanied by the same photo of the two leads from the display case.

There were a few brief quotes from the playwright, a middle-aged local named Nancy, who had always been involved in theater. She told the reporter it was "a dream come true" to have her musical, which she'd written on and off for over a decade, find a home thanks to her director friend.

"It's a different type of musical for the high school stage, but we have enough standout actors this year, particularly in our two leads, that I was confident it was the right time to do it justice," said Carole Finch, the director.

No actors were interviewed. The rest of the article shared the synopsis of the play, which had drawn inspiration from *A Christmas Carol*. It also listed the dates of performance, the ones that had never come to be. The playwright must have been terribly disappointed to see her musical canceled, never to be resurrected—at least for decades.

There were no other headlines about the musical. The newspaper hadn't even reported on its cancellation, which seemed negligent.

The information in the article was helpful, but what had happened between that report and opening night? Daphne doubted his death was as dramatic as a fall from the catwalk or a hanging, as Chad had suggested.

A direct search for his name put forth a more likely cause of death. A new headline, "Motorcycle Accident Kills 1," confirmed that any rumor otherwise was false.

According to the report, a motorcyclist had lost control on a curve and struck a tree at high speed. A neighbor, who heard a loud sound late at night and went to investigate, called in the accident. Michael was pronounced dead at the scene, and an autopsy revealed that alcohol was a factor in the crash.

A mental image came to her of Michael lying lifeless on his side as sirens flashed in the background. In her imagination, he was still wearing the costume. She forced the morbid thought away with a shudder.

An obituary was next. The right Michael Buza was easy enough to find. To Daphne's frustration, it was rather brief and didn't include any significant details she didn't already know.

He had "died unexpectedly" a mere three days before the musical was to debut and was survived by two younger siblings, his divorced parents, and some grandparents. The only other personal detail was that Michael was active in school activities.

To add how he loved to ride his motorcycle would have been in poor taste, Daphne noted darkly.

Michael's name was listed as part of the supporting cast in articles on other Drama Club productions, and on honor rolls. With no further follow-up, he simply vanished from history. On paper, anyway.

The story was simple on the surface. Musical planned, musical canceled. Actor dead. Meeting Michael's shade did nothing to connect her to the man in the headline. They might as well have been separate people. Separate ghosts.

Daphne drummed her fingers on the keyboard. That simple narrative didn't explain why the shade of Michael Buza was still haunting the stage decades after his passing. And apparently he wouldn't let her get near enough to ask him, which also meant she couldn't order him to leave the production alone.

Many of the shades she'd met stayed behind for nobler reasons. Most were like Heather or Robin from the cemetery, having a strong desire to see what became of someone they loved. But she sensed Michael was different.

Whatever kept him from moving on, the toppled drill proved he had a vendetta against the resurrected musical. Was he angry about dying before getting the full spotlight in his first lead role? Could shades be envious of the living?

Daphne closed her laptop, in a haze from her research. She had enough problems to deal with, including Heather, but this new shade intrigued her. If only she could talk with Michael, she might get to the bottom of what was keeping him behind. But he had proven slippery.

She glanced at the time, almost eight o'clock, and groaned. Researching dead, vengeful actors was far more interesting than completing homework.

9

HAPPY RETURNS

Daphne arrived at Jessica's house, a present bag in hand. A silver *18* and some balloons decorated the black front door. The party was already much more festive than she imagined her own birthday in a week would be.

Although she was late, Daphne hesitated on the porch. The party would be the first one she'd attended all school year, an unpleasant reminder of the state of her social life since the Veil. At least Beth would be inside as a friendly face. And with any luck, she'd have some time to chat with Nathan—something Heather would approve of.

It'll be fine, Daphne reassured herself, gathering courage on the Welcome rug. *You're just out of practice.* The idea of calling home for a boost of encouragement tempted her, but her mom was out celebrating her own birthday with a friend.

Before leaving for Jessica's, Daphne had handed over a present of chocolate as Phillip stood in the middle of the living room couch nearby, his legs eerily fused with the cushion. The shade's distracting presence reminded her of Michael, who she had searched for at Stage Crew that week without success.

Since there were no meetings on Fridays, Daphne had tried her usual door to the theater after school, but it was locked.

Another minute had passed. *Get it over with.* She rang Jessica's front doorbell and bounced on her feet.

Next door, a woman walked down the driveway holding a cardboard box, her blonde ponytail swinging. Daphne frowned. The air was edging close to freezing, but the woman wore shorts and a tank top as though it were the height of summer—and she was misting.

Jessica's door opened. Daphne snapped her attention back. "Happ—" she started to say.

An older boy she had only seen in dated family photographs stood in the doorway with a friendly smile. He wore a graphic T-shirt, and his dark hair was swept up like Nathan's. Daphne forgot for a second why she had knocked.

"Hey, welcome to the party," he said.

"Hi," Daphne said shyly, resisting the urge to glance over at the woman as she stepped inside the foyer of dark wood floors strewn with red and black balloons. "Where is everyone?"

"Out in the garage," he said, kicking the balloons aside as he led her past the staircase and down a short hall. It ended in an open kitchen and living room area that had changed little in half a year. "They're dyeing each other's hair with these spray can things."

"Oh," Daphne said. She resisted the urge to touch her own dark hair, hoping she could get out of it.

Frosted red cupcakes and other party snacks covered the granite countertops. He stopped at the punch dispenser as Daphne set down her present on a nearby table.

"Actually, you came at the perfect time," he continued conversationally. "Jessica was trying to get me to do green when you rang the doorbell, so I volunteered to see who it was."

"Glad I could help," Daphne said, noticing his arms as he

poured. He was more good-looking and muscular in person than she had expected, like he had learned how to do reps since the senior picture on the nearby wall.

"You're Daphne, right? I'm Leon, Jessica's brother," he said. "Want a drink?"

"You mean—"

"Nonalcoholic," he said, reading her pause correctly. "It's a watermelon margarita, since it's a Vegas theme, I guess."

Daphne hesitated. Laughter she recognized as Veronica's came from the garage beyond the nearby mudroom. She shouldn't avoid the rest of the party, but dyeing her hair wasn't her idea of fun.

"They were almost done, if you wanted to get out of it," Leon added.

She laughed and accepted the cup, surprised that he had read her so well and that he already knew her name. He clinked his own plastic cup against it with a dull sound. "Cheers," he said.

Her party anxiety was easing in Leon's calm presence, which was unlike his sister's energetic aura. Besides the fact he was Jessica's brother and a college sophomore, Daphne knew little about him. She recalled Jessica shopping for his birthday on the day they'd met Claire.

"Are you home from college for the weekend, then?" she asked. Just to have something to do with her hands, Daphne took another sip. The drink was decent, but too sweet.

Leon leaned against the kitchen island, relaxed. "Yeah. I don't normally make it home except during school breaks, but I wanted to surprise Jess for her birthday."

"Aw, that's nice you could make it," she said, then frowned inwardly. Since when did she say things like *aw*? Still, she liked him even more. He couldn't have looked forward to hanging out with high schoolers, but had come home anyway. Daphne wished, not for the first time, that she had a brother or sister. It was just her and her mom now. She took another sip.

"Also, don't tell her," Leon said, "but I was *really* missing real food, and her birthday just happened to be this weekend."

"I take back my 'aw,'" Daphne said, surprising herself again. Maybe she wasn't as awkward as she feared. "Though I wouldn't call this real food," she added, glancing at the microwaved chicken wings.

"True," Leon said, plopping a wing onto a small plate, "but my mom's cooking is worth the drive. I almost considered becoming a chef because of her."

"Really? What are you going for now?" She couldn't remember if Jessica had mentioned it.

"Design. I'm taking a lot of art classes. Actually, I painted *that*." He pointed to a small painting of a dove in flight on the nearby wall. "It was for class last year."

"That's great," she said honestly.

"Thanks. There's some better ones hanging up around here. I could show you if we get the chance," he said, a hint of passion infecting his voice. "You do anything with art?"

"I do photography. But I mean—" she stammered under his interest. "I do like art, I mean, too."

The opening of the mudroom door spared Daphne from further tripping over her words. Jessica burst out, giggling and wrapped in a pink feather boa, which matched the streaks in her long black hair.

"Hey guys, Daphne's here!" she called behind her. Privately, Daphne felt that her arrival wouldn't contribute all that much to the life of the party.

"Oh. I hoped it was the pizza," Veronica said with disappointment, entering next. Her hair had a few streaks of purple in it, which strangely suited her.

Nerves spasmed in Daphne's stomach, and she set her cup down firmly. *You can do this.*

She took stock of who was there. To her relief, Beth walked through the door with her boyfriend, Ethan, and waved. Her cropped red hair was absent of artificial color. Nathan, who now had an uncharacteristic lock of green at his temple, came in next and smiled at her. Her stomach flipped.

There was Maria and a few other junior girls Daphne knew vaguely. Last was a boy with short dreadlocks—Jessica's new boyfriend, Zeke. Besides Nathan, only the girls had dyed their hair. She wondered if Veronica had pressured him into it.

"Is everyone hungry?" Jessica said, throwing the feather boa over a shoulder.

Answering her question, the doorbell rang. "I'll get it," Leon volunteered.

Daphne tried to catch Nathan's eye again. He stood near Veronica with a hard-to-read expression. Was he not enjoying the party? Veronica scrolled on her phone, idly twirling one of her new purple locks of hair.

Daphne checked her own phone and mentally counted the hours until she could reasonably leave—hours during which a dyszoon might arrive for the third night in a row. Her made-up excuses to leave the party seemed flimsy now.

Leon came back up the hall with a stack of pizza boxes. Glad for something to do rather than because she was hungry, Daphne loaded up her plate. Leon disappeared. While she didn't blame him for not wanting to eat with them, she hoped that he would reappear before the party was over.

She stood at the kitchen island and talked with Beth and Ethan, who she hadn't properly met before, as they too seemed like they didn't quite belong in that group. He shared his plans to join the Army after graduation, a family legacy, and how he enjoyed restoring cars with his dad.

Daphne thought having a clear direction was refreshing, as she was undecided on her major and future career. She wondered if the separation would lead to a breakup, but Beth only nodded at his plans, unconcerned. Maybe their relationship would survive.

She stole glances at Nathan. Next to him, Veronica laughed obnoxiously with Jessica and the other girls. Just that morning, the couple had embraced by his locker, and now they seemed distant. More cheerfully, Daphne returned her attention to her plate.

The cupcakes on the other counter were free to grab at any time. When she had finished her pizza, Daphne walked over for one at the same time as Nathan, not entirely by accident.

"Hey, how's it going?" he said, grabbing two. The green in his hair would take getting used to.

"Good." Daphne shrugged. "I forgot to ask today, but when's your next home meet?"

"Next Wednesday afternoon. Want to come?"

She smiled at the invitation. Finally, something was easy. "I'd like to go. I've never been to a track meet. When would you be running?"

"If you get there right after school, you'll probably catch at least one of my events. But if you wanted to stick around longer, you could see more."

"Okay, I'll see how it goes."

Nathan smiled back, but it seemed weighed down. He returned to the couch in the nearby living room. Veronica looked up from her phone and took the cupcake without comment as Jessica began opening presents.

Daphne joined the larger group, looking forward to the meet. They would have time to talk and hang out—that is, as long as Veronica wasn't coming.

To her relief, the necklace she'd purchased from Claire's

shop went over well. "I love it!" Jessica declared, and unwrapped her feather boa from her shoulders to put it on. "Thanks, Daph!"

When Jessica had finished opening her gifts, which included a stack of lottery tickets from Veronica, she set down a stack of board games and sat on the living room rug. "All right, gather round, peeps. Whose plate is this?"

"Mine," Nathan said, standing to throw it away. As soon as he left, Veronica pulled out her phone. Daphne glanced at her own. To her shock, only an hour had passed. Resigned to her fate, she joined the circle on the carpet and wasn't displeased when Leon reappeared and took the spot next to her.

"So, I've got poker..." Jessica was saying.

"I don't know how to play poker," Veronica complained.

"Okay, how about this one..."

The card game, which involved a lot of slapping the middle space in the group, distracted Daphne from her worries about dyszoons. After several rounds, they paused, and she leaned back to stretch. Veronica whispered something to Jessica and then left the room.

"I'm getting a drink. Want anything?" Leon said to her.

"I'm good, thanks," Daphne said, pleased that he had bothered to ask.

Veronica soon returned with a slim box and sat. Daphne glanced at the cover. Instantly, the pizza turned sour in her stomach: It was Vivian's Ouija board.

"Ooh, I haven't done one of these since I was, like, twelve," one of the junior girls said.

"Did anything happen?" Jessica asked, bright with interest.

"No. Everyone just kept moving the piece. Then we all got food poisoning." She shrugged and took a drink.

Daphne quickly thought through the situation. Could she get out of it? She would have been reluctant to play even without dyszoons in her life, but the game now seemed that much more dangerous. Claire had once warned her that messing around with the board could allow something evil to slip through.

Her mouth was dry, and she wished Leon had grabbed her a drink after all. All evening, she had worried about how to leave the party without attracting attention if a dyszoon emerged from the Veil. That some form of one could enter Jessica's living room, she hadn't considered.

"All right, lay a finger on the piece!" Veronica said gleefully, her phone put away. The junior girls and Jessica obediently touched a finger to the planchette, along with Zeke and even Beth. Nathan and Ethan sat on the edge of the circle by their girlfriends, but didn't join. Leon had disappeared again.

Daphne remained on the couch, a ghost that had come to watch the party but could never fully participate. It was unlikely that she could stop them from playing, but she could refuse to take part in it. She should have known that Veronica would somehow ruin the party.

Jessica looked over. "Hey, Daph, don't you want to try it?"

"There's not any room." It was a legitimate excuse.

"We can make room." To Daphne's horror, Jessica scooted aside until there was a gap between her and Veronica.

"That's okay, I just want to watch." She kept her voice neutral, as though the board didn't much interest her.

"Why not?" Veronica said with a touch of disdain. "Come. Sit by me. It'll be fun!" she patted the floor beside her.

The others were growing quiet. Veronica was drawing attention to her choice and soon would make it weird.

"No, I'm just going to watch," Daphne repeated. She had already promised Claire, however reluctantly, that she wouldn't touch the Veil and expose herself to its power. Playing with a

Ouija board probably belonged in the same category of things that wouldn't impress the psychic.

But Veronica had caught on to something, and it would be difficult to get her to let go. "How come? Does it make you uncomfortable?" she said in a sympathetic tone that was anything but. "Don't worry, it's just for fun!"

Jessica had once said something similar to convince Daphne to get a psychic reading at Madam Moon. But Veronica was not her friend. She refused to give in.

"I'm good, really," Daphne said, keeping calm with difficulty. It was so easy for Veronica to get under her skin.

"C'mon, you should *totally* try it—"

"If she doesn't want to, she doesn't want to," Nathan interrupted sharply. Both of them looked at him in surprise. Daphne had never seen him irritated before.

Veronica's open mouth morphed into a smirk, as if she couldn't care less. "Okay then, let's start," she said, mock-sweet.

Daphne settled at the edge of the couch, struggling to calm her annoyance at Veronica, and at herself for being annoyed. She tried to catch Nathan's eye again to show she was relieved and grateful, but he was watching the board.

A little of the cheerfulness she'd felt earlier with Leon returned. Nathan had stood up for her. And against his girlfriend, of all people. There was no time to puzzle out what this meant, for Veronica had begun.

"Turn the light off," she commanded, straightening with authority. Ethan was nearest the light switch and obliged. The overhead light plunged them into semidarkness, a scented candle the only source of light.

"If there is anyone here with us today, we invite you to speak with us." Her smile cut into her otherwise solemn tone. Jessica pressed her lips together to stop giggling. "Is there anyone here with us tonight?"

The piece moved forcibly to *Yes*.

"*Zeke!* Don't move it." Jessica nudged him. He snickered.

When it was returned to the center, Veronica solemnly repeated the question. This time, as Daphne expected, the piece didn't budge.

"Try a different question?" a junior girl suggested.

"What's your name?" another called out.

"Shh, it won't answer if more than one person asks the questions," Veronica said, waving them down. "Is there anyone here? Can you tell us your name?"

After a few questions, it was clear the piece wasn't going to move by itself. Even Jessica was looking disappointed. From behind Veronica, Leon reappeared. Daphne looked up and caught his eye, grimacing. It was obvious she was the only one not participating.

"Is there something you'd like to tell us tonight?"

There are a lot of things I'd like to tell you, Daphne thought with resentment.

"What do you want?"

Nathan's eyes were on the board, his darkened face impassive. *Something I can't have.*

"Can you give us a sign of your presence?"

Something prickled at the edge of her awareness. Daphne sat up, straining to determine what had changed. Was she sensing something amiss with the Veil, or was an evil awakening in the room, just beyond her ability to perceive?

"What is your name?" Veronica called.

The prickling grew. Something was moving in the room, she was sure of it. Daphne sat on the edge of the couch. *Stop asking questions*, she wanted to snap. But no one would take her seriously.

"Are you a friendly spirit?"

The planchette moved slowly and stopped on a word. Jessica gasped.

No.

A stunned silence fell over the room as the candle flickered.

Darkness swallowed them. But before anyone could draw a breath, the flame relit like someone had merely blown on it.

The tension broke. "Ooh..." Several jeered in unison. Jessica fell into Veronica, overcome by laughter.

Relieved, Daphne unstiffened her shoulders. The prickling sensation was gone. There had been little danger of a dyszoon getting through, she knew that now. Daphne looked over at Nathan and, pleased to catch his eye, smiled at him.

"Wait, we have to keep going," Veronica said, pushing Jessica back up into a seated position. "We can't end it without saying *goodbye*, anyway."

Daphne stood up under the pretense of getting a drink and filled half her cup with the margarita.

"Want to go do something else?" came a low voice. Leon stood next to her, hands in his jeans. "If you want to get out of that, I can show you some of my artwork for a few minutes."

"Sure," she said without hesitation, setting the cup back down. Veronica was asking questions again. Daphne's absence would go unnoticed.

She followed him down the balloon-decorated hallway and took a left into a large room with polished hardwood floors. It was sparsely furnished with only a piano and stool. Daphne couldn't recall being in it before.

"This is kind of my mom's space," he said, walking backward. "She wanted to turn it into a creative room, so she hung up all my paintings."

Stunned, Daphne stopped in the middle and rotated. Canvases covered the walls, in some places from floor to ceiling. The different styles were mesmerizing.

"Are *all* of these yours?" she asked, overwhelmed by the number of paintings.

"Like, eighty percent," he said. "Pretty much anything I've made since the beginning of high school. And there's some of Jessica's, too."

"Did you do that one?" Daphne pointed to what was easily the largest canvas, as tall as the wall it hung on. It was a chaos of color with randomly splattered paint, but the final result was clearly intentional.

"This one was my summer project." They approached it, and more colors came into view. Daphne wished she knew more about art to say something intelligent about it. She wanted to be separate, to appear deeper and more mature than the giggling high school girls in the other room.

Leon pointed at the splotches. "I wanted to paint something where I didn't think about my choices. I just chose the first color that came to my head and chucked it at the canvas. No second guesses. Just whatever came to mind right away."

"Sounds like something I could do. Though it wouldn't turn out as well," Daphne said, looking it up and down. The painting was good enough to hang in a gallery.

Leon laughed. "I just kept chucking paint until it became what I wanted. I didn't have a plan."

"The process was more important than the result," Daphne observed.

He brightened, as if he hadn't thought of it that way, but it made perfect sense. "Yeah! I'll put that in my artist's statement, if I ever display it."

"You should. Display it, I mean. It's really good," she said, wishing again that she had the art vocabulary to better compliment it.

"Thanks. Can I show you this one?" he said, leading her to

a much smaller watercolor painting. "I did it last semester. I'm pretty proud of it."

A realistic owl gazed at them with a stern brow, its two pupils the size of quarters, with a faint dusting of white.

He was growing more animated, Daphne noted. It was charming. Leon gave her a brief tour of a few other pieces of artwork, passing over ones from high school that were no longer up to his standards but still prized by his mother.

One detailed portrait captured her attention, black and gray like her own photos, where most of the paintings were a riot of color. An unknown woman looked over her shoulder at the viewer, her highly freckled face half cast in shadow and tendrils of untamed hair. Her gaze was like one caught between shots—neither smiling nor coy, but a touch melancholy.

"Who is she?" Daphne asked, pointing.

"Oh—just out of my head." He shrugged.

"She seems so real." Daphne leaned closer, taking in the only visible eye that rested on a point just below the observer's gaze, like the woman hadn't noticed she was being watched. Darkness hid the other eye.

"Yeah. I wanted to try drawing a portrait without a model, and in black and white to focus on the shading. Then I imagined it like a story." His tone turned professional, like he was presenting to an art critic or an interested buyer.

He gestured at the bottom of the canvas, which dissolved into a charcoal tempest. "I pictured her as someone who stands in a shadow, but it's a shadow that she created in order to hide the weight of the problems she carries. And it's something no one else notices. But in this moment, when she lets down her guard, you can see it."

Daphne straightened uncomfortably, feeling as though she were standing before her own likeness. He couldn't know how closely the story of the woman hit. But his artist's eye had made him attuned to her thoughts all evening—from her reluctance to get her hair colored to taking part in the Ouija board. She hid her thoughts from even those closest to her, but he could somehow read them.

To her surprise, she felt more relieved than exposed. Comfortable. It was like a reprieve from secrets before the weight was hidden once again.

"I understand what you mean," Daphne answered after a pause, remembering that he needed a response. She looked up at him and was startled by how close their faces were. His eyes widened slightly as though realizing it, too. The distance between them was far enough to seem casual, but close enough that the space between them was charged.

Without thought, she drew closer to him just as he began doing the same—

"Leon, you're not showing off your boring artwork, are you?" Jessica's voice broke in. A bolt of panic ran through Daphne and she leaned closer to the portrait, pretending to inspect some detail closer.

"Says the girl with no artistic talent," Leon retorted, then pulled her into a headlock. She squealed and wriggled away.

Daphne forced a smile, heart still thumping wildly as if Jessica had caught her in wrongdoing. It skipped a beat— Nathan was there too, an odd expression on his face, like he knew what they had just interrupted. She blushed and turned away. Why had he followed Jessica?

"C'mon, we're going to watch a movie!" Jessica said, taking Daphne's hand.

Avoiding Nathan's eyes as she passed, Daphne followed her to the living room and sat on the floor as though someone else were steering her body.

Despite their tense moment earlier, Veronica cuddled up to Nathan on the couch. Beth and Ethan had settled on the other couch, but with less nauseating PDA. Daphne's stomach fluttered when Leon sat on the floor near her, but in front of Jessica, who took full advantage.

"Good, I need a footrest," she said, planting her feet on both of his shoulders.

"Is that so?" he replied, and tickled them until Jessica shrieked and brought them up to her chest protectively. Zeke returned and flopped next to her.

Daphne was highly aware of Leon throughout the movie, which passed unseen. She relived the charged moment in the art room. Had they really almost kissed? What might have happened if Jessica hadn't walked in? Her face heated again.

She was careful not to look in Nathan's direction, though his gaze pressed on the back of her head more than once.

Perhaps she'd surprised him. It was a different Daphne who had leaned in at that moment, someone more impulsive and reckless. Or perhaps it wasn't a different Daphne at all, but a version of herself feeling the sting of loneliness, who just wanted to forget everything and not care, just for a minute...

The movie finished. To her relief, Beth and Ethan left soon afterward, which made it more natural to say goodbye to Jessica a few minutes later. They hugged, and Daphne strode to the front door, trying not to look too eager to leave.

"Hey, Daphne, are you headed out?" came Leon's voice. He jogged toward her, upsetting balloons in his wake.

"Yeah," she answered, feeling the air charge. Underneath the excitement, however, was a faint sense of disappointment that he wasn't Nathan.

"It was good to meet you. Would you mind...Could I get your number?"

"Oh—sure." Daphne hoped she sounded confident and not surprised, like she had never experienced this scenario before.

It was nice meeting you, she almost said after entering it into his phone, not sure what one was supposed to say after giving away a number. Thankfully, the lame, formal response went unspoken.

"Well—talk to you later," he said with a smile. Daphne smiled shyly over her shoulder before stepping gratefully through the front door and into the freezing dark.

The neighbor woman carried a box down the lit driveway and set it down in midair inside an invisible car. She mimed shutting the door, and the box vanished. The shade returned to the house and walked straight through the front door.

Daphne considered her, and then, shaking her head, headed to her car. *Another time.*

10

———

PITY

Daphne pushed open the cabin door and stepped inside the dim room. A discarded chip bag crinkled under her foot. Startled, she kicked it aside and closed the door, cutting off the frigid, snowy air.

An air of unkemptness hung about the place. Discarded socks littered the floor along with dozens of crumpled up pieces of paper that had missed the paper bag being used for trash. Unrinsed food cans and more chip bags cluttered the limited counter space.

Despite what seemed like an endless amount of free time, Ashley had long given up on tidying. The bedsheets were bunched in a heap at the foot of the bed. Its occupant lay on her side, her usual baggy black sweatshirt swallowing her skinny frame.

Daphne approached her cautiously, fearing that her stillness meant death.

"Ashley?" she said, but no stirring came from the bed. Daphne crouched down to inspect her former classmate's face, half-hidden by uncombed hair and the drawn-up hood.

Ashley stared ahead without reaction, not even at the hand waved in front of her face. She was like a shell, almost lifeless except for the shallow rise and fall of her shoulders, which Daphne noted with relief, because at least she wasn't dead.

But her face was pale and sickly. The simmering rage Daphne used to sense beneath the surface was extinguished, replaced by emptiness.

Pity seared her. If only she could reason Ashley back to sanity. To convince her to stop being a tool of the demon, if only for her own sake.

Daphne moved to shake her shoulder. But time sped up, the light in the room dissolving into shadow. Ashley remained still as the cabin shrank into darkness like a dying candle. The light extinguished, and Daphne woke.

Several hours later, Daphne picked her way through the woods behind the house, replaying the short vision. The rising sun made a flashlight unnecessary. Unlike in the dream, there was no heavy snow, only a damp March chill.

Did the vision happen in real time? The heavy snow seemed to answer the question. Unless Ashley was far in the north, the vision showed a time in the past. It was unlikely that Mr. Burnes had sourced a hiding spot more than a few hours' drive away.

The blank expression on Ashley's face disturbed her. If Mr. Burnes was the only person aware of Ashley's whereabouts, that meant most of the time, she was alone. Daphne enjoyed stretches of quiet, but knew that dwelling too long inside her own head would edge her down the path of insanity. And with a demon twisting her thoughts, Ashley's situation was worse.

Daphne checked the time and turned to head back to the

house. There were shades farther on that she didn't want to bother with that morning, including a small boy.

The sun was risen by the time she hopped over the sagging bottom porch step. Her mom closed the front door, purse in hand. "Oh, good, I was hoping I'd see you before I took off," she said, dragging a lanyard of keys out of her purse. "I'm going to run to the grocery store. Need anything?"

Daphne considered. "Can you get more chamomile tea? I can pay for it."

"Nonsense." Her mom waved a hand and pulled her phone out to add it to her shopping list. "Anything else?"

"No. I think that's it," Daphne said, moving to pass. "Oh—how was your night out with your friend?"

Her mom's face became thoughtful, as if assessing the evening. "It was good," she said at last. "I had a good time. It was nice."

"Good," Daphne said, confusion tugging at her.

"I'll want to hear about your *par-tay* when I get back."

Daphne entered the house and ran upstairs, jumping at the sight of Phillip. The shade, stationed at his favorite spot in front of the long mirror, was facing her direction. His handsome face stared as she ducked into her room, where he thankfully didn't have permission to enter. A soldier in the house was always intimidating.

She collapsed on the bed. With the house to herself, besides the shade and the cat, it would be a good time to call Claire with the update about Ashley without being overheard. The time showed it was eight in the morning, and the psychic would be awake.

Daphne rested the phone on her chin, thinking through what information to share. Should she inform her of Michael and the falling drill at Stage Crew? Claire wasn't enthusiastic about delving into shades' histories, preferring to leave them and their problems alone. *No, I'll just handle that one.*

There was also the Ouija board last night and the sense of something moving at a level beneath Daphne's awareness. But she wasn't positive, in retrospect, that anything had happened. A sense of unease was nothing to bother Claire about.

With a short agenda, they had little to discuss. Claire hadn't received the vision but was unconcerned about this. She agreed that the vision most likely took place in the past, and beyond that, there was little new information. Ashley was in the demon's employ, and it was costing her.

Daphne hung up, picturing Ashley's dark eyes boring into her own. Calm and dark like the Veil at the surface, but hiding a great turbulence underneath.

Ashley should be their enemy. If she hadn't helped the demon with its plans, the Veil would have remained dormant. Heather would still be alive. And yet, Daphne's pity grew, if possible, even stronger.

She checked her phone. The screen showed no notifications. Was it too early to expect a text from Leon? He had asked for her number barely ten hours ago.

I'll probably never hear from him, she coached herself with a faint sense of disappointment, trying to suppress the memory of his face leaning toward hers. He would be just one more thing to worry about. For example, if he started texting, was she obligated to tell Jessica? Would she be mad?

Daphne curled on her side and closed her eyes. Yet she couldn't shake the image of Ashley doing the same thing, imprisoned by dark thoughts. And all alone.

The vision of Ashley hung over Monday morning like a dark cloud, one that foreboded bad things to come.

Despite the sense of doom, the rest of the weekend had passed with no activity from the Veil. Daphne's worries that dyszoons would emerge in a steadier stream because it had widened hadn't come to pass—yet.

She carried her lunch tray back to the table and found Veronica sitting opposite Jessica. Her stomach squeezed in dread. Nathan's spot at the table was empty, which explained the change in seating arrangements. This meant there would be no walk to class together after lunch, and she would brave the journey to Mr. Burnes's hour alone.

Her resentment from the party returned. She half expected Veronica to bring up the Ouija board and make fun of her again as a subtle punishment for Nathan coming to her defense. As she took a seat, though, her fears turned to confusion. Veronica was red-faced from crying.

Hope that she'd suppressed over the weekend strained to run free. Veronica and Nathan weren't getting along at the party. Could it be—had they broken up?

Taylor leaned over. "Hey girl, what's wrong? You need anything?"

The question brought fresh tears to Veronica's eyes. She dabbed them away, trying to keep her makeup intact. Annoyingly, she was still pretty despite her blotchy face.

"My granddad died last night," she said, voice strained.

"It was sudden," Jessica added solemnly.

"I'm so sorry!" Taylor said, which was echoed in various ways around the table. Even Beth, who cared little for Veronica, looked sympathetic.

The hope that had fought to run free inside Daphne went limp, replaced by pity mixed with disappointment. Veronica explained with further tears that the funeral would be on Friday and much of her extended family would be traveling in.

Daphne felt a twinge of jealousy at the close relationship

and expected size of the funeral. Her own extended family was rather small in comparison, and she had few memories of her grandparents. Her grandma had died of breast cancer while her mom was in college, and her grandpa had lived in another state and passed away when Daphne was in second grade. Her dad had been estranged from his parents, and so they had never been in her life before they passed away. Uncle Lloyd was the only family she saw with any consistency.

"Where's Nathan?" she asked Jessica in a low voice as Taylor got up to offer a hug.

"He's sick today. I know he felt bad for not being here."

Daphne nodded. Selfishly, she was relieved to be spared seeing Nathan's arm around his girlfriend's shoulder. With his own loss fresh in memory, he would be able to say the right things. Had possibly already messaged them.

Maybe they'll bond over it. She bitterly speared a piece of broccoli, then checked her thoughts with guilt. If she became any more resentful and jealous, she'd become just as moody as Ashley. Whatever the demon thought, they were *not* alike.

As if through a dream, Ashley's blank eyes met her own. *You're already on your way.*

11

———

TRACK

Right after Stage Crew on Wednesday, Daphne walked to the track field for Nathan's meet.

There was no cost to enter. She walked along the bleachers until she found a row near the middle that wasn't occupied by blanketed spectators or duffel bags.

"Third and final call, boys 3200-meter relay." The announcer's voice boomed over the sound system, and Daphne flinched. One row down, a young boy was arranging his haul of food, which included a full box of doughnuts, two bags of cheese puffs, and a half dozen energy drinks.

While no events were happening on the track yet, it was nevertheless a busy place. Small groups of runners stretched and warmed up on the green field. In an area on the left, a standing crowd watched a runner with a pole launch herself over a bar and fall neatly onto a cushion, a move captured on the screen at the opposite end.

"Attention, Mr. Harrington. We need a baton at the finish line," the announcer said with a touch of exasperation.

Daphne stood to better view the athletes spreading out on

the track. The runner in the innermost lane was stationed farthest behind the others, which she guessed made the distances fair.

"Gun's up." The referee's neon-orange arm lifted. With a snap, the gun went off, signaling the start of the race. The time clock rolled.

"Go Trace!" a nearby woman shouted. Daphne sat, wondering if Nathan would appear soon.

The orange runner in the outermost lane outpaced everyone to take the lead, but he was only a few paces ahead of a home runner in Falcons green. In under a minute, the athletes were passing by the bleachers to scattered cheers.

"Yeah! Keep it up, Trace!"

"First call, boys 110-meter hurdle."

The top three runners far outpaced the rest in the next lap, and more stepped up to the finish line. As the leading orange runner finished, his teammate began running, holding out a hand behind him for the baton. The green runner handed off his baton a few seconds later, and his teammate hurried to catch up to the lead.

"Okay, so they trade off," Daphne muttered, better understanding the relay.

The boy with the doughnuts overheard her. "Yeah, each runner does two laps, and there's four on a team," he said with authority. "Each lap is four hundred meters. Do you know how many laps you'd have to do for a mile?"

Daphne was fairly certain that 1,600 meters was a mile and quickly did the math. "Four?"

"Yeah." The boy looked disappointed and turned back to the relay.

After a quick two minutes, the second set of runners handed off their batons. Dom, Nathan's friend, was next.

Although she was silently cheering for the Falcons, Daphne felt a sudden desire for him to fumble the baton.

Dom lagged behind the lead until he was directly ahead of the purple runner a distance back. A fourth runner wearing blue, who Daphne hadn't paid attention to before, brought up the rear.

The athletes clustered together, and she inwardly yelled at Dom to go faster. At the very least, he could get the purple runner off his heels.

The crowd cheered as the first athlete ran past the stands.

"Push it, Elton!" shouted the nearby woman, who Daphne guessed was cheering on the orange team. The blue runner was almost on top of the purple one now, his steps quick but heavy with lost steam. He'd likely pass him soon. No—he was passing *through* him.

Daphne gaped as the blue runner came up next to Dom's heels. They merged in a bizarre entanglement of limbs. He sprinted through the finish line without a baton.

Her focus switched to the shade. Now aware of him, she could faintly feel his presence in spite of the distracting crowd. The shade ran through the orange runner.

Dom gradually narrowed the distance between himself and the lead so that by the end of his second lap, he was only a short distance behind. Breathlessly, he handed over his baton. Daphne stood again to see over the crowd, seized by excitement. Nathan grabbed it and dashed off.

"Go Nathan!" she shouted, casting away restraint. Not to be outdone, the woman nearby screamed her support for the last orange runner.

"Look—he's going to pass him," the boy predicted. Sure enough, Nathan had closed the gap and slipped past the orange runner. The Falcons were now leading the relay.

The blue runner passed by the bleachers, and Daphne

frowned in concern. If shades could draw real breath, he was quite out of it.

There was no time to dwell. Nathan ran into view a few meters behind the shade, the orange runner almost literally on his heels. The crowd clapped and cheered.

A woman near the time clock rang a bell as they crossed the finish line. It was the last lap.

"Go Jamie! C'mon, Jamie! PUSH IT!"

Nathan was on the opposite side of the track, maintaining pace. But the orange runner on his heels was edging to his right—he was passing. Someone screamed. He had reclaimed the lead, increasing the gap between him and Nathan with each second, giving all his energy for a final sprint to the finish.

"Oh no!" Daphne covered her mouth.

The two runners curved around the track for the last stretch. The bleachers erupted with encouragement.

"Push, Falcons! PUSH!"

"GO JAMIE, YOU GOT THIS!"

Nathan was gaining on the lead, closing the gap. He was drawing level. They were neck and neck. Just a few meters from the finish line, he sprinted ahead as the clock struck the nine-minute mark.

Daphne joined in the clapping at this victory and for the remaining runners, who finished up their lap. Nathan and the winded orange runner shook hands.

The shade continued his solo run. She tracked his progress, pursing her lips—was he another shade stuck in a loop—literally? How long had he been at it?

"Did you want one?"

Daphne looked down. The boy held up the doughnut box.

"Oh—no, I'm good. Thanks. I have to go find my friend," she said, unsure why she was telling him this. The boy shrugged and bit into a doughnut.

Daphne left the bleachers and walked along the fence. A gun popped, and female runners dashed over the hurdles. She paused and watched, but it was over in a flash.

The shade curved around the track. Under cover of watching the next set of athletes take their spots, Daphne concentrated on him, reaching out a mental hand. As he drew level with her spot, huffing, she yanked his arm.

Abruptly, almost comically, the shade lost his balance and toppled to the side, rolling over with a heavy groan. Daphne stepped back in alarm—she hadn't meant to harm him, only to release him from the purgatory of endless running.

The gun popped again, and the next heat of girls ran through the hurdles.

"First call, girls 100-meter dash. Please check in at the green tent."

The shade got to his feet, alternately looking at the sky and at the ground, hands on his hips as he breathed deeply. Daphne breathed with him. It seemed he would be okay. Or as okay as one could be while dead.

"Hey, Daphne! There you are."

Her stomach flipped, and she couldn't help but grin at Nathan's approach. He had thrown a green jacket over his tank top and carried a matching water bottle. His dusty brown hair was even more swept up than usual.

"Hey. That was a good push there," she told him.

"Thanks, it was close. I figured when he passed that early that he'd start losing gas at the end."

"That makes sense." Daphne nodded shyly. With no upcoming class to interrupt their time, the pressure to make the most of it was high.

"Did you just get here?" he asked helpfully. "Are you sticking around for a while?"

"I got here when the relay started," she said. "When's your next event?"

"The 1600-meter run. I've probably got an hour yet. The hurdles and dashes will be first."

"Yeah, I'll stay."

"Cool." Nathan broke into a grin. "Want to see the field events closer?"

They headed toward the crowd on the left. Daphne worried that Veronica would show up out of nowhere, but for now, it seemed like they had the next hour to themselves. She turned around to check on the shade in blue, who was still catching his breath.

He'll be all right, she reassured herself. Freedom from his looped thoughts had to be better than constantly running. After all, Phillip at home had never complained about being pulled from his endless trek up the stairs.

"Third and final call, boys 110-meter hurdle."

"What do the calls mean?" she asked Nathan.

"First call means you should go check in, and by the third call, you need to be in your place," Nathan explained. "The guys are doing the hundred-ten-meter hurdle next."

Volunteers were readjusting the hurdles. The girls' portion was already over.

As they walked, Nathan explained the field events and his upcoming races. After the 1600-meter event, he had the 800- and 3200-meter runs, but he didn't expect Daphne to stay for the entire meet.

"You never do field events?" she said as an athlete jumped over the bar.

"No. They're separate. Since I'm a distance runner, I just do the longer races." Nathan laughed. "Coach decided one time to sign me up to do the 400-meter dash. It's just a whole lap of sprinting until you collapse, basically. It was the worst race I ever did. I can't do dashes."

The announcer informed the crowd that the 100-meter dashes were next. Content to move on, Daphne returned with Nathan to the bleachers.

The blue runner was nowhere in sight. Neither, thankfully, was Veronica. It was understandable if she was skipping Nathan's track meet because of the death in the family. Unless she hadn't shown up because there was something amiss between them.

They sat in an available row. A woman behind them was recounting her vacation to a friend. "The puffer fish were *enormous*. I swam over one and it was *way* bigger than my fins..."

The dashes started. It was easy to talk with Nathan, confirming what Daphne had always sensed—that if nothing else, they could be great friends if given the time. An alternate reality filled her mind. One where she was sitting next to Nathan not as a friend grasping for time, but as a girlfriend cheering him on.

The stands grew louder and more crowded as more parents arrived. "Are your parents here?" she asked, realizing that she hadn't considered they might show up.

"They might be by now," Nathan said. "They both work, but I think my mom was getting off a little early."

She nodded, hoping that they wouldn't run into his parents, who she had only glimpsed once at his cross country meet last fall. There was a part of her that still recoiled at the thought of meeting them, knowing their dead daughter was close by and not yet at peace. Daphne shivered.

"You cold?" Nathan asked.

"A little," she said, though her shiver had been less about the cold.

"Hang on." Without further explanation, Nathan stood

and jogged down the stairs, heading in the direction of the field events. Below, runners sprinted toward the finish line with a speed Daphne knew she could never hope to beat.

A junior girl sidled into Daphne's row and sat on her knees, hanging on to the back of the bench to talk to the women in the row above.

As she waited for Nathan to return, Daphne half listened to their conversation. It seemed that the girl wanted to join a trip to Mexico with her mom and family friends, but would need to pay for her own plane ticket. However, the trip would use up much of her savings.

"Remember, what are you saving for?" her mom admonished.

"A car...and insurance," the girl said reluctantly. "But I worked all last summer!"

"Well, would you rather leave the house *one* time for *one* trip, or *lots* of times because you have a car?"

"One time," the girl said instantly, then added in a defensive tone, "What? Mexico is way better!"

Daphne smirked and buried her hands further into her pockets, thankful for her own car. If possible, she should get a job in the summer, ideally earlier in the day. Her and Claire's schedule for dealing with dyszoons had worked out so far, and her savings were dwindling with each tank of gas. If not for the Veil, she would have found a new job months ago.

She shivered again and willed Nathan to come back soon. A few minutes later, he returned carrying a large green-and-white fleece blanket. Since the junior girl was in the way, he slipped into the next row and hopped over the back with impressive finesse.

"Use this," he said, handing over the blanket.

"Thanks, you didn't have to do that," Daphne said, grateful

nonetheless as she sat on the blanket and wrapped it around her chilly legs.

"It's no problem. I had it in my duffel bag by the tent. Ran into Dom."

"What's he doing next?" she asked, though not caring much what Dom did. She was glad he hadn't returned with Nathan.

"Same thing I am, the mile."

They watched the 100-meter dash below, which transitioned into the boys' heats. While the girls were fast, Daphne noted that the boys were practically a blur. Being that quick would be useful in dyszoon battles.

She had barely thought of the Veil the entire event. With so much to watch and Nathan chatting next to her, it was hard to dwell on her worries.

"First call, boys 1600-meter run," said the announcer.

Daphne was disappointed. "That's you, isn't it?"

"Yeah. I can wait a few minutes, though," Nathan said easily. "The girls are going first, anyway."

"Oh, *you* can go. I just would hate to lose the nice warm blanket," Daphne teased, wrapping it tighter around herself.

"I see how things are," Nathan said, deadpan. "Well, I guess I'll just—" He stood with bravado.

"Wait!" Daphne grabbed his arm, then blinked. It was strange to touch him, even to pull him back down. As soon as he sat, she released him, face warm.

"Though, actually, I guess I should get over there," he admitted after a pause. "I have to warm up."

"All right," she said, resigned. "I'll stay to watch. But, here, you can have your blanket back. Good luck with the race."

"No, keep it. Just give it back to me tomorrow or something."

Daphne gratefully wrapped the blanket around herself again. He stood to go, then hesitated.

"Hey, I'm...glad you could make it out. I feel like the last few months have been so busy that we haven't gotten the chance to hang out at all. You should still come and see my cameras, even if it doesn't work out, you know, until summer."

He sounded almost rehearsed, even nervous, as if he'd been carefully thinking of the right words as they talked.

"I know," Daphne said, caught off guard by the unexpected speech. Then, feeling vulnerable, she admitted, "I've wanted to hang out too. I do want to see your cameras sometime."

"Good." He flashed a grin, then turned to head toward the green tent for check-in. Daphne watched him go, feeling the urge to leap up and cheer at something other than the Falcons. Maybe the end of the school year wouldn't mean their friendship was over. Summer could bring more flexibility.

A dozen female runners lined up at the finish line, almost half of them in Falcons green. The gun went off and the girls sped down the track.

"Go Reese!"

With the blanket wrapped around her, contentment she hadn't felt for ages warmed her as she reflected on the last hour. It had been so long since they'd properly talked. Or, if she were being honest, since she had hung out with a friend at all.

Nathan was *glad* she came. He had even hinted at what was also on her mind—something she had always chided herself to keep quiet about because he wasn't hers: that she missed spending time with him.

I miss our study time. He had messaged her that. Maybe Nathan had realized that the study session at her house in the fall was the last time they'd hung out alone, and what he really meant was that he wanted more time with her. Just her.

But as friends? Or was there a chance yet for something more? Clearer than ever came the image of herself by his locker, his hands sliding around her waist, pulling her close, whispering words only she could hear...

The last call was announced for the boys 1600-meter run, yanking Daphne out of her imagination. A dozen runners were spread out evenly at the finish line, shuffling and hopping, Nathan in the middle. Her cheeks heated, the fantasy washing away now that the subject of it was in view.

"On your mark!" the ref shouted. The gun cracked, and the runners sprang down the track, though at an easier pace than the relay. In a minute, they were passing in front of the crowd.

"Go Nathan!" Daphne shouted.

He seemed to stumble—there was a misstep—but recovered quickly. His position was in the middle of the pack, which was surprising since he was one of the higher-ranked runners. Even Dom was ahead of him.

Perhaps it was strategic, and he didn't want to wear himself out before his final two events. He had mentioned that he only needed to place high enough to qualify for certain meets, so it wasn't necessary to be in the lead.

"Let's go, Ezra! You got this!"

"Go green! Keep the pace!"

A cool presence brushed her mind. Daphne looked up mid-clap and yelped, a sound that luckily went unnoticed by the women behind her.

The blue runner looked down at her, expressionless and no longer breathing heavily. Sweat glistened in his hair and on his muscular dark arms that were fuzzy with the curling mist of shades. She stared at him, her heart returning slowly to its normal speed.

The shade nodded once, solemn. Then he ran down the steps, legs passing through the bleachers, toward the crowd by the field events and out of sight.

12
———

MICHAEL

Daphne's happiness from spending so much time with Nathan was buoyed by the absence of dyszoon attacks through that Friday morning.

Claire had handled the last battle, as it was during school hours. Having a weeklong reprieve felt like a gift that could be snatched back at any moment, especially on her birthday.

It had been easier to cope with her eighteenth by ignoring its approach. Gloom was rolling in like a heavy storm, promising the reliving of old memories of her dad that stung because she couldn't create any more.

"Happy birthday, Daphne!" Jessica hopped next to her locker before the first bell, holding out a small gift bag. "Got you something."

Daphne took it with surprise, the dark clouds pausing in interest. She hadn't expected any presents from friends or, if she were honest with herself, any birthday wishes. The tissue paper, pulled aside, revealed a light blue leather wallet.

"Thanks, Jessica!" She unzipped it and peered inside. "I love all the pockets."

"You're welcome!" Jessica beamed and leaned in for a hug, which Daphne was long conditioned to accept. "I saw it and thought of you. I don't know why. Then I realized it was going to be your birthday!"

"Wait, it's your birthday?" Nathan had come over to visit and overheard. Daphne's face warmed, something that had been happening each time she saw him since the meet.

"Yeah, we're both adults!" Jessica said.

Daphne checked behind him before realizing, like an unexpected birthday present had dropped in her lap, that Veronica would be gone because of her grandfather's funeral. It meant a full day without annoying laughter or any PDA by his locker.

"Sorry, I didn't realize." Nathan looked put-out. "Happy birthday, Daphne."

"That's okay," Daphne said with honesty, though she appreciated his birthday wishes more than anyone else's. "It doesn't really feel like my birthday."

The bell rang. She stowed the wallet away, hoping that neither of them would ask about her plans. *I'll go home, maybe chat with the ghost for a bit...*

"See you later," Nathan said in a gloomy tone, leaving as Jessica headed for her own class.

Once he was gone, Daphne pulled out her phone and felt her face. It was still warm to the touch.

Happy birthday, Daphne! Enjoy your day.

Daphne smiled at Claire's midmorning text. It occurred to her she didn't know the psychic's birthday. Maybe it had already passed without acknowledgment. She resolved to ask the next time they met.

As she passed by the side theater door after lunch, Daphne itched to try the handle, on the slight chance it was unlocked, but didn't imagine that her birthday would make her any luckier than last week's attempt. If only she could pass through solid doors like a shade.

Since the previous Monday, when Michael had knocked the drill from the top of the ladder, he had only manifested around the stage in glimpses. It was as if the shade was keeping out of her reach, perhaps mindful that she could order him away once they made contact.

Whatever kept him tethered to the stage, he didn't want Daphne's help in resolving it.

She continued to her locker. To her surprise, Nathan was already waiting for her, a plastic cup in hand.

"Hey, I bought you this." He handed over the blended drink, which was piled high with whipped cream.

"What is it?" Daphne asked in disbelief that he had bothered to get her something.

"I went through a coffee shop over lunch. I know you don't drink coffee, so it's like a cookies-and-cream-blend...thing."

"It's so good," she said blissfully after taking a sip. Though the drink was icy, Daphne's face had flushed again. "This is my favorite flavor. Thanks!"

It was a turn in fortune. Only a week ago, she was overwhelmed by loneliness and had almost kissed a stranger. Now two friends had remembered her birthday, and she hadn't battled any dyszoons for a week.

Nathan grinned, evidently pleased by her reaction and the luck of getting the right flavor. "No problem. Happy birthday, again."

"Thanks. Burnes better not confiscate it," Daphne said, half-serious. In her current glow, it was impossible to feel her usual dread over history class.

"Tell him you'll buy him one," Nathan joked. Their walk was over too soon, but Daphne was glad that they'd had a month's worth of walks together at the track meet. And who knew? They could hang out that summer. She said goodbye and entered the history classroom.

Without Veronica to talk to, Vivian was slouched against the wall with a bored expression. Feeling bold, Daphne was tempted to ask her how the musical was coming along on the actors' side of things, but thought better of it as she settled in and set the drink on the desk. She could ask Chad next week.

Daphne tried and failed to picture him and Vivian together as the two romantic leads. They didn't seem alike at all. *I guess that's where the acting part comes in.*

"What do we have here?" came a deep voice beside her. "That looks good."

A shard of ice pierced the warm glow. Daphne looked up at Mr. Burnes, attempting to keep the horror out of her expression. He had paused in the row between desks and was peering down at her, his long sideburns stretching halfway across his face. Before her eyes, in a cabin far away, he kicked over a pile of cans in rage.

"It's...a blend I got."

"Where's mine?" It was an attempt at a joke, and therefore menacing. His eyes were dark and deceptively friendly. She half expected them to narrow in acknowledgment. *I know who you are. I know what you can do. Stop me, and I will end you.*

Daphne forced herself to laugh. It sounded fake even to her ears. "I guess I forgot it."

Where's Ashley? Where are you hiding her? Is she still in that cabin?

"Shucks," he said mildly. "Next time, then."

To Daphne's immense relief, he moved on. The bell rang. She straightened with the sense of having sidestepped a land mine.

It's fine. He's still not going to murder you. Daphne took a sip of her drink and felt slightly better. *It's my birthday.*

The rest of the school day passed with no sudden attack by Mr. Burnes. At the last bell, students rushed to their lockers and fled for the weekend.

The warm glow had faded with the empty drink cup that Daphne tossed. What awaited her was a too-quiet evening at home with only her mom, Mystique, and Phillip for company.

Daphne regretted not planning something special for her birthday to distract herself, but a party wasn't an option. Besides having a depressingly short list of people to invite, she couldn't leave her own party to go to the Veil.

I bet Claire would have covered, she realized. It was too late now.

Daphne packed her backpack, hoping without success to see Nathan again before the weekend. She ambled down one of the empty hallways that led past the theater, not in any hurry to go home. But at least she *could* go home. Michael and Heather would remain tied to the school for lifetimes unless she helped them let go.

A janitor who looked young enough to be a student was passing by, rolling a trash bin. An idea came to her. Before she could second-guess it, Daphne hurried forward.

"Sorry. Do you by chance have a key to the theater? Or know someone who does? I'm in Stage Crew, and I left my jacket behind. I think it's still in there, but I'm going to need it for this weekend."

The lie was making her wordier than necessary.

"Yeah," the janitor said simply. To Daphne's astonishment, he walked down the stairs and unlocked the door, propping it open for her.

"Thanks so much, I'll just be a second."

He shrugged. "I'll lock it back up in a few minutes."

Daphne hurried into the theater, hardly believing her luck. The open door provided some light, but most of the room was pitch-dark except for strips of light along the steps. Dropping her backpack, she rummaged for her flashlight.

Where should she look for Michael? Even with the better light, the darkness was unpleasantly solid and somehow more menacing than the woods. Daphne swung the light beam over the stage, more for the benefit of not being in the dark than because it was necessary to perceive the shade.

The completed dining room set had been rolled off to the side. The beginnings of their next project, a wide staircase she was looking forward to painting, was in the middle. Daphne stopped next to it.

"Michael?" she called as loudly as she dared. Then, louder, "Michael? Where are you?"

No response. The ramp leading downstairs looked horribly dark, but she might have to go down it, and soon. The janitor would be back to lock the door.

Daphne shone the flashlight at the catwalk, the first place she had seen the shade. A faint presence brushed against her mind, and her heart flipped. Michael was looking down at her, one misting hand on the railing.

"Michael, come down here!" she called, fearful that he would disappear again before she had the chance.

The shade uncurled his hand from the railing. Keeping a haughty gaze on her, he trudged down the length of the platform. Daphne followed his progress with impatience. He was obeying, but barely.

Suddenly, he was no longer there. She pointed the flashlight toward the middle edge of the stage. Michael stood in a prime spot to be seen by the imaginary audience, his face smug.

Daphne swallowed, flicking off the flashlight. The photograph in the glass case outside the theater had, in death, come to life before her eyes. In reality, he was less present than the dust that floats across a stage light.

Michael glowed like a pale moon. Superiority dripped from him. She could only imagine how much more it had done so while he lived.

"I've been searching for you," Daphne said, unable to completely quell the fear stirring inside her. No matter how many times she saw shades, there would always be a part of her that feared ghosts.

She stepped forward until they were only a few paces apart and was relieved that he didn't move. Whatever bound him to obey her summons was keeping him nearby. His smirk quieted her usual guilt over this.

"Why did you stay behind? Why are you here?" Daphne asked. At any moment, their time could be over. And with shades, she had long learned that getting to the point was the best way to interact with them.

Michael strode almost right up to her nose. "This stage is mine! I deserve it!" he shouted, gesturing with a wild arm. "It was taken from me!"

Daphne stepped back, heart hammering as much as if a living person had confronted her, despite the lack of actual danger. In his anger, Michael seemed alive. The worst he could do to her was pass through, but words were another matter.

His reason for staying matched Daphne's best guess. Death had robbed him of his starring role, and this had evidently prevented him from moving on.

"I'm sorry you died," she said, meeting his livid face without reacting to his outburst. "But that was almost thirty years ago. You had your time on the—"

"It's MY part. MY musical. *No one* gets to take it from me," Michael bellowed, now walking in agitation around her, mist trailing in his wake. His blond hair was combed into sleek waves, forever groomed for a part that he could never perform.

Daphne matched his pace. They were like animals circling each other, each angling for dominance.

"I understand you didn't get to perform, but—"

"I *deserve* this part. I *worked* for it. *No one else* gets to have what *I* worked for!" he said bitterly, pointing a misting finger at the set.

Daphne noted the present tense with a sinking feeling. *So that's why he interferes with performances.* He was still in the present. *His* present.

"This isn't your musical anymore. Yours never happened," she told him, still matching his pace in a slow circle.

"This *show* isn't going on without me," Michael declared. "*I'm* the lead. *I* put in the work. *I* don't get to be thrown out!"

He was like a child throwing a temper tantrum, and Daphne fought to keep patience. "But you died. Your stage isn't here anymore."

Michael stopped, a dark sea of empty seats behind him. He was an actor without an audience. Daphne also paused. Had her reasoning gotten through to him or made him remember that fateful night on the motorcycle?

"*No one* gets to take my part from me," he whispered with menace. "*No one.*"

In a blink, he was gone. Bewildered, Daphne felt outward for his presence, but there was nothing.

"Michael? Michael!" she called. There was no answer.

Daphne turned on the flashlight and returned to the entrance, grateful the janitor hadn't witnessed the conversation. The hallway was empty, and she kicked the door closed with a shiver. Her legs were shaky from fading adrenaline.

Michael unnerved her more than any other shade. He was volatile and hard to reach. His anger tethered him to the stage, and even death was an unimportant obstacle to the glory he had once imagined for himself.

She had encountered shades who had died horribly or were concerned about a loved one left behind, but Michael was different. He'd died with his dreams unaccomplished and was determined that no one else could supplant what was, to him, his rightful place as the lead. It was a selfish reason.

Claire's long-standing caution about shades' problems being too difficult to solve came to mind. It seemed to be true in Michael's case. Short of casting him in a musical, was it even possible to help him move on?

Even if she couldn't help him, there were stakes Daphne couldn't ignore. He'd toppled the drill from that ladder and almost injured someone. And there was Beth's story of the prop that fell and ruined a scene during a performance, an incident that appeared far less innocent now.

Maybe the best she could do in Michael's situation was to prevent him from interfering with the musical. But their conversation had been short, and she hadn't had a chance to order him away.

Going forward, Daphne decided as she opened her car door, she would keep an eye out for the shade and take the next opportunity to protect others from his wrath.

She grimaced. Stage Crew was no longer the normal activity she'd once hoped for. Wherever she went, ghosts would always haunt her.

13

───────────

EIGHTEEN YEARS

Daphne cast off her shoes and dumped her backpack in the entryway. The kitchen light was on, which meant her mom was home already from work.

"Mom?" she called, then halted in amazement. Streamers and balloons covered the kitchen entrance. Daphne pushed them aside.

"Whoa."

Two giant foil balloons spelled out *18*. A professionally decorated cake was on the table, crowned by chocolate truffles, wafers, and macarons.

"Happy eighteenth birthday!" her mom cried with a small hop, a one-woman surprise party. "You're an adult!"

"You got me a cake from the bakery?" Daphne said in amazement. Normally, they bought a cake from the grocery store or a cupcake each.

"Of course! They did a great job, didn't they? I thought 'Death by Chocolate' sounded nice, so that's what I ordered."

Mesmerized, Daphne inspected the cake closer. "Wow, they even have truffles on here."

"I know! I resisted eating one of them and rearranging the spot. You wouldn't have noticed, I suppose."

Daphne laughed. In her growing gloom, now kept at bay again, she hadn't considered that her mom would go to any special effort beyond the usual. Everyone else had given more thought to her birthday than herself.

"You got off work early?"

"Yes, I wanted to have time to prepare everything. I made fish tacos too."

They settled into the early birthday meal. It felt like a time before she had heard of the Veil, before she'd lied to her mom repeatedly about her whereabouts and struggles. Daphne put off thoughts about shades, dyszoons, and anything that was bothering her as she showed off the new wallet and even braved sharing that Nathan had bought her a drink.

"He did, did he?" Her mom raised both eyebrows suggestively.

"Not like that," Daphne said hastily, having feared this reaction. She hoped that the gesture was a sign, at the very least, that Nathan valued their friendship enough to not let it die at graduation. To hope for anything more was to be set up for disappointment.

"Mmm-hmm." Her mom took a sip of water. "Well, that was very nice of him."

After getting a picture of Daphne with the cake and balloons, her mom cut her a large piece with plenty of toppings.

"This is the real reason for birthdays," Daphne said, biting into a macaron with a satisfying crunch. "Chocolate."

"Exactly!" her mom agreed. She cut a much smaller piece of cake for herself and tossed in a truffle. When they finished, she handed over a present bag.

"Wow, Mom! You bought me the telephoto lens?" It wasn't a cheap gift.

"I hope it's the right one. I followed the link you sent me that one time," she said. "It has the built-in stabilization and all the fancy-ness."

"It's perfect." Daphne turned the box over with reverence.

"Good. Now you can do all the telephoto things!"

"I can get long shots, yeah," she said. Her standard lens was adequate for most uses, but the new lens would make photographing wildlife easier.

Daphne set the box aside, her mood lifting further in anticipation of testing out the lens later. Dreading the time when she was finally alone with her thoughts, she allowed herself to be drawn to the living room for a movie.

"You can pick, I don't have any preference," she said, flopping onto the couch. Thankfully, unlike last week, Phillip wasn't standing in the middle of it.

"I thought this one looked interesting," her mom said, remote in hand. "It's about a couple who broke up after high school and then they run into each other in Italy twenty years later. She's divorced, and he concentrated on his career, so he never married."

"Ah," Daphne said. A bushy tail walked by, and she patted the cushion. Mystique leapt up to examine the spot. "So they're going to fall in love, but first, obstacles."

"We shall see-ee," her mom replied in a singsong voice, starting the movie.

Daphne's phone lit up. With a happy jolt, she saw Nathan's name on the screen.

Hey, I hope you're having a great birthday.

I am, thanks! she replied, and sent a picture of the cake.

Wow, he replied, unknowingly echoing Daphne. *Now that's a cake.*

I'll save you a piece, Daphne typed, in a joking mood, but deleted it. It might come off weird, maybe a little desperate.

Death by Chocolate, she sent instead, and then turned off the phone to resist the temptation to respond again.

The movie was enjoyable enough, though Daphne was tempted to turn her phone back on more than once. An hour and a half later, the man rushed to the airport to catch his love interest before her flight out of the country. He made it just in time to declare that he couldn't spend another twenty years without her.

"That was sweet," Daphne said, yawning prematurely. It was barely seven. Mystique was curled up at her feet, a fluffy black rug.

"Want to watch another one? Or choose something yourself?" Her mom held out the remote from the armchair.

"No, I think I'm going to just chill in my room," Daphne said, yawning again. "Is that okay?"

Watching another movie would only postpone the gloom she could still feel rolling in like storm clouds. It could only be postponed so long before it must be felt.

"It's your birthday. You get to do what*ever* you want."

Daphne smiled and rolled her eyes. She retrieved the lens before heading upstairs, saying hello to Phillip as he stared misting before the mirror.

Hopefully there would be no need to rush out to the Veil that night. Daphne flopped onto her bed and turned on her phone, waiting impatiently for the screen to light up with Nathan's response.

Her heart sank in disappointment. There were no new messages.

Daphne reviewed her last message critically. *Death by Chocolate.* Was that lame? Should she have gone with her first choice?

Or he's busy. He might have messaged her on the way to his girlfriend's house, and they were right now curled up on a couch, watching a movie of their own while Daphne lay next to her cat. But no—Veronica had family over for the funeral. They wouldn't be spending a romantic evening alone.

She shook her head. It was pointless to obsess over something so small, or torture herself imagining them together. A distraction was necessary.

Daphne attached the new lens to her camera and pointed it out the window, testing its capabilities. It was too close to sunset to test it properly in the woods, but she could try it out tomorrow. She set it aside and opened up her laptop.

Now that her birthday was almost over, it was somehow easier to look up ideas to celebrate. She paused over an article that suggested "18 Insanely Fun Ways to Celebrate Your 18th." The weekend was ahead of her. Maybe she could cross off at least one thing on the list.

Book a hotel room. It was too late for that one. Daphne hadn't taken her mom up on an offer to go away for the weekend. It was too risky to go out of town and leave Claire alone to deal with the Veil.

Get a tattoo. A few classmates had booked tattoos right after their birthdays, but Daphne wasn't attached to any design she'd want inked forever on her skin.

Stay out all night. Outside of bars, there wasn't exactly any nightlife in Long Haven for newly minted adults not of drinking age. The last time she had stayed up late was on Halloween, to fight dyszoons.

Her phone lit up. Daphne checked it, hopeful that Nathan had finally gotten back. However, the message was from an unknown number.

Hey Daphne, thought this was pretty cool. Maybe we could try it sometime.

The sender had shared a reel that showed a splatter paint

project. Leon's large painting came to mind, though the art in the video was simpler.

This is Leon btw. Jessica's brother.

Daphne felt a tiny shock that she wasn't sure how to interpret. Exactly a week had passed since the party, and though she had tried not to expect anything, part of her had been disappointed not to hear from him.

Her thumb hovered over the keyboard, then lifted away. Would it appear desperate if she responded only a minute after his message, especially since it had taken him a week to reach out? Would it imply she didn't have any plans on a Friday night? But if he was messaging her, maybe he had nothing going on, either.

It doesn't matter anyway, Daphne told herself, annoyed that she was already overthinking it. It wasn't like she was looking to *date* him, was she? His college was a few hours away, for starters. Her thoughts shouldn't have even gone that far. He might just be bored. Yet, a memory of his face coming closer to hers intruded, and her face heated. *Stop it.*

That looks like fun, she wrote back. *I need some art for my wall.* Daphne sent the message and was pleased to see that he was already typing back.

Hey, I could paint you something if you wanted. We could do some fun art projects this summer.

Daphne smiled, her mood lightening again. It wasn't a happy birthday message—she didn't want to reveal it was her birthday, in case he asked what she was up to—but texting was a decent distraction.

That would be fun. Daphne deleted the text before sending, realizing it was almost the same as her last reply. *I'd be up for that,* she sent instead.

Was that too available? She analyzed it, worry growing as a long minute passed without a return message. He was probably out with friends, bragging about the high school girl he had hanging on his every word.

She had only met him once, but Leon didn't seem like that type. Besides, imagining the worst of him wasn't a good strategy to avoid being disappointed. Daphne turned back to the list of birthday ideas.

"Go mini golfing," she said aloud. It had been at least six years since she'd putted a colorful ball around a course. She had been...Yes, her dad had been with her, just the two of them. Daphne struggled to bring the memory to the surface, particularly of him, but could only recall fishing a golf ball out of a concrete pool.

The gloom she'd held back all day washed over her. In the memory, he was only a faint presence, fuzzy and out of focus, like a shade. He was becoming a remnant in her mind, slipping away. It was her eighteenth birthday, and he would never get to see her as an adult.

Daphne pressed her palms against her eyes. *Stop it.* The shadows around her desk light sharpened, ready to cocoon her in self-pity and regret. No, she wouldn't go down that melancholy path. Not on her birthday.

Another text from Leon helpfully distracted her. The dark cocoon brightened.

Actually, are you free spring break? My family's going on vacation, but I should be back on Thursday. Want to meet up at Central Cafe later? At 6?

A stronger shock zapped her. Just like that, after a week of silence, Leon asked her out for her first date ever. Her suspicious imagination softened. Perhaps he'd been nervous of rejection and had only now worked up the courage. And he had gotten straight to the point, which, according to everything she had heard from other girls, was entirely refreshing.

But how to respond? Daphne imagined him staring at his

phone, wondering in turn why it was taking her so long.

Nathan popped into her head. For a moment she fantasized about him finding out about the date and being jealous, discovering feelings that he hadn't realized were there...But no, he was dating Veronica. Would still be in the summer.

Daphne had a choice. She could either spend the break dwelling on Nathan and what could have been, or she could learn how to paint from a guy who was certainly not unattractive.

Sounds like a date, she sent with a burst of excited nerves. There. She had done it. Her first date. It was something to look forward to, a spark of heat in the miserable fog of uncertainty that shrouded the last few months. Battling dyszoons wasn't her whole world.

Daphne rubbed her eyes. It was only a little after eight, but fatigue was settling into every muscle, and either a nightmare or a dyszoon would likely awaken her in the early hours.

Leaving her phone untouched, Daphne instead clicked through one video after another of easy art projects, gathering ideas for discussion, until she could no longer fight sleep.

At least I didn't have to fight any dyszoons on my birthday, Daphne reflected with gratitude as she settled into bed.

The bedroom was large and stylish, with pillows artfully arranged on a queen-size bed. Strings of white lights and tacked-up photos hung above it.

Veronica sat cross-legged on the wooden floor in a dark dress, her finger on the planchette of a Ouija board. A pretty blonde with a similar nose who looked just a year or two older also touched the piece, a lit candle in a glass jar nearby. The door was closed.

"Granddad, can you hear us?" Veronica said. The piece

didn't move.

"It's not going to work," the blonde girl said with a hint of disdain, removing her finger.

"Makayla. Just let me try, okay?" Veronica's eyes filled. "I just need to try." There was no trace of the arrogance she'd had at Jessica's party, laughing as she removed the board from the box. Only desperation.

"Okay, fine." Makayla put her finger back on the piece. "Try asking something less specific."

Veronica took a deep breath. "Is there anyone here with us?"

The piece moved to *Yes*. She squealed. "Did you move it?"

"No, *you* did—"

"I didn't—wait, don't get up," Veronica pulled her back down, keeping a finger on the piece. "I don't want him to leave."

"This is stupid. He's *dead,* " Makayla said, sitting down heavily.

"I just want to check if it's him. Okay. Granddad? Is that you? Are you with us?"

Just as she had a week ago at Jessica's party, Daphne sensed something stirring in the room. Uneasily, she moved closer to them. They had no idea of the danger.

"It doesn't want to talk," Makayla said, and was shushed with urgency.

"Shut up. I need to be the one to talk, or it won't work. Granddad? Are you here with us right now?"

The piece stayed in place.

"If it's you, can you give us a sign?"

The candle flickered, but stayed lit. "It's him!" Veronica said, her face lighting up with excitement instead of the misery of a minute ago. Makayla's face, in contrast, was drawn into a skeptical frown.

Daphne watched, dread increasing with each second. The unseen force was growing stronger, like an encircling snake looping itself tighter around its oblivious prey.

"Okay, Granddad? I just wanted to tell you I'm sorry I didn't get to say goodbye, and—and I love you." Tears spilled over onto Veronica's pink face. With her free hand, she wiped them away, sniffling. Daphne had never seen her so vulnerable, and her heart clenched.

It's not your granddad! She wanted to shake her, cruel as it would be to shatter the moment. Makayla seemed to have swallowed any further comment in pity. Yet the snake was squeezing, the pressure building—

"Can you just speak with us?" Veronica sniffed.

The piece moved to the letter *I*. Daphne was breathless, wrapped in horror. The unseen creature had paused, the wall separating it and the room cracking under pressure. The piece moved again, to the letter *M*.

"V, I swear, if you're moving it—" Makayla said, her annoyed tone back.

"I'm not!"

It moved back and forth across the board in a frenzy of letters. Both girls leaned over, mouths open. Skepticism was on Makayla's face, growing fear on Veronica's.

The piece paused. "'*I'm coming*'...Really, Makayla? You're such a—" Veronica stopped talking as the piece moved abruptly across the board and rested on the letter *D*. "What are you—"

The piece shot out from underneath both of their fingers and bounced off the wall. Both girls gaped as the lights over Veronica's bed flickered violently. The glass jar of the still-lit candle trembled as if caught in an earthquake.

And beneath it all, Daphne felt a pale brush of cold, faint but unmistakably like a dyszoon emerging from the Veil.

14

SCREW

With a gasp, Daphne woke and flung aside the covers. The alarm clock on her nightstand showed it was just before ten. She had only been asleep for an hour.

Half in the fog of the vision, she yanked on a jacket and sweatpants, then checked the hallway. Confident that her mom slept, Daphne crept down the stairs and, once outside, sprinted to her car.

Veronica's house...She knew vaguely where it was, in a rich neighborhood north of Long Haven. If she could get there, it might be possible to sense where the thing had ended up.

She fumbled with the car key. The sensation of the dyszoon coming out had felt far less potent than usual. Did that mean it was a weak dyszoon, or worse, some other evil that she and Claire hadn't yet encountered?

Whatever it was, even if it dissipated soon on its own, Daphne couldn't just let it run free to cause more chaos. Not even Veronica deserved that.

Twenty minutes later, Daphne turned sharply onto a winding drive lined with budding trees. Smooth shrubs accented a sloping brick wall, the neighborhood's name in metal letters. Despite the urgency of her mission, the immaculate houses awed her. Each was worth several times her own.

She focused outward for any sign of a dyszoon, but there wasn't anything yet, not even a shade.

The road curved and dipped, splitting off into other lanes. Daphne slowed, squeezing the steering wheel. Without Veronica's address, the search for the dyszoon was proving more difficult than she'd thought. This was assuming that the vision had taken place in real time and it wasn't already long gone.

A number of cars were parked on a side lane, which struck her as out of the ordinary in a neighborhood of long driveways. Daphne reversed and turned down the street. Redbrick houses with sloping lawns lined one side. On the other, a walking path edged with pine trees added a sense of privacy to the lane.

Vehicles spilled out of the driveway of an enormous home with white pillars, black shutters, and a double front door. Despite the late hour, the windows were brightly lit.

Daphne parked alongside the walking path and focused. The faintest cold flickered at the edge of her awareness, far weaker than any dyszoon she was used to.

She assumed the house with all the cars was Veronica's, hosting a multitude of relatives for the night after the funeral. Was the dyszoon still inside? All seemed quiet, which perhaps meant the creature was too weak to cause any more havoc.

Even so, she couldn't leave it alone. Yet she could hardly knock on the door, asking to take a look around.

Daphne exited the car, glad that the other cars on the road gave her a cover story for any neighbors who might be nervous about a lone figure strolling at night without a dog. A presence, like a faint breath, came from the opposite direction to the row of houses.

She stepped onto the walking path to follow the presence,

expecting a dark shape to swoop down, but no attack came. When she had drawn level with the next house, Daphne ducked between two pine trees and emerged onto an expanse of grass. There was a small grove of trees a stone's throw away, one of the few features in the pricey neighborhood that didn't appear there by design.

"There you are..." Daphne approached one of the more mature trees, no longer afraid of an attack. The dyszoon wasn't a threat, not even to Veronica.

She crouched down, sensing more than seeing the quivering wisp of dark fog at the base of the tree. Slowly Daphne reached for it, curiosity trumping fear, and poked it.

It was like reaching through cobwebs. The creature snarled and quaked more than ever. She removed her hand, none the worse for wear. With the smallest pressure, the wisp dissolved.

Daphne returned to her car. The victory felt anticlimactic. All that worrying, and there wasn't even a fight. It was a situation she could have handled before she first practiced battling dyszoons. The weak dyszoon would have dissolved soon without her help, but at least she had ensured it did.

Thankfully, the dyszoon had caused more mischief than lasting harm. The most exciting thing it had likely done was to throw the planchette across the room. Soon, the incident would become a good story.

Daphne settled behind the wheel as a silver car drove up the lane and pulled into Veronica's driveway on the open side. One of the front doors of the house opened. In the entrance light, Daphne recognized the figure running with her arms outstretched.

Veronica threw herself into Nathan's embrace, shoulders shaking with unheard sobs. He rubbed her back, speaking calming words Daphne couldn't hear.

Instead of the expected jealousy, her heart clenched as it

had in the vision, watching Veronica telling her dead grandfather the words she wasn't able to say.

To Daphne, battling dyszoons was as normal a morning routine as brushing teeth. The attack, if that was the right word, was minor for someone used to seeing dyszoons snap branches like twigs. But for Veronica, who didn't live in that reality, the experience was frightening.

She had vowed that no dyszoon would ever harm someone again. Now, a crack had formed in that promise in a way that neither she or Claire could have expected.

Despite their best efforts, the evil of the Veil would always threaten to spill over beyond their ability to contain it. The dyszoons that had almost attacked the two women on their morning walk just a few weeks ago were proof of this.

As the Veil's power increased, so too would the possibility for more attacks like tonight. Veronica wasn't the only person who would try to connect with spirits. With those attempts, more dyszoons could emerge from a network of mini Veils, perhaps not as mere wisps, but strong enough to cause serious harm.

It was only a matter of time before their containment problem grew out of control.

I'm coming, D. That taunting message, like a late response to a birthday party invitation, had been meant for her—she was certain of it. Was it from the demon? And if so, which one? And how had it known she was watching? Did it mean the "inferior" demon, called so by the demon eager to rise to Earth, was arriving sooner rather than later?

Daphne came to herself, realizing she had been staring at the couple for the last few minutes, lost in grim possibilities. They broke their embrace and entered the house. Starting her car, she turned around toward home.

Likely, the whole incident would smooth over any recent

friction and bring them even closer together as a couple. She pursed her mouth. *Some birthday...*

Daphne's resolve strengthened as a plan formed. She could already hear Claire's objections, but it was easy to dismiss them out of necessity. It was clear their problem was bigger than they had realized.

And to solve it, she would need to try something Claire wouldn't like.

Daphne approached the stone bridge nervously, second-guessing her decision now that she had arrived. The Veil was solid black despite the bright sun. Unremarkable except for the fact that it existed at all.

Its larger size again took her aback, but she rarely saw the Veil anymore. Dyszoons had always traveled farther down the road by the time she drove out, and there wasn't any point in visiting a gate she couldn't shut.

Unless she could.

Daphne picked at her gray shirt. Despite the warm day, she wore long sleeves. The last time she'd touched the Veil, it had thrown her backward onto her elbows. It was like a guard stationed in the center of the bridge, barring her from crossing. Or was it daring her, willing her near?

It was difficult to picture the lower-ranking demon squeezing through the black gate. Her imagined demon was a giant ball of shadow, like a hundred dyszoons rolled into one evil creature. Or a tall figure cast in flame, setting down an enormous boot from above. Laughing as it crushed her underneath it.

In reality, they didn't know what to expect when it arrived. She and Claire only guessed that their abilities would likely be next to useless against it. But if they *closed* the Veil so it could never arrive...

Her eyes fell to the pothole that a dyszoon had created on Halloween night when it was aiming for her head. Many battles since then had sharpened her instincts. If repeated today, she could fight that battle in a minute, with no extra strength needed from Claire—or it *would* have been quick, before the dyszoons grew more powerful with the larger Veil.

I need you, Daphne. I can't do this alone. Claire's earnest gaze pierced her with guilt, and Daphne hesitated at the threshold of the bridge. Was she really about to go back on her promise to Claire? What if the Veil injured her?

But nothing happened last time. At worst, the Veil would knock her over again. It was stronger now, but she too had grown in power. And like Claire said, by sending through all the dyszoons, the demon was accidentally training her to be a more formidable opponent.

"I'm an adult," Daphne reminded herself, as if it were a reason above all others. She was eighteen, free to make her own choices. And her choice was to take action when it was clear a decision had to be made, even if Claire had advised otherwise.

I'm coming, D. They were running out of time. The Veil would expand again, and there could be more incidents like last night. And even if there weren't, the demon was coming. Something had to be done.

The memory of a sobbing Veronica, wrapped up in the embrace of a person affected by the Veil's horrors more than anyone else she knew, pushed Daphne's foot forward onto the stones of the bridge.

Her heart quickened with nerves. She wasn't connected to the Veil in the way Ashley was, by blood, but that was an advantage. It didn't control her. The demon, whatever Mr. Burnes implied, couldn't twist her to its purpose.

She paused after a few feet, keeping to the middle of the bridge. The creek below was shallow, with sharp rocks not far below. To be thrown onto them would cause greater injury than a knock backward onto the pavement.

The Veil hung before her, high out of reach. She wasn't sure how she had touched it the first time, as it had just appeared close. But this time, her attempt would be deliberate.

Daphne reached out a phantom hand like she did for shades and dyszoons, extending it directly toward the Veil. To her surprise, the hand slowed in the few feet before its surface, as if there were thick cobwebs around it, a sensation like last night's dyszoon.

The Veil was reluctant to let her touch it, Daphne considered with triumph. Last time, it had drawn her in before she had the chance to improve her abilities. If the Veil was defending itself now, it had recognized that she *could* damage it.

She grimaced, pushing the phantom hand through the web. Inch by inch, it gave way under pressure. Outside her concentration, the whistling wind intensified into screams.

The black circle grew, filling her vision. The Veil itself seemed to be screaming. Her triumph grew. She was so close.

The last inch of its defense gave way, and Daphne struck hard at its surface.

The early afternoon sun beamed down cheerfully. A white butterfly fluttered across the lawn as Daphne waited for instructions, holding a fistful of screws. A handsome dark-haired man was crouched below her in dirty jeans and a T-shirt. He fit a board into place, the new porch step.

"Hand me one of those, Daph."

Daphne picked out a screw that looked good to her and

held it out. He grasped it with strong and callused fingers and drilled it into the board.

"All right, next one," he said.

She picked out another screw, but as her dad moved to take it, her grip tightened.

"You need to let go, Daphne," he said calmly, holding the sharp end.

Daphne blinked, confused. "What?"

"You need to let go, now!"

His urgency was scaring her. "I don't—"

"Let go! Let go, now!" She was still gripping the screw, wanting desperately to understand what he meant. His eyes widened at a point over her shoulder. Daphne looked behind her and gasped in terror.

A huge black tempest swirled within arm's reach, an abomination on that beautiful summer day. Horrible, distant screams were coming from within it. Soon, she would join their chorus.

"Let go of it! Daphne, let go!" her dad shouted, standing. "Let go, now!"

Daphne gritted her teeth and attempted to yank her fingers away. It was like they'd been glued.

"Let go!" The tempest brushed her shoulders.

"Let go!" her dad was yelling, the project forgotten.

"*Let go!*"

With a cry, Daphne ripped her fingers off the screw and fell backward into the dark void, where she would be lost forever.

Daphne woke on the pavement, drenched in sweat and lying on her side. For a disorienting minute, she stared at a small rock in her line of vision, scrambling furiously to understand where she was, and why.

Her sluggish thoughts were slowly coming into focus until,

abruptly, the missing piece of the puzzle set into place. She gripped the pavement and sat up, head pounding. The Veil was in its normal position, no crack, real or imagined, on its unchangeable surface.

She stood, shaking and likely to throw up at any second. Had she managed to do anything to the Veil? Something *had* happened.

There was the dream, for one, so vividly real. It had been years since she'd seen her dad so clearly. Usually, her only dream of him was of him burning to death, and that nightmare hadn't haunted her for months. Fixing the porch steps was a buried memory her mind had resurfaced as it attempted to retreat, sensing danger if she held on any longer.

Despair clung to Daphne as if she'd just battled a dyszoon. *At least I tried.* She had wrestled with something of great evil and power and come out mostly unharmed. *It wasn't completely worthless.* Or so she hoped.

At the very least, they could cross off harming the Veil as an option. Despite Claire's worries, nothing worse had happened to Daphne than fainting. She leaned on her knees, willing the nausea to pass.

A cold finger pierced her senses. To Daphne's disbelief, a dark mass shot from the depths of the Veil with a piercing cry. As if to punish her for the attempt to harm it, it had unleashed a dyszoon. The weeklong break from any battles was over.

Daphne straightened, her knees encouragingly not quite as weak as a few minutes ago. The dyszoon veered in her direction, and she wearily struck.

The dyszoon's scream turned from glee to rage. It had met a stronger opponent than expected.

She blocked it again. Its blows, though as difficult to repel as ever, hit dully against her mind. It was just one more thump to match the headache already banging beneath her skull.

The creature grew more enraged as each attack failed. When it returned too quickly to launch a solid attack, Daphne took her chance. With a firm hit, the dyszoon burst into pieces. The particles hovered, then were drawn into the cracks of the bridge. It was gone.

Daphne tottered forward but kept her balance, breathing heavily. She was tempted to lie down in that spot, but the battle had awakened her enough to know that the middle of the road wasn't an ideal place for a nap.

She looked up, perched at the edge of the pavement where it met stone. The Veil hung unmoving.

The fatigue that clouded her mind abruptly snapped. What the Veil was had never seemed so clear. What they were up against. Swallowing her dread, Daphne walked to her car, wondering what she would tell Claire. Her broken promise.

At least nothing permanent happened, she justified, as if to practice. But it was true. The nausea was already passing, and the rest of her symptoms were nothing a nap and a painkiller couldn't fix.

Daphne shut the car door and winced at the noise. She imagined Claire's *I told you so.* Maybe her anger. But at least Daphne had tried.

She warily glanced once more at the bridge, making a different promise—to avoid it for as long as possible.

15
____

VIVIAN

The aches from her encounter with the Veil faded by Monday.

Her full recovery made Daphne feel justified for trying to strike back at the Veil. She planned to tell Claire about the attempt when they met the next day to discuss Veronica, who the psychic hadn't dreamed about.

Despite her nerves over how Claire would react to her broken promise, Daphne looked forward to seeing her after three weeks apart. Texts and brief phone calls only went so far. Their meetings encouraged her that neither of them dealt with the Veil alone.

She wondered what Claire would make of Veronica's Ouija board incident or how they would address a potential army of weak dyszoons in private homes. Friday's incident could repeat itself at any time, and without a vision, they might not know about the attack.

Daphne dipped a paintbrush into the can at her feet. Stage Crew was painting a wide, shallow staircase to look like concrete for the scenes in a city park, the last set they'd build for the musical. She had looked forward to painting it the most.

We could do some fun art projects this summer. Leon's words made her stomach burst with nerves. Daphne filed away any thought of the date as her brush ran dry over the wood. The less she dwelled on next week, the more relaxed she would be. He hadn't messaged much since her birthday, and she was impatient for the silence to break.

With less than three weeks until showtime, there had been a noticeable uptick in the number of people moving around the stage. Actors continually descended the ramp to visit a small room where a few older women with sewing machines busily adjusted dress hems and pants lengths.

Chad, who was the lead in the musical, disappeared to get the final alterations to his character's brown suit pants and jacket. He emerged from the ramp with his arms spread wide.

It was strange to see him dressed up instead of in a T-shirt. Daphne compared him with the photo of Michael Buza on display in the glass case outside the theater. The costume was mostly the same, but Chad's unruly hair was dark instead of a sleek, wavy blond.

Since her last talk with the shade, she hadn't seen so much as a curl of mist around the stage, to her unease. She doubted Michael had left permanently.

"It looks a little big," Beth told Chad skeptically, holding her dripping paint brush over the bottom step.

"It's supposed to be." He tugged at the cuffs of his sleeves. "That's the *point.* It's symbolic."

"Symbolic of what?" Daphne asked bravely. Chad was never mean to her, but his unpredictable energy made her nervous. Despite this, she liked him.

"Victor's taking on something too big for him, something he's not suited for," he said with the stuffy air of an actor who had studied his part well. "Basically, he wants to make a ton of money because he thinks he needs to, for his fiancée, so he's playing a part."

"So wait—you're playing the part of a guy who's playing a part?" Beth teased.

"Exactly. Beth, you get me. Come here, I love you..." He moved to give her a big hug.

"Wait, I've got paint! No, Chad! Wait! Stop!" Beth set down her wet brush hastily. "Okay, now you can."

After an exaggerated hug, Chad marched downstairs to change out of his costume, belting out a tune that may have been from the musical or perhaps out of his own head. Daphne shared a look with Beth, who shrugged with a smile that said, *Yep, he's a little weird.*

Daphne scanned the stage again for Michael, and her insides fell. Veronica was chatting in an aisle with her junior friend, Vivian, who was playing Victor's fiancée, Ginny. Veronica was an assistant director and had been bound to turn up at some point.

If not for the vision on Friday night, Daphne would never have guessed how Veronica's weekend had taken a turn. She had appeared normal during lunch, though a little subdued, and sat close to Nathan.

Daphne had firmly set her back to them, trying not to dwell on the fact that they looked like the top couple of the year.

Although she had fantasized about making Nathan jealous over her upcoming date with Leon, he might tell Jessica, whose reaction she didn't want to deal with, regardless whether it was good or bad. She hoped fervently that Leon wouldn't bring it up to his sister either. Her mom was the only other person who knew about the date, and Daphne had quickly downplayed it.

It's not a big deal. We're just going out to supper, she repeated to herself, wondering in the next moment what to wear as she refreshed her paintbrush. Beth, painting next to her, might have advice on first dates.

"Hey, when you and Ethan—"

Just then Chad reappeared, now in his usual T-shirt and jeans. "Daphne, I need to ask you something."

"Yeah?" She stood, apprehensive.

"Would you be interested in running the curtain for the show?"

It wasn't anything close to what Daphne had expected him to say. "Like, pull it for scenes, you mean? Is it hard? What do I have to do?"

"Hey, whoa, one question at a time. But, yeah, it's simple. I've done it. You just have to write down your cues. All you do is pull the gold curtain when it's the end of an act, or the black curtain at the end of a scene."

Daphne stared at him in panic.

"It's really easy," he reassured her. "Don't worry."

"Have you done it?" she said, turning to Beth. "You'd probably do better..."

"Oh, I'm doing the lights!" Beth said brightly. "I've never done curtain, though."

"Think about it and let me know," Chad said. "You were the first person I thought of when Mr. Heigelman asked me to find someone."

Daphne was touched. She'd only been part of Stage Crew for less than a month, and because of her limited skills hadn't contributed much to the set. But Chad had thought of her right away. "I'll let you know."

"Sounds good." He saluted them and walked away.

Daphne reflected on the offer over the next hour. Thanks to Beth, she was growing confident that the task wasn't difficult, but she worried about the commitment. Taking on the role would mean attending musical rehearsals in the week leading up to the weekend performances—rehearsals she couldn't easily leave to battle a dyszoon. And she couldn't ask Claire to cover, since her shop hours overlapped.

And even if Claire *did* cover—Daphne's mind sank further into the obstacles—what if there was a massive outbreak of dyszoons during a show? She would have no choice but to leave and deal with the fallout later.

They left the set to dry overnight. Collecting everyone's used brushes, Daphne went downstairs and rinsed them in a paint-stained tub. The sewing room was closed. She was half-tempted to tell Chad that she couldn't run the curtain, but paused. Before she made any firm decisions, she would run the offer by Claire.

She turned off the tap and shook out the brushes, then paused to listen. The sound of sniffling was coming unmistakably from the girls' dressing room.

Daphne hesitated, uncertain whether to investigate or leave whoever it was alone. She could retreat and leave the girl to cry in peace, like she would have preferred if their roles were reversed. The sniffle turned to a sob.

"It's so STUPID!" the girl cried out in a strangled voice.

Feeling now that the choice was made for her, Daphne approached the open dressing room with a mixture of dread and duty, doubting that she was the best person to help.

Vivian sat on a folding chair next to a room-length counter and mirror, out of costume. Her curly hair was loose and wild around her red and blotchy face. At Daphne's approach, she dabbed angrily under her eyes with a tissue, wiping off the mascara that had run down her face.

"Hey, Vivian," Daphne said with caution. "Are you all right?" Had Veronica told her off for sharing the Ouija board that had set off the weekend's disaster?

Vivian hiccuped in response, obviously attempting to pull herself together enough to speak.

Daphne waited awkwardly. They shared history class, but she didn't know Vivian well. Anyone who was close to Veronica, she disliked instinctively, Jessica being the only exception since she had been friends with her first.

"Do you need anything? Do you want me to go get someone?" she ventured, at a loss for what to say. Jessica, who was warmer toward people, would do a lot better in this situation. Then Daphne remembered Vivian disliked Jessica. And probably herself.

"N-No." Vivian sniffed and hiccuped again. "I'll be fine."

"Okay," Daphne said, turning to go uncomfortably but uncertain there was any other option. *I tried, I guess.*

"It's just—" Vivian burst out. Daphne straightened her turning foot. "This *stupid* part. It's been *so* stressful. Like, I've done parts before but I just, like, thought it would be a lot more fun being the lead."

So it wasn't about the Ouija board after all. "I suppose you have to memorize a lot, right?" Daphne said, not knowing much about the work being a lead entailed.

Vivian hiccuped. "Yeah," she said distantly, in a way that Daphne took to mean she was simply agreeing with her, but the problem was more complex. "I mean, I've got most of my lines down. Like, the director gets pretty pissed if you're still reading from the script. She yelled at me for that last week."

Before Daphne could respond, Vivian continued in a rush, "And afterward Chad was on her side, being all like, '*Well, you have to memorize your lines,*'" she imitated angrily. "So I got mad about it and it was hard getting, like, into character and being a loving fiancée and all that. I guess that's why leads shouldn't date, right?"

Daphne hid her surprise. She couldn't have pictured a

more unlikely couple than Chad and Vivian—their personalities were too different. But then again, there were an unusual number of couples in Drama Club, many of them popping up at the beginning of rehearsals.

The long mirror reflected Vivian as she dabbed again at her eyes. Daphne leaned against the counter, sensing that the reason Vivian sat crying alone went deeper than a minor disagreement with her boyfriend.

It was strange to try to comfort someone who she suspected had gossiped with Veronica about her. Stranger still that Vivian was confiding in her. Daphne couldn't picture herself doing the same with the roles reversed.

"I'm sure you'll work it out," she said. "I mean, it seems like everything is coming together."

Fresh tears welled up in Vivian's eyes. "I don't know," she whispered. Daphne waited without comment, feeling useless. "I just...I guess I don't want to let down my mom. She's, like, so happy that I got the same part she did."

Daphne did a double-take. "Your mom played Ginny last time? In the show that got canceled?"

"Yeah, so she really wants to see me perform this role because she never got to. It's all coming full circle, or whatever. But in rehearsal, I just feel like..." She gestured with the hand that held the wet tissue. "I don't know...like I'm not supposed to be here? Like I'm not welcome, or good enough, or something."

Vivian's mom would have known Michael—the living, unshadowed, fully himself version—but it would be heartless to press for details just then.

"But you've been in a few other performances, right? Did you feel that way then?" Daphne asked in a reasonable tone.

"Well...no. I guess not. I don't know why this feels different. It just does." Vivian gestured helplessly and hiccuped. Her hands collapsed into her lap.

Daphne imagined Michael turning a glowering face in Vivian's direction. *No one gets to take it from me.* Dyszoons deepened negative feelings. Could a malevolent shade affect the people around him the same way? Or did Vivian just have normal self-doubt brought on by her first leading role?

"I mean, it's probably like you said. It was your mom's part too, and so it's, like, extra pressure." Daphne checked herself—she was starting to mimic Vivian's way of talking. "But I mean, you have your lines down. And if you got the part, you're obviously supposed to be here."

Vivian hiccuped again, but it wasn't quite as forceful. "You think so?"

"Yeah. You have to be really good to be a lead. I definitely couldn't do that." Daphne second-guessed being self-deprecating, but then reminded herself that Vivian wasn't Veronica, who would have pounced on the comment and used it against her at some point. Even so, she didn't quite trust Vivian, despite her vulnerability. "You've done bigger parts before, right?"

"Yeah. This is my biggest role, though."

"But like you said, you've got your lines down."

Vivian clutched her mascara-blackened tissue, though someone who walked in might not be able to tell that she'd just had a hard cry. Daphne noted the normal color on Vivian's face with relief. Maybe she wasn't so terrible at comforting people.

"I'm also worried..." Vivian said, staring into the distance. "If me and Chad break up, what if history, like, repeats itself?"

"You're worried that the show will get canceled?"

"Yeah. It's just a lot of pressure. I mean—" She ran the tissue across her nose and sniffed. "My mom was going out with the guy who was the lead last time, and from what she's told me, I know they had, like, issues. So it made me think of me and Chad, and—"

"Your mom was going out with Michael?" Daphne interrupted in surprise. That fact wouldn't be written in a newspaper article. Michael died in a motorcycle accident, but something had led to that point.

"During the musical, yeah. My mom said she broke up with him the week of the show, so after he died she felt like it was her fault it got canceled. That maybe if she'd waited, he wouldn't have gotten drunk and crashed his motorcycle."

"I'm sure that's not true," Daphne said, her dislike for Michael increasing. His poor choices were still reaching beyond the grave to affect Vivian's mom, and now her daughter, decades later.

While she didn't believe the breakup was to blame for his death, Daphne understood the worry. From experience, she knew that guilt was common after a death. Over choices made and words not said. Veronica had attempted to talk to the dead because of it.

"And anyway," Daphne continued, "I can't picture Chad drinking and driving. And one of you would have to die for the musical to be canceled. So unless you're planning to murder each other..."

For the first time, Vivian laughed, to Daphne's relief. "No. At least, *I'm* not."

"Then I think you'll both be great."

Vivian smiled, her face no longer blotchy. "Thanks, Daphne. Sorry, I didn't mean to dump on you. It just kind of came out."

"It's okay." Daphne smiled back in reassurance and pushed herself off the counter, relieved her time of comforting was over. "We've all been there."

"Well...thanks."

"Good luck with the show," she said, and left the dressing room. The dread she'd felt at the start of their conversation was gone, replaced by satisfaction that things hadn't gone horribly wrong. Somehow, she'd done a halfway decent job of being helpful to someone in a crisis.

As she walked up the ramp, Daphne filled in Michael's final week. Vivian's mom had broken up with him the week before the performance. No doubt that had been a blow to his enormous ego. But had it really been a factor in his death?

She stopped before the old show poster painted on the concrete wall, his large signature difficult to miss. Something was occurring to her about the timing of Michael's death. He had died a few days before the musical's opening night, which meant his accident had occurred in the middle of the week.

Daphne had assumed without thinking about it that he'd come from a party, which explained the drunk driving. But in retrospect, the day of the week made that unlikely. So either he was a drinker or something unexpected had happened that coaxed him to the bottle that night. The bad breakup, and with his co-lead, no less, could have been that very event.

Not that Vivian's mom was right to harbor guilt. Before Vivian's story, Michael had seemed like a bad-tempered shade who was fixated on how death had cheated him of his big moment. But it was becoming clearer that it was Michael's ego that had been his downfall. His own bad choices.

Vivian felt like she wasn't welcome on the stage, which fed into her self-doubt. Was it possible he was doing everything he could beyond the grave to make sure the show didn't go on? Was the daughter of his estranged ex his special target? It would be hard to prove.

More urgently than ever, Daphne knew she needed to locate Michael before the musical and order him to stay away. But he had disappeared. She didn't trust for a second that he was gone for good.

Daphne signed out. If she wanted to stop him from inter-fering with the performances, she'd need to station herself nearby. Accepting the curtain role would be the best way of doing that. But if dyszoons emerged during those times…

A slight headache was pounding at her temples, an echo of the one she'd had on Saturday. Daphne massaged her forehead and resolved to put ghosts out of her mind until the next day.

16

———

SECRETS

Daphne opened the door to Madam Moon and shut it behind her with a jingle of the bell. The psychic's head rose from straightening the glass display case. A large pendant rested below her neck, matching her patterned black-and-white shirt.

"Oh good, you're here. Meet me in the back?"

"Sure," Daphne said, squeezing her hands inside her jacket pockets. Though she had looked forward to their meeting, the prospect of confessing her attempt with the Veil was nerve-wracking. *Nothing happened,* she defended herself, entering their usual room.

A short time later, Claire emerged through the beaded doorway with two mugs of chamomile tea. "So. You had an eventful weekend?" she asked, setting the mugs on coasters.

"What?" Daphne started guiltily before realizing that she was asking about the vision on Friday night, not the Veil. Though Claire was perceptive to the point of passing off as a psychic to those eager to believe, Daphne had never seriously thought she could read minds.

"Yeah, I did," she said, recovering.

"I almost forgot." Claire disappeared through the beaded doorway. The strings didn't have time to settle before she was back with a small present bag, which she set on the glittering tablecloth. "For you."

"What for?" Daphne said in confusion.

"For your birthday, of course," Claire explained, sitting.

To Daphne, her birthday already seemed like ages ago instead of a few days. Her face warmed a few more degrees with guilt. In a few minutes, Claire might regret her present.

She removed the tissue paper and a small jewelry box containing a necklace. A small silver star with eight points shone up at her.

Claire evidently had an eye for their different tastes in jewelry. While the psychic always wore large statement pieces, Daphne had only the simple owl bracelet her dad had given her a few weeks before he passed.

"It's beautiful, Claire," she said, tilting the box so the star gleamed in the lamplight. "Thank you."

"You're welcome. Did you have a good birthday?"

Daphne summarized her celebrations with her mom. She had accomplished nothing from the online list of eighteenth-birthday activities and hoped that Claire wouldn't judge her for the quiet weekend.

But Claire would understand more than anyone why it had been quiet, Daphne realized. They both had responsibilities. Veronica's encounter with the Ouija board was proof that they could never completely let down their guard.

"By the way, when's your birthday?" Daphne said. "I just remembered I wanted to ask you."

"August 27. But I won't tell you which year," Claire answered with a laugh.

With birthday talk out of the way, Daphne described in greater detail Veronica's attempt to use the Ouija board, the sense of something moving in the room, and the message on the board that chilled her more than she wanted to admit. A demon, a powerful one, knew her by name.

I'm coming, D.

Claire's ringed fingers pressed together in grim thought, though over which part of the tale, Daphne wasn't sure.

"What do you think of the message? It's like the demon knew I was watching." She was eager to get Claire's thoughts before moving on to her main worry—how to address the dyszoons that would emerge from portals other than the Veil.

"A taunt," the psychic said finally, her eyebrows drawn together. "And a rather crude one. I wouldn't trouble yourself too much, Daphne. I'm sure it merely meant to frighten you."

Daphne didn't want to admit that it had succeeded. That it had pushed her to conclude that they were running out of time, which had led her to confront the Veil.

"But how could it have known I'd see it?" she pressed, not able to dismiss the message so easily. The demon's presence—whichever demon it was—had rattled her. "It can't read minds, can it? I mean, it's not like I was actually there and it sensed me."

"No, it can't read your mind, Daphne," Claire reassured her. "But as to whether or not you were there, I'd say that you were, in a way. Enough for it to realize you were."

"What do you mean?" Daphne said, frowning. Surely the psychic didn't mean that a part of her had been physically in the room with Veronica. "How could I be there? Isn't a vision like a dream?"

"Yes, and also no," Claire said, fingers still pressed together. "The way we experience the two may be similar, but I've long concluded that we couldn't feel visions so vividly without being present in some way."

"What do you mean?"

"In visions, we don't just observe, but take part. When we saw dyszoons attack Heather, we *felt* the crash."

"Isn't that just imagination? And if we're there in the vision, why couldn't I warn Heather?"

"I doubt she could have sensed us without having our abilities," Claire answered.

Although Heather's last moments hadn't visited Daphne since the night before Halloween, parts of it remained imprinted in her memory. Feeling weightless as the car upended. Glass splitting lines of fire on her skin. The sticky wetness of blood as she crawled out of the shattered window...

Blood turned into the maroon walls of Claire's studio. Daphne rubbed her hands together under the table, working the phantom memory of broken glass out of them.

Although still skeptical about the theory, Daphne went along with it. "So you're saying that the demon sensed that some part of me was there at Veronica's? Like, as a spirit?"

"Not just your spirit, but also your body, I'd say."

Daphne stared. "But how would that work? I mean, it's not like I leave my room whenever I have a vision. That I know of, anyway." She was, of course, alone when they took place.

"A spirit can't sense or feel the way a body does," Claire said. "It's another reason shades, who have lost their bodies, could never be a substitute for their living selves. They're missing an essential part of what makes them who they are. All of them are fractured, though some more so than others."

Daphne pressed her lips together, trying to grasp the implications. The theory made sense only because there had to be a reason the demon knew she was listening. But the idea of being present in visions, and not just an observer, was terrifying. She had always scraped through with only the memory of pain, but could some visions be dangerous?

To her, visions were nothing more than dreams that took

place in real life. But she had tried to communicate with both Heather and Ashley. Which meant that, in the moment, she had believed they might hear her.

"If the entire vision of Heather was real," the psychic said softly, "were your injuries the only part you imagined?"

Daphne was about to say that Claire had a point when something occurred to her. "But these visions, they take place in the past," she pointed out. "They don't always happen in real time. So if part of us is present, that would mean we had traveled back to the past."

Claire nodded as though she hadn't considered it that way. "I suppose we would have, wouldn't we," she agreed.

Daphne buried her face. "My head hurts."

Claire laughed. "It's strange to think about, isn't it?"

"I'm not going to. All I know is that the demon knew I was there." Daphne unburied her face. "But anyway, moving on. Long story short, I found the dyszoon and it was barely there anymore. Like, see-through."

"The first dyszoon I ever met was like that, though perhaps not quite as weak as this one. Mine still had a last fight left in it."

"And this is the first dyszoon that we've had outside of the Veil," Daphne said. Her pent-up anxiety was spilling over. It was the topic she was most eager to discuss, though it would lead to her confession.

"Is it?" Claire said mildly.

"Well—yeah." Daphne was caught off guard. "The dyszoons could come out anywhere, and we might not find out about it in time."

"True, but they're too weak to cause any actual damage."

"But if the Veil gets any bigger, maybe they'll be strong enough to hurt someone," Daphne said, baffled that Claire wasn't grasping the enormity of the problem.

"I expect that those who mess with things they don't under-stand may encounter more than they bargained for," Claire said. "But as far as the danger, your friend's experience was nothing more than what I've heard about from others, even before the Veil grew."

"You mean this has happened before? A dyszoon coming out like that?" Daphne said in astonishment. She swallowed the urge to correct that Veronica was most definitely not her friend.

"Certainly. The Veil would be the first time, at least that we know about, that the dyszoons have been able to emerge with greater strength. Outside the Veil, they can only squeeze their way through whatever narrow opening they can find, and the journey will always weaken them greatly."

"So you're saying dyszoons have always been able to find a way through, *outside* the Veil," Daphne said, incredulous.

"I've been told of similar experiences. Things moving on their own, that sort of thing," Claire said. "That's why I've always warned others not to play with Ouija boards. They can't control who they invite in. In this case, a dyszoon."

Daphne absorbed this, taking a sip of tea to buy time. She had expected Claire to agree with her that the situation had grown much more serious. Now, with a sickening feeling, it was dawning on her that it was possible she had overreacted, primed as she was for bad news ever since the Veil had grown once more.

Closing the Veil had seemed so urgent that she hadn't paused for Claire's perspective or caution. The speed at which she moved against it now seemed, at best, foolish. At worst, it could have put her out of commission.

The tea in her stomach soured with dread, and she set the mug down. Had she made an enormous mistake? By trying to battle the Veil, she might have played directly into the demon's hands.

But I didn't, Daphne comforted herself for the umpteenth time, twisting her owl bracelet. Nothing bad happened. She had pulled away from the Veil in time.

"I am sorry for her," Claire added with compassion, her ringed fingers curled around the mug. "I hope it made her aware of the dangers."

Veronica's shaking shoulders appeared before Daphne's vision. "She was really upset. I'm so used to things now that I didn't think about how it's, you know—scary."

When she'd first started seeing shades, it had struck Daphne how the supernatural seemed so normal to Claire. And though she had expected otherwise, it had taken only a few weeks for her to view shades the same way.

She hoped that there would be no further need to go to Veronica's house. But after the shock wore off, Veronica might convince herself that her grandfather had thrown the object in an attempt to communicate and try the Ouija board again. Daphne knew, painfully at the moment, how easy it was to misinterpret things.

Face warm, she steeled herself to admit the other half of her eventful weekend.

"How has the last of the school year been for you?" Claire broke the silence, folding her hands on the table.

It would be a brief reprieve, but Daphne took it. Maybe she didn't need to confess yet.

"It's all right. I'm kind of wishing classes would just be over," she said. "I feel done already."

Claire chuckled. "I remember that feeling."

"At least spring break is next week. I'm not doing anything, so it'll be nice." Her upcoming date with Leon came to mind, and Daphne flushed. She didn't need to tell Claire about that. "Drama Club has been fun, though. We're almost done with the set for the musical. Actually, I haven't told you about the shade I met there."

"Oh? Have a theater ghost, do we?"

Daphne summarized what she had discovered so far about Michael and his fateful end, and his fury over the musical continuing without him.

"I've never met a shade like that. Usually they're worried about their family, but Michael is different," Daphne said. "He knocked a drill off a ladder and it almost landed on someone. I always thought shades were supposed to be good, or at least not evil like a dyszoon."

A shadow passed over Claire's lined face. "It depends what you mean by good," she said. "Shades are still as they were in life, to a degree, with those flaws. Some, as you've found, are more aggressive. But are they spirits bound for Hell? No."

"I'm trying to keep an eye out for Michael, but he hasn't shown up yet. I don't want him to mess with the show. Like knock something over, or on top of someone."

She imagined pulling open the curtain as Michael nudged a drill from the catwalk. The audience screaming as it landed on Chad's head. The musical would be canceled once more due to the tragic death of its lead actor.

More likely Michael's interference would be small and mischievous. Shades were limited in how well they could interact with their solid surroundings. The likelihood of some-thing death-inducing being left on the catwalk was slim, not to mention the shade would need very good aim.

"Perhaps you can keep an eye out at the performances?" Claire suggested. "Are you required to be there?"

"No, not without a backstage role. I was just asked to pull the curtain, but I said I'd have to think about it."

"Are you going to do it?"

"I don't think so. I mean, you have your shop open, so I

can't ask you to cover for me," Daphne explained. "And if a dyszoon came out, I couldn't easily leave the show."

Claire touched her fingertips together. "Do you want to do it?"

"Well, I *would* do it, since they need someone," Daphne said, flustered by the question. What did it matter what she wanted? There was only reality. "It didn't sound so bad. My friend Beth is doing the lights. And if I were closer to the stage, I could make sure Michael doesn't do anything if he shows up."

"When is the show?"

"A little over two weeks from now. The seventeenth through the nineteenth, and the last one's on Sunday afternoon. Three shows altogether."

"I see," Claire said briskly. "I think that's doable."

"I can't ask you to do that," Daphne said, her face warming again. "And even if you covered for me, what if a bunch of dyszoons came out at once?"

"Oh, we can risk it."

"I..." she began, then stopped. How could she explain that Claire wouldn't make the offer if she knew Daphne had broken her promise? Between the birthday present and Claire's willingness to help, her guilt was only growing.

"I actually..."

It would be difficult to watch the kindness on Claire's face turn into disappointment and maybe anger. No doubt she would regret having given Daphne the star necklace, or having trusted her at all.

Nothing happened, she defended herself. Did it matter if she had broken her promise? When it came down to it, she hadn't been harmed. It wasn't as if the Veil had swallowed her whole. And if she accepted the curtain role, she would be well-positioned to keep an eye on the stage and stop Michael from sabotaging the performances.

Pushing down her guilt, Daphne forced a smile. "Okay, I'll tell them I can do it."

"It sounds like fun," Claire said. The door to the shop jingled, and she stood. "Pardon me. Did you want to continue after I'm finished?"

It was her last chance to mention the Veil.

"I—no, I think that's everything we needed to—I'm good." Daphne stood as well, collecting the present bag. "Talk to you later. Thanks again for the necklace."

As she pulled her car away from the curb, loneliness hit Daphne as hard as a dyszoon attack. Never before had she hidden something important from Claire. But now the psychic was another person she was keeping secrets from. Another casualty of her lies of silence.

Nothing bad happened. It was becoming a mantra.

How long that would stay true, only the Veil knew.

17

SIDE EFFECTS

Daphne signed into Stage Crew and scanned the stage. As usual, Michael was absent.

Beth looked up eagerly at her approach. She was painting details on the staircase to make it look like concrete.

"Daphne! Hang on, I've got to show you something!" she said. Setting down her brush, she rummaged in the purse at her feet and pulled out a ring case. "I didn't want to get paint on it. What do you think?"

Beth opened the case, beaming. Daphne blinked at the white gold ring set with small diamonds for a few seconds, uncomprehending.

"Wait, are you—did Ethan propose to you?"

"Yes!" Beth said giddily. "We were watching a movie at his house last night, and then he paused it and proposed!"

"Congrats! Wow." The news stunned her out of any thought of the Veil or Michael. Beth's comfort with Ethan's future Army plans at Jessica's birthday party now made more sense. They were a serious enough couple to take the next step and had probably been discussing it. "Are you having the wedding soon?"

"We're thinking this summer before he has Basic Training, so possibly June. It would just be a small ceremony. There's not a lot of time," she said in an excited rush. "I can't believe I'm getting married!"

Beth talked more in-depth about their plans as Daphne joined the painting effort. When Chad walked by, she let him know her decision on operating the curtain.

"Excellent!" He high-fived her. "I knew you couldn't resist it!"

"Right," she answered, wondering if accepting the role was a mistake.

If there wasn't a chance Michael might try to ruin the show, she wouldn't have risked the commitment. With each passing day, Daphne's suspicion that the shade was staying away from her on purpose only grew. Without her being able to order him not to interfere, his next move could be during the performance.

Beth glowingly resumed sharing her wedding plans and the type of dress she wanted to look for that weekend with her mom, who'd been surprisingly ecstatic about the news. Daphne recalled that she was strict and had only reluctantly allowed her daughter to date Ethan.

Although Daphne was genuinely happy for Beth, underneath it was panic and a twinge of jealousy over how well the couple had it together. A friend was tying the knot, and she hadn't even had her first kiss yet. Well, she *almost* had, with Leon. She blushed again at the memory.

With help from a few others, they finished painting the staircase, then collected all the paintbrushes to wash in the big sink downstairs.

"I can't believe you're getting married. I'm having my first date next week," Daphne risked saying, grayish water running through her hands. Beth was the first friend she had told about the date, and it was freeing.

"You're going on a date? That's great! Who with?" Beth said with glee, and Daphne grinned. Excitement was contagious. She could picture Veronica having the same reaction, but for a reason other than being happy for her. Veronica would tell Jessica as soon as possible and ask endless mocking questions.

Daphne double-checked the large room was empty. Although the women's dressing room and the sewing room were both lit, the sound wouldn't carry if she talked quietly.

"Don't tell anyone, but it's Jessica's brother," she said in an undertone. "I haven't told her."

"I won't," Beth promised, matching her lowered voice. "That's exciting! He seemed nice, you know, at the party."

"Yeah. I'm a little nervous. I've never gone on a date before." Usually, she would have hesitated to admit this, but she didn't think that Beth would judge her lack of experience.

Beth nodded. "There's nothing wrong with that. Ethan's the first guy I went on a real date with," she said, her voice normal again. "We've been friends since junior high, so I wasn't sure about being anything more than that. It took me a long time to think of him that way, actually."

"No love at first sight?" Daphne joked.

"Not at all." Beth shook her head, serious. "He liked me first, but I was kind of hesitant because I didn't want to ruin our friendship. But, I gave it a chance."

"And now you're getting married."

"Yeah." She smiled blissfully. "It's worked out. And hey, maybe it will work out for you too."

Daphne shrugged. "I've never had a boyfriend."

"Anyone close?"

"I mean, there've been guys I've liked, but it's never gone

anywhere. And it's too late to date anyway, since we're graduating," Daphne said, voicing out loud the other obstacle she'd thought of with Nathan. Even if they started dating tomorrow, what would be the point if they just broke up before the fall semester because of the distance? In that case, they were better off staying friends instead of suffering heartbreak later.

"I don't know," Beth said thoughtfully. It was one thing Daphne liked about her—she took the time to reflect on what people said, and didn't just accept their conclusions. "I think you could make it work if you wanted it to. And you'd still have good memories, right?"

"I guess," Daphne said, gloom cutting into her happiness over the engagement news. The closer graduation came, the more it was likely that Veronica and Nathan's relationship would continue through the summer and beyond. It would be too late, no matter what happened. If only feelings could be rationalized away.

"Is there someone you like?" Beth asked. Coming from her, the question didn't feel prying, just straightforward and without ulterior motive.

Avoiding her eyes made it easier to skirt closer to the truth. The last brush in Daphne's hand was clean, but she continued to twirl it around in her palm. "It doesn't matter. He's dating someone else."

Her dismissive tone could almost convince herself that it was no big deal. That she didn't wonder what might have happened had she stayed with their group at the event on Halloween, instead of being called away by dyszoons.

"I'm sorry." Beth shook water out of the brushes and murmured, "You know, it surprises me that Veronica's lasted this long, honestly. I expected them to break up months ago."

"You know I like Nathan?" Daphne said without thinking,

forgetting in her surprise to lower her voice as well. She looked around, but there was no one nearby to have heard.

"Don't worry, I won't tell anyone. I just thought you did since I know you're friends with him, and he's dating someone."

"Oh," Daphne said. Her flushed face cooled. She felt exposed, but knew without a doubt that Beth would keep the secret. "Thanks for not telling anyone."

"I won't," Beth promised again, drying her hands. She slipped her engagement ring back on. It glittered in the light.

Daphne signed out of Stage Crew, feeling lighter than she had in weeks. Her new star necklace swung out as she wrote down the time. At last, she had a secret that didn't have to be carried alone.

The clipboard blurred, then vanished before her eyes. She stared, confused, as she was no longer standing near the stage but in the middle of a vast woods with budding leaves. A cool breeze touched her face.

Leaves crunched behind her. Daphne jumped out of the way of Ashley, who passed almost close enough to brush shoulders. Judging by her slow, sullen pace, she wasn't in any hurry.

Daphne attempted to speak, to shout Ashley's name, but it was as if her mouth was painted over.

"Daphne?"

Her name echoed in the wind. The edges of her vision grew fuzzy. She strained to call out to Ashley as her mind lost its grip on the scene.

"Daphne." A tap on her shoulder.

The clipboard reappeared. She was still holding the pen.

"Are you done with that?" said the voice. Daphne turned to see the freshman girl she'd followed downstairs on her first day in Stage Crew.

"Sorry," she said in confusion, setting down the pen and stepping aside.

Dazed, Daphne collected her backpack from the front row and headed up the stairs, only half-certain that the steps were under her feet. The fresh scent of the woods clung to her nose, as vivid as if she'd just returned from there—which if Claire's theory was correct, she had. Was Ashley on a leisurely stroll at that very moment?

A vision had never come to her while awake. Her feet slowed. Daphne clutched the railing, sickened by a thought.

She had touched the Veil. The timing couldn't be a coincidence, unless she was wrong and Claire would message soon that she'd also seen Ashley. This was unlikely since Claire had never had a vision of Ashley before.

Her encounter with the Veil had to be the reason why the vision had come to her while awake, when visions only came— she had thought—while dreaming.

Daphne winced. Claire would need to know, which meant admitting she had broken her promise and had failed to mention it during their meeting.

She paused at the top of the stairs, frowning at the floor tiles. Something was moving at the edge of her awareness, just out of sight. It was like standing on a frozen lake, the elusive flash of some unknown creature swimming below. A creature that might burst through the ice at any moment.

Was the presence another weak dyszoon threatening to emerge somewhere in the school? But this movement felt far away, like the tremors of distant steps. Maybe from more than one set of feet.

The fluorescent lights were hazy, spreading like fog. Distant, distorted voices echoed down the hallway. Daphne brushed a finger along the wall, reassuringly solid as she walked half-blind, listening to the steps.

They quickened. The creature struck the ice, cracking it,

and the fog vanished. Daphne stopped with sudden comprehension, her path clear. She needed to get to the Veil.

Not bothering to check if anyone was watching, she shoved open the front doors and broke into a sprint.

Daphne ran down the hill toward the Veil with a sense of déjà vu. The last time she'd run toward the bridge was on Halloween night.

She expected a dyszoon to bombard her. During the drive, the creatures had slid like snakes along a narrow tunnel, but now they were quiet.

At the threshold to the bridge, she paused and caught her breath. She wasn't cut out for sprinting. The Veil hovered above her, a menacing pupil.

A full minute passed, then another. Daphne paced restlessly and checked the time. Her mom would be home already, if not soon, and wonder where her daughter was. *Stage Crew went late today,* she rehearsed. *Beth got engaged! I'm happy for her, but is it okay that it freaks me out a little?*

Claire had sent no message, which meant that whatever was happening with the Veil, she hadn't sensed it. They always connected when a dyszoon arrived to make sure one of them was on the way and each had their battles handled. What happened next would be Daphne's responsibility.

She bent over. It felt like a snake was wrapped around her mind, squeezing it in a death grip. Daphne clasped her head, fighting to push the pressure away. But the snake squeezed even tighter.

Creatures were trying to pass each other in a too-narrow passage that was ripping them apart. One slid past the others toward the wide-open space ahead. Daphne clutched her head tighter. It was as if she were the wall of the tunnel itself, pushed against as they forced their way through.

The snake uncoiled itself and she gasped, knowing with absolute certainty what was about to happen.

A black shape hurtled from its depths with a high-pitched shriek. Judging by the lingering pressure in her mind, the others weren't far behind.

Daphne ran toward the dyszoon as it soared to meet her, matching its scream. Perhaps caught off-balance by meeting an opponent so soon after its arrival, the creature exploded into a black cloud that surrounded her before the remnants were pulled into the ground.

She braced herself, unable to celebrate the victory. More were coming. She could feel them—

A dyszoon shot from the Veil, and then another. They darted back and forth as if celebrating their freedom from the stifling journey.

The two creatures spotted Daphne at the same time and pivoted, attacking from different angles. She raised her hands, closing her eyes to better focus. The one on the left was faster, but sloppy.

The dyszoon shattered at her touch, its final shriek ringing in her ears, but the one on the right was lucky. Daphne had timed her blow a half second too early. It struck like a boulder and then bounced upward with a whistling scream.

She steadied herself and spun around, throwing out a phantom hand in the same motion. The dyszoon dissolved like a black firework. Tendrils fell and faded toward the ground.

Daphne braced for the next attack, but the pressure surrounding her mind had stopped. There were no more distant footsteps, no sliding of snakes along the passage. The Veil was dormant.

Her phone dinged with a message—likely Claire, checking to see if she had the battle handled, not knowing it was already over in less than a minute. Meeting the dyszoons right after they arrived had given her the upper hand, despite their strength.

She looked upward warily. The pupil stared back, blank and silent. Though the creatures were gone, the victory was stale. Sensing dyszoons ahead of their release was a new ability. Touching the Veil had affected her after all.

Daphne unstuck her gaze and ran to her car, wanting to put as much distance between herself and the bridge as possible.

18

AMBUSH

Daphne dashed between two burning trees, worried that she had lost sight of the owl.

Wings flashed above the blackened tree branches. Her heart leapt, and she sprinted in its direction. Sweat poured from her temples—the heat was suffocating. Half of the forest was crackling with flame, the sky a sickly peach color.

The owl came to rest on another dead branch. Daphne slowed to a walk, careful not to make any sudden moves. It swiveled its white head to look at her, its dark eyes like gaping holes, and then silently flew off.

"Wait!" she called in panic, following its direction but getting entangled in prickly underbrush. Once free, she collapsed on the ash-covered ground with a sob. After hours of tracking it, the owl was truly gone. A nearby branch fell in a burning heap only feet from her head.

Daphne allowed for a minute of self-pity and then stood, brushing ash off her pants. Somehow, she'd need to find a way forward. But where was she?

A cabin appeared farther ahead, a green oasis in that

dead forest. Hope seized her heart. Whoever lived there might know the way. At the very least, she could rest there before striking out on a fresh path that might lead her to the owl.

She pushed open the door, which was ajar. The bright sun stopped at the grimy windows. While gloomy, the room was tidier than the last time she'd seen it. Its sole occupant sat cross-legged on the bed, sketching with a pencil. Her hair, for once, looked clean.

She stopped drawing and brushed away bits of eraser. Daphne approached, curious to see the result. Her own calm face stared back at her from the page.

Ashley looked up. Pity was on her face. "You know you can't stop it," she said, as if puzzled Daphne might even try.

Daphne's eyes widened. She stumbled back, desperate to hide behind whatever invisibility had always cloaked her. Her heel caught on the tattered rug and she fell, hands flailing for something to grasp. There were only shadows.

After lunch, Daphne shut her locker and waited for Nathan, who was trading out his books down the hallway. She grimaced at Heather, who stood misting nearby. The shade's watch over her brother was a distracting reminder that there was a promise to be fulfilled.

She suppressed a yawn. A series of nightmares, concluding with Ashley, had ended her sleep early that morning. Once awake, her heart stampeded as the vision's implications hit. Daphne was always like an unseen phantom in her visions. But Ashley had *seen* her.

Was it a vision or a nightmare? It would be easy to confuse the two. And if it were a vision, why would Ashley notice her now, when she had walked past Daphne in her vision at Stage

Crew just a few hours before? But if the dream *was* real, and Ashley had noticed her...

Did the Veil have something to do with it? Daphne could no longer think that touching it had been without long-term consequences, not when she could sense dyszoons before they arrived. Ashley was connected to the Veil, and now so was Daphne in a different way.

Perhaps that was why she had visions of Ashley, and not Claire. Since the first time she'd touched the Veil, it had been tying them together. And that connection had evolved. The visions, after all, had only begun once the Veil grew again.

Was that connection a bad thing? The glimpses allowed her to keep tabs on Ashley, and she could meet the dyszoons at the bridge instead of tracking them down. She would no longer have to speed to Laurel Road and worry that a scene like Heather's smashed-up car awaited.

Each dyszoon only makes you stronger. The demon is training you to be more formidable to it, Claire had told her. Daphne couldn't help but think she had gained another advantage over the demon.

Nathan shut his locker and jogged up to her. She returned his grin, though was sad realizing that tomorrow would be their last walk together before spring break.

"You were going somewhere next week, right?" Daphne asked as they started down the hallway.

"I'm heading to Virginia Beach with my parents. We're visiting my brother for a few days," he said. "I haven't really talked to him much since Christmas."

Daphne glanced over her shoulder. Heather followed a distance behind, her darkly lined eyes solemn. If the shade were still alive, she might have been a part of that trip. *We were close,* she'd said of her relationship with Nathan, who didn't share that closeness with his only brother.

"That sounds nice," she said, choosing to ignore Heather. "Are you gone the whole week?" While it was unlikely, she clung to a slight hope that he wouldn't wait until summer to invite her over.

"For most of it, yeah. You?"

"I'm not going anywhere," she said, blushing. Her date was in exactly one week, next Thursday. Jessica had mentioned nothing about it, so Daphne assumed that Leon hadn't told her and hoped it would stay that way.

They had only texted a few times since then, mostly to share art project ideas, and her nerves grew with each passing day. She still had to decide on an outfit.

A short walk later, she said goodbye to Nathan, who continued to his math class with Heather following. Daphne shook her head. She had once told the shade not to cling so closely to him, and would have to add to the definition of *space* the next time they spoke.

She entered the history classroom. Vivian was deep in conversation with Veronica, but smiled when they made eye contact. Daphne smiled back a second late, wondering if helping her to overcome an emotional breakdown meant they were friendly now. She hoped not, remembering loyally the way Vivian had talked down to Jessica about the Ouija board.

Vivian would no doubt ignore her again soon. There was only one more Stage Crew meeting before break, and the sets were almost finished, so it wasn't as though they would have many chances to talk.

Daphne sat at her desk. Mr. Burnes was still in his office. Had he visited Ashley recently? Or did the fact that she looked more put-together in the vision mean her work on the Veil had paused? *Maybe widening the Veil isn't working,* came the hopeful thought.

If the nightmare had been real, it was possible Daphne had

a way to speak with Ashley and try to convince her to stop helping the demon. She couldn't imagine having only Mr. Burnes to talk to. Ashley clearly despised him, and the feeling seemed mutual.

His office door opened. Daphne jumped and took out her notes, pretending to be busy. Just one more day, and then she would be free from Mr. Burnes for a week.

At Stage Crew after school, someone handed her the daily rehearsal schedule for show week, which was right after spring break. As the curtain operator, she was required to attend all the rehearsals.

Daphne folded the paper and made a mental note to send a picture of it to Claire, who would be covering any dyszoons during those evenings. Chad had dubbed the long, intense days of rehearsal "Hell Week."

"Are you ready for the show?" she asked him. If he was nervous about his leading role, he didn't show it.

"I was *born* ready, curtain girl," Chad said, making shooting motions at her with his fingers. He walked over to where Vivian, in costume, stood chatting to—Daphne's heart sank—Veronica. Neither seemed to have anything important to do.

Vivian laughed at him. *So they did make up,* Daphne observed. Barring any tragic accidents, the show would go on.

The schedule included a party hosted at Veronica's house for all Drama Club members on the Thursday before opening night. Daphne would have skipped the party if Beth hadn't mentioned it as though both of them were going to be there. She could hardly explain that Veronica's house was far away from the Veil.

In an attempt to feel better about it, Daphne reasoned that even if a dyszoon came out, the distance wouldn't matter. She would have a head start. And since the party was at Veronica's house, Nathan might show up.

More cheerfully, she nailed a small set of shelves to the wallpapered dining room wall as Beth held it in place. Stage Crew was placing the set's furniture, while others took care of any final touches. The two sophomore girls she'd met on her first day were walking backstage, marking with tape any spots that creaked so the actors could avoid stepping on them.

Beth was planning to devote her break to wedding planning. Even though the guest list was short, the event sounded like a lot of work.

"I can do the ceremony and everything at my uncle's place," she was saying, standing back to check the shelf's placement. "I might do a late-morning ceremony and have a lunch reception, so that would save some money. And my cousin could be my flower girl. She's his daughter…"

Daphne placed a chipped porcelain bulldog on the top shelf and faced it outward. It had seen better days. "Do you have a date set already?"

"Not yet," Beth said as she added an antique clock to the middle shelf. "I want my grandma to come, but she goes to Vegas every summer and hasn't gotten back to me."

Half an hour later, both of them had run out of meaningful tasks to do. Beth left to meet up with Ethan, while Daphne hung around the edge of the stage, reluctant to leave without attempting to find Michael before the break.

Under the pretense of looking over the finished set, she felt outward for his presence. In the distance, she could sense Heather wandering the senior hallway.

She glanced upward, squinting against the bright lights. The catwalk was empty.

"Hey, Daphne—sorry, didn't mean to make you jump— could you do me a favor? Could you take this down to the girls' dressing room for me?" Vivian smiled brightly at her, holding out an old-fashioned hat.

"Oh—sure," Daphne said, shaking off confusion. Bright spots danced in her vision. "Just anywhere?"

"Yeah. Thanks!" Vivian pressed it into her hands and walked away.

Daphne headed down the ramp, wondering why Vivian didn't take it herself. But maybe she had somewhere to be and Daphne hadn't seemed busy.

She navigated through the clutter downstairs and entered the women's dressing room. Veronica was at the far end, adjusting her curled, highlighted hair in the long mirror. She met Daphne's eyes through the reflection, unsmiling.

"Hi," Daphne said with a tight smile. There was space on the counter. She would drop the hat there and Vivian wouldn't be able to miss it.

There wasn't an answering hello. In awkward silence, she set the hat down and moved to the exit. Veronica turned toward her, arms crossed.

"Hey. Before you go, I was hoping to talk to you, actually."

Daphne stopped, taking this as a bad sign. "What's up?" she asked warily. It was possible that, as an assistant director, Veronica had instructions to pass along for rehearsal week.

"Nathan," Veronica said. Her face was grim.

"What about him?" Daphne asked, taken aback. Had something happened to him at track practice? He had been ill and fainted once last fall, but it was unlikely the episode repeated itself—or that Veronica would be the one to tell her about it.

"It's just that I *thought* the two of you were only friends. And I was totally okay with that." She walked closer, extra tall in high-heeled ankle boots. "But *now*, I feel like maybe I was dumb to believe that."

"What are you talking about?" Daphne's insides were

sinking into a black abyss of dread. Only two people knew how she felt about Nathan, and Beth wouldn't have told anyone. Had Veronica learned they'd hung out at the track meet and become jealous? Or was this delayed revenge because Nathan had defended her at Jessica's birthday party?

Whatever the reason, a storm cloud was gathering above their heads, with Veronica directing the lightning strike.

"Look, I'm going to be completely honest here." She was gaining steam, almost towering over Daphne. "He's my boyfriend, and I want to make sure you understand that."

"Okay?" Daphne said, hoping her tone sounded incredulous enough that such a thing needed to be brought up. It was difficult to stay calm when her stomach sensed the blows ahead.

The first one came. "I know you have feelings for Nathan. And before you deny it," Veronica added as Daphne's mouth opened to do just that, "Vivian heard you talking to Beth about it."

She was speechless. *That was a private conversation.* One where she'd taken a chance at revealing a secret. And to have it overheard by almost the worst person possible...

That was why Vivian gave her the hat. The two friends had schemed together to give Veronica the chance to pounce in private. Her smile when handing it over seemed, in retrospect, rather insidious.

"So, I wanted to clear things up," Veronica continued, her tone reasonable but edged with knives.

Daphne unstuck her voice, but to her frustration, it sounded quiet. Meek, compared to Veronica's confidence. "Me and Nathan are just friends. I'm fine with that—"

"A friend doesn't have a crush on their friend while he's dating someone else," Veronica said coldly.

Daphne closed her mouth. There was truth to the words, even though it came from one of her least-favorite people. And she had admittedly lied—she *wasn't* fine with staying friends with Nathan.

"So, I think it's best for both of us if you keep your distance from him. Can you agree?"

The lightning bolt had finally struck. It felt much like a dyszoon had pummeled into her and flipped her backward, a feeling Veronica seemed to excel at creating.

"I...I don't think that's—"

"Or we can talk to Nathan about it and see what he thinks?" Veronica smiled, no doubt at the panic that unwittingly crossed Daphne's face.

Would Veronica really tell Nathan? She could hear it already. *Hey, I found out that Daphne has a cute little crush on you! Isn't that adorable? I think you should still be nice to her. I mean, it's not like she has a lot of friends.*

Their friendship would be over. And to add insult to injury, Veronica might go to Jessica if she had also learned of the date with Leon. Besides Beth, Daphne would become entirely friendless. All because of an overheard conversation.

"Okay. Yeah. Fine. I'll keep my distance," Daphne said, anger bleeding into her voice, but it was too late for confidence. She'd lost.

"Good." Veronica smiled again. "I'm glad you understand." Without further comment, she swept past Daphne and out of the dressing room with the clicking of heels. The lingering smell of her perfume was sickeningly sweet.

Daphne remained in the dressing room, her thoughts racing. The conversation hadn't been long, and yet it had upended everything. Heat flooded her face from shame.

Only the fear of Vivian coming to collect her hat and change out of her costume motivated her to move. Veronica was likely sharing with her what had happened. Daphne's face warmed further at the image of them whispering together as she passed, laughing in the corner.

She could escape out the back door—but no, all her things were in her backpack in the front row.

The urge to cry came sharply. Daphne's anger turned on herself. Once again, she had allowed Veronica to get to her.

She replayed the conversation, trying without success to frame it in a way where she hadn't been knocked flat on her back, gasping for air. But no, Veronica had controlled it from the beginning.

At least I didn't slap her. A different confrontation with Ashley came to mind. Daphne grinned, but without humor.

She left the dressing room and went up the ramp. There was no sign of Veronica or Vivian around the stage. They were probably catching up in a more private spot.

"Hey!" Chad interrupted her halfway across. "High five."

Daphne forced a smile and stood on tiptoe to reach his hand, deliberately held high. She wasn't in the mood for playing around, especially not with the boyfriend of the girl who'd pushed her into Veronica's trap.

She collected her things and left, thankful that Beth was already gone so she didn't need to share the embarrassment of how easily she'd given in.

How would she step away from Nathan? One part was easy: They never hung out alone outside of school. If it came up, she would have to turn down an invitation to come over to his house to see his camera collection.

Messaging? They usually only shared links and memes. Veronica could find out about them through an offhand comment, though. *Hey, Daphne sent me this. It's hilarious.*

Lunch? Daphne wasn't sure how she could avoid walking with Nathan to class afterward. Their walk was brief anyway, and Veronica always rushed ahead. She relaxed slightly. Their daily walk felt like a small foothold to stand on. Her favorite part of the day could remain intact.

Daphne's phone dinged at the top of the stairs outside the theater. Her heart squeezed at Nathan's name. He'd shared a video of a fluffy black cat similar to Mystique that kept sticking its paw into a glass of water before trying its head.

It was as if Veronica stood nearby, crossing her arms. *So. What are you going to do?*

Daphne hesitated. She could ignore it, but that would make him wonder. The goal was to back off, not pretend he didn't exist. That would be suspicious.

Lol, she typed. *That cat looks like—* She reconsidered and deleted the extra sentence. There could be no additional comment, like she would normally have done. Nothing that could continue the chat. Only distance.

Was she going to let Veronica win? Daphne reopened the chat, determined to type more, but hesitated again. A better question—did she want extra drama from Veronica while she was dealing with visions, shades, dyszoons, and demons?

And that was only the supernatural-related stress. To say nothing of finishing high school, preparing for college, looking for a summer job...

Cold touched her mind like a breath. Heather stood at the entrance to the senior hallway, expression forlorn, as if she'd heard her name in Daphne's thoughts. Daphne stared back, phone loose in her hand.

Her promise. She'd told Heather she would help Nathan. If she listened to Veronica, she'd be going back on it.

But if Nathan found out about how she felt about him, it would be impossible to fulfill that promise anyway, as they would stop being friends. Considering everything she was already dealing with, Daphne couldn't stand avoiding him for the rest of the school year and willing graduation to come as soon as possible so that she could leave the drama behind.

Curling mist rose from the shade's shoulders and hair, a reminder that however alive she looked, Heather was only a fragment of herself. A fragment who cared deeply about what happened to her brother and wasn't satisfied that Daphne had done enough.

Go away. Daphne turned her back on the shade. It was out of her hands. She couldn't keep the promise.

And what was more—Daphne's eyes burned as she slammed open one of the front doors—she should never make them in the first place, because promises were always broken.

19

UNCREATED

As expected, her brief response to Nathan had stalled any further conversation. He'd sent a smiley face back, and that was it.

Daphne, sitting cross-legged on her bed an hour later, fought the temptation to send him a better message. Each time, she pictured Veronica leaning over to tell him about her crush and closed the chat again.

A notification popped onto the screen. Leon had sent her a video of an easy painting project, saying, *Hey, what do you think of this?* Before she could tap on the video, another text came through. *Looking forward to next week.*

Her heart skipped a beat. She replied, *Me too.* Since he'd said it first, she hoped it didn't sound desperate. They messaged back and forth for another ten minutes. Her mind seized on the distraction feverishly. When her mom called up the stairs that dinner was ready, Daphne reluctantly put down the phone.

Maybe Leon was the answer, she considered as she headed downstairs, sidestepping Phillip as he marched his way up, trailing mist. Letting go of Nathan would be easier if there was someone else she could turn her thoughts to. Someone who'd already made it clear he was interested in her.

While she feared Veronica would tell Jessica about the date and ruin their friendship, her former best friend probably wouldn't care. Might even *like* that her brother was going out with someone she knew.

After the first date, depending on whether there was a second, Daphne would let Jessica know about the situation. She could hardly sneak around doing paint projects with him and expect him to keep quiet about hanging out. It would be one less secret to balance.

Her mom stirred a bubbling pan on the stove. "You can move the binder if it's in the way," she said.

Daphne sat down and slid the open binder aside. The pages showed photocopies of a diary written in cramped cursive. She casually glanced over a small entry sandwiched in the middle of the page.

The days are like gray fog. It feels as though I pass through the valley of the shadow of death. I am surrounded by ghosts. Hers, I know, will always haunt me the most.

Daphne raised her eyebrows. That was the entire entry. The next one picked up months later, an update about visiting relatives in the west.

"Is this the diary you were typing up for the historical society? Didn't you finish it?"

Her mom mumbled something that sounded like, "I might not have worked on it at all this year." More loudly, she said, "Yes, it's Thomas Blakely's diary. He was one of the bigger Joe Schmoes a century ago."

She set two bowls of curry on the table. "It's got interesting parts, actually. There's some stuff in there about setting up the first free library..."

They settled into the meal. While it was delicious, Daphne

itched to return to her phone. Leon's messages had made her feel reckless, and she was rewriting the confrontation in the dressing room. In that version, Veronica was told where she could stick her concerns.

"How was your day?" Her mom's eyes showed concern, apparently having noticed her daughter's mood.

"It was fine. I did have an interesting conversation with my favorite person."

Face heating, she recapped the ambush. Her mom was aghast over Veronica's demands for Daphne to stop being friends with Nathan.

"And she basically told me that if I didn't, she'd tattle to him and tell him I like him," Daphne concluded.

"If she *were* to tell him, would that be so bad?" her mom said with defiance, her eyes bright with anger. "Maybe he likes you too and needs a reason to act on that, and that's why she's so threatened by you all of a sudden. If he knew how you feel, he might realize he'd rather have you."

"He doesn't like me that way, Mom," Daphne said. It stung to be blunt.

"Well, Veronica really should be going to *him* if she's so concerned. See what *he* thinks about being told who he can be friends with—What?"

Daphne suppressed her smile. "Nothing. Sorry. I just like that you're on my side."

Her mom huffed. "Of course I am! The fact that she went to *you* all sneaky just means she's a little—"

After another few minutes of this, Daphne's confidence grew. Veronica had caught her off guard, but she didn't owe her anything. She and Nathan could still be friends. And if he learned about her feelings for him, she could downplay it. *I actually just started seeing someone.*

"Just one more day until break," her mom reassured her.

.   .   .

By lunchtime on Friday, the fiery confidence that Daphne had felt the night before had waned. She avoided Veronica, who luckily sat by Nathan at lunch. It was one thing to talk to him despite the consequences, and another thing to brace herself for more drama. However, she couldn't avoid walking with him to history class.

Unless that choice had already been taken away from her. When Daphne reached the senior hallway, Veronica was at his locker. It was clear that she was going to prevent their walk, and had known about it all along.

Daphne grabbed her books, eyes stinging. *It doesn't matter.* The couple walked up the hallway, not saying anything to each other. She met Nathan's eyes.

"Have a good break," he said. His smile seemed apologetic.

"Yeah, you too," Daphne replied, and then pretended to sort through her books, though she'd already grabbed what she needed. The last thing she wanted to do was trail behind them.

Once they'd turned the corner, she slammed her locker shut just as dizziness overcame her. She laid a hand on the cool green metal, fighting for focus.

As if through a thick pane of glass, Ashley appeared before her. She was facing a tree, gesturing wildly with her arms. Her shouts were garbled.

Daphne took a step closer, and the scene cleared. Fresh air filled the hallway. Trees melded into the roof as if the school was giving way to a forest. Ashley stumbled into the tree and clawed at the bark. "Stop it! Let go of me! Let go—"

No—Daphne wrenched her focus away, and her back collided with the lockers. The vision was still there, pulling for her attention, but the trees were receding. Ashley was gone.

The bell rang.

A shock went down her spine. Daphne swore and jogged around the corner.

Despite her panic, she was only tardy by half a minute. Most of the class was standing yet, and Mr. Burnes was in his office as usual. He emerged as she set down her books, none the wiser that she'd been late.

She avoided looking to her right, where Veronica and Vivian sat. They might be talking about her, noting her lateness and gossiping about it. She flipped her notebook open and tried her best to ignore them.

Another vision had come while awake. Was it a glimpse of the recent past, or was Ashley losing her mind at that very moment? She risked a glance up at Mr. Burnes. What might they be planning in the long week ahead? At the very least, she might expect a dyszoon outbreak.

At the most, a demon's arrival.

The grass was brittle. Lifeless. Daphne walked barefoot, weaving in and out among the blank headstones. The heavy air trembled with thunder.

She paused before a red headstone, its earth freshly dug, and peered into the hole. It plunged into the far depths—perhaps into the very heart of the earth.

Something was behind her. Daphne turned and nearly fell backward into the abyss. Fear clawed her as a human-shaped creature stepped forward, cloaked in black. It ripped away the darkness from its face like a mask.

Ashley's expression showed pity. "You know you can't stop it," she said. Without warning, she kicked Daphne hard in the stomach and into the grave.

Daphne desperately reached for anything that might slow her fall but came up empty. The red sky became a pinprick, and then vanished altogether. There was nothing to do but descend into darkness.

Finally, she struck the bottom of the hole with lung-shattering force and punched through the earth. The world turned upside down, all sensation collapsed into a single point. She was a speck of dust, invisible against the dark void that stretched in all directions.

A galaxy-size spiral of matter floated in her vision. She was being gathered into the cosmic storm along with the rest of creation that had met the same fate.

The spiral shuffled toward a black circle that was even denser than the nothingness that surrounded them. The only sound in that endless, uncreated universe was that of a slight scream, vacuumed into silence whenever the circle pulled in the next fragment.

At least it was peaceful before the end of it all. Daphne was grateful for that. She had failed, but it wouldn't matter soon. Nothing would.

What may have been a millennium later, if time still existed, her turn came. The black circle filled her vision. Just before it drew her in, Daphne woke.

20

———

DATE

Daphne lay her head on the steering wheel, willing her rapid heart rate to slow.

In about ten minutes, she could enter the downtown cafe Leon had chosen. While she was looking forward to their date, her nerves weren't unlike those she had before facing dyszoons.

At least the Veil was quiet. Since the creatures mostly preferred the early morning hours, they were unlikely to come out during dinner. And if they did, she'd have a head start.

Her new ability to sense dyszoons before their arrival had proven useful twice so far that week, although it came with the usual unpleasant symptoms. A creature had come through the Veil before sunrise on Sunday and two more on Tuesday. Each battle was over in less than a minute.

Daphne was careful to wait until the dyszoons vanished before texting Claire that she had them covered. Messaging too soon meant explaining how she sensed them in advance, and she wasn't ready to admit that secret except in person. The psychic wouldn't be pleased but would have to admit they needed an advantage—it was the only one they had.

She checked the time again. Five more minutes, and then she would get out of her car.

Ashley hadn't appeared to her either awake or dreaming. While the waking visions were intrusive, Daphne was anxious to glimpse what was happening at the cabin and what Ashley and Mr. Burnes were up to. Spring break was more than half over, and with no change to the Veil.

It was time to enter the cafe. A firework bouncing around her insides, Daphne checked her reflection one last time in the rearview mirror. Her outlined gray eyes were striking, though the mascara tube had needed several drops of oil before it was usable. She'd even dug out a straightener to smooth out her dark hair, which was still irritatingly frizzy.

"You're fine. It'll be fine. You've already met him," Daphne repeated her mom's encouragement as she exited the car. The sky rumbled, heavy with storm clouds.

Why should she be nervous, anyway? Hadn't they hung out at the party? This wasn't all that different. And they had messaged each other.

Daphne entered the cafe, struck by another anxious thought—what if Leon told Jessica his plans for that evening? Was she inviting drama by going on a date with him? *I've got a date with your friend. She didn't tell you? Sorry...*

With any luck, Jessica was with Zeke and unaware of her brother's whereabouts. And honestly, did it matter? Jessica hadn't texted her all week. If dating Leon was the death blow to their friendship, it had been close to dead already.

Leon waited in the small entryway before the inner doors, dressed in a graphic T-shirt. Daphne, after trying on more outfits than she wanted to admit, had picked out a black top and light jeans.

"Hey!" he said with an easy smile.

Her face flushed. The last time she'd seen him, they'd almost kissed. "Have you been waiting? Sorry, I was—"

"No worries—"

"—didn't want to be too—"

"Ever been here?" Leon asked, holding open the door for her.

"I think once, when it was called something else. That was a really long time ago," Daphne babbled, gripping her purse strap like a lifeline. Time had slowed from moment to moment. The hostess greeted them, and they followed her past a glass case filled with tantalizing slices of pie and settled into a window booth.

Daphne crossed her legs. She was highly conscious of how she positioned her body. Where was she supposed to put her hands? It felt masculine to rest her arms on the table. Yet she felt uptight keeping them in her lap, twisting her owl bracelet.

In contrast, Leon was easygoing, like she remembered. It relaxed her a minuscule amount.

The hostess deposited laminated menus. Menus! There was something to hold! Daphne opened hers up, although she had already reviewed it online earlier.

"What's good here?" she asked, forcing a smile. If she pretended to relax, it might become a reality.

"I usually go with the Southwest chicken wrap, but I think I should mix it up."

The waitress arrived and set down glasses of water. Daphne took a tiny sip and examined the menu. With her stomach twisting, none of the options were appetizing.

"What was Jessica doing today?" she asked. Maybe taking one worry off her plate would help.

"I'm not sure. I haven't seen her since we got back. I think she's been with Zach all day."

"Zach?" Daphne said, momentarily puzzled. "Oh, you mean Zeke?"

"Right. Only met him once, at her birthday party."

"So she hasn't asked about us having dinner?" Daphne dared to say more directly. Leon would assume his sister, her friend, knew about the date. Would he find it weird that she'd kept it a secret?

"She doesn't ask about what I get up to. Plausible deniability." He grinned and set the menu aside. She smiled back, relieved.

The waitress returned. Daphne asked for the veggie wrap and fries, and Leon ordered the Southwest burger.

"You're really venturing out," she observed, reluctantly giving up her menu. It had given her something to do. However, the fact that Leon didn't seem to hate her company several minutes into their date made her feel less self-conscious.

"What can I say? I like what I like," he said, glancing up at her. "Are you a vegetarian?"

"Kind of," Daphne replied, rubbing a finger over the owl on her bracelet underneath the table. "I'll eat fish and stuff. I'm not against meat, but I've never liked it all that much."

"My roommate is vegan. Actually, gluten-free too. Honestly, I don't know how he can eat..."

For the next few minutes, Leon shared some of his roommate's odd behaviors and misadventures. After a recent middle-of-the-night stroll, he had climbed a tree, and it was an hour before his friends could coax him back down.

"Why did he climb it, then?" Daphne laughed in amazement, now stirring the ice in her water instead of spinning her bracelet. She was grateful that Leon was carrying the conversation so far. Her mind was steeped in fog.

"He's afraid of heights, so he did it on a dare," he explained with a grin. His dark hair was attractive, swept up. "At least he hadn't been drinking. He doesn't drink anything but sparkling water. Literally."

"He sounds interesting. I hope I get a decent roommate. But that'll be after I transfer."

"Oh yeah? What are you thinking of doing?"

Conscious of his gaze on her, Daphne shyly answered his casual questions about her plans to take classes locally to save money on housing. The plans sounded like another person's, a vision of what would be if a demon wasn't in the picture. The sky outside grew darker, threatening rain.

"I don't know what I want to major in yet," she admitted. Unlike Leon with design, no clear passion or talent that could be turned into a career had magically revealed itself to her. Daphne poked an ice cube with her straw, considering a soda. Whether it was the thought of her blank future or anxiety over the date, she felt lightheaded.

"That's okay," Leon said. "Don't worry about it yet."

"I'm looking into clubs, though," she added. "I might join Drama Club."

"I can see you onstage." He grinned at her.

"No, I meant—right now, I'm just building the set, though we actually just finished—I'm not one of the..." Daphne stammered, caught off guard that he thought her outgoing enough to be an actor. "I'm pulling the curtain next weekend."

She took a deep sip of water. If the date made her this nervous, delivering lines in front of a large audience would be that much worse. She could suddenly sympathize with Vivian's self-doubt.

"Oh yeah?" Leon said, straightening with interest.

Daphne nodded in response, swallowing. There'd been enough focus on her. "Are you involved in anything fun?"

Her attention slipped away as he talked about the camping club. Or was it the climbing club? The light hanging over their table was far too harsh, a spotlight on her every nervous thought. The ice in her drink swirled faster.

"Daphne? Are you okay?" said a voice.

The dining room came into focus. The ice stilled. "What?"

"I asked you something, and you didn't say anything," Leon said, no longer smiling.

"Oh, I'm sorry." Daphne blinked in confusion. "I think I— I'm sorry, I'm just going to head to the bathroom quick." She could regroup there.

"Sure," he replied, now frowning.

Daphne slid out of the booth, and amid the hazy room, full of muffled talk, she spotted the sign for the bathroom. Thankfully, it was empty.

Her reflection was pale. She rubbed cold water on her forehead, and the fog in her head receded a little.

Each second that Leon spent alone felt like a strike against her dating skills. She had been excited for the date and now wished more than anything that it was over. Was she having a panic attack?

A presence brushed her mind. Recognition toppled over her as if the booth light had fallen on her head. *Not now. No.*

Focused on Leon, she hadn't recognized the brewing signs. Her outlined eyes in the reflection widened in horror and then blurred. The creature brushed past the bathroom walls, although it was far away.

A dyszoon was coming. It didn't care that she was busy, and could have chosen any other time to arrive. It was coming.

Twenty minutes, give or take. That was all she had before the dyszoon came through the Veil. She and Leon hadn't even eaten their meal.

Her thumb hesitated over her phone. She could text Claire and ask her to cover. But doing so meant explaining how she knew the dyszoon was on its way.

There was no choice but to cut the date short. Daphne pressed a hand against her forehead, sorting through her options. She didn't *have* to meet the dyszoon right at the Veil. It was only lately that doing so was even a possibility, but it was a risk. Once the time was up, she could feign an illness. Apologize and say she was unwell.

Daphne dried her face and emerged from the bathroom, relieved that the chatter in the dining room was clear. The room was no longer hazy.

Two plates were on the table when she slid back into the booth with an apology, and Daphne wondered if she'd been away longer than she thought. Leon, she was touched to see, though it was tinged with guilt, had waited for her before digging into his meal.

"No worries," he said, and picked up a knife to cut his burger apart. Daphne did the same with the wrap, not wanting to risk eating messily with her hands.

Distantly, she knew that the food was delicious. But her insides were tight with tension, and the first bite was tasteless. The dyszoons would arrive soon. If she left now, she could still meet them at the bridge.

They ate half a minute in silence. Pulling her thoughts away from the Veil, she scrambled for a new topic. Leon didn't seem as easygoing as before. What had they already talked about? They'd started with Jessica.

"I take it Jessica didn't win anything from her lotto tickets? I never asked her," Daphne said in desperation, remembering Veronica's birthday present. The dyszoon's movements pressed deeper into her mind, and she strained to focus.

"She did not, unfortunately. But she never told me, so she could be a secret millionaire."

Daphne forced a laugh. The silence lulled again, broken by

the waitress, who checked on their food. Behind them, another couple chatted effortlessly.

An obvious topic came to her. "How was your vacation, anyway? Where in Florida did you go?" she asked. Claire's three sons lived in Florida, she recalled. She'd forgotten to ask for an update on her upcoming grandchild. The due date had to be soon.

Daphne finished her wrap at a record pace while doing her best to ask questions. She glanced out the window several times as if the dark clouds would reveal the dyszoon's progress.

It helped if she didn't look at Leon, or else he might see the pressure building behind her eyes as the creature slid along. The first drops of rain splattered on the pavement. With any luck, the dyszoon wouldn't travel far into the woods before she could arrive.

Daphne set down her fork. She'd left a few kettle chips. "You know, I don't feel all that well, actually."

Leon was chewing slowly. "In what way?" he said, after swallowing.

"My stomach is off. I noticed it earlier."

Leon's eyes dropped to her demolished plate. In contrast, he'd only eaten half of the burger and hadn't touched the majority of his fries. Daphne realized her error. She should have feigned indigestion after her bathroom trip, though that would have been embarrassing, or else come up with a believable family emergency.

The waitress stopped by to check on them, helpfully giving her a moment to think. Daphne took out the pocketbook Jessica had gifted for her birthday to avoid his gaze.

"I have some cash for mine. I'm sorry, I guess I should probably go," she said apologetically, dropping a bill.

His lips pressed together grimly. "I'm sorry, you know, if I bothered you," he said. "You didn't have to go out with me, for Jessica's sake."

"For Jess—?" Daphne repeated in confusion. "No, that's not the—"

"It's just that I can tell you haven't been into this. And that's fine, whatever. But I'd rather you just canceled."

Daphne stared, aghast. The last hour flashed through her mind from his perspective. She had been distant almost from the beginning, and had rushed her meal and stared out the window. Capped by her weak excuse just now, she had given him all the signs of being uninterested.

Leon had read her well at the party, and might even suspect she'd fled to the bathroom to ask someone for advice on how to end the date early. How long had she been in there?

She might have known he would see through her excuse, as it hadn't worked on Halloween, when she'd pretended to be unwell so she could go battle dyszoons. Nathan had suspected the lie too.

But what could Daphne say to reassure him? That she could prove Jessica wasn't the reason for the date since she had kept it a secret? It would make things worse. She had been so successful at lying for months, that to have a lie backfire...

Daphne opened her mouth to confirm she was interested. To share, with vulnerability, her hopes for the summer. Hopes that mostly involved him. But at that moment, the snake sliding around her mind squeezed it in a death grip. Her estimates had been off.

The dyszoon had arrived.

"I'm sorry," she managed to choke out through the pressure, and exited the cafe without looking back.

21

WASTELAND

Numbness spread through Daphne as she sped to the Veil, the sky dimming as night approached.

Earlier that day, she'd been excited. She'd imagined sitting across from Leon, laughing together and making plans to meet up again once summer came.

And afterward, there might have come a moment where his face drew near hers, without interruption this time. A tangible promise that something good was on the way. And while she had hoped that kiss would be with someone else, she would get over Nathan with time. For once, she wouldn't have to long for something. It would be hers.

She pulled the car over a few miles from the bridge. The dyszoon was in the woods nearby. Daphne zipped up her jacket, wishing she'd thought to pack a raincoat, and marched into the trees.

The date was supposed to be a stepping stone toward a summer filled with something other than worry over the future. But that was over. The dyszoons, the demon, the Veil...Once again, they had ruined that hope.

Leaves rustled ahead. The dyszoon hadn't ventured in as far as she feared. She'd grown comfortable confronting the creatures at the Veil. It was much more inconvenient to track them down, worrying all the while that they'd harm someone before she arrived.

Daphne clung to the numbness. It was the only thing keeping her emotions together, and she needed to concentrate. She crept forward, feeling outward for any clear sign of the dyszoon. Cold rain flattened hair she had so carefully styled that afternoon. All for nothing.

A sudden urge to cry seized her. Daphne stopped, wanting nothing more than to curl up on the ground. Hadn't she learned? A normal life wasn't possible for her. Not while the Veil was open. As benign as it seemed, its evil would never leave her alone. It infected everything.

As if sensing her emotions, the dyszoon's presence grew stronger. Daphne flinched at the sound of a small branch breaking and gritted her teeth. A dark blur blasted into a nearby tree with an ear-numbing shriek.

Daphne deflected its first blow with a cry and stumbled back. In her current mood, the dyszoon felt twice as strong as the others. It soared away, but it would be back in seconds.

The sky rumbled with thunder, and rain soaked through her coat. If life were fair, she would still be sitting in the booth with Leon, trying one of the sliced pies from the case. Instead, she was freezing and alone except for the creature that wanted her dead.

It curved back for another attack. "Just *go away!*" she shouted. Her hit was sloppy. The dyszoon careened onto the ground and glided upward, unfazed.

Daphne sobbed. The dyszoons would never stop coming. Powerless to stop the Veil, she would deal with them her entire life until one killed her. Like a storm, there was no way to prevent what was coming. The demon would arrive. All her efforts to thwart its dyszoons would mean nothing.

"*Go away!*" she screamed, pushing the creature away. It barely moved and shrieked with glee at her weakness, her despair. Its presence would only drive her down further.

Her next feeble push was as effective as brushing a hand across a pane of glass. Pathetic, to expect the window to shatter. She was too weak to face the demon—she couldn't even fend off a single dyszoon.

The dyszoon pressed its attack, its shadowy form spreading across her invisible barrier. Daphne pushed back, unable to do the same to the grim thoughts welling up in her mind, cutting through the numbness. They intensified each moment she spent in the presence of a creature whose hatred washed over her skin as much as the rain.

This battle was one in a thousand. If—when—she defeated this one, more would follow. She'd never live a normal life. They'd make sure of that.

Leon. She might have moved on with someone good for her, but the Veil had once again taken it from her, like it had with Nathan on Halloween. That chance had gone to Veronica, who was better at these things. Better at getting a guy. Better at being beautiful. Better at being a best friend to Jessica.

"*Just go away!*" Daphne sobbed. Her attempt to push it away failed. As soon as she let her defense fall, it would be on her.

But what was the point in stopping it? No matter what she did, the Veil would be there. Watching her every move. Destroying every chance for something good. Poisoning every relationship she had.

"*Stop it!*" Daphne pushed outward with all the force she could muster. The dyszoon was only knocked back a few feet, but it gave enough space to launch a better attack. She struck it with each word.

"Leave!" It writhed and snarled.

"Me!" She forced it back.

"ALONE!"

Daphne's blistered scream matched the dyszoon's. It shattered like black glass.

A pressure lifted from her mind, and Daphne let her knees buckle. She rested her forehead on the wet ground, shaking with sobs, past caring about getting wet as the woods vanished into night.

Storms kept at bay were threatening to drown her. For months, she'd been strong. Failure wasn't an option, not with dyszoons. Every other responsibility paled in comparison to her duty to protect others from harm and stop the demon's plans.

Any heartache over Nathan, over her failed friendship with Jessica, over a future written by the Veil could be cast aside as she battled the symptoms. Now, that pain was making itself known with a ferocity she'd denied it for months.

The Veil was her present and could be her future for years. Up to this point, she'd always assigned an end date to the problem, even if it wasn't until next year. Because surely there was an end, and they would figure out how to close the Veil and end its dangers once and for all.

Her life after graduation had no purpose except to battle dyszoons. Sure, she was enrolled in fall classes, but this was more out of necessity. A plan she had made in another life, and not because she had a clear direction. In that future, a book-carrying Daphne made of mist blew away the moment she tried to look closer. As intangible as a shade.

A dark thought, always pushed aside as an impossibility, blackened her already dark vision. The idea of failing. Of never stopping the demon. Or maybe—the possibility loomed above

her like a growing Veil, blocking out the stars—of a fateful end
to the struggle.

Daphne shivered the thought away, pushing herself
upright. She wouldn't approach that edge. They would not fail.
The demon would not win.

"We're not going to fail," she whispered, willing the stars to
reappear in her mind. They did reluctantly, one by one. "You're
not going to die."

Heavily, Daphne stood. There was nowhere else for her to
go but home. One more battle was won.

Another would follow.

As she turned into the driveway, Daphne relaxed at the sight of
home, its lit windows warm and welcoming in the dark. Things
wouldn't look so bleak when she was dry, and blasting the heat
in her car had already helped.

Daphne gathered her soaked jacket and hurried up the
porch steps. The front door closed behind her, and she sighed
in relief.

"You're back! How was your date?" her mom called from
the kitchen with an optimism Daphne couldn't bear just then.
All at once, her carefully filed emotions came tumbling down.

"It was fine," she choked out, rushing up the stairs before
her mom could question her wet clothes.

"Daphne?"

She furiously changed into leggings and a T-shirt and then
slammed the wet outfit into the bathroom laundry basket,
wanting to punish anything that had given her hope.

Her gray eyes were blotchy, black like a raccoon's. Daphne
removed her owl bracelet and vigorously rubbed her face clean.
As expected, the floorboard outside the door creaked. She shut
off the tap.

"Daphne? Are you okay?" her mom asked gently, trying the door handle.

"I'm fine," Daphne said in a voice that was clearly not, wiping her face dry with a towel. Her hair was still wet, but there wasn't anything to be done about it.

"What happened? Did your date not go well?"

Daphne didn't respond. She could hardly explain that all her relationships were doomed because of the Veil. The memory of Leon's grimace, catching her in a lie, made her stomach sink.

"Can I come in?"

She sighed into her towel and then unlocked the door. Her mom's cropped blonde head poked in gently.

"Things didn't go so well?"

The room became blurry with tears. "No."

"Oh, Daphne." She wrapped her in a worried hug. "Were you out in the rain? What happened?"

Daphne stared at the owl bracelet on the counter rather than meet her mom's eyes, which could read her so well. "It was going fine until it didn't. He said...it was clear I wasn't interested in him, and that I didn't have to go out with him just because of Jessica."

Her mom's mouth fell open. "What? Why on earth would he think that?"

Daphne settled on a partial version of events that was nevertheless somewhat truthful. "I don't know. I started not feeling well, so I got quiet, and I went to the bathroom before the food came. And when I came out, he seemed kind of bothered. I tried to stick it out, but then I explained why I needed to leave, and he told me all of that."

"I'm so sorry, Daphne!" Her mom pulled her into another squeezing hug. "Forget him, if that's how he treats you. You don't need that."

"Thanks, Mom." Daphne gently extricated herself. She didn't deserve a comforting hug, but she couldn't share that Leon was right to be suspicious, just wrong about the reason. No one could know that, least of all her mom. That burden was hers to face alone.

"I feel so stupid about everything," she murmured.

"Yeah?" her mom prodded gently.

Phillip walked past the door, mist trailing behind him. Like a shade, Daphne occupied the room and yet was caught up in some other place. For years, a fragment of herself had sleepily acted out a normal life. And now she was awake.

"I've just been realizing that everything I care about gets blown apart." Her calm voice was someone else's. Years of pent-up thoughts she'd locked away, unacknowledged, strained to break free. The bracelet lay on the counter, the owl's brow deeply furrowed. A poor stand-in for the father who'd given it to her.

"What do you mean?"

"Whenever I think about the future, it's so empty, Mom." Her voice was barely above a whisper, and she hugged herself, straining to keep from falling apart. "Nothing's there. After school is over...it's just blank." There was only the growing Veil, ready to swallow her and the stars.

"It'll be a change, Daphne, but you'll figure things out." Her mom smiled, though her eyebrows had pinched together in concern, perhaps realizing that the problem ran deeper than a bad date. She gripped her arm, attempting to make eye contact. "You have plans. You're going to college, for starters."

Daphne moved out of her grip and paced the bathroom, moving to twist her owl bracelet before realizing she hadn't slipped it back on. It was almost like having a purpose, this restless pacing.

"It's just, I'm graduating soon and I have no idea what I'm

going to do with my life. It'll be summer and—" She gestured outward into the void beyond the room.

"You have a plan," her mom put in gently. "You can figure it out as you go. You're only eighteen."

Daphne only half heard her as she continued feverishly, "I'm an adult. I should have some idea by now, but I don't. I'm almost done with being a senior, and it's supposed to be the best year of high school, or whatever. But it *hasn't* been and I have *no* friends—"

"You have Jessica—"

"She dropped me. I might as well face it." The blunt truth didn't sting. She was hurting too much already. "We haven't even—" Daphne stopped short of admitting that she and Jessica hadn't hung out for months. She'd used going to her house as a cover for her trips to the Veil too many times.

"And Nathan—"

"He's got Veronica. I probably won't see him after we graduate." What he'd said at the track meet about seeing his cameras had made her hope otherwise, but tonight had taught her that hope was foolish.

"Beth—"

"We're only friends because of Drama Club. She's getting married in June anyway, and moving. I doubt we'll keep in touch," Daphne said. Weariness was soaking into her bones.

"Well, even so. Life after high school is different. I think you'll be surprised by who sticks around. Trust me. This is just a season. Give it time, and things will work out."

"No, they won't," Daphne said, knowing that she sounded obstinate, but it felt good to argue. The dam she'd tried so hard to keep in place all these months was finally breaking, washing her away.

Oddly, letting go was freeing. Caring had bruised her to numbness, so that it was like she no longer cared at all.

Her mom attempted to grip her again and stop the pacing. "Daphne, you've had a bad evening, but it'll be okay—"

"No, it WON'T," Daphne yelled, barely recognizing her own voice. Distantly, she knew her mom wanted to help, but she was already falling. "It WON'T be okay. Everything is awful and I can't—I can't fix anything! No matter what I do, everything falls apart and I can't do anything about it." She sobbed.

"Daphne, what is so awful? What's the matter?" Her mom seemed close to tears herself.

She was perilously close to revealing everything. Months of lies and secrets, but also a deeper sense of loss that had come well before the Veil, and would continue long after it.

"Nothing," Daphne choked out.

"You can tell me."

She stared intently at the bracelet, attempting to calm her hiccuping breaths. "Nothing...has been okay for years. Dad died on us. He made a mistake, and it killed him, and *we're always going to be paying for it!*"

Her mom flinched. Of all the things she had confided, this had struck.

"Your dad didn't mean to go," her mom said, voice small. "Trying to save that girl wasn't a mistake, even though it turned out she wasn't inside. His passing was the hardest thing I've ever lived through, but we're making it. Our lives aren't so bad."

"I'm sorry." Daphne crossed her arms, mildly ashamed, and angry for it. First she'd been caught out on a lie, and now she'd made her mom feel bad. She hiccuped. "I don't expect you to understand. It's just how I feel."

"It—"

"And *don't* say it'll get better. You don't know that, okay?" she snapped, conscience pricking. None of it was her mom's fault. She was only trying to listen.

"Daphne…" her mom said. Her tone was gentle, but also reproving.

"I'm fine. Whatever." She turned away, not able to look up. "I'm sorry to bother you. You can go back to what you were doing before."

"You're not bothering me. I'm just trying to help you see it's not the end of the world."

It will be if the demon wins, she thought. And with each day that passed without an answer for how to stop it, that future was more likely to be the only one any of them had. *I'm coming*, one of the demons had said, through Veronica's Ouija board. It could arrive any day.

Why did the date matter? Nothing would come of it anyway if she didn't close the Veil. To get distracted by anything else—dates, Drama Club, college—was foolish. It was time to face the fact that a normal life wasn't for her.

"Daphne?"

The house that had seemed like a refuge half an hour ago was now unbearable, choked with memories. She couldn't stay there, under her mom's gaze, which might pierce through her defenses to discover the whole truth. That was a conversation she had no strength to have.

"I'll be okay," Daphne said with calm, hiccuping unhelpfully. "I just…I need to get out for a bit. Go for a drive."

"It's after eight and raining. I don't think you should be driving like this—"

Her irritation flared. Why couldn't her mom understand? "I'll be fine." She pushed past her.

"Daphne—"

"I'll be *fine*, Mom! Just leave me alone!" Daphne yelled over her shoulder.

She jogged down the stairs, barely turning aside in time to

dodge Phillip, who was coming back up. His solid-looking elbow passed coolly through her arm, and she flinched.

Daphne grabbed a spare coat off the wall and flung open the front door. The faster she went, the less time she'd have to second-guess her decision to go. She had to do *something* other than be home, her mom prodding at what was wrong.

When everything was.

22
____

THE CAFE

Light rain splattered on the windshield. Daphne barely noticed the direction she was driving, except that it was toward town.

She was numb again, as if she'd spent a year's worth of emotion in a single evening and had now lost the capacity to feel anything. As she reached downtown, she wanted to stop somewhere, anywhere. Not thinking twice, Daphne turned into the parking lot of a cafe. Leon's car was long gone.

Are you safe? Her mom texted.

Yes. Stopping somewhere for a bit, Daphne wrote, a sliver of guilt cutting through the numbness. Hopefully the calm response softened her sudden, dramatic departure.

She entered the cafe, uncertain why she was returning so soon, except that she couldn't muster the energy to think of another place to sit quietly by herself.

The waitress, thankfully not the same one as before, seated her at a booth on the left side. Daphne grabbed the menu and stifled a flash of Leon's face, his tightened mouth. *I'd rather you just canceled.*

Voices floated from behind the wooden partitions. The booths were empty except for a balding man two tables behind her. She was grateful to not be the only person sitting alone.

When the waitress returned, Daphne ordered a hot chocolate and a slice of chocolate cream pie. It was a small victory over the dyszoon that prevented her from ordering it earlier.

"I'll take some more coffee, thanks," the old man told the waitress as she passed.

The order came, and her fingers wrapped gratefully around the mug. She hadn't warmed up properly since the woods.

The overhead fixture was once more like a spotlight on her predicament. She typically turned to her mom with her problems, and now she was alone in a booth with nobody to talk to about them. They hadn't fought so badly in recent memory, if it could be called a fight, when Daphne had carried it.

Her fingers went to twist the owl bracelet, faithfully worn every day since her dad presented it to her as a Valentine's Day gift a few weeks before he died. With dismay, she realized it was on the bathroom counter at home. Her wrist felt bare without it.

Who, then, could she talk to? Daphne sipped the hot chocolate and mentally scrolled through her contacts.

Uncle Lloyd flashed through her mind first, as her next-closest family member, who was often halfway across the world. She had always looked up to her mom's younger brother, but he was removed from their day-to-day lives. Explaining what was bothering her that wasn't demon-related would take more effort than she had energy.

Besides Uncle Lloyd, there was no other family she could turn to. Her grandparents had passed away, and she had no other uncles or aunts or close cousins. That left extended family, most of whom she had never met.

Friends? Daphne laughed grimly and stabbed the pie. Hadn't she admitted half an hour ago that she had none? There was Jessica...but they didn't even message each other anymore, and Daphne couldn't tell her about the disastrous date.

Even if they were still best friends, she'd hesitate. Jessica had been a good friend when they griped about work, which had bonded them when they'd been fast food cashiers together, but she had never been someone Daphne would turn to in an emotional crisis. She had always known that Jessica was more bubbly than mature.

Beth? There was a maturity there that Jessica lacked. But while their friendship had grown thanks to Stage Crew, they weren't quite close enough for Daphne to lay out her problems.

Or could she? Beth had confided her own family difficulties, especially the spats popping up around the wedding. She hesitated, a thumb over their most recent chat on her phone. Below Beth's name was Nathan's.

Daphne stared at it. There was never anyone she wanted to see more, and never anyone she could talk to less. She imagined him reaching for his phone as her name popped up on the screen. Veronica, sitting next to him, asking, "Who is it?"

The next mouthful of pie, though delicious, was less enjoyable. *Of course she'll be with him,* Daphne thought with a fresh dose of pain. His girlfriend's presence ruled him out as someone she could message, not with the threat to stay away hovering over every conversation. It was too risky.

For a moment, Daphne was tempted to abandon all restraint and admit how she felt about him. How could she feel any worse than she already did? Her recent nightmare resurfaced. Nathan, squirming with embarrassment as he suggested they were better off as friends.

Then, of course, they would no longer be friends. Not after

that. She would take friendship—even restricted by Veronica—over nothing at all.

Another wave of despair overwhelmed her, and Daphne hid her face in her hands. She had no one. Her mom was her best friend and understood her the most of anyone, but she couldn't talk to her tonight.

Plus, her mom was only aware of half the problem, and that was the way it had to be. The coming battle was Daphne's responsibility. And Claire's...

Claire! Daphne opened her eyes, stunned. The one person who knew about the hidden part of her life and might be up for listening to all of it.

Madam Moon was just a few blocks away. The solution was perfect. Why didn't she think of it before? The explanation must be that her life was divided into two worlds, and the psychic was, for obvious reasons, fixed firmly on the supernatural one.

The decision filled Daphne with purpose where she had previously been adrift. If there was anyone who could understand what she was going through, all of it, it was Claire.

Relieved, Daphne sipped her hot chocolate, and then promptly spat it out. The person she least wanted to cross paths with on a night like tonight was entering the cafe.

Veronica wasn't alone, but was with Nathan's best friend, Dom. No doubt Nathan would be joining them soon. Despite admitting how much she wanted to see him, Daphne would rather smash through the window to escape than run into him with his girlfriend.

Her mug paused in midair as she raced through her options. If the waitress led them to the left, there would be no avoiding Veronica. Sneaking to the bathroom wasn't possible. In seconds, they would spot her.

Daphne looked down at her half-empty plate, imagining

Veronica clocking it all. *Are you having high-calorie substances all by your lonely self? That's a little weird, don't you think?*

The waitress greeted them and picked up two menus. Not thinking twice, Daphne ducked under the table.

She hugged her legs and made herself as small as possible. The awkward position would be difficult to explain if they spotted her. Three pairs of nearby feet walked past the booth, but none paused.

A minute passed, and Daphne's legs ached. Where were they seated? That admittedly was the flaw in the plan. There was a chance they'd recognize her when she sat up, but she had no other option. Nathan hadn't walked by, but he could arrive any second.

Cautiously, Daphne worked her way up the seat and peered over the top. To her relief, Veronica and Dom had disappeared behind a wooden partition. A long head of curled blonde hair was half visible.

Her eyes dropped to the balding man down the row, who was peering down his nose with interest, as if reading a newspaper. He glanced to his left and brandished an invisible mug. "I'll take some more coffee, thanks."

Startled, Daphne took in the mist rising from his buttoned-up shirt. Preoccupied, she had failed to recognize him as a shade who was perhaps sitting in his favorite booth with an imagined mug.

Pity surged through her. It was a relief to feel it for someone other than herself. While most shades walked freely, a fair number were stuck in a loop. However, now wasn't the right moment to pull him out of it.

Daphne risked one last bite of pie and then removed some cash. Again, she was leaving before the bill arrived. Bursting with nerves, she strode to the door and then dashed to her car, which was parked near where the shade was sitting. Nathan's car was absent.

From this angle, Veronica's side was clearly visible through the bright windows, and Dom was partially hidden. The waitress set down drinks and took out her pad.

Daphne frowned, a hand paused on the car handle. If Nathan were coming, wouldn't they have waited for him before ordering? Their menus were taken.

Veronica laughed and flipped a length of hair over her shoulder. A sense of déjà vu filled Daphne, difficult at first to place. Only, Veronica was acting with Dom the way she had with Nathan at the beginning—flirtatious.

A memory slid into place, and Daphne cursed her forgetfulness. Nathan *couldn't* join them. He wasn't in Long Haven, but visiting his older brother on the coast for at least another day. She had worried about bumping into him for nothing.

Daphne gripped the phone in her pocket, uncertain what to do. Maybe Veronica acted that way around all guys, laughing and annoying. But...everything she did was intentional.

Even if she let Nathan know about the dinner, the scene was hardly incriminating. He might know his friends were meeting up. Veronica and Dom seemed an unlikely pair, but they must have gotten to know each other through Nathan. But if he *wasn't* aware they were out together...

An angry, sweet triumph warmed her better than the hot chocolate. After an evening of defeat, a victory had landed on her lap. The opportunity to strike at Veronica, who was now out with his best friend behind his back—possibly.

The anger turned lukewarm. Daphne pulled her hand from her pocket, shaking away her suspicions. She had enough problems without creating more drama that would, in all likelihood, hurt him. The temptation to send a message was strong, but who would she be sending it for—Nathan, or herself?

Daphne pushed Veronica out of mind as she drove the few blocks to Claire's studio, grateful that most of the shades on Main Street were on the sidewalk. A man loitering on the centerline brushed her side mirror. She gritted her teeth and turned left to park in front of Madam Moon.

The neon Open sign was lit. Daphne approached the door, more sure-footed than she had been all day. Claire would listen. And that was all she needed.

She opened the door to the jingle of bells, soothed by the strong scent of the perfumed room. Claire appeared through the curtain, a glimmering wrap around her shoulders. Her painted eyebrows rose in surprise, but she smiled warmly.

"Daphne! It's good to see you. How are you? We didn't arrange a meeting, did we?"

"No, I was just nearby," Daphne reassured her, balling her hands self-consciously in her jacket pockets. She doubted her decision to come—how would she begin sharing all that was on her mind?

"Well, come join me. It's been a quiet evening."

They sat down in their usual spots in the reading room. Claire's curly hair was freshly dyed a brighter shade of red, its edges glowing in the lamplight. Daphne noted the tissue box on the nearby shelf and vowed that she wouldn't need them.

"Oh—I should ask if you want tea."

"I'm good," Daphne said hastily. "I had some hot chocolate at the cafe. And then I thought, since you were nearby..."

"Well, I'm glad you stopped. I've been thinking we were due for another chat. I saw your message about the dyszoon. How did that go for you?"

Daphne's voice echoed, seared with hopelessness and rage, screaming at the creature so difficult to defeat. *Go away!* She touched her wrist before remembering, yet again, that the owl bracelet was at home.

It went okay, she nearly said. But she had come to unload, not hold back.

"It...it was hard." Daphne clasped her hands on the starry tablecloth, gazing into a turquoise stone set into one of Claire's rings. "Harder than it should have been. I was actually...I was on a date when it happened, so obviously I had to leave. He didn't...he didn't like that I had to go all of a sudden." To her embarrassment, her eyes stung.

Claire leaned forward and placed a weathered hand gently on hers. "Are you all right, Daphne?" Not long ago, she had been asked that same question, and Daphne had dismissed it by saying, *I'm fine.*

But she wasn't. The sympathetic touch undid her caution, though thanks to determined effort, the tissues weren't needed. The last few hours—it was difficult to believe it had only been a few hours—poured out without a filter. Daphne was careful not to reveal she had sensed the dyszoon before it arrived, but the rest of it was true.

Claire listened patiently and offered no comment, instead listening with an intent gaze. Daphne told her about Leon's reaction to the lie, her despair as she battled the dyszoon and broke down at home, and her return to the cafe.

"And then my least favorite person comes in. Veronica. And so, I hid under the table." Daphne laughed, the sound strange in her ears. "That's actually kind of embarrassing."

Claire laughed with her. "I'd have been tempted to do the same, but I'm afraid my hip would tell me otherwise."

Daphne smiled, and it came easily. As she suspected, Claire was good at listening. The chat had been exactly what she needed. For the first time, she was able to confide a problem that combined both worlds. The main downside was being unable to tell Claire the full truth about what the Veil had done to her, but she would do it soon.

She half-seriously considered asking for permission to collapse on one of the couches in the shop and forget the world for a night, but home was waiting. Her mom hadn't texted further, giving her space as always, but was no doubt worrying. It was close to ten.

And yet, Daphne couldn't leave and simply dismiss the overwhelming feeling that they were running out of time. There had to be an answer to how to defeat the demon, which meant she was overdue to tell Claire everything—they could have no secrets.

She steeled herself, but the psychic's reaction to her touching the Veil would need to be the least of her worries. The amount of sharing she'd done made it easier, somehow, to confess. What was one more problem that evening?

"Claire, there's something else I need...to..."

The stench of body odor and spoiled food, tinged with sharp antiseptic, filled her nose. She stared at the hanging strings of beads over the open door, bewildered. Was it coming from outside?

"Daphne, what's wrong?" Claire frowned. The lamps dimmed, and Daphne gripped the edge of the table while knowing that it would be of no use.

The room vanished, and she was standing in a dark cabin. Garbage and crumpled paper were scattered across the dirty floor, dimly lit by a battery-powered lamp.

Ashley lay on the bed, incredibly pale and staring up at the carved symbols on the ceiling. Dark blood ran through a tube from her bandaged arm to a clear bag on the card table. Without her black sweater, her frailty was evident.

A figure emerged from the shadows and bent down to check the bag.

"How much more...?" Ashley mumbled weakly.

"Just a little more, and then we'll have enough." It was the calmest Daphne had ever seen Mr. Burnes in Ashley's presence. Usually, they were at odds.

"Okay..." Ashley's voice was very faint.

She continued to pump the ball in her right hand. He monitored, resting his chin on the tips of his fingers, his face harshly shadowed. Daphne couldn't tear her eyes away from the line of blood as it was drawn little by little, pump by pump.

"I don't like this part," Ashley murmured.

"I know." He almost sounded compassionate.

Daphne was nauseated. Once, she had imagined the work the demon was making Ashley do. Of terrible rituals, a knife slicing a hand underneath an orange moon, and deep chanting.

Somehow, this was worse. It was sterile, clinical. A helpless girl giving her blood not to save a life, but to bring about the end of the world.

"Almost there," Mr. Burnes said.

The blood was how Ashley forged a deep connection with the Veil and expanded it for the demon. Daphne had to stop them from getting the amount required. Otherwise, there would be no preventing what happened next.

If a part of her was physically at the cabin, as Claire had theorized about their real-life visions, then maybe she could interfere. Daphne swiped at the tube, but her hand passed through it like air. It was useless.

She tried to overturn the table next, but it didn't budge. Mr. Burnes held up the bag, examining its contents in the light. The corner of his lips twitched in a self-satisfied smile.

The triumph in his face filled her with panic. He had almost collected what they needed. What the demon needed. Daphne went around him, stepping over an unrinsed soup can, and attempted to shake Ashley's shoulder without success. She was less than a shade, unable to move things.

At least once, Ashley had heard her in a vision. If touch didn't work, maybe sound would.

"Ashley. You've got to stop. Ashley!" Daphne bent near her ear and screamed her name.

She stopped squeezing the ball. "Keep going, just a little more." Mr. Burnes glanced up, possibly to check if she'd fainted. "We're close."

Daphne shouted louder, "You have to stop!"

"I can't," Ashley moaned in response.

"You can," Mr. Burnes said with a touch of his usual impatience. Daphne's excitement paused, and she was uncertain whether Ashley had been talking to her after all.

"You can stop it!" she contradicted him. "Pretend you've fainted."

Ashley's eyes closed and her head lolled to the side. Mr. Burnes clocked the change and shook her shoulder, swearing. There was no response. He pulled the tube from Ashley's arm, and Daphne scanned her pale face. The faint was convincing and could be real.

But if Ashley was faking it, she might be willing yet to resist the demon's grip. If only Daphne could speak with her alone and encourage her to make a break for it.

Muttering swear words under his breath, Mr. Burnes bandaged Ashley's arm. Daphne hoped he hadn't collected enough blood and that the demon's goals were delayed, even by a day.

The lamp began to flicker. Mr. Burnes moved his hands cautiously from Ashley's bandage, the action jerky like in a strobe light. It was like the haunted trail last Halloween, with dark figures reaching evil fingers toward her...

She slammed her hands against her head and bent over. A familiar terrible presence was wrapping around her mind tighter than the strongest python. Her head would soon collapse in on itself.

The light stopped flickering. Through the strain, she looked up.

Ashley turned her head on the pillow toward Mr. Burnes, eyes white. Her voice was low and hoarse.

"*It's here.*"

23

HELL WEEK

The touch on her shoulder came from a great distance, as did the voice.

"Daphne." It was like hearing underwater. Darkness covered her eyes.

The voice came again, sharper. "Daphne!" It mingled with another voice. Someone, perhaps her, was screaming "No!" over and over.

There was still pressure around her head. Her hands, as in the vision, were pressed tightly against her skull. The room was so cold.

"Daphne!" The voice was pulling her to the surface, toward a growing sliver of light in the dark. The pungent scent of rotting food faded into something else that was strong, but far more pleasant.

The woman shook her shoulder hard. Why hadn't that worked with Ashley?

"Daphne. Are you with me? Daphne."

Abruptly, she pierced the surface and gasped. The hand snapped back. Daphne realized she was rocking in the chair and stopped, lowering her shaking hands. Although the cabin had felt as real as the reading room, Ashley had vanished. So had the terrible presence.

"Are you all right?" Claire asked, her stare penetrating.

Daphne shivered, feeling as if she'd just been violently ill. The air was chill against her sweaty face. Claire looked grim, but her calm anchored Daphne in the present.

The realness of the cabin faded. She touched a section of the glittering tablecloth and bunched it up with a trembling finger. *This* she was a part of.

"I think so...How long was I..."

Claire exhaled, clearly relieved that Daphne was talking lucidly. "About a minute."

"It was...it was just a minute?" She rubbed her damp forehead. The feeling that she'd been sick was passing, though the pie moved unpleasantly in her stomach.

"More or less." Claire still looked at her intently. "I wasn't sure whether to touch you. You faded just a little until you started shouting. What did you see?"

Daphne slouched and closed her eyes. "I was at the cabin. Ashley's cabin. She was giving blood. A lot of it." Nausea traced a route through her insides, recalling the red tube. "Mr. Burnes was there, helping. He said they almost had enough. I tried to stop it and speak to her. I told her to pretend to faint, but I think she actually fainted, and then..."

She shivered and met Claire's dark gaze, lowering her voice although the presence was long gone. "I felt it. Ashley said it was there."

Claire sat slowly. "You sensed the demon?" The lamp behind her flickered.

"Yes. The greater one, or whatever. I don't know if it came because of what they were doing, but it seemed"—the prospect was chilling— "as though the demon knew I was there, like it did at Veronica's house."

"Has this happened to you before? Having a vision while you're awake?"

The hesitation was enough of an answer. "Yes," Daphne admitted, adding, "I was going to tell you right before this one happened. Normally, they're just flashes. This is the first time I was taken away for that long."

She straightened. The lingering grogginess was helping her to overcome any fear. "I'm sorry, Claire. I...I tried to touch the Veil a few weeks ago, after the dyszoon came out at Veronica's house. I was worried we didn't have much time left, and I had to do something."

"What happened when you did?" Claire said after a moment, her face giving no hint of dismay or anger, which encouraged Daphne to continue. The reaction was different from her worst fears, as she might have known.

"Nothing. Or at least I thought so until I started getting visions of what Ashley was up to while awake. I can also sense when a dyszoon is coming about twenty minutes before it happens, so something useful came out of me trying, I guess."

Daphne sighed and buried her face in her hands. More than anything, she wanted to fall asleep in her own bed and forget the last twelve hours. To wake up as a normal teenager who wasn't worried about how to prevent a demon from taking over the world.

She lowered them. Thankfully, her fingers had stopped shaking. "I'm sorry, Claire. You were right. It didn't help anything."

"I'm just glad you're okay. I won't lie, Daphne, I was quite worried for a minute. I wasn't sure how to help you." Claire's calm mask slipped, and the strain showed. She must have felt as helpless as Daphne had when a dyszoon possessed the psychic last Halloween.

"You said I faded?" Daphne asked. The curious statement came to her as she grew more alert.

"Yes, that's perhaps the best way I can describe it. You weren't transparent by any means, but you weren't fully present. That terrified me more than the shaking."

Daphne frowned. "Maybe a part of us *is* there when we have visions. Ashley spoke to me before, but I thought there was a chance I was dreaming it up," she explained. "Just now, though, I thought I could try telling her to stop giving blood, and it almost seemed like she heard me."

"Did they collect what they needed?"

Daphne picked up one of the smooth stones decorating the table and turned it over, reassured that she was present in the room—all of her.

"I think so, at least by now. What I saw was probably from a few days ago. I mean, he's on break too and tomorrow's Friday, so why wait to draw blood until now?"

She had wondered what Mr. Burnes's plans were to further the demon's cause during his time off. Now they had the answer, though what the blood would be used for, they could only guess. Daphne dropped the stone, a more pressing question on her mind.

"Claire...what do you think will happen when the lesser demon comes? Can we do anything?"

The psychic folded her ringed hands together and sighed. She looked as tired as Daphne felt.

"I wish I could admit otherwise, but tonight has shown that we're dealing with things neither of us understands. Even if we did, even if we knew *exactly* when that demon would arrive, that wouldn't help us."

A faint chime came from the other room. The grandfather

clock, declaring it was ten. Time moved relentlessly forward, toward the inevitable battle.

"I've feared defeating it may be beyond either of us," Claire continued. "When that day comes, which could be soon, it may be that we can only determine how to battle it *after* it arrives. When that happens, we will find out our limits and strengths. My hope is that these last few months will have trained us for its arrival."

It was no different from what she'd said before, but Daphne felt no frustration, only tired resignation. Their best chance at success seemed to be counting on their experience with dyszoons to help them face off against a much greater evil.

The lesser demon would come first, its purpose to pave the way for a demon still more terrible—the one she had encountered on the bridge as it spoke through Ashley, and felt once again tonight.

Even if they managed to push the first demon back to Hell, the next would follow, presumably once the Veil was large enough to let the demon's entire terrible presence through.

And the blood...Daphne had no idea if the amount collected was enough for Ashley and Mr. Burnes to do the demon's work, whether that involved a Veil expansion or something worse, or if another bag was required. She could hardly stride into his office and ask him for a progress update.

"If Ashley gave enough blood to expand the Veil again, the demon could come out this week," Daphne speculated. The five-month wait for the lesser demon had stretched on for so long, its arrival felt unreal.

"Perhaps," Claire said. "I hesitate to say for sure, or what we can do."

"I guess nothing has really changed, then." Daphne yawned. Her capacity to sort out difficult problems was drained, and if she didn't leave soon, she would never make it past Claire's couch. "I'll try to give you a heads-up during school if I sense something coming."

Worry filled Claire's face. "I'm glad you're all right, Daphne, but I don't like these new abilities of yours."

"They're useful, though, aren't they?" Daphne said. Being able to keep tabs on Ashley and the dyszoons was invaluable, despite the cost.

"I'm afraid that nothing good will come of it in the end. I don't think the Veil is a giver of gifts. It's left its mark on you, Daphne, and I'm not sure what will happen."

"I won't touch the Veil anymore," she said, standing. "I'd better get home. I should be okay to drive." Two visions in one night was unlikely.

Claire stood with her, her wrap shining. "Yes, your mother is no doubt worried. That reminds me, I enjoyed her article this week on the history of the building two doors down."

"I didn't read that one." Guilt stabbed her. Really, she owed her mom an apology.

"It's worth reading. I like to think it helps me better understand the shades who haunt here, if I know some downtown history. This building, for example, was once a grocery store."

Daphne turned a yawn into a sound of interest. On any other night, she'd be happy to delve into the finer points of Long Haven history. They walked into the shop. The sidewalk outside was awash with yellow light, holding off the night.

"Your musical is next weekend, correct?" Claire asked.

Daphne processed this. *Right, the musical.* Impending demon invasion or not, normal things would continue.

"I'll have rehearsals every day after school this next week."

"Good luck, then. And don't worry, I will cover you."

"You still want to?" she said, amazed. After the broken promise, Claire was willing to help her?

"Yes, I'll manage," the psychic said briskly, opening the

jingling front door. "Now go and get some rest, and leave your thoughts to the morning."

Daphne hurried up the ramp to the senior hallway a few minutes later than her typical arrival at school.

A glimpse of wavy brown hair caught her eye, and her heart squeezed painfully tight. The problems postponed by spring break flooded back. How would she avoid Nathan? It had been easy enough last week, but the school year didn't end for another month.

For the moment, he was occupied by Veronica's tight hug. Anyone looking at them would think they were as much of a couple as ever. A prom king and queen.

Veronica's late night out with Dom must have been innocent after all. Daphne was grateful she'd thought twice about messaging Nathan about it, or else the first day back would be quite different.

The first bell rang. Daphne unlocked her locker and threw materials into her arms. A notebook slid off the top of her pile.

"Hey, let me get that for you." To her horror, Nathan bent down to grab it off the floor. He handed it to her with a grin that made her heart squeeze again, though more pleasantly.

Defiance fought against caution, and she gave him a small smile. She could still *smile* at him, couldn't she? Was that breaking the law? After all, why should *she* care what Veronica threatened? If Veronica told him everything, she could always deny it.

Even so, Daphne checked the hallway for his girlfriend.

"You have a good break?" he asked. She snapped her attention back, unable to finish looking.

"Yeah," she lied, slamming her locker closed. "How was your brother's?"

"Decent, I'll tell you more later."

"Okay," Daphne said, turning away in case Veronica's eyes were on them.

"Well, good to see you," he said, taking the cue.

"Yeah. I mean, you too," she said over her shoulder, cursing her own cowardice, when Veronica likely hadn't witnessed them. And Vivian, a natural informant, was also absent from the crowd. Even Heather wasn't around—perhaps Nathan's weeklong absence had made her lose track of him.

I'll tell you more later. Daphne's heart sank at what was likely going to be an unfulfilled promise. If he expected to talk on their usual walk after lunch, that was going to be impossible. Veronica would see to that.

Cheerlessly, Daphne sat at her computer for class. She had worried about losing Nathan's friendship once summer arrived, but if she gave in to Veronica and avoided him, that fear was all but guaranteed. In a way, they were already separated.

At least nothing had happened yet with the Veil besides a dyszoon on Saturday. Despite her breakdown last week, hope had stubbornly trickled back in with the continued absence of the lesser demon. The blood hadn't led to another move with the Veil quite yet.

She was looking forward to rehearsal after school, although Veronica would be there as an assistant director. The show premiered that weekend. *Once the musical is over, I'll risk talking to him,* Daphne decided. With only a few weeks left until graduation, what did she have to lose? She could endure the consequences.

Once Drama Club ended, she'd only have to see Veronica in history class and at lunch. Whenever Veronica joined their table, Daphne could sign out and find food elsewhere.

The bell rang. She checked her messages. *Have a great day, sweetie!* her mom had texted. Daphne smiled and stowed the phone away.

The theater was in a state of organized chaos by the time Daphne arrived for rehearsal.

A small orchestra sat in a pit at the front of the stage, tuning instruments and practicing snatches of melody. Actors hurried downstairs, a few in 1930s-style gray suits or pretty dresses.

Veronica sat near the director in the center row, her legs draped over the cushioned chair in front of her. Daphne glared.

As expected, Veronica had taken over walking with Nathan after lunch. The message was clear, that her threat to expose Daphne's secret wasn't forgotten. If any lines were crossed, Nathan would learn everything.

The only upside to the Monday was that history had passed normally. An irritable Mr. Burnes went over the day's lesson without any hint of his activities on break. Though Daphne remained on edge in his class, his presence increased her hope. If he was showing up to work, far from Ashley, the lesser demon wasn't on its way.

Ashley had visited her nightmares over the weekend as a sunken corpse on the bed, a black tube pumping death from its veins. The corpse wouldn't wake up no matter how loudly Daphne shouted. Beyond the lantern light, shapeless creatures circled the room like sharks.

"Daphne!" Beth waved to her from a few rows up.

She shook the vision out of mind and dropped into a seat near her. "Any idea what's happening?"

"Nothing yet," Beth said, rummaging in her purse. "By the way, I have something for you. I picked them up over lunch."

Daphne took the plain envelope and pulled out a card.

Beth and Ethan beamed from the photo, and underneath it were details for a June wedding.

"Oh wow! You set a date?" The excitement that rushed through her felt as though it belonged to someone else. While Beth had talked endlessly about the wedding and the family drama surrounding it, Daphne had half worried that she wouldn't be invited due to the limited guest list. A lack of invitation would be another strike that confirmed her loneliness.

But the postcard was physical evidence to hold on to, much like the stuffed owl that Nathan had won for her last Halloween. Someone had considered her, and however lonely she'd thought herself while sitting in the cafe booth, she still had a friend.

"Yeah, my grandma *finally* booked her trip to Vegas, so I set it for the weekend after. My uncle was okay with me having it at his place."

She settled into wedding talk. Her ten-year-old cousin, the daughter of the uncle in question, was the only bridesmaid. Her friend Taylor was playing the cello for the walk up the aisle, and then a catered lunch under a large tent would follow the ceremony.

"Also, I know you take good photos," Beth said. "Would you want to take pictures at my wedding?"

"Like as your official photographer?"

"Yes! If you don't want to, no big deal."

"No, I'd love to!" Daphne said with another burst of excitement. Her experience was nature photography, but capturing people couldn't be too difficult a transition. "You don't have to pay me either. It'll be my first wedding, so that can be your present from me."

"Thank you! That's one more thing I can check off. You can start your portfolio!"

Daphne privately doubted she would photograph more

weddings but looked forward to it all the same. "How's the planning been going?" she asked.

Beth explained that she was nearly done, but emotions were running high. Her mother was upset with her dad for wanting to bring his new girlfriend as a plus-one and was demanding that she be excluded from any formal pictures.

"Let's get organized, folks!" called Miss Rand, the director. The noise lowered a half decibel.

Veronica chatted animatedly with Vivian. Daphne didn't plan to tell Beth that their conversation about Nathan had been overheard. Mentioning it was an invitation for more drama, and she would rather not admit her cowardice.

Daphne glanced at the catwalk out of habit. To her shock, Michael was peering down his nose at the stage. The elusive shade had finally reappeared.

There was a brief window to get his attention. Daphne stretched out an invisible hand. If she grabbed him now, she could order him to stay away from the shows.

A man with graying hair that stood straight on end stopped by their row. "You can head on up, Beth. The booth's unlocked. And you're curtain?" he said to Daphne.

The invisible hand broke. "Yeah," she answered, and put away the wedding invitation.

"I'll get you situated," he said. "Follow me."

As they walked down the side aisle, the orchestra went silent. Chad, in costume, paused above the pit.

"LET HELL WEEK—BEGIN!" he bellowed.

Most laughed, though Daphne noticed Vivian cross her arms and glare in his direction. If she was mad at her boyfriend again, Daphne wasn't going to try cheering her up. Her eyes flicked upward, but she couldn't see Michael from her position.

The man, who Daphne learned was a longtime parent volunteer and had programmed the lights, led her behind the curtain. A plastic chair and overhanging lamp were set up in the corner by the wall.

"Right, here are the cues to look out for." He pointed at a sheet of paper underneath the headset on the chair. "I'll show you the ropes. Literally."

There were two pulleys with heavily marked-up ropes. "This one's for the yellow curtain," the man explained. "That'll be for the end of the acts. The black curtain is for the scenes. You'll need to pull at about this pace..."

Daphne nodded along with the instructions until the man left. She sat down and turned on the headset that connected her to the booth. The air crackled, and she removed it.

Actors rolled the stairs set into the middle of the stage. Daphne closed her eyes and reached an invisible hand toward the catwalk. It was empty—Michael was gone once more.

"Curtain girl! Wake up!" Chad called. Daphne opened her eyes and waved.

The shade's absences filled her with unease. If Michael was so elusive, presumably to avoid her, she couldn't help but suspect even more that he planned to disrupt the performance. At least she was in a prime position to stop him.

Chad approached Vivian, who stomped off. Daphne gritted her teeth in sympathy for him. Between relationship drama and Michael, they would be lucky if the musical wasn't cursed to be canceled once more.

24

THE DIRECTOR

Daphne approached the black-shuttered home, which loomed even larger in the fading daylight than it had at night. The long driveway was once again filled with cars.

If Beth hadn't been expecting her, she would have skipped the Drama Club's pre-opening-night party at Veronica's house. A week ago, almost to the hour, she'd ducked underneath the cafe table. That instinct slowed her steps now.

You just have to avoid her. And Vivian.

Although the Veil had been quiet, she would welcome a dyszoon interrupting her plans, unlike during her date with Leon. Judging by Jessica's normalcy that week, Daphne assumed he hadn't brought it up to her, and was grateful.

Her heart skipped a beat as she spotted a silver car—Nathan's. She had wondered if he would come to the party since it was at his girlfriend's house, but had no chance to ask. That week she was careful to avoid him, not even looking up as he passed by her locker with Veronica after lunch.

Heather's reappearance made the situation worse. Daphne

felt guilty every time the shade appeared. She was breaking her renewed promise to be a friend to Nathan.

One of the front doors was ajar. She pushed it open and stepped into a hallway with polished hardwood floors and an impressive staircase. A chandelier glittered from the tall ceiling.

The sound of voices led her to a stunning kitchen. Pizza boxes covered the large island, and two sophomore girls from Stage Crew were helping themselves.

"What's in this one? Ew, no, I don't *want* pepperoni."

Daphne grabbed a paper plate, noticing the other curly-haired girl too late to avoid her.

"Oh. *You* showed up," Vivian said bluntly, cutting short a yawn. The pressure of having a leading part was showing its strain even though she had nailed all of her notes in rehearsal.

"Yeah, I did," Daphne replied with a wide smile, realizing with a gleeful surge of power that Vivian didn't intimidate her the way Veronica did. She plucked two slices of veggie pizza from a box and turned on her heel. "Nice seeing you."

A sense of rebellion calmed her. Attending the party might send a subtle message to Veronica and show her she wasn't in complete control. Sure, Daphne had avoided Nathan all week. But now that rehearsals were over, tonight she could start fighting back against Veronica's threat a few days early. She just needed to find him.

Daphne followed the sophomores down the hall and into a large entertainment room. It was full of Drama Club members and a handful of adults. Beth was huddled with a group by a retro pinball machine. She started toward them, past the air hockey, but pivoted as they broke into cheers, feeling it would be awkward to stand with them while eating.

There weren't many places to sit, and Daphne realized with anxiety that, when it came down to it, she didn't know most of the Drama Club members. Chad wasn't anywhere to be seen, and to her disappointment, neither was Nathan. Maybe—she had just noted the other absence—he was with Veronica somewhere.

An open spot on a couch nearby was the only seating option. A large woman with short silver hair occupied one side, looking rather out of place surrounded by high schoolers.

Well, I'm out of place surrounded by high schoolers, Daphne thought with amusement as the woman caught her eye.

"Sit here, I don't bite," her brusque voice boomed above the noise. Jumping, Daphne shyly thanked her and sat.

The woman was looking at her, expectant. Daphne chewed through her first bite and swallowed, wondering if the stare meant she was supposed to recognize the woman.

"Sorry, are you—are you Veronica's grandma?"

"Who?"

"This is her house—never mind," Daphne said, squirming. She became interested in taking another bite.

The woman shifted toward her with interest. "Are you a part of the production?"

Daphne swallowed her ill-timed bite of pizza and felt it slide down her throat. "Kind of. I'm just on Stage Crew."

"Stage Crew's important," the woman said firmly, apparently thinking that Daphne was being self-deprecating. "They put in as many hours as the actors, and more." She nodded.

"There's a lot of work, yeah," Daphne agreed, wishing for some soda to help the lump in her throat move along. The run-in with Vivian had stopped her from getting one. "I'm running the curtain for the show."

"Oh! You are, are you? Is this your first time?"

Daphne answered her questions about the show's progress. More cheers came from the pinball machine, and she wished she had headed there first. When there was an opportunity, she asked, "Are you involved with this at all? The musical?"

"In a way, yes. I directed *all* of the Drama Club productions for twenty-three years," the woman said with pride.

"That's a long time," Daphne said politely as the memory clicked into place of a repeated name from the display case outside the theater. "Wait, are you—you're Carole Finch?"

"Yes, I am!" Carole smiled broadly.

"I've seen your name on some of the past shows." Another realization came to her in a dizzying rush. "You were the director the last time we did this musical, weren't you?"

Carole nodded. "Yep, I was."

"I know it got canceled. Are you happy to see it come back?" Daphne asked, containing her eagerness and the reason for it. Michael's director was the person closest to his situation that she'd met, at least who was still living. Her memories might be the best chance Daphne had to unlock his last week of life.

"I am, if only for Nancy—that's the writer," she added at Daphne's puzzled look. "Oh, she was *devastated* that it was canceled, of course."

"I'm sure."

"Not that I didn't *try* to make it work, but our lead was killed in a motorcycle accident, and the death was hard on the entire cast. My leading gal didn't feel she could move forward with it—guilt, I think."

"Could the show have gone on after that?" Daphne asked, surprised. She'd thought the production died with its leading actor, unless someone who knew Michael's role was able to take over with less than a week's preparation. Professional actors might have alternates, but it was a lot to expect from a high school production.

As if to prove her point, a group of male actors playing air hockey broke into loud jeers.

"I thought so," Carole said when the noise died. "I had another actor who I had almost chosen for the leading role, but

I ended up giving him a different spot. *Michael* had the better voice, though I must say, I came to regret it."

"You didn't know he would pass away," Daphne said in sympathy. Canceling the performance was a deep blow, but not a predictable one.

"It was his own fault anyway, drinking and driving," Carole snapped with sudden bitterness. "I suspected he did it out of spite, just to ruin it for everyone."

The accusation took Daphne aback. She hadn't expected her to be so candid, especially about the dead. "Why would Michael do that? He was the lead." The shade's angry words came back to her. *This stage is mine! I deserve it!* That he would try to ruin the role he wanted to play, so much so that he had stayed behind as a shade, made little sense. But Carole, of course, couldn't hear Michael beyond the grave.

"He *was* the lead," she said with emphasis. "I fired him."

Daphne gaped at her, astonished. This reaction was enough encouragement for the old director to continue, or else thirty years of pent-up bitterness had found a new, willing listener. Carole gave her the impression of enjoying an audience as much as any actor.

"Yes, I lost all my patience and told Michael he was *done*." She slapped a knee. "I was going to replace him and give some lines to the others. I knew Nancy would understand having to change up the writing. She was always just grateful someone was willing to produce her show."

"Why did you fire him? If I can ask."

"I don't mind. It was so long ago. I fired him, frankly, because he was the most narcissistic idiot to act on my stage," Carole said, looking pleased to admit this. "I chose him for the lead because he was, unfortunately, a natural actor for his age. He'd been in a few plays before that. I remember him being so quiet as a freshman, and then he came out of his shell. The Drama Club does that to kids."

She stared into the air, more somber. "But I'll tell you, he was one of those who only came off nice when he was quiet. There were so many problems right from the start of rehearsals. He was dating my leading gal, Rachel, and they were on and off, on and off, all the time. She'd cry up a storm to me," Carole said with an eye roll. "Then he'd be bossing around the others and arguing with me about this or that scene, like he knew just how things ought to be done. But it was all mostly going well, and I thought we'd pull through."

"So what happened?" Daphne asked. Here, more than anything printed in a newspaper, was the insight into Michael she had wanted. She'd quite forgotten the unfinished pizza on her lap.

"It was the last week of rehearsals. We had a tense evening, and then Michael went too far. He'd been acting erratic by then. At the *time*, I thought it was him being nervous." Carole shook her head. "I'll admit, I excused him too much. Anyway, he yelled at a freshman girl and made her cry over something I can't remember anymore. It wouldn't surprise me if she had just *giggled* at the wrong moment."

She shook her head again. "I put a stop to it, and then he tried turning on me instead. So I told him he was replaceable. And he didn't think so, being the hotshot lead he thought he was, so I fired him," Carole continued matter-of-factly. "Shocked him to the core."

Daphne's thoughts whirred. *No one else gets to have what I worked for*, the shade had said. She'd assumed that Michael had been referring to his death and his jealousy of the actors in the current musical. But what had made him angry enough to stay behind after death was being fired and replaced. Maybe the words he had shouted at Daphne were the very ones he'd hurled at the director.

"What happened next?" she asked, holding her breath.

"He left in a huff, and that was the last time I saw him. Not *heard* him—he called my house that night to tell me off." Carole rolled her eyes. "At first I thought it was a prank caller, and I almost didn't recognize him. He was so emotional. But I realized later that he was halfway through his mom's bottle. I suspect I was the last person to speak with him before he died."

This thought seemed to cool her irritation, and she sank into a reflective silence.

Daphne's imagination took over. A mistless Michael, his normally neat blond hair messed up, sank into a rage with a bottle in hand. He hopped on his motorcycle, possibly to deliver his tirade in person, and turned too sharply. His life ended like the cue of darkness on a stage.

"I'm sorry it canceled the show," Daphne said, uncertain what else to say. Did the director feel as though she'd contributed to his death, like Vivian's mom, Rachel? She didn't have the right to ask.

Carole slapped both hands on her knees, brusque once more. "Well, I'm glad I get to see it put on again, after all these years. It kind of brings everything full circle." *Full circle.* That's what Vivian's mom had said too.

"Is the writer able to see it? She's not here, is she?"

"Nancy?" The director seemed distracted now, perhaps by memories. "No, but I'll be attending opening night with her."

It had to be a big moment for the playwright. More than ever, Daphne resolved to keep Michael away from the performances that weekend.

A woman tapped Carole on the shoulder and greeted her with enthusiasm. Daphne stood up. "It was nice to meet you," she said honestly.

Carole looked around. "You too, dear."

Leaving the newcomer to take her seat, Daphne left the room, craving a quiet place to reflect on what she'd learned and how it might help her approach the shade. The kitchen, thankfully, was empty. She drank a soda thirstily and took in the bright space.

Though Veronica's home was beautiful, Daphne couldn't picture living in it. *Too much to clean,* her mom would say. And yet, if they were this rich, they wouldn't do the cleaning.

She finished the cold pizza on her plate, mulling over Michael. All this time, she'd assumed he stayed behind because death had robbed him of his chance onstage. But it was his temper that had ruined it, though he blamed the director.

It was a stroke of good fortune, running into Carole. Daphne wished that she had done more to uncover Michael's story earlier. The shade was too fixated on his resentment to share, and sorting through old newspaper clippings could only give her a limited view.

A living witness was far more valuable. She could have tracked down Carole's number and worked up the nerve to cold call. *Hi, you don't know me, but I've been speaking with a former student of yours. He's dead, but I was wondering...*

Daphne tossed her plate in the garbage. It was time to join the party. Maybe, she thought with hope, the pinball machine was open.

Angry voices came from above as she entered the hallway. To her horror, she recognized them as Veronica's and Nathan's. Footsteps thundered down the stairs.

The kitchen was the nearest retreat. Daphne ducked out of view, the sense of power after her exchange with Vivian curdling into fear. She didn't want to face Veronica in her own home. And an angry Veronica, apparently.

"I don't know what you expect me to say. Plans change—" she was yelling after him.

"Just leave it." Nathan stomped toward the front door.

"You're taking it so wrong..." Veronica said. Daphne recoiled at her condescending sigh and instantly took Nathan's side in whatever argument was happening—not that she'd ever be rooting for the other side.

Daphne stayed out of sight as the front door shut, muffling their voices. She hesitated, wondering whether to dash for the other room, but the front door opened seconds later. Veronica was returning.

What if she spotted her alone and vulnerable? Daphne assessed her options. Then, hating herself, she ducked behind the kitchen island. At least it was more spacious than hiding under the cafe table.

As she'd feared, a pair of heeled boots clicked into the room. Daphne breathed shallowly as Veronica poured a soda. If discovered, it would be impossible to pretend she had dropped something and wasn't hiding. *Please, please, please don't come around the counter.*

More splashing sounds came from above Daphne's head. Another cup was angrily poured and downed. A vision of Veronica discovering her flashed across her eyes, as vivid as any of Ashley, and she suppressed the urge to laugh.

Veronica burped loudly.

Daphne pressed both hands over her mouth to muffle a bubble of laughter, a feat almost as difficult as fending off dyszoons. She quaked from the effort.

With a click of boots, Veronica left the kitchen. The sound continued down the hallway and back up the stairs. Apparently, she wasn't interested in joining the party.

The bubble of laughter burst. Daphne released her mouth and pulled herself up using the quartz countertop. The idea of

Veronica and Nathan fighting should have made her happy, but her heart filled with pity for him.

She glanced upstairs and then followed his path outside.

The porch was well-lit, like a stage, and the dark shapes of cars were faceless audience members. Daphne stepped off the porch, only half hopeful that Nathan's car would still be there.

"Daphne." The voice stopped her in surprise, and her heart leapt. Nathan stood near an unlit section of wall, hands in his jacket pockets, perhaps deciding whether to go back inside and make amends.

She approached with a thrill at the danger of being seen. Maybe she wasn't as cowardly as she feared, despite hiding.

It was pointless to pretend she didn't know the cause of his glumness. "Are you okay? I kind of heard..." She trailed off.

"Yeah. Just thinking," Nathan said to the night sky, his sour mood drifting from him like mist from a shade. She stepped closer and looked skyward as well. The waning moon was a sliver, deepening the night.

"What about?"

The enormity of thought filled his face, too big to translate into words.

"I guess I'm just ready to graduate," he finally said.

Her brief laugh acknowledged the truth of it. "Me too."

She itched to ask what their argument had been about, but that would push it. However, it seemed she wasn't the only one approaching the end of the school year with baggage too heavy to carry.

Nathan's phone dinged, and he sighed. It was obvious that he was too preoccupied to talk now that a message was waiting for him.

"Well, I'll see you tomorrow?" Daphne said, disappointed. She'd been happy to run into Nathan alone, a chance to make good on her resolve to start talking to him again. A wall was growing between them with each day that passed without meaningful conversation.

But now that the opportunity to talk had arrived, Daphne knew it wasn't the one she wanted. What she wanted was to hang out with Nathan on their own terms, neither weighed down by problems—and, ideally, not in front of his girlfriend's house.

"Yeah." Nathan was already dragging out his phone as though bracing himself. "See you later."

Daphne went inside, wanting to hang out with Beth for a while. Even if the rest of the party wasn't fun, Carole's insights had been worth the trip. Still, a cloud of defeat swirled around her.

She ought to have been happier that Nathan and Veronica were on rocky ground at the moment, but Daphne couldn't bear to get her hopes up. Graduation was just around the corner, and the closer it got, the less time she had to fix the growing cracks in their friendship. The cracks that she had let Veronica create even before the ambush.

And why? Assuming the Veil stayed as it was, none of the drama would last beyond high school. Life would move on, and it wouldn't matter how hard she had crushed on Nathan Grey. But if he knew...

The tiny, reckless flame that had sparked during her chat with Vivian grew brighter. She could take Veronica's power away by telling him her secret. What did she have to lose? She had survived worse embarrassment.

Daphne stopped in the middle of the hallway, her pulse quickening. She could turn, walk up to Nathan, and say...

Her feet steered her back to the party. *Not yet.* She returned Beth's cheery wave from across the room. The pinball machine was occupied.

She joined her, wondering what Veronica had texted

Nathan and whether he would come inside or go home. *Before we graduate, I'll tell him how I feel*, Daphne decided. And if rejection was the answer, the Veil could swallow her like it did in her nightmares.

Before graduation arrived, maybe it would.

25

OPENING NIGHT

"Curtain, get ready."

The parent volunteer's voice came through the headset. Daphne gripped the white rope, hands cold with nerves, as she waited for the orchestra to play the notes that were the cue for the first scene.

"Open!"

The gold curtain split, unveiling wide cement stairs in a city park. Chad, as Victor Savage, hurried onto the stage with his head bent. He carried a shabby suitcase, a newspaper tucked under his arm.

Daphne sank into her chair with relief. Her first live curtain pull was a success.

"Good job on the curtain," Beth said over the headset. Daphne whispered a thanks.

Extras lounged on the steps or mimed conversation as the orchestra plucked away. Another actor, credited as "Homeless Man/Ghost" in the show program, jingled a cup at Victor.

"Brother, can you spare a dime?"

Victor dug into his coat pocket and dropped it in the cup.

The old man touched a hat to his cap with a grin. "Thanks, brother. It's a beautiful sunny morning, isn't it?"

"Oh...yes. Yes, I suppose it is," Victor agreed without bothering to look around.

"Say, does that paper have a crossword? I used to finish one every morning!"

"Yes. Yes, I suppose it does," Victor said. He opened the paper and ripped out a section. "Oh, and I suppose you'll need a pen." He dug in his pockets and handed one over to the man.

"Thank you, sir! You don't meet many kind strangers nowadays! It's all hurry, hurry, hurry. Always going from one thing to the next! Why, my uncle used to say—"

"Savage!" A girl dressed in a striped suit and wearing a mustache walked toward Victor with a confident stride. She greeted him with a vigorous handshake. "It's great to see you, the man of the hour! Excellent work on that account. I hear you're up for a promotion!"

"Yes, I am, thank—"

She clasped his upper arms and marched him away. "As my uncle used to say, diligence is the mother of good luck! In hard times like these, we're one wrong move from ending up like *that* guy." She bobbed her head in the direction of the homeless man now happily looking over his crossword.

Daphne looked over her cue sheet. Up next was an opening number about doing whatever it took to get ahead in the middle of a Depression, and then the black curtain would signal the end of the scene.

"Curtain ready."

She shot to her feet and grabbed the thinner rope. The song finished, and she pulled the curtain closed to applause. In the semidarkness, the hidden crew sprang to life, rolling away the steps and swapping it for the dining room set. Vivian lifted her dress and stepped onto the platform.

"Okay, they're ready," Daphne spoke into the headset.

"Lights ready, open curtain."

Vivian, playing Victor's fiancée, Ginny, carried a pie with pot holders as Victor entered through the door in the middle and removed his hat.

"Hello, dear! You're just in time! I've finished my pie." She set it down on the table, a real pie baked by one of the elderly costume makers. The cast and crew were under strict orders not to inspect its quality.

Victor removed his hat and inspected it. "Looks delicious... Is it safe?"

"Oh yes. This time I used flour instead of baby powder. Did you know it makes all the difference?" she said cheerily, removing a checkered apron.

There was a rumble of audience laughter. Daphne was tempted to peer around the curtain and pick out familiar faces. Carole and the playwright, Nancy, would be there, and likely Vivian's mom, Rachel, the original Ginny. Her own mom was going out to dinner with a friend and would attend the Saturday night performance, a plan Daphne had reassured her was still supportive.

If Vivian and Chad were on rocky ground as a couple, it only worked in their favor. Victor was gruff, worried despite the potential promotion about his position getting cut in a Depression economy, and obsessed with gaining wealth for his future family's security. There were only two outcomes in his eyes: to become like the homeless man he passed in the park, or else to join the ranks of the wealthiest men featured in the papers.

"Would you like me to cut you a piece?"

"Thanks for the offer, Ginny, but I was only stopping by for a moment. I have an important meeting with a client soon."

"But I thought you had off today!"

"I'm up for a promotion. There *are* no days off."

"But Victor, I've hardly seen you! You've been working so much lately."

"I promise, Ginny, it'll pay off," Victor said earnestly. "Success is so close, I can taste—" He turned, coming face-to-face with a spoonful full of pie, and yelped.

"Just one bite, then?"

The audience laughed. Daphne smiled, jiggling her knee impatiently for the cue. There were over two hours left for something to go wrong.

A faint presence flickered into existence. She blinked, and a glowering Michael appeared at the far end of the table. There were two Victor Savages on the set.

Daphne's pulse throbbed. *It's okay. No one can see him.*

She reached an invisible hand to pull Michael away from the two actors. It hovered uselessly as he strode to the shelf that she and Beth had hung and swiped at it.

A porcelain bulldog toppled to the ground, the sound as subtle as a bomb going off. Miraculously, it didn't shatter.

Chad and Vivian stopped in surprise, the spell of the scene broken by stunned silence. Over the headset, Beth gasped.

If the actors ignored the moment, the audience would laugh about it during intermission. *Wasn't that awkward, that thing falling from the shelf?* No matter how flawlessly the rest of the musical went, everyone would remember that incident the most.

Vivian recovered first. "Oh dear, the house is *falling* apart," she said in the hushed silence, sweeping over to pick it up. Someone chuckled from the seats. She placed it charmingly on the shelf and then stepped back with an angled head to check its placement.

"I shouldn't worry. It's the ghost, no doubt," Victor said in his character's gruff tone, not realizing how true that was. Michael had disappeared.

"A ghost!" Ginny cried, spinning around with a hand on her chest. "I should hope not."

"Anyway,"—here was the transition back to the script—"I should be going." He put on his hat.

Daphne's shoulders slumped in relief, her hands trembling on the rope. Her dislike of Vivian aside, she admired the way the scene had been put back on track. It was a clunky moment, certainly, but given that Victor spent most of the musical dead and reflecting on his ambition, most might think it was a part of the script after all.

"But you'll be around later, darling?" Ginny asked.

"Don't count on me. I don't know when I'll be finished," he said, dismissive. "Goodbye."

Ginny closed the door behind him and leaned against it, unhappy at the cold parting. She sang a solo about the lack of time he had for her, compared to the earlier days of their relationship. Darkness swept the stage, courtesy of Beth, and Daphne pulled the curtain closed.

She remained vigilant for any hint of mist, but Michael didn't reappear. In the following scene, a business associate broke the news to Ginny of her fiancé's death.

The associate told an animated tale of how a car had almost struck Victor while he crossed the road, and how he was immediately robbed at knifepoint on the sidewalk. After surviving these brushes with death, a piano nearly crushed him when its rope snapped while it was being lifted into an upper apartment. As Victor dived out of the way, a bug flew into his throat, and he choked.

"He...choked," Ginny said in disbelief.

"It was a very large bug," the man answered helpfully, to audience laughter.

The homeless man reappeared, leading a now-dead Victor through scenes of his life, including his relationship with a younger Ginny that was more carefree. They waltzed up and down the steps between couples, him promising to work hard to give her the world, her clear soprano voice sweetly answering that she would "never need anything more than this." Their love was enough.

Daphne remained in her chair during intermission and chatted with Beth. So far, the curtain and light transitions had gone smoothly, and while she would keep an eye out, she felt confident that Michael would make no further mischief. The theater grew noisier as members of the audience returned, and the next act began.

Victor relived another scene of his life. He was determined, along with his group of young friends, to rise to the top. Ginny spun around the stage like a ghost, reprising the song from their waltz as his voice questioned, and then answered, that he needed "more than this!"

This transitioned to the next song. The group of up-and-coming men shed their shabby jackets for nicer suit coats and energetically danced on and off of briefcases.

"You gotta hustle, hustle, hustle if you wanna get ahead!" they sang, wagging fingers at the audience.

Daphne grinned at the standing ovation as they finished and held their pose, wanting to join in the clapping. It was the best song in the musical, one the actors had struggled with up until the final rehearsal.

Later, Victor learned that the homeless man had been wealthy before the stock market crashed. He lost everything but was happier now than he'd once been. The worst had happened, and yet he was still alive and well, no longer consumed by those things he thought were so important.

"I've been so caught up with succeeding, that..." Victor was saying.

A force slammed into Daphne's mind. She stiffened, the thread of the scene slipping away in a blur.

"...sometimes I feel as if I'm barely tethered to the present."

Daphne pinched herself, fighting to regain focus. The words were coming from a great distance. Thankfully, she had seen the musical enough to recapture her place.

A lot of them, she thought worriedly, blinking at the bright stage lights. At minimum, a few dyszoons were on their way—possibly more. She sent a warning text to Claire. Even with the head start, could the psychic handle them all? If she didn't have to pull the curtain, Daphne wouldn't have hesitated to join her.

She counted the time left. There were at least twenty more minutes, not counting the presentation of the cast. After that, she'd need another few minutes to get to her car, and then there was the drive to the Veil.

Daphne sat at the edge of the hard seat, willing the actors to say their lines faster. Victor had almost resolved to let go of his unfulfilled dreams and pass on. But first, a song...

Cold filled her like a fierce winter wind, signaling the arrival of the dyszoons. Daphne poised icy hands on the rope. Her phone lit up on the chair and she itched to check it. Chad was still in the midst of his solo, his impressive voice soaring through the theater.

"I'm ready," Victor said to complete silence, donning his hat. He grabbed his suitcase off the floor and walked solemnly up the smoke-filled stairs toward the open doorway at the top. The orchestra picked up the music, which thundered as he reached it. She closed the black curtain.

The crew rolled on the dining room set at high speed. Daphne checked the text. It was from Claire.

Come quick.

Her stomach dropped. What did that mean? How many

dyszoons had come out? But, despite it all, she couldn't abandon her responsibility, not at the final scene. Daphne hoped fervently that Claire could hold on for a while longer. And yet, if the psychic were hurt, or a dyszoon got away because she had waited…

The curtain reopened. Ginny was carrying a pie.

"Hello, dear! You're just in time!" she said, setting it down on the table.

"I-I am?" Victor stuttered.

"Yes, I've finished my pie. Did you know using flour instead of baby powder makes all the difference? Now, it's a *little* hot —" She removed her oven mitts and picked up a pie server.

"But—I-I thought the door went to—am I really here?" Victor gripped the chair as if reassuring himself it was real.

"What do you mean, dear?"

"It's just that—you know, I feel rather funny." He touched his forehead.

"You *do* look a little pale." Ginny pulled out the chair and sat him down. "Don't worry, you just need to eat something!" she said cheerfully, and dished up a plate. Victor stared at the slice of pie.

"Do you need anything else?" she asked him, a caring hand on his shoulder.

There was a long pause. He looked up at her. "No, nothing more than this."

They smiled lovingly at each other as the orchestra played the tune from their waltz. Daphne yanked the gold curtain shut to loud applause.

The orchestra struck up a bright tune, and once the actors had lined up, she opened the curtain. The actors strolled across the stage, waving and smiling. Chad and Vivian went last to renewed cheers and whistles.

Daphne donned her coat. The actors gestured to the

orchestra in the pit below, and then lined up and bowed again. She yanked on the rope, hiding their energetic waves.

"Good job, guys!" Chad began high-fiving everyone within reach. Daphne ripped off her headset and then slipped behind the curtain. The audience was already pouring out of the theater, and she needed to get ahead of them to avoid being delayed. She sprinted up the side stairs and slowed to a brisk pace as she reached the lunchroom.

"Daphne?"

She stopped before the front doors. *Not now.* "Oh, hi, Nathan," she said, a little breathless from running. "I didn't realize you were here."

"I came for opening night." The girl behind the flower table caught his attention, and he took the bouquet. For Veronica, no doubt. Maybe he had gone back inside last night and they had made up. She grimaced.

"I saw your name in the program. You did the curtain? That's cool," Nathan said, thankfully not noticing her reaction.

"Yeah, first time, but I think it went okay. Anyway, I need to go, but I'll see you later?" she said, laying a hand on the door. The crowd passing through the front doors was thickening. Soon the exit to the parking lot would be flooded with cars.

"Oh. Yeah, talk to you later."

She pressed through the door, relieved to hear it click shut behind her. Under normal circumstances, she would be happy to have another chance to speak with Nathan. He seemed to be in a better mood than at the party, and if he was getting Veronica flowers...

Part of her felt strangely satisfied at brushing him off. The jealousy that sparked over seeing him holding the bouquet was petty, of course, but it was there.

The defiant flame she felt last night was useless. What was

the point of confessing her feelings, anyway? Nathan had chosen Veronica.

Daphne brushed her thoughts aside and sprinted down the sidewalk, not caring about attracting stares. Claire needed her, and she had a battle with dyszoons to think about instead of picturing how happy his girlfriend would be to see the flowers.

26

———

UNSEEN EYES

Daphne ran through the woods, her flashlight parting the solid darkness. "Claire!" she shouted. "Claire!"

The psychic's car was parked near the Veil, but there was no sign of her. It seemed the fight had moved into the woods.

A faint voice answered. Daphne pivoted toward the sound, on high alert in case a dyszoon separated from the night. "I'm coming!" she called, almost tripping over a fallen branch.

Claire sat on a log, bundled in a scarf and leather jacket. She was clearly out of breath. Relieved, Daphne assessed her shadowed face. "Are you okay? What happened?"

"I'm fine," she said, waving a ringed hand dismissively. "I just need to catch my breath...Three of them went into the woods when I showed up...I handled the next two that arrived... but I couldn't go after the others fast enough."

"What direction did they go?" Daphne said with urgency. Further details of the battle could wait.

Claire pointed behind her. "That way. They can't have gone too far."

"I'll find them," Daphne said. "You can rest. I'll call you in twenty minutes, tops."

Claire didn't insist on accompanying her, perhaps recognizing that she would only hold up the search. "Daphne, do be careful," she said, serious. "These are a vicious bunch."

Daphne clenched her teeth at the warning as she went deeper into the woods, which was like pressing through an ink wall. Thankfully, she didn't need to rely on sight to find the dyszoons. Instead, she aimed the flashlight at the ground to avoid tripping over dips and fallen branches.

After a few minutes, a presence touched her mind, too faint for her to determine its direction. Daphne considered her options. She could try going a different way, but getting lost in the woods with spotty reception was unappealing.

Even if Claire was correct about which direction the dyszoons went, they could have changed course or separated. In which case, she might be tracking them for a long time.

Daphne stopped and turned off the flashlight to focus. Darkness swept across the woods like a heavy black curtain, and her eyes bulged, seeking any source of light. Her breaths shortened, teetering toward the edge of panic. Three dyszoons were on the loose, and she was alone.

Or was she? A pair of eyes pressed into her neck, and Daphne spun around, half expecting to see Claire, though no leaf had rustled.

"Claire?" she called uncertainly, just loud enough for someone close by to hear. There was no answering call. Of course—Claire had a flashlight and wouldn't sneak up on her. No person could without making a sound.

It could be a stealthy animal unafraid of humans, but the eye contact was at her height. Daphne's thumb rubbed the flashlight switch but didn't turn it on. Her panicked breaths were slowing, soothed by an outside feeling of calm. Or perhaps peace.

A prick in her awareness brought her attention away, breaking the invisible staring contest. The presence was stronger farther into the woods. Daphne looked back where the eyes had been, but they were gone.

She turned on the flashlight and jogged through the woods, adrenaline replacing calm. As she drew near the presence, however, Daphne became convinced it wasn't a dyszoon.

The shade turned at her approach, confirming her suspicions. The faded T-shirt, jeans, and cropped hairstyle could have placed him at any time period from the last few decades. His dark skin glowed with a faint silvery light, like the moon.

At less urgent of a time, she would have taken time to learn more about him, but she had told Claire to expect a call in twenty minutes—more than half of that had passed. Could the shade point her in the right direction?

"Which way?" she asked.

He pointed a misting hand south.

"Thanks."

Daphne jogged, shivering from anticipation more than the cold. She preferred a sudden fight rather than these drawn out minutes that were deceptively quiet, when at any second the battle could begin.

"Hey!" she shouted, the sound swallowed by the open air. "Hey, come get me!"

The trees were grim phantoms overhead. She stumbled against a hidden root and dropped the flashlight with a curse. It spluttered but remained lit. As she reached for it, three new shapes sprang into her awareness like fast ships on a radar screen.

Dyszoons.

A black mass blasted through the light in a blink and

slammed into her defense, thrown up too late. She flew through the air and hit the ground as the dyszoon soared past with a whistling scream.

Daphne rolled and hurried to her feet, rubbing her arm. Claire's warning was accurate. This dyszoon wasn't more powerful than the previous ones, but it was bursting with chaotic energy. Judging by a nearby shriek, another was closing in.

The first dyszoon attacked as a second came from the left. On instinct, Daphne blocked both creatures and was proud to see them blasted away. Practice *was* making her stronger.

Her triumph was short-lived as a third dyszoon joined the others. It was the highest number she had battled at one time since the Veil had expanded over a month ago. With their increased strength, it was a worse scenario than the battle on Halloween night.

"You can do this," Daphne muttered aloud as they closed in. Claire trusted her. If only she could receive some of the psychic's strength and feel a rush of power like during that fight, but she would have to make do without it.

She closed her eyes and blocked.

The dyszoons soared in all directions. The one in the middle bore the brunt of the hit. To her astonishment, it burst into dust. The remaining creatures screamed, piercing the woods with a battle call that made the hairs on her arms bristle.

Daphne braced herself for their attack. Her foot nudged the flashlight, plunging the woods into darkness.

A dyszoon charged her. Distracted, Daphne weakly blocked the unseen blow as it smashed into her shield. It rushed by, forced to change course but unharmed. With little warning, the other one dropped like an anchor on her head, cracking her defense. She pushed it away, screaming from the effort.

The dyszoons darted between the trees at a dizzying pace,

two shapeless masses that stood out against the dark. Daphne stepped back and struck something hard.

Light returned just as they switched course and charged.

The combined hit was almost too much for her. Daphne staggered but remained standing, fending off alternating attacks that forced her backward, step by step, away from the flashlight.

Her confidence flickered. The dyszoons would continue attacking long after she no longer had the strength to parry the blows. Someone would find her pummeled body cold and lifeless in the woods. She was all alone...

The creatures blew away as if caught in a violent windstorm, shrieking in rage. Bewildered, Daphne looked up at the bobbing light coming toward her.

"Claire!" she yelled, relief dissolving the despair she now realized was being heightened by the dyszoons. "What are you doing here? I was going to call you."

"No need. I always intended to follow you. I'm only sorry I wasn't here sooner," Claire said, less out of breath than before. "I drove a mile up the road before I sensed them."

"I had to walk farther in than I thought. There's two left."

"Then let's take care of them," Claire said with grim resolve, stowing away her flashlight. The dyszoons were circling back with a cry, and her presence boosted Daphne's courage. With a touch of nostalgia, she realized that they hadn't fought dyszoons together since Halloween.

Instead of risking a direct attack, the dyszoons split directions, a tactic that gave them a greater chance of lasting longer. Daphne turned to the one closest, swallowing with unease.

The dyszoon attacked, and she blocked. Claire cried out nearby, but Daphne didn't dare turn and see how she fared. It bounced away, snarling, and flew at her again.

Her defense quivered, dashing hope for an easy victory. How could she think Claire's help would improve her chances?

The psychic had lent her strength once, but that wasn't available now. She was weak.

Stop it, Daphne scolded her thoughts, breathing as heavily as Claire before. The attacks had already distanced them by a few yards.

She struck at the dyszoon. To her frustration, it returned unfazed and pounded at her barrier, fended off only a few feet each time she countered. Eventually, it would break through.

A terrible shriek rang out, loud enough to wake the entire woods—Claire had won her battle. The final dyszoon echoed the call in rage. Although it was faceless, it seemed to turn toward the psychic.

"Claire!" Daphne yelled, heart in throat.

She realized her mistake too late. The dyszoon struck like black lightning—but the blow was aimed at her.

Her eyes widened in surprise. It was just a streak, stretching out in terrible fury. Far too slowly, her mind worked to defend while her body steeled itself for the fiery pain, however temporary, that would follow.

A silver blur rushed ahead of her and met the dyszoon in a bizarre entanglement of mist and shadow. Astonished, she recognized its face—the shade she met had interfered.

The silver disappeared, defeated by the dyszoon. But the seconds delay had given her just enough time to prepare. She met the onslaught with a matching scream.

Like a violent wave, a black mass collided with her barrier and exploded in all directions. Its scream rang through the trees and was gone. In the calm, the woods thrummed once more with unseen creatures, none of them supernatural.

Claire hurried forward with a flashlight. "Are you all right?" she asked worriedly, echoing Daphne's question earlier.

"Did you see that?" Daphne said, staring at the spot where the shade had collided with the dyszoon.

"See what?"

She gestured, at a loss to describe the strange scene. "The shade I met a few minutes ago. The dyszoon was coming for me, and the shade just...He flew in and slowed it down."

Claire pointed the flashlight at the spot. "Where is he?"

Daphne felt outward. No presence made itself known. "I think...I think he's gone. Where could he be?" she asked. Dyszoons returned to Hell when defeated, but shades had bound themselves to the earth until their most pressing problem was resolved, or else they faded with the centuries.

"I'd say if he doesn't reappear elsewhere, he's become untethered," Claire answered.

"You mean—that forced him to move on?"

"Yes. And that's not a bad thing, all things considered."

Daphne's heart twinged with sadness. It wasn't as though the shade had died a second time, but his second exit from the world was sudden and without a chance to remedy whatever had kept him behind. She would never get to know his story or even his name.

But she also got Claire's point. The shade, if forced from the land of the living, no longer existed as a shadow of himself in a self-inflicted purgatory. He was finally at peace, and his final act was heroic.

"I thought shades couldn't fight dyszoons," Daphne said. "Didn't you try it once?"

Claire's silence was thoughtful. "Yes, in my first dyszoon battle I tried pulling one in to help me out of instinct, but he wasn't able to help—it went right through him. I assumed shades weren't strong enough, and I wouldn't risk getting distracted in a fight by trying it again. But perhaps the issue was never strength."

"Maybe because the Veil's grown twice since then, the dyszoons are more present? And shades can interact with them better because of that?" Daphne guessed, recalling the transparent wisp in Veronica's neighborhood. Any weaker, and she might not have even sensed it.

"Something like that," Claire mused, peering at where the shade had vanished. The flashlight harshly illuminated the trees. "And if that's the case, shades could become essential in the coming days."

Daphne shivered, almost hearing the psychic's thoughts matching her own as they grasped the implications.

"Do you think they could help with the demon?" she said.

"The demon, I doubt. But if we were to face any large outbreaks like tonight or worse, it's possible a few shades might make all the difference."

They lapsed into silence. In Daphne's opinion, it would be too much to expect even a few shades to win a fight against a dyszoon—they shouldn't rely on it, anyway. But in a tight spot, the shades could tip a battle in their favor.

The possibility of a dyszoon outbreak that she and Claire couldn't handle had long haunted the back of her mind. Even a small advantage was better than nothing.

Daphne collected her dropped flashlight, feeling outward for a sign of the shade without success. His disappearance bothered her more than she cared to admit to Claire, who was tougher about such things.

She had often wanted to do more to help shades move on, and a face-off against a dyszoon was a shortcut. However, the idea of a shade like Heather disappearing with her last request unfulfilled felt wrong, akin to a failure to carry out a promise made to someone dying.

Shades were dead, but she hoped to minimize the casualties of using them in battle. Older shades whose problems were unsolvable would be best for this purpose. It would be a kindness to release them into peace when she knew no other way of granting it to them.

There was another reason not to dismiss the help of shades outright. While weeks of battles had improved her abilities against the stronger dyszoons, it bothered Daphne that the victories didn't come as easily as before, especially once she began to feel the effects of their evil presence. If—when—the Veil grew again, the risk was high that the next level of dyszoons would overpower her. As Claire said, interference from a shade could make all the difference.

She dwelled on these thoughts as they made a straight path to the psychic's car, and was quiet as she concentrated on stepping over fallen branches.

At least the time wasn't so late that her mom would question her delay in coming home. Daphne silently thanked the friend who'd invited her mom out to dinner and prevented her from attending opening night. Leaving right after the musical would have been tricky to explain.

More than once, Daphne rubbed the back of her neck, the memory of an unseen pair of eyes pressed into her skin.

27

DEMOLITION

Daphne signed in to Stage Crew a final time after school on Monday. The cast and crew were already making quick work of pulling apart the sets.

"We need folks to haul the wood down, mostly," the technical director said when she asked for an assignment. "By the way, you did a great job with the curtain. Want to do it again next year?"

"Oh—thanks," she said, flustered. "But I'm actually graduating soon."

He seemed disappointed. "Well, good luck with the rest of the year."

Mimicking others, Daphne picked up a long piece of wood and carried it down the ramp, taking care not to impale anyone. Chad stood waist-deep in the scrap bin, which was filling rapidly with salvageable pieces.

"Hey, curtain girl!" he greeted her, taking the piece. "Great job this weekend."

He held up a gloved hand. Daphne grinned and high-fived it. "You too," she said. "You have a really good voice."

"Thank you," he belted out in falsetto.

Daphne smiled all the way back up the ramp. It was bittersweet to pull apart the sets in mere hours when it had taken weeks to put them together, but she was relieved Hell Week was over. She had missed any discussion about the toppled bulldog during the opening performance. Perhaps it had refueled rumors of a haunting, or caused doubt that lighting the candle before each show was enough to appease the mischievous spirit.

Thankfully, the final two performances had gone smoothly. Her mom, handing over flowers after the Saturday performance, effusively praised her daughter's rope-pulling skills.

"I guess I've found my calling," Daphne had responded drily. Nearby, Vivian talked cheerfully with her mom, Rachel, who was oblivious that her ex-boyfriend lurked around the stage. Rachel's highlighted hair was in sleek curls instead of the wild ones she'd had as a teenager playing the part of Ginny. Daphne hoped she felt closure with the successful return of the musical.

No one was aware of Daphne's double role of pulling curtain and keeping Michael from the bulldog. He'd reappeared during each show like a persistent fly, spiking her anxiety each time the crew rolled on the dining room set. His appearances were unpredictable.

The woodpile on the stage was shrinking. Veronica, she was happy to see, was sweeping scraps into a pile and looking disgruntled about the manual labor. Vivian supervised the halfhearted effort, laughing.

Her heart quickened with renewed recklessness. Veronica and Nathan had barely exchanged a word on the way to history class while she followed at a comfortable distance. It appeared that the flowers on opening night hadn't been a sign that they'd made up after all.

"Can you load me up a few more pieces?" Beth asked Daphne, holding out her arms.

"Is that too much?"

"No, I think I got it."

Daphne grabbed a few small pieces and walked with her down the ramp, saying, "This is going a lot quicker than I thought it would."

"I know, right?" Beth said, slightly out of breath from the weight she carried. "It helps when the cast joins in."

They went outside. Chad was singing the song about hustling from the musical.

"I'm glad everything went okay. I know Vivian was worried, but she and Chad seemed to get through it," Daphne said. It had been three weeks since the dressing room breakdown, but she had kept it confidential.

"They've actually broken up now," Beth said casually.

Daphne almost dropped her own load. "Wait. What?"

"It happened this morning. Chad told me," Beth said. "I'm not surprised, honestly. People usually couple up when rehearsals start, but then they don't last once the show's over."

"I didn't think they had a lot in common, anyway," Daphne admitted. There wasn't time to say more, as Chad was close enough to overhear. Neither he nor Vivian seemed broken up about it. And if they had uncoupled, maybe it was contagious.

Over the next hour, the Drama Club dismantled the rest of the sets, organized props, and swept sawdust. Those who hadn't yet signed the painted poster went downstairs and grabbed a permanent marker. Chad's signature, Daphne noticed, was much smaller than Michael's—although, so was the poster, a dark rectangle squeezed into an increasingly rare blank section of wall.

Many left for lack of work, but Daphne hung behind with the broom Veronica had abandoned. This part of her high school experience was over, and though the stage was as clean as it could reasonably be, she felt reluctant to sign out. The remaining handful of helpers were downstairs.

A cool finger brushed her mind. Daphne looked up, the broom handle resting on her shoulder. Michael glowered down at her from the catwalk.

She shot out a phantom hand before he could disappear and tugged his arm. The shade came down in a silver blur and solidified a few feet from her, his expression as haughty as ever.

Any sympathy she normally felt for shades stopped at Michael. He was proud and self-centered, the type of person who blamed anyone other than himself for his problems. Shades often stayed behind after death because of someone they loved, and Michael was no exception—he loved himself.

Daphne approached Michael until they were only an arm's distance from each other. She couldn't help but compare him with Veronica in how he had once tried to bully and control others. There was a choice when it came to people like him, though the solution was far from clean.

Maybe that was why the original director had put up with his behavior rather than fire him. It was easier to manage the damage than to face the explosion. In the same way, Daphne had given in to Veronica's demands in order to avoid drama rather than push back. But giving in had caused its own drama. She needed to decide which type she could live with.

"Michael," she whispered, in case someone appeared from downstairs. The sets were gone, and the role of Victor Savage was laid to rest for another few decades. Just not the original actor. Not yet.

The shade stared down his nose, his dead eyes narrowed in contempt. He was reluctantly remaining in place, compelled to obey her since he remained in the realm of the living.

She'd considered carefully what to tell Michael for weeks.

An order to stay away from the stage wouldn't stop him from interfering. More needed to be said.

"Michael. You can't stay in this theater, or touch anything, or...or try to harm anyone."

The command didn't sound all that impressive to her ears, and Daphne doubted her wording. She hadn't given such an order before.

Michael held his gaze long enough for Daphne to wonder if he was immune to her orders. He turned and sauntered to the edge of the stage, an actor demanding the full attention of the audience beneath lights that could no longer illuminate him. She blinked, and he was gone.

No sense of peace surrounded her like when she'd helped Robin in the cemetery pass on. She guessed that, exiled from the theater, he would linger elsewhere until time closed the curtain on his final act. That, however, was his choice. Doubtless, the legend of the ghost actor would be passed down for years to come.

Daphne looked around at the stage, now truly vacant. She propped the broom against the wall and signed out of Stage Crew for the last time.

The hallway talk buzzed as Daphne hung up her backpack.

A strange energy had thrummed beneath her skin since confronting Michael the previous day. With the end of Stage Crew, graduation loomed large. She had a few short weeks to make good on her resolution to talk to Nathan again.

To confess her feelings for him was too high a cliff to jump off of, but she could stop being afraid of talking to him. And if Veronica retaliated and told him about her crush, what of it? It would be easy to avoid him for a few weeks.

For once, Nathan stood alone at his locker. Daphne's heart

beat faster. She'd expected to put her resolution into practice by joining him after lunch, whether or not Veronica liked it, but this was an easier beginning.

Even so, Daphne hesitated. They hadn't talked properly since before spring break. She had been shaking him off, and it was too optimistic to hope the change went unnoticed.

Stop being a coward. Clutching her books, Daphne forced her feet forward. The buzzing in the hallway grew distant. Her nerves echoed the first time she'd met Nathan, when his sister had helpfully knocked his books out of his hands to give her an opening. However, Heather wasn't here to help now.

She was close. There was no retreating. If Veronica witnessed the moment, Daphne would take the consequences.

The first bell rang. She halted a few feet from him as lockers slammed up and down the hallway. It was too late to strike up a conversation. Nathan shut his own locker and noticed her, mild surprise on his face.

Heat exploded in hers. "Oh. Hi. I-I'd better—" she stammered. Daphne turned on her heel, wishing that she had the ability of shades to vanish into thin air.

By lunch, she had replayed the attempt enough times in her head to recognize that it wasn't, perhaps, as embarrassing as it had felt in the moment. When the hour ended, Daphne resolved, she could try again. Veronica was nowhere to be seen, which boosted her bravery.

She sat down. Jessica played with her food, subdued. "What's up?" Daphne asked, her thoughts jumping to Chad and Vivian's breakup. Had something happened between Jessica and Zeke?

Jessica shot a suspicious look at the rest of the table. Taylor was sitting down, talking to anyone who might be listening.

"Can I tell you after we eat? Let's go up there." She pointed to the carpeted platform outside the theater doors.

"Sure," Daphne said with a frown. It wasn't like Jessica to be secretive. She ate her pizza quickly and was one of the first to drop off her lunch tray.

"Okay, let's go," Jessica said, gathering up her wrappers and chucking them in the garbage can. Daphne followed her up the wide steps and sat before the flat carving of a falcon that hung between the two sets of theater doors. The railings along the edge of the platform partly shielded them from view, and away from other students, their conversation would be private.

"So, if you don't know yet," Jessica began matter-of-factly, "Veronica and Nathan broke up last night."

Daphne blinked at her, uncomprehending. Then, all at once, the impact of the news slammed into her. It was the reason Nathan was by himself at his locker that morning. *They broke up.* She was in an alternate reality, or a cruelly realistic dream. The words she'd never expected to hear clanged in her mind. *They broke up.*

"What? Are you sure? Why? Is that why she's not here?" Her shocked questions tumbled out.

"Oh, Veronica's here today. She's just avoiding me," Jessica said with a dark laugh, smoothing her high ponytail.

"What do you mean?"

Jessica took a deep breath. "Last night we were messaging about prom, and Veronica said Nathan wasn't coming along in the limo. So I'm like, 'Um, okay?'" Jessica mimed confusion. "'Is he meeting us later?' But then she told me they'd just broken up."

Daphne absorbed this, trying not to show the full extent of her shock. She had never told Jessica about her feelings for Nathan, and now definitely wasn't the right moment.

"I was like, 'Oh my gosh, I'm so sorry. What happened?' But then Veronica said it was fine, and she was bringing someone else in the limo. Like, a date."

Daphne did a double-take. "What?" she said in disbelief. However, an inkling of the answer crept into her mind. Veronica's laugh through the window at the cafe...

"Right? So I was thinking, okay—who? And she said she was bringing Dom!"

"*Dom?*" Daphne said, her suspicion confirmed. "But he's his best friend!"

"I know! She said he asked her to go to prom, and she said yes, like it was no big deal! So...I got mad." Jessica laughed again darkly.

"So, wait, she was going behind Nathan's back?" Daphne said, grappling with the quick turnaround. Even for Veronica, cheating seemed low. As recently as last week, she was cuddling up to Nathan at his locker.

"Well, she *says* she didn't cheat on him. That Dom asked her out to prom once he heard they'd broken up." Jessica twirled her ponytail in agitation. "But no, I'm sorry, *something* was going on. No one moves *that* quick."

Daphne looked over at Nathan's table, which was obscured by the railings along the steps. However, she knew Dom wouldn't be sitting there.

Veronica had sat at that table plenty of times. How long had Dom secretly wanted his best friend's girlfriend? Daphne never liked Dom and thought him a poor friend, and now here was solid evidence she hadn't been wrong. Their absence at lunch likely meant they had signed out for the period.

"Did Veronica break up with him? Or did Nathan with her?" Daphne asked, curious to learn all she could without raising suspicion. She thought of Veronica, laughing with Vivian as she swept the stage as lazily as possible. The mood didn't seem to match someone about to break up with their boyfriend that evening, which could mean Nathan had done it.

But then again, Chad and Vivian hadn't been torn up by

the end of their relationship, either. Since Veronica had moved on with Dom so easily, she might have taken the initiative. Or else Nathan had found out she was secretly hanging out with Dom and ended things, but Veronica didn't care because it was what she wanted.

Who had told Dom the news? Did Nathan tell his best friend, who then immediately made his move? Or had Veronica texted Dom casually, hoping he'd ask her out? Without more info, Daphne could only speculate.

"I'm not sure," Jessica said. "I didn't get to ask. She got upset when I said I didn't want to do the limo anymore."

"You don't?" Daphne suppressed a laugh. All of it was suddenly very funny. A strange feeling was spreading through her heart and all the way to her fingertips. It had been so long since she'd felt it that it took a moment to identify it as hope.

Intermixed with it was pity. She willed the clock to move faster so she could see Nathan. To lose not one, but two relationships in one stroke was a hard blow. She had almost been a third. Could still be.

"No. Because, first of all, I do not like Dom." Jessica held up a finger as her first point. "Second, I'm friends with Nathan too, so I mean, for V to ditch him for his best friend *kind of* rubs me the wrong way."

"That *is* pretty cold," Daphne said mildly.

"My brother's friend"—luckily her flinch went unnoticed at Jessica's casual mention of Leon—"the *same thing* happened to him in high school. His friend's girlfriend was going to this guy's house to work on a 'project' for class, and he was even dropping her off! And then later she admitted they were just making out."

"Wow," Daphne said before changing the subject. "How did Zeke feel about not doing the limo?"

"He doesn't care about that," Jessica said confidently. "I mean, it would have been fun, but..."

The bell rang, and they stood to leave. It occurred to Daphne that their chat was the deepest conversation she'd had with her former best friend in months. However, she doubted that Jessica and Veronica would be on the outs for long.

They said goodbye, and Daphne joined the moving crowd. When she compared her lonely feelings two weeks ago, as she hid underneath the cafe table, to now, her entire social life had turned around. She was invited to Beth's wedding, Veronica and Jessica weren't talking, and Nathan was single.

But that doesn't mean anything. Despite the hope in her chest, Daphne was determined to be realistic. It wasn't as if he would develop feelings for her at the same speed Veronica had attached herself to Dom. She'd be lucky if they stayed friends.

Another relationship probably wasn't on his mind, especially with graduation coming up. If he had wanted to be with her—Daphne forced herself to look this fact squarely in the face—he would have done so and not been with Veronica.

Regardless, there were several immediate improvements. No longer would she have to see their embraces in the hallway or listen to Veronica laugh at his every remark. And best of all, Daphne could talk to him without looking over her shoulder.

She pushed through the slow-moving crowd, eager to stretch her time with Nathan. It might not be too late to repair their friendship. *They broke up.* It was the best news she'd heard in months.

Nathan was still grabbing books when she shut her locker. "Take two..." Daphne muttered to herself. "Don't be awkward." *Highly unlikely.*

This time, her approach was less complicated. "Hey, Nathan." Her tone was cheerier than normal and, to her own ears, overdone.

"Hey." His smile was automatic.

"What's up?"

"Not too much, you?" he said, dropping another book onto his pile. His wavy hair was stuck up more than usual, as if he'd been running a hand through it.

Panic crept at the edges of Daphne's thoughts, when she should have been relaxed at Veronica's absence. In her imagination, they'd slipped into conversation as easily as they'd done at the track meet a month ago, as if the last few weeks had never happened. But he couldn't have failed to notice how she'd avoided him.

Maybe if she called herself out, it would help. "Not much. We tore down the sets yesterday. By the way, I'm..." It was hard to get the words out. "I'm sorry that I couldn't talk more after the show. I was in a hurry, but I felt bad about it later."

"Oh. Yeah, that's okay. Don't worry about it." He slammed the locker closed, and together they set off as if Veronica had never interrupted their routine. She was relieved he didn't ask why she'd been so eager to leave.

"What did you think of the musical?" Daphne asked after a few moments of silence, resigning herself to carrying the conversation. He was no doubt having a bad day, and it had nothing to do with her.

"It was really good," he said. "I'm jealous of anyone who can sing like that."

"Chad's great," Daphne said, choosing to omit Vivian, under the circumstances. "So, you can't sing?"

"Let's just say the choir director begged me to quit freshman year." Whether it was because of her lighter tone or the apology, he seemed to be warming up.

She smiled, but then second-guessed and glanced sideways to see if he was joking. "Did he?"

"I assume he was thinking it." Nathan shrugged.

They reverted to silence. Panic warred in Daphne's mind as she struggled for another topic. Talking to him didn't usually take this much effort. Should she admit she knew about the breakup? Or were they not close enough to talk about it?

"Do you have any more track meets at home?" she asked in desperation, already knowing the answer.

"Not any more this season."

"When's your next one?"

"Saturday."

"I wish they were closer. It's fun to go to them. There's always a lot going—"

They were almost to the history classroom, and Nathan had stopped, mouth pressed thin. Daphne left the sentence unfinished and followed his stony gaze.

Veronica was rushing from the other direction, a route likely chosen to avoid this very encounter. She was late coming back from the lunch hour, and judging by the coffee drink in her hand, Daphne suspected she had spent it with Dom in a drive-through somewhere.

She spotted Nathan, and her eyes widened. Her expression was sheepish, as if he'd caught her in wrongdoing—a look Daphne couldn't have pictured before. Veronica retreated into the classroom.

"I...heard what happened. I'm sorry. That sucks," she said, deciding it would be impossible to pretend not to have noticed the moment. She burned to know how the breakup had played out. Who had broken up with whom? Did Nathan still want to be with Veronica?

"Yeah," he said, his face grim.

"If it makes you feel any better, you didn't deserve that." She was walking on a balance beam, backward. It would be so easy to misstep. "I've never liked her. And vice versa."

Daphne turned before catching his reaction, squeezing her

books to her chest. It was a risky thing to say about his ex-girl-friend, who he might yet have feelings for, and he could be angry at her for it. There was always the possibility that Veronica could crawl to him and beg to get back together.

She sat at her desk, shivering at her own daring and second-guessing herself. Veronica and Vivian, who now had a recent breakup in common, were whispering to each other.

Mr. Burnes emerged from his office, and she ducked her head. She was too distracted to wonder about how his plans with Ashley were progressing, and wondered instead for the full hour if she had struck the fatal crack in her and Nathan's friendship.

28

THE DARKROOM

If Nathan was angry with Daphne for admitting her dislike for his ex-girlfriend, he didn't mention it.

Instead, to her surprise, he appeared at her locker the next morning, and then the next. She guessed he was trying to avoid Dom, who shared the same circle of friends, as much as possible. If Veronica had switched to cozying up to Dom at his locker, she didn't see.

Daphne couldn't muster the courage to ask more details about the breakup, and the few extra minutes weren't enough time to discuss it anyway, but the awkwardness between them had lifted.

The freedom to speak to him without backlash would take a while to get used to. Whenever he stopped by, Daphne caught herself checking the hallway for Veronica before realizing that it was no longer necessary to worry.

Despite the breakup, Nathan seemed happier with each passing day. Veronica remained absent at lunchtime the rest of that week to spend it with Dom off-campus, something that Jessica had taken to commenting on negatively.

On Thursday, Daphne stood in the hot lunch line and received a scoop of overcooked whole-wheat noodles. Next to her, Nathan held out his tray.

"I'm hosting some of my team for pasta night at my house tomorrow," he said. "We have a meet on Saturday. Want to come?"

"Pasta? At your house?" Daphne heard herself repeat stupidly, after asking for meatless sauce. "That sounds fun," she added, recovering.

"Cool. I thought it would be a good time to show you my camera setup."

"Right," Daphne said, grabbing a roll. "Can you send me your address?"

"Sure."

They parted ways. Daphne sat down at her table with a sense of unreality, only half hearing as Jessica gossiped about Veronica and Dom's absence to the others and shared her satisfaction that canceling the limo was the right punishment. After months of talking about their passion for cameras, going over to his house was finally happening.

Dom, who was on the team, might be part of the reason he'd invited her. It would be awkward for Nathan to have his former best friend over at his house, to say the least. And who knew what sides were being taken on the team? He needed an ally outside of it all.

A noodle slid down her throat like a sour worm at a new realization. She would meet Nathan's parents. And Heather's.

The shade hadn't recently come to mind due to her absence. Daphne pictured meeting his mother and compulsively spilling her secrets, followed by the stunned silence of Nathan and the entire track team.

She internally rolled her eyes at the ridiculous vision. No, she would *not* work this up in her head. It was just a casual party. She would attend and then leave with a greater appreciation for old-fashioned photography. *It's not a big deal.*

The Veil, however, could interrupt their plans. No dyszoons had come out since the opening night of the musical—all the more reason to believe that they would during the party. Or worse, maybe the Veil was only calm because Mr. Burnes and Ashley had drawn more blood and were planning to summon the long-awaited demon, timing it during suppertime on Friday...

Or, her luck would *hold,* and she wouldn't be called away to battle a small army of dyszoons.

Daphne speared another noodle, appetite gone. She hadn't been all that lucky so far.

Daphne pulled into Nathan's driveway and parked at the end of a line of cars.

A tan one-story house was nestled in a sparse section of woods. *I'm here,* she messaged Nathan while walking up, hoping he'd be the one to meet her at the front door. She'd deliberately arrived late to the track party so that everyone would be too preoccupied with dinner to pay much attention to her. As the only girl, she would stand out.

She hesitated at the entrance. Should she knock, or walk in? Daphne raised her hand and then withdrew it as the door cracked open.

"Hey, glad you made it," Nathan said with a grin, standing aside to let her in. Her chest fluttered. The entrance was chaotically homelike, similar to her own, with twenty pairs of scattered shoes and dropped coats. Two small sets of stairs led upstairs and down.

"Sorry I'm late," she said nervously.

He waved her off, relaxed in his own territory. "Doesn't matter. Find it okay?"

"I used my phone. Your house is a little out of the way."

"Yeah, I didn't realize how far we were from each other the first time I came out to yours."

He led her upstairs. Many of his teammates were in the living room, devouring plates of spaghetti on the floor while watching others play a racing video game. Dom was absent. Perhaps he'd been able to excuse himself from coming and was with Veronica instead, a thought that angered Daphne for Nathan's sake.

He led her into a warmly lit kitchen. The coach was deep in conversation with Nathan's gray-haired dad by the kitchen island. Daphne's stomach clenched, but she experienced no sudden urge to tell him all about his daughter's shade, as feared. There was no sign of Mrs. Grey.

"Help yourself," Nathan said, pointing to the large pots of spaghetti and sauce. Daphne scooped a small helping as he drew her a glass of water.

"Thanks," she said, hoping that something interesting to say would occur to her soon.

"No problem. I'll be right back," he said. "I gotta finish setting up downstairs."

"Okay," Daphne said. Nathan left the room before she could follow up with the obvious question. *Finish setting up what, exactly?*

With no desire to enter the living room, Daphne ate her spaghetti alone at the counter and avoided eye contact with the two men, who didn't pay her any attention. A few teammates came to refill their plates and then disappeared.

She felt much more comfortable in the outdated kitchen than in Veronica's glossy one. A sliding door off to the side revealed a large deck and a sizable yard that ended in trees. The sun dipped closer to the horizon.

A latecomer arrived. Mouth full of spaghetti, Daphne stared at Dom as he entered with a self-important swagger that reminded her of Michael. He made eye contact and then ignored her with a smirk as he dished up a plate. It was astonishing that he was there at all, at the house of his former best friend, when he was going out with that friend's ex-girlfriend.

Dom left without comment, though she hoped that he felt her glare on the back of his head. Unnoticed by either Nathan's dad or coach, she trashed her paper plate and moved toward the dining area, unsure of where else to go. She was thankful Nathan hadn't been present.

Her breath caught at one of the large pictures on the wall. Heather's senior portrait hung prominently between her brothers. It had been shot outdoors, Heather smiling radiantly in a pretty light-green dress, the scene full of sunlight.

Was the portrait painful for the family to look at? Ever since her dad passed away when she was thirteen, Daphne had generally avoided looking at pictures of him. At some point, her mom had removed a family portrait from the wall that had been taken the previous summer. None of them knew their lives would be blown apart within the year.

Maybe it was a comfort to have the picture so visible. A sign that their daughter wasn't forgotten or erased, but watching over the family dinners.

Heather's family didn't know that she was still in Nathan's life, in a way. *He's so alone.* Had she noticed that Veronica was slipping away? That his best friend would betray him? If she had, the timing of the shade's reappearance and their conversation in the bathroom made more sense. Maybe it hadn't had anything to do with the Veil after all.

Daphne looked over Nathan's brother's photo with interest.

There was some resemblance between the two, but Caleb's hair was dark and wavy. He was good-looking in his own way.

"Hey, thanks for waiting." To Daphne's enormous relief, Nathan appeared at her elbow. In reality, he'd been gone for less than a few minutes, but it felt much longer. "Want to see my cameras quick? They're in my room."

She swallowed any mention of Dom as she followed him down the hallway to a door on the left. His bedroom was rather plain and uncluttered, a few old trophies and some pictures in frames the only real personal touch. A twin bed was pressed against a dark blue accent wall, and a desk and lamp sat by the window, his backpack deposited on the office chair. Daphne imagined him messaging her from it as he did his homework.

She considered her own bedroom, with its clothes strewn on the floor and the wall of photos, and was thankful he had never seen it. His bedroom was far neater.

Nathan walked over to a shelf and removed a boxy maroon camera with a handle on top. Daphne took it carefully, but it seemed sturdy despite its obvious age.

"This was my great-grandfather's. It's an Ansco, from the late 1920s," Nathan said. "He bought it for my great-grand-mother when they started seeing each other."

"Where do you look to take a picture?" Daphne asked. There wasn't a viewfinder on the back of the camera.

Nathan moved closer. She held her breath as he pointed out a metal-lined opening on the top. "You would look there, and the picture would have been upside down. The view is kind of blurry, but I think that's because it's old. And then this"—he flicked down a small lever on the side, to the sound of a mechanism inside—"is how you would take the photo."

Excitement filled his voice, Daphne noted, exhaling as soon as he moved away. His passion was endearing. "I take it you can't shoot film in here anymore?" she asked, moving the lever.

"Nah, this camera wouldn't work. But I think my Brownie would still take photos, if I could get the film. I haven't looked into it, though."

He removed a few more cameras from the shelf. There was a Kodak Duaflex II that his grandma had used and a Hawk-Eye model B that his dad had purchased at an auction. Lastly, Nathan showed her a black-and-silver camera.

"This is my thirty-five millimeter and what I take pictures with, mostly. I can get film no problem," he said, passing it over. "Here, there's one more photo left on the roll. The front ring focuses."

Daphne looked through the viewfinder and pointed it at him. He grinned at her, which she couldn't help but mirror as she took the shot.

"Not sure if that turned out or not." She handed it over, jittery with nerves. "You develop them yourself?"

"That's what I was setting up downstairs. I was going to show you my darkroom, if you want to. My negatives from spring break are ready to print."

"Sure," she said shyly. Though they had talked about it for months, the tour of his cameras had taken only a few minutes. It was natural to see the rest of the setup.

Daphne followed him through the kitchen, past the living room, and then down the stairs to the lower level. They crossed the common room into a hallway.

He opened the first door and flicked on the lights, revealing a narrow windowless room. Three shallow trays of liquid and a piece of equipment she knew was called an enlarger were on the long counter, which had a small sink close by the door.

"The guy who built this house was a photographer, so he had a real darkroom put in," Nathan said. "That's how I got into film photography, already having the setup."

"Did you take all of these?" Daphne pointed to the pictures clipped to the wall to dry.

"Yeah. They're not that good, though, like yours," he added hastily. "I think I'm getting better, but I also like taking pictures just so I can develop them."

"They look great," she said with honesty, hoping the praise would mean a lot to him, coming from her. "Were these from one of your meets?"

"Yeah. So anyway, here's the setup..."

He handed her a strip of negatives and a magnifying glass so she could decide which photo to print. Daphne selected a shot of him and his brother standing by the pier. Nathan placed the negative in a small black carrier with a window for the image and blew air at it with a puffer brush.

"Removes the dust," he explained, sliding the carrier into the enlarger. "Next thing we need to do is turn off the light so we don't ruin the paper. You can close the door and hit the safe-light switch."

Daphne obeyed. The room was plunged into darkness and lit again in a wash of red. Nathan turned on the enlarger. It projected a red-tinted photo onto the clear easel below. He twisted a dial to adjust the size of the projection and then placed a tubelike object in the middle of the frame.

"You look through this, and then focus the image up here," he said, twisting another dial. "Want to try?"

Daphne bent down to look through the focus finder, highly conscious of how close he was in that small space. *Focus,* she told herself, twisting the dial.

"Like that?" she asked, leaning away as he checked the sharpness of the image.

"Perfect," he said, to her irrational pleasure.

Nathan unsealed a packet of photographic paper and slid a glossy sheet underneath the easel. He hovered a plain sheet of paper above most of it and, following the timer, moved the sheet an inch every five seconds until the entire sheet had been exposed. This method would show them different exposure times that they could choose from once the picture developed, he said.

"So after that, you slide the sheet into this first tray...and then set the timer." Nathan said, tipping the tray to slosh the liquid chemicals over the glossy paper. A black-and-white image blossomed onto the page, to Daphne's fascination. "After a minute, you take it out with these tongs and slide it into the next tray. That'll stop the developing. Then in another ten seconds...it goes in the fixer tray."

When half a minute had passed, Nathan used a third set of tongs to remove the photo from the last tray of chemicals.

Daphne turned the white light back on as he rinsed the photo in another tray of water at the sink and then wiped it clean with a silicone blade.

He laid the striped image flat. "These are the five exposure times?" Daphne asked, pointing at the bands that ranged from light to dark as she leaned on the counter.

"Yeah," Nathan said, near enough that she was finding it difficult to concentrate on the photo. "This light side is five seconds' exposure, and the darkest is twenty-five seconds."

"I think ten or fifteen look best."

"We could do twelve seconds," Nathan said as his phone dinged with a message.

Daphne examined the picture of the pier. His brother's hair was much longer than in his long-ago senior portrait, and he was less baby-faced. He was an indie musician, she recalled.

Nathan's phone dinged again, and he sighed, turning it silent without looking at the screen.

"You okay?" she asked.

"It'll be someone telling me Dom's here. I don't care, honestly."

"I saw him upstairs," she said. When a pause told her that he didn't mean to say anything more about the subject, Daphne switched the red safelight back on.

He slid a fresh sheet of paper underneath the easel and let her adjust the focus. Her thoughts turned back to Dom and Veronica in the cafe, the flirtatious hair flip over the shoulder...

Maybe she should have let Nathan know about the outing after all. Yet, if she had, his smile in the trip photos would be forced. Either way, it didn't matter if she let him know about it now.

"I should have said something, but I saw her and Dom eating out on break," Daphne confessed, continuing to adjust the dial, although she had already achieved clear focus twice. "It seemed weird, but I think I wanted to assume you knew about it."

"Oh yeah? I figured."

She looked up in surprise. "You did know about it?"

"Not about them hanging out on break, no. But I guessed that they were probably hanging out." His voice was dark.

"Was that why you broke up, because you found out she was seeing Dom?" Daphne asked, unable to suppress her curiosity over how the relationship ended.

Nathan turned the timer on and exposed the image. "No. I mean, I guess it was because of Dom, but I didn't know about that until one of my buddies told me she was going to prom with him. Then I assumed that he was the real reason why she'd been canceling on me lately."

Daphne stepped aside as he removed the paper and let her submerge it into the first tray. "I'm sorry it happened that way," she said, leaning her elbows against the counter to watch as the blank white paper gave way to the pier scene.

Nathan shrugged, leaning over with her. Their shoulders were only a few inches apart. "It's fine. I mean, it sucks. But I'd rather know the truth, you know?"

If it were that simple, Daphne thought, biting her bottom lip. She'd told so many lies in order to camouflage her new reality of dyszoons and shades, and he hadn't been immune to the dishonesty. Really, after everything, it was a miracle that she was here in the darkroom with him at all. That they were friends.

The question gnawed at the edge of her mind like a dyszoon whose presence she couldn't ignore.

"Can I ask—what made you break up, if it wasn't Dom?"

Nathan stared at the tray as if seeing Veronica in its depths. "I think I was tired of trying. Lately, it was like we were only together out of habit or something, and when she started canceling on me, I realized that maybe she didn't want me to try. So I stopped at her house and said I wanted to talk."

"So she was okay with breaking up?" Daphne said. "But she wanted you to be the one to do it?"

"I wouldn't say she was okay with it."

"But if she wanted to be with Dom—"

The timer ran down. Afraid the interruption would shatter this moment of trust, Daphne hurried to move the picture into the next tray.

"I don't know, honestly, if she does or not or if she's just getting back at me, or sending a message," he continued. "She didn't take it very well when I said it wasn't working."

Daphne shook out the photo and submerged it in the third tray. "Lots of swearing?"

"Let's just say things were said. She wasn't happy with breaking up right before prom and said I couldn't handle her having a life outside of us. Stuff like that."

She dropped the photo into the tray of water. They waited

in silence. At his direction, Daphne removed it and used the spatula to wipe off the liquid—a satisfying step.

"We can hang it up to dry." Nathan clipped it to a line strung above the counter.

"It turned out nice," she said, wanting to do another. "Anyway, that sounds like a fun time."

"Yep, it was. Oh, right, and she brought you up," he added casually.

"She did? In what way?" Daphne whipped her head around, struck with fear that in the heat of the moment, Veronica had blabbed her secret. She comforted herself that if that were the case, Nathan would have mentioned it days ago.

"She thought that you were saying bad stuff about her to me."

"Really?" Daphne said, relieved. "Like I was trying to turn you against her?"

"Yeah. It makes more sense now, knowing that she doesn't like you," Nathan said. "And I told her that we've never talked about her, and that we haven't really talked that much in the last few weeks."

So he did *notice that.* "Yeah, I guess we haven't been able to walk to class," she said. Hopefully, he would agree that was the main cause.

Nathan picked at the seal on the packet, seeming to hesitate. "It wasn't just that. It sometimes felt like you were avoiding me, like you didn't want to talk to me, or something."

Her stomach clenched. If she told Nathan the truth, that Veronica had ordered her to stay away from him, he would want to know why. She could tell him that Veronica had only *thought* that she was suddenly a threat after months of dating. But if the reason for it was untrue, and Daphne didn't have any feelings for him, there was no excuse for her to have given in.

It was no good.

"I didn't want to—to *stop* talking to you, I mean," she hastily added.

"Then why did you?"

Daphne was glad the red light hid the color on her face. Although they weren't quite in darkness, the different lighting was making it easier to be reckless, as if it were an alternate room where anything could be said and then erased from memory with the return of normal light.

"Right before break, Veronica told me to stay away from you. I'm sorry." His hazel eyes were on her, impossible to meet.

After a long moment, Nathan spoke. "Don't be. I wish I'd known that."

"I guess I didn't want the drama."

It occurred to her that Veronica hadn't made a similar request to Nathan to end their friendship, citing Daphne's hidden crush. Instead, she'd kept it to herself. But why do that, unless she wasn't confident in who he would choose?

"But why did Veronica think you were a threat all of a sudden?" Nathan asked.

Daphne's heart was thumping. She'd been hoping the logical question wouldn't follow.

I don't know, she wanted to say. But that wasn't believable either. Suddenly she wanted badly to escape the room, the questions she wasn't ready to answer. The photo on the wall was quite interesting. "Veronica said...she got this idea that I like you...more than just a friend."

Nathan's face was unreadable at the corner of her eye, as was his pause. "And do you?"

It was hard to lie to someone who was looking at her so intently. "Nathan, I—I like our friendship. I don't want to...I wouldn't want you to...to feel weird if I—"

Her words stopped abruptly at the touch of his hand as it brushed hers. Daphne looked up at Nathan, and she was close enough to see that his eyes, like a hidden scene unfurling on a blank page, were revealing a picture she didn't dare try to understand, in case she was wrong.

"Daphne." Her name was a question that only wanted one answer. The picture abruptly snapped into focus.

Daphne moved forward without conscious thought at the same time as Nathan. This time, there was no one to interrupt, no one to stop her from seizing his shirt or his hands from pulling her in. No one to pull their faces away as they connected with ferocity.

Six months of pent-up longing exploded in the press of her mouth against his. Her lack of experience didn't matter or even come to mind. His lips guided hers, searching frantically for something neither could name, only explore. Daphne slid her hand around his neck, swept against him like a tidal wave and then pushed back with the urgency of the opposing wave. Her back collided gently with the closed door.

Daphne grabbed fistfuls of his shirt and clung there, pinned tightly between him and the door, which helped support legs that were dissolving beneath her. Her fingers explored his shoulder blades and then ran through his wavy hair, a sensation better than she had often dreamed, as the next kiss swallowed her whole.

She shuddered at the release of her lips. He seemed to slow in concern, but Daphne coaxed his mouth open, telling him wordlessly that she was far from done. That she might never be done. She was rewarded with an answering shiver as his hands trailed up her arms and cupped her face.

Maybe that was the whole point of film in a digital world, it occurred to Daphne much later. Delayed gratification.

29

ABSENCE

If Daphne was tempted to wonder if her time in the darkroom was a wishful dream, Nathan's messages on Saturday were proof that things had changed forever between them.

Unable to stop smiling, Daphne caught up on their chat after a rare late morning of sleeping in without nightmares. The kiss washed fresh over her mind, the memory vivid enough that her lips tingled.

Enjoyed last night :)

Glad you could come over.

Also I never got to show you the color process. Another time? :)

Leaving for the meet. What are you up to today?

Actually…what are you up to tomorrow?

Her insides bubbled with anticipation as she wrote that Sunday was free and that she had enjoyed coming over to see his setup, deciding on one smile emoji instead of a more suggestive winking face.

They settled on Sunday afternoon at her house for a movie. Luckily, upon arriving home, Daphne had let her mom know right away that Nathan was no longer just a friend, and so asking if she could have him over was only a formality. Her mom had reacted with much delight and thankfully didn't probe for too many details.

Nathan messaged her throughout the day while at the track meet. She grinned at each one that popped onto her screen, wrapped in a happy glow.

The wait for the next day was both quick and excruciatingly long. To keep busy, Daphne channeled her energy into preparing. She ordered Phillip to stay upstairs, browsed movies that Nathan might like, organized the shoes in the entryway, and tried on outfits.

Her mom, fortunately, would be out grocery shopping when he arrived. Therefore, the house was quiet when Daphne heard the crunch of gravel in the afternoon. She ran to open the front door with a white-hot burst of anticipation. Phillip was settled upstairs in his favorite spot by the mirror and wouldn't distract her.

"Hey," Nathan said as he walked up the porch steps, tall and athletic in school gear.

"Hey," she answered back with a shy smile. There was no red light to hide the flush in her face. Even so, she was relieved to see him in person. He was still himself, despite everything.

Nathan followed her through the tidied entryway and into the living room. Most of the third cushion was occupied by a furry black throw.

"I don't think we've met," he told the cat, stroking the top of her fluffy head as he sat. Mystique rumbled loudly in response and stood.

"She'll want to sit on you," Daphne warned him, scooping her up. "You can go here." The cat promptly hopped off the armchair with a jingle and sauntered away to nap elsewhere.

"Didn't want to party, I guess," Nathan observed. His arm

lay across the back of the couch, and Daphne wondered if it was an invitation for her to sit there. Or was that too close, too soon? After months of putting him firmly in the *friends* category, it would take some practice to act like—was she his girlfriend? Not officially.

Of course, they'd gotten much closer Friday night. Her face grew warmer. Looking elsewhere, she grabbed the remote and sat next to him. *There, that wasn't so hard.*

"What do you want to watch?"

"I don't care. You can choose," Nathan said. Daphne could feel his eyes on her instead of the screen. His arm touched the back of her shoulders. She itched to slide closer, to create more points of contact.

The movie started, one of yesterday's options, but she barely registered its title. She casually adjusted herself so that their legs were touching. His arm dropped down and curled around her shoulder. Daphne stared ahead, but the opening credits passed unseen.

"By the way...were you planning on going to prom?"

Daphne paused the movie and looked at his knee. "I wasn't sure yet," she said, not wanting to say that she'd made no plans to attend. He might conclude that she was uninterested in the dance and discontinue the thought.

"You didn't make any plans to go with someone?" Nathan said, his face relaxing in relief.

"No, I think Jessica still has plans with Zeke, and I don't know what Beth or anyone's up to," Daphne said, willing him to continue.

"Somebody mentioned it yesterday, and it hit me that it was coming up this weekend already. I wasn't sure if you'd made plans with someone."

Confusion pulled her eyebrows down. Someone, as in another guy? "No, I don't know who I would go with."

Nathan picked at something invisible on his pants, saying, "I thought maybe you'd be going with Jessica's brother."

"*Leon?*" she said, startled. Not even Jessica suspected that anything had happened there. "No, I'm *definitely* not going to prom with him."

Perhaps realizing from her tone that the topic of Leon wasn't a neutral one, Nathan asked, "Did you and him...Was there anything between you? It just seemed like, you know, at Jessica's party..."

Daphne recalled Nathan showing up just as she and Leon had almost kissed. While Jessica had missed the moment, she had gotten the impression that Nathan hadn't. She blushed, embarrassed all over again. Comparing the two, she'd been foolish to think Leon could have worked as a distraction.

"We just texted a bit. Then over break we went on a date, and that was it. We weren't going to work," she said. It was a light description of the train wreck, but dyszoons and her mental breakdown were unnecessary details. "We never talked about prom."

Nathan smiled. "Cool. If you didn't, you know, have any plans, would you want to go to prom? With me? But if you don't," he added hastily, "that's cool, I mean..."

Fireworks set off in her stomach. Daphne shifted around to see him better and grinned. "I'd love to go to prom with you."

"Yeah?" he said, breaking into an even wider smile that made her lips tingle again.

"Yeah," she answered, and leaned forward as he did.

The movie remained paused.

Daphne walked to her locker on Monday morning as if emerging from a dream.

Her mind had been occupied with little else besides

replaying her time with Nathan, so that she had hardly given any thought to dyszoons, the Veil, Ashley, or indeed, any problems at all.

It had been months—no, years—since she'd felt this happy. Daphne was afraid to reflect on this fact too closely, wanting to pretend as long as possible that the only thing she had to worry about planning for was prom, not a demon's arrival.

The first prickling of reality started with a voicemail from Claire, who asked if she'd like to meet after school. Daphne hadn't seen the psychic since the opening night of the musical over a week ago. The Veil had also been quiet, and the long week without more dyszoons was beginning to seem ominous.

Their reprieve would be broken sooner rather than later, but Daphne relished the break. For a few days, she had felt almost like a normal person who wasn't anticipating a battle with a demon.

Daphne sent a quick text to Claire that she was available and opened her locker. With a burst of excitement, she realized that the studio was located near a dress shop. She had last year's dress as a fallback, but surely it didn't hurt to look?

"Hey," came a voice.

She grinned and faced him. "Hey, Nathan. It's been a while. How was your weekend?"

"I'd say it was pretty good." He leaned against the locker next to hers, books slung at his side.

"What'd you do?" Daphne bit her bottom lip in an attempt to stop smiling like a maniac.

"I hung out with a friend," he said. "We didn't do much talking, though."

"That sounds kind of boring." She was finally able to school her face into a semi-neutral expression.

"It wasn't." It was clear from Nathan's eyes that their time together in the darkroom, as well as the gentler moments on the couch, until the front door opened, were foremost on his mind. Electricity struck her core.

The bell for first period rang. "Shoot. I have to grab my books yet," she said.

"Okay. See you at lunch." Nathan leaned forward to give her a quick kiss that took her aback, though the surprise wasn't unpleasant. She'd imagined him kissing her by the lockers more times than she cared to admit.

The reality wasn't disappointing, exactly, but the watching eyes would take some getting used to. Those didn't exist in her imagination. Kissing in public was like making an announcement to the school over the loudspeaker that they were together. There was no going back.

Though she would have preferred otherwise, Daphne knew that Jessica, Veronica, and Dom would find out soon enough. Their peaceful bubble couldn't last forever.

On the way to lunch, someone pinched her arm.

"Hey! I can't believe it. You and Nathan! I'm so happy for you!" While normally calm, Beth was nearly squealing.

Daphne's smile back was nervous, but she was relieved that there was at least one positive reaction to the news. "Thanks. It just happened. Who told you?"

"Taylor. She overheard Vivian talking about it."

This bit of intel twisted her stomach. If Vivian knew, so did Veronica. Though she should care less about what either girl thought, Daphne could only imagine what they were saying. *It doesn't matter.*

"Are you going to prom together?"

The question gave her focus. An echo of her giddy excitement over Nathan's invitation yesterday pushed the worry away. "Yes. I'm going to go look at dresses in town later."

"Do the shops still have them this late?"

"I hope so," Daphne said, worried again. This possibility

hadn't occurred to her. "I guess if they don't, I'll just wear the one I wore last year. Not a big deal."

"That's what I'm doing," Beth said. "Buying a new prom dress *and* a wedding dress in the same year is a bit much."

"Maybe your wedding dress can be your prom dress!"

"*That's* an idea. But it's being altered right now, so I couldn't anyway."

They entered the lunchroom and separated. As she joined the hot lunch line, Daphne considered where she was supposed to sit. Would Nathan join her, or was he expecting her to head to *his* table? Neither choice sounded appealing. She didn't want to hear Jessica's opinion about their relationship, good or bad, or try to have a conversation in front of Nathan's friends.

As if summoned by her thoughts, Nathan appeared as abruptly as a shade. "Daphne. Sorry, this is last minute, but would you want to sign out for lunch?"

"Oh—sure. Anything wrong?" she asked, anxious that he'd caught wind of whatever Vivian had been spreading.

"No. I just realized that I would rather it be the two of us."

Daphne's mind cleared, leaving with it shame that even the mere mention of Vivian or Veronica was enough to get under her skin. It would take more than a few blissful days of a relationship with Nathan to banish the ghosts of her old fears. "I'll need to grab my jacket first," she said.

They stopped at her locker and then doubled back to sign out at the entrance desk. Ten minutes later, she was glad for his quick thinking after biting into a bean burrito that was far superior to school enchiladas.

Her phone sounded with excited messages from Jessica—Beth had told her. Daphne smiled, relieved that Jessica wasn't angry at Nathan for moving on to a new relationship almost as quickly as Veronica. *It just kind of happened*, she responded.

Too soon, the clock hurried them back to the school parking

lot. She was dreading the next period, when she would be close to her least-favorite people.

As Daphne switched out her books for the next few periods, Nathan said, "You heard history was canceled, right?"

She weighed this news, history materials in hand. "No, I didn't hear that."

"Yeah. My class was canceled this morning. It's canceled tomorrow too."

"Do you know why?"

Nathan shrugged. "He's probably ill or something."

If Mr. Burnes were ill, that wouldn't be any cause for alarm. But if he was calling in sick to extend the weekend for a different reason, one that involved Ashley and their work on the Veil...

Erasing her frown, Daphne shut her locker. Nathan kissed her goodbye again, shooting another electric bolt through her, but this time she was more prepared for it.

Instead of heading in their usual direction, she turned down the stairs that led to the Study Hall auditorium underneath the library. On the bright side, the new arrangement would make it easier to keep a healthy distance from Veronica and Vivian.

Should Mr. Burnes's absence worry her? He'd never missed a day all year, but could simply be ill. *Or something's wrong with Ashley,* came the other worrying thought. The name was like a bucket of ice water that woke her up from the weekend's dream to a normal existence of demons and an ever-expanding doorway to Hell.

No glimpse of Ashley had come to her since spring break. The lack of visions, coupled with the quietness of the Veil, had lulled her into a false sense of security. Ashley gave blood three weeks ago, and yet nothing had happened to the Veil. This had to mean her work was incomplete.

Was the toll of the task catching up to her? Daphne shuddered, remembering Ashley's paleness in the last vision. Her frailty. How often was she being pressured into giving blood? Perhaps Mr. Burnes had an emergency medical situation on his hands.

Daphne signed in for the canceled class and took a seat far from Veronica and Vivian. If only she could force a vision to glimpse how Ashley was faring. But the visions were random and uncontrollable, as far as she knew. At best, she could share news of the canceled class with Claire and get her opinion.

She opened her French workbook, turning her thoughts more pleasantly to prom and what a new dress might look like.

30

———

ESCAPE

Daphne parked in front of Claire's shop downtown but didn't enter. Instead, she walked back up the street to the dress shop.

She paused to let a misting woman in a buttoned-up black dress stroll by, and then entered. A crystal chandelier dangled above, its light bouncing off the gleaming wooden floor and the racks stuffed with glittering formal wear.

The shop girl came over to assist. "How can I help you?"

"I'm looking for prom dresses," Daphne said, worried the girl would tell her there weren't many left.

"Oh, sure! They're all back here."

Daphne followed and was relieved to see there was plenty of inventory to choose from. Left to browse, she lifted the price tag of a sequined gold dress and winced. Was it worth spending that much? She texted her mom for advice.

After a few minutes of browsing, she mentally noted a few dresses to try on later and then left for Madam Moon. The entry bell jingled as she entered the shop.

"Hello?" she called.

There was a shuffling sound, and Claire poked through the curtain to call her back to the reading room. "How are you, Daphne?" she asked, pulling aside the strings of red beads over the doorway.

It was a valid question. The last time they'd met in that room, Daphne had broken down. It had also been over a week since they'd battled the dyszoons in the woods, and they needed to catch up.

"I'm good," Daphne answered, realizing it was sincere. "I was just looking at prom dresses next door."

"Is that coming up soon?"

"This Saturday. But I only knew I was going yesterday."

"Oh? Someone ask you?" Claire said with interest as she sat down in her usual chair. She seemed to be in a cheerful mood. The break from battling dyszoons had done both of them good.

"Yes." Daphne blushed. "You kind of know him. He's the one Heather wanted me to help last fall. We've been friends for a while, and so, yeah."

"I hope you have a wonderful time. And don't worry about the Veil. I will watch it."

"Thanks. I figured you would, but thanks," she said, relieved. The supernatural hurdle to her prom plans was now sorted out with little difficulty.

Claire took out her phone and tapped at it with a glossy green nail studded with a tiny diamond, which matched her emerald cardigan. "I have some good news to share," she said, and slid the phone across the sparkling tablecloth. "Meet my new granddaughter, Jade Iris Moon."

The screen showed a small baby in a hospital crib fast asleep, delicate, and pink. "Wow!" Daphne said, stunned. "Congratulations! She's your first grandkid, right?"

"Yes." Claire took the phone and smiled at her granddaughter with a happiness Daphne had never witnessed from her before. "My son called this morning. She's two weeks premature, but both mom and daughter are doing well. Here's a picture of them both, and then him holding her..."

Daphne realized this was the first time she'd seen Claire's family. Often in her mind, Claire seemed to only exist in Long Haven, but the photos broke that bubble. There was life, even joy, beyond their conflict with the Veil.

The last time she'd sat at that table, she couldn't have expected how much more hopeful things would seem in a few short weeks. She had a date for prom, Claire was a grandmother, and there might be a wrench in the demon's plans.

"Are you going to visit them?" she asked when they'd finished with the photos.

"That's what I wanted to run by you, Daphne. Obviously, I'd very much like to meet my granddaughter, but I'm also reluctant to leave you to deal with the Veil alone."

"I can handle the dyszoons, even if it's a bigger group," Daphne said at once, infected by an optimism that had entirely to do with the past weekend. "I mean, you didn't go see your family for Christmas because of the Veil. And I owe you for covering me for the show."

"Not at all. I ended up needing your help."

"You would have covered me during the week if a dyszoon had come out during rehearsal," Daphne pointed out. "And the Veil's been quiet."

"The more reason to think it won't be soon."

"Like I said, though, I can handle it," Daphne said, eager to not allow their problems to deflate Claire's happiness over the birth of her grandchild.

"It's not that I doubt you, Daphne. I've always had faith in you," Claire said. "My hesitation is if something unforeseen were to happen, since I would never want you to carry that burden alone."

"It would only be a few days. But I think the Veil will stay quiet for a while. Mr. Burnes's classes were canceled both today and tomorrow."

Claire's eyebrows rose in surprise. "They were? Is he ill?"

"I don't know. They don't normally give a reason. But if he was planning to be absent, he'd have a substitute, so I don't think he's skipping work to help expand the Veil," Daphne reasoned. "So either he's ill, or Ashley is and he has to take care of her."

Far from agreeing that this was good news, Claire's lips pursed in concern. "I would hate to assume that and leave you here by yourself, Daphne. He could be absent because they needed a few more days to get things in order."

"But if that were the case, and he was planning it, I think he would have gotten a sub," Daphne pointed out. Under normal circumstances, she'd be agreeing with Claire that the worst-case scenario was the most likely outcome, but her good mood had cast everything in an optimistic light.

"Perhaps, but I wouldn't want to take any chances," Claire said, fingering her jade necklace. "Until we know what's happening with your teacher, I will remain here."

Daphne felt disappointed but understood the caution. She could only imagine how much Claire desired to be holding her grandchild by morning. It was unfair that the threat of the lesser demon and dyszoons infected everything.

"I wish I could have a vision of Ashley and check for sure," she said. While the visions were unpleasant and intrusive, at least they would know what was happening.

"Have you had any other visions while awake?"

"No, not since I was last here."

"Good," Claire said firmly. "I hope that ability doesn't bother you anymore, despite its uses."

"Visions I could do without, but I want to keep sensing dyszoons ahead of time. Maybe I'll also have some warning if they're doing something with the Veil," Daphne said.

"Perhaps."

Daphne's phone dinged, and she read the text. "My mom's going to meet me next door after she's done with work," she said in surprise. Was a new dress a realistic dream? Her good mood, dampened somewhat by her sympathy for Claire, returned with a glow.

"Have fun. This was all I had for you. I wanted to show off my granddaughter, and check that you're doing all right," Claire said, standing. Although she was likely disappointed, her smile came readily.

"Congrats again on Jade," Daphne said, also standing. "I like the name."

"Thank you. I do wish my husband had lived to see her. He would have loved that she was a girl," Claire said, eyes softening with fondness. "Iris was his mother's name."

Daphne left, promising to keep Claire informed of her prom plans, which were yet to be decided fully. Her excitement grew with each step toward the dress shop, and she couldn't shake the confidence that everything would work out.

An important part of her weekend was settled the next day.

"I've got the prom invitations," Nathan told her, handing over two cards. Each showed a romantically foggy forest with a swirl of shimmering gold around the text.

"*You're invited to an enchanted evening*," Daphne read. "I like it."

"Seems cool," he answered, stowing the invitations away in

the sun visor of his car, where they were eating their sack lunches. "I didn't actually go to prom last year."

"You're not really into dances, are you?" she noted. "You missed prom, homecoming..."

"How'd you know I didn't go to homecoming?"

Daphne froze, realizing her mistake. Heather had mentioned it the first time they spoke as a sign Nathan wasn't okay. *He skipped homecoming. His last homecoming.*

"I don't know. I just knew it, somehow," she lied, and changed the subject. "By the way, I got my dress yesterday. It's light blue."

Nathan nodded, chewing. He seemed to have accepted her explanation. She was tempted to show him a picture of the dress but wanted her appearance to be a surprise on Saturday. Her mom agreed at the dress shop that the dress was too perfect to pass over and not only purchased it, but added in a hair accessory as well.

Caught up in the excitement, her mom had also taken the initiative to contact hair salons for any available appointments that Saturday. When Daphne worried about the expense, her mom waved her off, saying that she had extra cash stowed away for special occasions.

All too soon, she and Nathan were at her locker again. After months of making the most of their short walk to history class, the longer stretches of uninterrupted free time with him felt like a feast after famine. Since her next period was canceled, Nathan kissed her goodbye and then turned the corner. Daphne smiled in his direction and headed to Study Hall to check in.

The fluorescent lights dimmed as the smell of rotten food filled her nose. Daphne realized what was about to happen in time to collapse into the empty bathroom on her left. She stumbled into a stall and turned the lock.

The bathroom tiles vanished. She was lying on a dirty wooden floor littered with garbage and crumpled socks. A figure in a black sweatshirt was hunched on the bed, her back to the rest of the dimly lit room. The window panes were black.

"I got you more vitamins," Mr. Burnes said, tossing a bottle on the bed. Ashley didn't react. Despite knowing she was invisible to him, Daphne fought an instinct to hide.

"I see you haven't used the garbage bags I brought."

Again, Ashley was silent. Mr. Burnes sighed, kicking aside a pile of empty wrappers as if to prove his point.

"Sit up. We've got work to do."

The hunched figure stirred. "No," a faint voice answered.

"The sooner we do it, the sooner all this is over. Don't you want that?" He dropped the paper bag of supplies on the floor and moved toward the bed. Feeling braver, Daphne stood and followed him.

"Ashley." Mr. Burnes laid a hand on her shoulder.

The figure sprang to life so quickly that Daphne at first didn't understand why he reeled from the bed, a hand pressed to his temple. He stepped on a soup can and toppled to the ground with a heavy grunt of pain.

Instinctively, Daphne walked forward to help but stopped as Ashley flew out of bed and launched at him. Instead of attacking him, she reached into the pocket of his jeans and pulled out keys. Shoes were already on her feet.

"*No*," she yelled, her eyes wide and crazed. Daphne got out of the way as she ran for the door and wrenched it open.

"Wait..." Mr. Burnes groaned, removing his hand. Blood was running down his temple, and a sharp rock lay abandoned at his feet.

Daphne followed her through the open front door. His truck headlights cut into the deep night.

"Wait!" came a cry from within the cabin. Mr. Burnes got unsteadily to his feet. "Wait!"

The truck reversed with speed. He stumbled to the door-frame. "*Stop! You don't know what it'll do to us!*" he screamed.

But Ashley either didn't hear or was too desperate to care. The truck fled down the gravel pathway. She was gone.

31

THE WARNING

Fog was lifting from her mind. Daphne came to the present, her head resting at an uncomfortable angle against the corner of the stall. The air was cool on her damp face.

She looked down. A pair of legs was visible in the gap and she groaned, hoping fervently that the girl hadn't heard her shouting or noticed her fade.

"I'm all right," Daphne mumbled, rising on unsteady legs, feeling much like she had after touching the Veil.

She unlocked the door and yelped. Heather, reappearing for the first time since before Nathan's breakup, stared at her with wide hazel eyes. Mist rose from her thick hair.

"Can you step aside a second?" Daphne asked, suppressing a groan. After what she'd just witnessed, Heather was low on her priorities list.

Heather moved away. Daphne went to the sink to wash her hands on the assumption that the bathroom floor was an unclean spot to touch. At the moment, she cared little whether she'd been in the stall for five or fifty minutes.

"I'm going to prom with your brother," Daphne said,

splashing cold water on her face. "If that's enough for you to move on, I don't know."

She glanced at the mirror, forgetting as always that it couldn't reflect shades, and turned. Heather stared at her in silence. Why had she followed Daphne if not to talk about Nathan? Had she been drawn by the vision in the uncanny way that spirits could sense evil at work?

Daphne dried her face. Compared to her dreams, it was ironically most difficult to feel awake after her waking visions.

It was clear why Mr. Burnes hadn't shown up for work, if she assumed the vision had taken place over the weekend. The nasty gash Ashley left on his forehead might even need stitches. Or it looked worse than it was, and his priority was to locate her without having to alert the police that a known runaway had stolen his vehicle.

Even without an injury, Mr. Burnes would be in a tricky situation. He needed to find a ride out of the forest. If the cabin was located in a remote place without cell reception, that might mean a long walk with an injured head. And that was assuming his phone was in his pocket and he hadn't left it in the truck.

His terrified scream disturbed her. It was a loss of control, similar to when he'd kicked the cans over in rage during her first vision of Ashley. It was as if he expected the demon to rise from the earth and swallow him and the cabin whole. Was his panic about the demon's wrath over Ashley's escape attempt warranted? What the demon could do to them from afar, Daphne didn't want to consider.

And Ashley? She had finally done what Daphne willed all along. With adequate transport, she could find her way to the nearest police station or hospital. But if she had done so, surely the news would have spread. It was possible Mr. Burnes had already located her, perhaps with the demon's help, and was busy forcing her back in line with its goals.

But if Ashley was still on the run, that meant the demon wasn't about to rise anytime soon. The worst the Veil could throw at her that week was a few dyszoons.

The hour bell rang. Daphne checked the time—only a few minutes had passed. She could risk slipping into Study Hall late, but first, she needed to update Claire.

Claire answered her call on the first ring. "Daphne, are they coming?" she asked right away.

Still groggy and thinking how best to summarize the vision, Daphne was slow to understand. "Dyszoons? No, I didn't sense anything. I just wanted to tell you I had a vision of Ashley."

Daphne recapped what she'd seen. With a last look at Heather, who remained silent, she left the bathroom.

"So, long story short, I haven't heard anything about Ashley, so he must not have found her yet. And if she's run away, we have some time." Her voice dropped as she descended the stairs to Study Hall with trembling legs. "And even if he does find her, she's not very willing to cooperate. You could go see your granddaughter this week."

There was a long pause on the other end.

"I'm still not sure, Daphne," Claire finally said. "I don't like this, regardless of it seeming like good news. I don't like leaving you alone with the Veil. If more dyszoons—"

"I'll be able to handle them, I promise. I know when they're coming. And you'll be back before prom anyway," Daphne said, almost whispering as she approached the open door to Study Hall. "Leave Wednesday and come back Friday or Saturday morning."

There was another long pause.

"Let me think about it, and I'll text you what I decide."

"Okay. I just...after this year, I feel like you deserve a break too," Daphne said. "This could be the only one we get before it all starts up again."

"Yes, that could very well be true."

They said goodbye, and Daphne joined the line of students from history class who were signing in yet at the front of Study Hall. No one raised an alarm at her tardiness.

Daphne collapsed into a chair, wishing she could see where Ashley was now. The escape was good news, but some of Claire's unease was infecting her. Even so, she wanted the visit to work.

She checked her phone under the table and smiled at the text, her unease ebbing away.

I will go.

Jessica sat across from her at the table, tapping a pen as the lunchroom materialized. A handful of early arrivals were biding time until the first bell as snow fell softly beyond the front doors.

The pen stopped. "No, I'm not going to."

"What's the worst that would happen?" Daphne heard herself say.

Jessica hugged herself and shivered. "What if he finds out?"

"Does he know your handwriting?"

"No."

"Then he won't."

Jessica bit her lip, uncertain, but the decision was building up in her face. She'd regret the missed chance, Daphne knew.

"Okay. I'll do it. I am *going* to do it!" she declared, standing.

Daphne followed Jessica's determined march up the wide carpeted steps by the theater. A senior girl sat behind a table decorated with a glittering pink banner and grinned at them.

"I'd like to buy"—Jessica counted out a few dollar bills and threw them down—"a Valentine's cookie."

"Awesome, here's the form," the dark-haired girl said, filing away the money that would benefit the Student Council.

Jessica wrote down Zeke's name as the recipient, taking pains to write the letters without any of her usual flourishes. In a few days, an anonymous heart-shaped cookie would be delivered to her crush for Valentine's Day.

"Did you want to send one?"

Daphne, busy watching Jessica, realized the girl was talking to her. The hazel eyes looked familiar. "Oh—no," she said, face heating. It was true. She was between crushes at the moment, or at least ones strong enough to send a cookie to. In turn, she had no reason to believe her own cookie-less streak wouldn't continue for the third year running.

"All right. I did it," Jessica said, folding up the piece of paper twice and handing it over.

"See, that wasn't so bad."

"Thanks, guys," the girl said. They turned to go, but something yanked Daphne's arm back. Jessica kept walking, chatting to empty air.

Daphne glanced at her hand, and then up at the girl's serious face. The hazel eyes were so familiar.

"Heather," she said.

Heather's thick hair reached her shoulders, not yet cut short, as it would be that summer. No mist rose from her form. She was alive and fully herself, something she could tragically never be as a shade. The lunchroom began to collapse.

"Daphne. Don't give in, no matter what it says." Heather's hazel eyes, so like her brother's, were urgent.

"I know," Daphne answered. In truth, she didn't know.

"Don't give in!" Heather's grip remained clasped around her wrist. Her plea echoed around the collapsing scene. *Don't give in! Don't give in! Don't give—*

The floor vanished.

. . .

Daphne startled awake and squeezed fistfuls of the bedding to stop her fall.

Satisfied that the bed was indeed solid and unmoving, she sighed and glanced at the alarm clock. It was almost half past three, an unfortunate waking time on the day of prom. Daphne rubbed her eyes in the dark, the finer details of the dream already vanishing into smoke as her surroundings had done.

But was it only a dream? During junior year, Jessica *had* anonymously mailed a cookie, which she confessed to Zeke after they became a couple in January. He had laughed.

However, the seller of that cookie was hazy in her memory. The dream had been so vivid, it was hard to believe Heather hadn't sat at that table. She'd looked so alive, even more so than in the nightmare of her final moments.

Perhaps there was a way to check. Daphne shook off the bed covers and pulled out last year's yearbook, opening it to the group picture of Student Council. Heather wasn't in the photo. She deflated in disappointment, but it was to be expected—she had already searched for Heather in the yearbook months ago.

Two chairs were at the table, one empty. It was possible a friend had been on the Student Council and Heather had informally kept her company, manning the table when needed.

Daphne put the yearbook away and slipped into bed. One thing was certain—Heather hadn't talked to her that way. Her imagination had carried the scene.

Don't give in. Her fear of being twisted to the demon's purpose was given a voice through Heather. But that worry hadn't been forefront on her mind lately, so why the urgency? *No matter what it tells you.* The demon had already failed to recruit her once. It was unthinkable that she would help the demon, especially after witnessing Ashley's decline.

Daphne settled back under the covers, determined to sleep a few more hours. Her hair appointment was later that morning, and Claire's return flight would touch down in a few hours. Everything was set for a smooth prom.

The only dent in her confidence was that Mr. Burnes had remained absent the whole week. By Wednesday, a sub was found to supervise the class and lead a review for the upcoming AP test. Daphne had expected any day to hear of Ashley's rescue and his subsequent arrest for imprisoning a student, but no news was worrisome. What if he had caught up to her?

He hasn't, Daphne reassured herself. His lack of a vehicle was a significant setback in a search. And while Ashley may have fled the cabin, that didn't mean she was eager for the outside world to find her yet. There was no telling how deep the trauma of isolation and her connection to the Veil went. One might escape a cell, but not the prison of the mind.

His unhinged scream rang through her ears. *You don't know what it'll do to us!* Had the demon reached them? And what had it done?

Daphne turned over. Her new dress hung over her bedroom door, and a shock of excitement pushed out the memory. She relaxed. Today of all days, she wouldn't worry about the Veil. Tonight, if no other night, she would be a normal teenager.

32

PROM

"There he is," her mom said, a smile in her voice as they turned into a parking space at a local park. Daphne's stomach flipped.

Nathan stood on a path that led to a gazebo, handsome in a gray tux and light blue tie, a hand in his pocket. Standing by him, her blonde hair lifting in the wind, was his mother.

Daphne squeezed the clutch from Jessica that matched her dress. She would finally meet the woman whose daughter's death she had witnessed a hundred times.

"Nervous?" her mom asked.

"A little," she admitted, fingering the silver starburst necklace Claire had given her for her birthday. She couldn't confide that, in addition to prom nerves, she was uneasy. Only a few hours ago, Claire had called to say that her flight out of Miami was delayed due to a storm, but there was a chance she would still be able to fly out that day.

Until she returned, any dyszoons would be Daphne's responsibility. However, the fact that none had come out of the Veil for two weeks made her optimistic that they would hold off until after prom. Claire's delay was unfortunate, but the excitement of the day was a distraction from worrying.

"Just think, you'll barely remember prom ten years from now," her mom reassured her. "So have fun and don't worry about anything."

"Okay."

She lifted her dress and stepped out of the vehicle. A cloud passed over the sun, signaling the chance of rain later. Her mom followed her along the path, holding Daphne's camera and boutonniere.

Her eyes were on Nathan. He turned, and the nerves in her stomach broke out into an excited dance. To think that he could have been riding in a limo while she strolled the woods at home, trying not to dwell on the fun she was missing and avoiding the pictures that confirmed it.

"Hey," he said. "You look amazing."

Daphne smiled nervously, but she believed him. For once, she felt beautiful. The dress was a glittering light blue with skinny straps, slim along her figure, with tulle fanning out near the bottom. The cut dipped low but was made modest by a strip of tan fabric. A diamond ivy-shaped hair clip accented her curled updo.

"You look good, too," Daphne entered his one-armed embrace while her mom introduced herself to Mrs. Grey. Nathan's free hand held a container with a corsage.

His mom approached her with both arms open. Her face was prematurely lined and framed by a graying bob in a style similar to her late daughter's. "Daphne, it's so good to finally meet you. You look so beautiful. I'll warn you, I'm a hugger."

Daphne accepted the hug, forcing away a sense of unreality as she breathed in the woman's pleasant perfume, but the meeting wasn't as strange as she had feared. Today, the past didn't matter.

"All right, ready for some pictures?" her mom broke in, the large camera held aloft. "I am armed and ready."

"Hey, Mrs. Cole. That's a nice camera," Nathan said.

"It's Daphne's," her mom said, twisting the lens in and out. "She's letting me touch it!"

"I let you touch it," Daphne said defensively.

She chuckled. "So, where do we want to be? The gazebo?"

Daphne linked her arm through Nathan's and ventured up the path, the green lawn swaying in the breeze. The camera clicked behind them.

They stopped in front of the structure. Mrs. Grey pulled out her phone and tapped away as Nathan slipped the pretty corsage of white-and-blue flowers on Daphne's wrist. She presented the boutonniere, shyness overtaking her in front of the active cameras as she tried to concentrate on his lapel, pin in hand.

"I watched a video, so I think it goes like this. Or maybe..." The shutter clicked, and she cursed herself for letting her mom use the camera.

"You're doing it right," Nathan reassured her. "I had to do one when I stood up in my cousin's wedding."

He helped her finish sticking the pin. When the lapel lay flat, the small bouquet rested securely in place. "Perfect," he said, looking at her, and Daphne relaxed. The shutter clicked.

"You two stand on that middle step there," Mrs. Grey said. "It'll be so pretty."

"Can you use my camera, too?" Nathan asked her, and then explained to Daphne, "I brought my thirty-five millimeter. I want to develop it later."

"That's so cool," she said, and hoped he would ask her to help him. They posed formally on the steps and then replicated the pose in the middle of the gazebo.

"We should do a fun one!" her mom called.

"You're right," Nathan said. Before Daphne could react, he dipped her backward. She shrieked in surprise but recovered, laughing, for the pictures. His hand pressed into her back, steady and reassuring.

They moved around the park, the moms growing more animated in their suggestions for poses and spots and insisting that she and Nathan kiss for a few. Although she was uncomfortable doing so before an audience, the short kisses were chaste compared to their first. Daphne blushed all the same.

Her smiles were starting to come naturally. Nathan, for his part, was good at making her laugh, cracking jokes as her mom snapped pictures. Daphne borrowed her camera to get Nathan with his mother, whose smile was radiant, and then handed it to him so he could return the favor.

Daphne posed next to her mom. Grief pierced her heart as the shutter clicked, and she impatiently shoved it aside. If not for tragedy, her dad might have stood on her other side. No doubt he would have given Nathan a few rules for his conduct throughout prom and especially after. She also didn't doubt that they would have refrained from kissing for photos.

After internal back-and-forth, she had removed the owl bracelet at home, since it wasn't formal enough for the dress. Now, Daphne wished it was on her wrist.

"I should borrow your camera more often, Daphne. This is fun!" her mom remarked after everyone agreed they'd taken more than enough photos.

"Dinner, then?" Nathan said to Daphne, his arm around her waist from their final pose. She nodded, nerves returning.

"Well, it was wonderful meeting you, dear," Mrs. Grey said. Daphne accepted another hug. "Have fun, you two." When she hugged her son next, her lined face was tight with the effort of holding back the tears pooling in her eyes.

"Thanks, Mom," Nathan said, rubbing her back. "It's okay."

"Yes, yes, I know," Mrs. Grey said, a few tears escaping as she stepped away. She swiped them and laughed. "Don't mind me."

"Have fun and be safe!" Daphne's mom said after a hug. "I'm going to go home and see if I got any good pictures."

"I'm sure they're great. Thanks for doing this, Mrs. Cole," Nathan said.

Her mom waved a hand. "Oh, I loved it. Have a good night, Daphne." With final waves, the two mothers returned to the parking lot.

"Will your mom be okay?" Daphne asked quietly.

"Yeah. She cries pretty easily," he answered. "Always has."

The two cars left the parking lot. Nathan held out a hand, and she took it. He squeezed.

"Ready?"

"Ready."

The next few hours passed in short bursts like the flash of a camera, and Daphne could see why one day she'd forget prom.

In one moment they were in a booth, conspicuous in formal wear as they waited for their food to arrive. In the next, Nathan was signing a credit card slip and calculating the tip in his head.

Daphne checked her phone. Claire had messaged that her flight was delayed yet again. As a helpful distraction from dwelling on this, her mom had already sent a few photos from the gazebo.

"I'm sending you what my mom took of us," she said.

"These are great," Nathan said, looking them over. "Mind if I post a few?"

"Go ahead," Daphne said, pleased. It felt like a formal

declaration that they were steadily becoming an official couple, not to mention acting as a jab at Veronica and Dom. She wondered what they were up to, but also found that she didn't particularly care.

Prom didn't start for another two hours, and neither wanted to arrive on time. Instead, they browsed through a sports store, entirely out of place among racks of leggings and exercise equipment. In one aisle, they tossed a kickball back and forth before fleeing the scene when it escaped control. Other prom-goers were likewise killing time at the nearby department store, drawing wary glances from regular shoppers.

On impulse, they turned into a small park with a man-made pond and sat down on a bench along the water. The sun lowered toward sunset, casting the park in a golden glow. Daphne rearranged her dress, the fabric sparkling, and sighed. If only she could stay here, by Nathan, forever beautiful in a dress she'd likely never wear again.

"Daphne."

She turned, and Nathan captured her small smile on his camera. He lowered his eye from the viewfinder. "I was hoping to get that moment. I'm looking forward to developing these."

"Hand it over. I'll take one of you." Daphne stepped away, focusing the shot as he'd taught her, and then rejoined him on the bench to stare at the water, head on his shoulder. It was blissful, and at the same time melancholy, to sit together quietly at ease in a moment that felt all too brief, and yet infinite.

An hour later, as the sun dipped below the horizon, they left for school. Her arm looped through Nathan's, Daphne checked in at the front table and then followed other well-dressed classmates down the hallway toward the lunchroom, the usual venue for dances.

Strands of lights and tree cutouts decorated the walls. They were half an hour late, but the colorfully lit floor was far from full, though several large groups were arriving behind them.

"Hey, Daphne! You look beautiful! I love your dress," Jessica said, gleefully coming over and taking both of her hands. She wore a silver dress, its cut pushing the dress code despite the alterations to the slit at the side. Nevertheless, she looked very pretty, her usual sleek ponytail now crafted into a wavy mass. Zeke was dressed in a patterned suit in a vivid shade of blue.

"Zeke, take a picture of us." Jessica handed over her phone and beamed. "Are you going to coronation? We should sit by each other."

"Sure," Daphne said, masking her surprise. It felt like a year ago when she'd considered them to be best friends. That bond could never be fully repaired, but she had to admit again that her social life had completely pivoted from the loneliness of just a few weeks ago.

A line formed outside the theater for the show. Daphne waited with Jessica while their dates chatted behind them. She retook Nathan's arm as the doors opened and students filed into seats to watch the prom court get elected.

While she didn't care about who was on court, Daphne was grateful for the opportunity to not put weight on her heels for a while. She checked her phone for a text from Claire, disregarding more pictures from her mom.

Flights are getting canceled. Exploring options.

"You okay?" Nathan asked, perhaps noticing she was staring at the phone without unlocking it.

Daphne smiled and stowed it away. "Yeah. Catching up."

Only half of her mind was on the stage, which she idly noticed was absent of Michael. If the storm was preventing flights out of Miami, the soonest Claire could realistically get back home was the following day.

But did it matter? When the coronation ceremony ended, the dance was already half over. Since dyszoons were more likely to come through in the early morning, the likelihood of an attack was growing slimmer by the hour.

When the ceremony concluded, they emerged onto a much fuller dance floor. Daphne let Nathan pull her deeper into the crowd. A teammate lightly punched his arm as he passed.

He stopped. Veronica stood nearby, laughing with Dom, her blonde hair in polished waves over a slim green dress. His mouth hardened, and he led her in a different direction.

A hand grabbed her arm. "I love your dress! It goes with your eyes!" Beth shouted over the noise. Her own was a light shade of green that complemented her short red hair. Nearby were Taylor and Maria with their dates, along with Ethan, who was chatting with a friend.

"I like yours too!" Daphne shouted as the DJ turned up the music volume and the dancing began.

For half an hour, she forgot her worries about Claire's flight and dyszoons. *This* was what she liked about dances, Daphne realized. To be swept away with the music, to not think about anything but moving her feet, which she only vaguely registered were hurting.

Their group swelled as Nathan's teammates found him. Nearby, a dance ring formed, clapping to the beat. Chad slid into the middle, energetically kicking and spinning. Daphne gave him a high-five as he exited.

Finally, at the end of another song, Nathan asked if she wanted a break.

"Yes," she said, bending over to rub her heel but realizing that the length of the dress made it impossible. They moved through the crowd to the cooler air at the edge.

Jessica was removing her heels. "My feet *hurt* already," she complained, rubbing them.

"Same. I'm protesting my shoes." With some difficulty, Daphne unbuckled her heels and tossed the pair into a corner.

The music slowed, and she turned toward Nathan. For the first time, she wouldn't have to wait awkwardly on the side of the dance floor, watching couples sway. His hand was already taking hers.

Daphne followed him through the gaps in the crowd until they were in the center underneath the disco ball. His hands gripped her waist. Copying nearby girls, she wrapped her arms around his neck, keeping a pace apart. She'd never danced a slow song before, but swaying was easy enough.

It was easier, being so close, to look at something else. Beth was swaying serenely with Ethan, her engagement ring catching the light as it rested on his neck. Ethan nodded, and Daphne smiled back. Next month, they would be more than just a high school couple.

She met Nathan's eyes, highly aware of their closeness. In a flash, she remembered what it was like to run a hand through his wavy hair in the darkroom.

"Thanks for coming to prom with me," he said with a grin, breaking the tension.

"No problem." It was impossible not to grin back.

"You look really great, by the way. I mean it."

"Thanks." Her smile grew wider, and without a word, they closed the gap between them. Over his shoulder, her eyes scanned the dance floor. Normally she hated how excruciatingly long slow songs were, but she appreciated it now.

A gap opened in the crowd. Veronica was energetically swaying with Dom, mouthing the words to the song. A new observer might assume they'd been dating for months.

Daphne closed her eyes. It seemed absurd that she'd once cared about what Veronica said or thought about her. But the drama of the last few weeks was slipping into the background.

There was a line that she and Nathan had crossed together, and behind it was everything that no longer mattered.

With any luck, they would move forward into a future that was far more hopeful than anything she could have imagined just a short time ago, when it seemed clear she had no future at all.

True, there was plenty of uncertainty ahead. At a football game last fall, Daphne had once sensed how she was both a part of and apart from time. Since the night on the bridge had changed everything, she had braced for what was to come to the extent that it was difficult to claim a place in the present.

But for now, for this moment, she was content. She was Daphne Cole, in the embrace of someone who made her feel beautiful, and that was enough.

"I was wondering..." Nathan said near her ear.

Daphne pulled back to look at his face. "Yeah?"

They stopped swaying. It seemed he was having a hard time looking at her.

"I don't want to assume anything, and I know all of this just happened, but I want you to know..." His eyes shifted to hers so suddenly that her breath caught. "I'd rather be here with you than anybody else. I just don't want you to think you're a—a rebound, or that I'm getting back at anyone—"

"I never thought you were," Daphne said in surprise, glad her voice worked. "I never thought you were doing that."

His grin returned in a startling flash, and he was clearly relieved. "Okay. Good. Cool. Just wanted to make sure."

"I'd rather be here with you too." Though he had gone first, saying it felt like stepping out into a freefall. More of her heart was exposed, free to be pierced by a simple *This has been fun, but...*

"Yeah? Cool. And I want you to know...this isn't just a prom thing for me. I want this to continue," he said. His words seemed carefully chosen, as if one misplaced could scatter whatever they were building in a thousand directions, like the lights against the ball above.

"I know." Daphne adjusted her arms, and they swayed again. If she was going to fall, it might as well be a clear break. "I've wanted to be with you for a long time."

She focused on the colored patches of light on the floor. It was embarrassing to admit such a thing. That he'd been on her thoughts for far longer than she'd been on his.

"I wish it had happened differently," he said. "The last week has been...A lot of things have cleared up for me. I don't know if it's graduation, or what. Honestly, I think it's you."

Daphne met his gaze again. Nathan didn't seem to find her embarrassing. "Really?" she said, her voice small.

"Yeah. I've felt better than I have in a really long time." He laughed in release.

In facing their problems, they had much in common. They were two souls touched by tragedy, grasping on to distraction. For Nathan, it had been the first relationship that came easily. For her, she had dived, almost literally, into the black abyss of the Veil.

"I've been feeling the same way," Daphne said. "This year has been...I'm glad it's almost over, put it that way. But I'm more hopeful about things now."

"Me too."

They swayed for a time without speaking. The floor was cold beneath her bare feet, but still a vast improvement from the heels.

"With that said..." Nathan broke the silence. "Would you like to be official?"

"Yeah?" Daphne asked, confirming the words she'd wanted to hear were real. "I mean, yes. Of course."

"Okay," he laughed, clearly relieved again. "Phew."

Nathan leaned forward, and everyone else vanished. Warmth traveled to her cold feet. If there was a moment she could be stuck in forever, this was it. The slow song came to an end.

Another pop song blazed through the speakers. Wordlessly, Nathan led her back to the spot claimed by their group before the dance floor became packed. Dancing no longer held much appeal, though there was over an hour left until midnight.

Daphne's hand swung in Nathan's. She would rather go somewhere with just the two of them.

A teammate caught his attention, and she excused herself to the bathroom. Catching up on her messages, Daphne read Claire's text that she was back at her son's place and would fly out first thing in the morning. However, the delay didn't matter anymore. Prom was almost over, and no dyszoons had interrupted the evening.

Retrieving her heels, Daphne maneuvered around an energetic group and found Nathan on the edge of the crowd, his tuxedo coat slung over a shoulder. *My boyfriend*, she thought with an electric jolt. That would take some getting used to, but it felt right.

"Hey," she said, taking his hand. "I was thinking—I'm kind of done with dancing. Would you want to go out somewhere that's still open?"

"I'd be game," he said. With a dramatic flourish, he slipped his coat back on. "Let's roll."

She said goodbye to Jessica as they passed and scanned the crowd for Beth, who was likely somewhere on the dance floor with Ethan. They could catch up on Monday.

They left the throbbing room behind for the cool night air, which rumbled with distant rain. Perhaps she should want to stay until the end of her last school dance, but she preferred Nathan's company without distraction.

Time came again in bursts. They were kissing outside his car and then taking a seat at a late-night grill. In the next moment, they were polishing off the plate of nachos that Daphne was being careful not to get on her dress as they held hands on the table.

The time was well after midnight, and though she wished to extend her time with Nathan, it was going to be a stretch even for her laid-back mother to accept much later than one in the morning as a curfew.

Nathan seemed to accept, without her bringing it up, that the next destination was home. All too soon, he pulled into her gravel driveway.

"I had a great time," Daphne told him. "Thanks for dropping me off."

"No problem. I did too. Talk in the morning?"

"You mean later in the morning?" she said, laughing. "I probably won't be awake."

"Right. Good point."

After a long kiss goodbye, she reluctantly exited the car to the warm, wet air and waved as he drove away.

Daphne entered the house and removed her heels. Her head was full of stars. No matter what happened, she would remember Nathan's words under the shimmering ball forever.

The stairs creaked, and her mom descended wearing pajamas. "You made it home!" she called. "How was it?"

"You're still up?" Daphne yawned. The energy that had sustained her halfway through the night was ebbing away.

"I woke up a bit ago and saw the time, so I decided to wait up. Did you have a good night? How was Nathan?"

"It was great," Daphne said, letting loose another wide yawn. "Can I tell you more later? I think I need to get some sl—"

In one sweeping motion, all the stars in her head were

snuffed out, leaving a black void. The deepest cold pierced the core of every atom, far worse than any dyszoon emerging from the Veil. Beneath her feet, a shrill scream rang out as if the ground itself was cowering in terror.

"No..." Daphne said. She dropped her clutch and pressed both hands against her ears in a desperate attempt to quiet the sound. The screaming grew louder. "Not now...no..."

Daphne was aware on some level that her mom had said her name. Was taking a step toward her. But nothing existed except the cold and the darkness. This was another evil entirely. From the depths of Hell itself.

And it was now unleashed.

33

ARRIVAL

Sound and warm air returned.

Daphne was doubled over, holding her head. The screaming had finally stopped. Or maybe it had been coming from her the whole time.

She straightened. Her mom's face was stricken with shock. One thing was certain—the lesser demon had arrived.

"Daphne?" a tentative voice drifted across her awareness. "What happened?"

"It's here," she whispered, backing into the entryway. Abruptly, Daphne shoved her feet into a pair of shoes and snatched the jacket that contained her car keys. There was no time to change out of her dress. No time to waste. She thrust open the front door.

"Where are you going?"

"I'm sorry, I need to go!" Daphne yelled over her shoulder.

"What?"

"*I need to go!*" She ran down the porch stairs and across the driveway, not bothering to lift her dress from the dirt. Her mom stepped outside.

"No, you need to explain to me—"

"*I can't! I have to stop it!*" Daphne yanked the car door open.

"*Daph—!*" The door shut, cutting off her name. She fumbled with the keys, hands shaking.

The tires skidded over the gravel. Her mom was on the porch steps, eyes wide and shocked, but Daphne couldn't pause to explain her sudden exit. All that mattered was getting to the Veil as quickly as possible and confronting the demon.

She sped down the road in the moonless night, flexing the wiper blades every minute. Her phone rang continuously, likely her mom calling, or perhaps Claire. Would Claire have felt the demon come out from such a distance? Even if the psychic had, she would be too late to help.

Daphne was alone.

Her calm was like a faltering candle flame. The terror of the situation crouched in the dark, ready to snuff it out. Her lack of fear wasn't bravery, but shock. Whatever lay ahead was unknown. She would get out there, and then—

Death, a voice whispered in her ear.

She turned left on Laurel Road and pressed the gas pedal nearly flat. *I'm coming, D*, the demon had promised through the Ouija board, and now it had arrived at last.

No battle insights came to her. The demon in her imagination was a giant shadow, an oversize dyszoon. How would she fight it?

An empty parked car appeared on the side of the road. Daphne frowned and braked hard, parking a short distance ahead. The light rain drenched the windshield as she closed her eyes and felt outward.

There was a faint presence, perhaps several, in the woods. Was it the demon, dyszoons, or both?

Daphne silenced her phone without checking the screen

and then exited the car. Holding up her dress, she marched into the woods with a small flashlight, rain splattering on her face. Her feet ached from the dancing, but if she stopped now, they would fail to move entirely.

For a minute, Daphne made her way through the trees, the presence acting as her compass. Her dress sparkled dully in the harsh, moonless night.

A clearing appeared before her. The presence was a distance away yet, but the flashlight beam lit upon a figure that lay sprawled on the wet leaves.

"Ashley!" Daphne rushed forward and directed the light to her face, at the open eyes that gazed unseeing in her direction.

For a long moment, she failed to comprehend. For the person wasn't Ashley at all—but how could he be here, in the woods? She had just seen him at the dance.

The earth tilted and her knees buckled. Daphne crawled closer to him, shaking uncontrollably, no longer caring about her dress, or the demon. Time was still. The world had reduced its existence to the shadows that surrounded them, and beyond their small circle of light, there was only an endless void.

"No..."

Daphne didn't know how long she knelt beside the body, not daring to touch it in case by doing so his death became a permanent fact. She looked at the face of her friend, unable to reconcile that the marbled mouth, slightly open, had spoken words only hours before. Had smiled at her. He was still wearing a tuxedo.

Her eyes dropped to the white-gold band, which gleamed palely on a finger that could no longer feel it or carry its promise.

"Ethan. *Ethan*," she pleaded. He did not stir.

A chasm split inside Daphne's chest, swallowing her whole. Despite her best efforts, her worst fear was reality. A dyszoon—

for it must have been a dyszoon—had killed someone once more. Tragedy would rip another family apart. All because she had failed.

A picture of Beth's anguish flashed across her eyes. The wedding dress that would stay on its hanger. It had never been so clear how fragile futures were.

"A tragedy, no doubt," a familiar voice said.

Daphne's veins turned to crystal, then shattered. No—it couldn't be him. She whipped the flashlight toward the sound and stood so abruptly that she almost swooned. A man wearing a gray tux stepped from the shadows.

Nathan.

He paused on the other side of Ethan's body, and though her flashlight lit his features, he would have been visible without it.

"You're not him," she said firmly, with a trickle of doubt. They had just said goodbye to each other. It wasn't possible.

Nathan smiled, dimples showing. The eyes pressing on her greedily weren't hazel, but entirely black. Otherwise, every detail was exactly as she'd left him not half an hour ago, down to the boutonniere she'd pinned on his lapel. Only one thing was off—a malevolence radiated from him, similar to the hatred from dyszoons.

Understanding punched her. "You're the demon," Daphne concluded with surprising relief. For a moment, she had thought...

Her mind kicked into high gear, scrambling over what defensive action she might take. Yet the demon didn't seem about to attack.

It tilted its head and appraised her. "Daphne Cole. I've been waiting a long time to meet you."

She flinched. It was jarring to hear Nathan's voice filled with the promise of danger when it normally comforted her.

"You killed Ethan," Daphne accused it, realizing the death would have happened while she sped to the Veil. If she had sensed the dyszoons coming in advance, he wouldn't have died. But arriving with the demon had masked them.

It shifted its gaze from her to the body. Daphne didn't dare do the same, on guard for any sudden movement that would break what felt like a fragile truce. Ethan's rigid face at the edge of her vision ripped at her conscience. *Don't look at him.*

"This was unfortunate," the demon said in a tone that could be mistaken for regret. "How do humans say it? He was at the wrong place at the wrong time? A dyszoon can't resist easy prey."

*In the wrong place...*Claire had said such a thing once about Heather, the first victim of a dyszoon attack. Reckless anger blazed through Daphne. He—it—could have easily commanded the dyszoons to leave Ethan alone.

She could only guess how Ethan came to be in the woods. He must have been traveling home from Beth's house when a dyszoon struck his car. If Ethan thought he hit an animal, he would have parked and searched for it. Then, the dyszoons attacked him.

The nachos she'd shared with the real Nathan were threatening to make a reappearance. It might not have been an instant death. Ethan had suffered.

"Why do you look like him?" Daphne asked.

It smiled faintly with Nathan's lips, which she could still feel on hers. He stepped around Ethan's body. Fear rooted her in place as the demon stopped in front of her, nearly as close as she'd been to Nathan during their slow dance. Every inch of her recoiled.

"I've learned much about you, Daphne Cole," it said softly, reaching a finger toward her. She was immobile. "The connection you forged with our passage isn't like the girl's, but it was enough to understand who you are. Your mind. How you...*tick*." Its finger stopped short of her temple.

The blood drained from Daphne's face. The Veil. She had touched it not once, but twice. It had given her the ability to sense dyszoons in advance, but also exposed who she was to the two demons on the other side.

She felt contaminated. Violated. If the demon were telling the truth, it could exploit any part of her mind. Even her memories weren't safe, for it had taken on Nathan's most recent appearance. The scene in the clearing was a sick reenactment of the dance—her in her damp dress, a demonic Nathan as her partner, and Ethan's motionless body nearby.

It withdrew its hand. "Where's Ashley?" she breathed, holding the flashlight between them as if the light could fend off evil. She stared back at its soulless black eyes. Anywhere but at Ethan.

"In our service," the demon said, smiling at her horror.

Ashley hadn't escaped. Either Mr. Burnes had caught up to her, or else she couldn't remove herself so easily from the greater demon's influence. An escape was futile from the start, and so was Daphne's hope of a setback in its plans.

"And you're here to kill me," she said. It was inevitable. She was the only barrier to the demon's goals, Ashley's efforts.

"No, Daphne Cole," it said, stepping around to her side. "If that was my goal, I would have had our worthless servant do it months ago. No..." It leaned close to her ear, devoid of breath. Daphne suppressed a whimper, shaking from head to foot.

It inspected the side of her head. "This, your mind, is valuable. You could be useful. We've already trained you so well."

"What do you mean?" she murmured. Nothing was blocking Ethan from her sight. *Don't look at him.* She focused on a branch above, a faint silhouette against the night sky.

The demon stepped aside, and she exhaled. "The dyszoons.

It sent so many, and you, Daphne Cole, grew stronger for it. All this time, it's been shaping you for one purpose, and that's to serve it."

Claire had encouraged her that all those battles were strengthening her to better fight the demon. To be told they were training her for its service instead...

She frowned at the demon, now a few paces away, her every sense on high alert. "If you aren't killing me, what are you going to do?"

"I have trod its path so it may rise. I have limited time, but my purpose is twofold." The grandeur in its voice was so unlike Nathan. "Before the night is over, Daphne Cole, you will know how desperate your situation is and that the only salvation lies with it."

The demon's words had the opposite effect, perhaps, as intended. A little feeling returned to Daphne's legs from relief. If it meant to recruit her to its cause, it had already failed. And if it didn't intend to kill her, she was safe.

Even so, her heart shook. She needed to banish it back to Hell somehow, but to assume she could simply strike it the same way as a dyszoon was foolish. If she failed in the attempt, the demon could change its mind and do its worst.

And there were dyszoons in the woods. No one could banish them but her. If they were part of the demon's plan that night, she needed to find them before they harmed anyone.

Like Ethan. A combined blow of grief and guilt nearly toppled her. She would never get to photograph his wedding.

"I'm not joining you," Daphne told it. Her voice sounded braver than she felt.

Nathan's lips tugged upward again. A confident smile. "We've only just begun."

Before she could ask what it meant, the air changed. It was growing warmer, stifling. The trees became charred and brittle, while the night sky melted into a sickly red through their spidery limbs.

A heart-stopping *bang* made the forest shudder. Daphne jumped and looked up. A fireball split into fiery lines that sliced across the sky.

The ground trembled as if a nearby giant had dropped a heavy footfall. Daphne stumbled and fell onto her hands and knees, only to find they were buried in an inch of gray ash. The dropped flashlight had gone out, but an eerie red glow lit the woods, enough for her to see her surroundings.

Startled, Daphne jerked her hands up. Her corsage had withered and shriveled, the beautiful blue flowers now the color of decay.

A second tremor came. Daphne steadied herself and leaned over to pick up the flashlight. She shrieked. A few dozen spiders were scuttling toward her hand, each the size of a fist.

"You'd better get going, Daphne Cole," the demon told her as she hurried to her feet. "There are things in these woods I think you'd rather avoid." The advice sounded like a taunt.

The ground shook. There was no time to consider a plan. The spiders and something huge were both closing in. She gathered up her ruined dress and fled from the clearing, looking once over her shoulder. The demon raised a hand in farewell, and then a tree hid it from sight.

The footfalls grew fainter as Daphne ran, panting in the stale air. She had to get as far away from the steps as possible.

Daphne might have mistaken the place for Hell, except everything was familiar. The red sky. An unknown pursuer. Even the spiders. It was her nightmare, now as real as the broken flashlight she shoved in her pocket.

And there was no waking up.

34

PURSUED

Daphne ran through the woods, spurred on faster by the vibrations under her feet. She'd left all thought behind in the clearing except one—to get far away from her pursuer.

The demon was right. It didn't matter if the footfalls were real or part of the nightmare. Whatever the thing was, she wanted to avoid it.

After a time, Daphne realized that the only steps she heard were her own and paused, pressing the sharp stitch in her side. *Don't panic.* Ethan's pallid face pressed into the darkness of her eyelids. His lifeless eyes. *Don't panic.*

She should be grateful to have survived her encounter with the demon without a blow swung on either side. It had let her go—unless the running was taking place in her head as it watched her. But the stitch felt real.

A deep fatigue infused every limb. There was no place to sit except in the ash, and so she stood, unpleasantly thirsty in the warm air, fingering the starburst necklace. If only Claire were there to give advice.

But—Daphne could call her! Hope rising, she pulled out

her phone and pressed the power button. The screen remained black. She held it down again, with no response.

"Turn on!" She tried repeatedly, hot tears springing down her face. "Work!"

It was no use. The nightmare that broke her flashlight had also drained her phone battery. Daphne put it away and hugged herself, shivering despite the heat.

I'm alone. The thought had never struck her so hard with its terrifying truth. No help was coming. Whatever strength she possessed was all she had to rely on. If she fell, no one was there to lift her up. She was alone.

A *boom* shook the ground as a fireball exploded overhead. Daphne stumbled and laid a hand against the nearest tree trunk to stop her fall.

Its smooth, chalky surface sagged. The dead wood bulged around her left wrist, leaving only a small gap framed by the decayed corsage. Daphne attempted to wrench free and was met with pain.

"What—?"

Panic devoured her. Although her wrist was stuck, she could still flex her buried fingers within the created hollow. Daphne rotated her hand with difficulty, wincing as she maneuvered it into a position that might allow her to squeeze it through the small gap.

Something snapped above. Black branches were curling in on themselves and slithering down the trunk.

Fear electrified her. In a past dream, the branches had bound her to the trunk, and she'd been helpless to move as spiders crawled all over her and heavy footfalls approached.

She tugged urgently at the wood around her wrist. Given enough time, she could extricate her hand, but it didn't move.

A branch snaked toward her shoulder. "*No!*" she yelled,

swatting at it. To her surprise, the branch recoiled, but another was reaching for her. She slapped it away.

The ground tremored. Daphne's stomach dropped. Her pursuer was closing in, and it would find her trapped.

Daphne tore her eyes from the dead woods and slapped more branches. They drew back, writhing like worms. As she rubbed her fingers against her dress to iron out the pain, an idea came to her. If the branches reacted that way when struck, would the trunk?

In desperation, Daphne began smacking the tree with her free hand. "Let me go! *Let me go!*"

More branches were coiling down the trunk. If her experiment failed, they would trap her. Fingers smarting, she hit the trunk harder.

"*Let me—!*"

The wood entrapping her hand vanished. Daphne gaped—her fingers were now pressed against an ordinary tree.

Flecks of rain hit her face. She looked up at the black sky, blinking at the cold drizzle.

In a blink, the dead woods returned, and her hand was stuck once more. Daphne touched her cheek, and her fingers came away dry. Those few seconds might have been a dream—if she wasn't already in the nightmare.

Branches reached for her. Daphne stared at them, both thrown off balance and reoriented.

The nightmare she was in...it wasn't real. She was wandering through the woods, awake but lost in a vision. The real world was there, just unseen.

Regardless, her hand was trapped. The rules of the nightmare still applied, and she didn't doubt those branches would hurt. Swatting a few more, Daphne turned her attention to the trunk. The opening didn't budge.

The ground shivered with more footfalls. She needed a

different approach. Flexing the fingers inside the tree, Daphne pressed her fingernails hard against the wood and scratched it.

The trunk shuddered. To her astonishment, the gap around her wrist widened. She wiggled free and then jumped beyond the reach of the branches just in time.

A tree crashed to the ground somewhere close, cutting short any celebration of her release. The thing that pursued her was closing in.

Massaging her freed hand, Daphne sprinted in the opposite direction of the footfalls.

When the ground was still, she rested, careful not to touch the fallen log nearby. Besides her own labored breathing, no other creature stirred in that dead space. The silence was eerie.

Sweat dripped down her back, but Daphne zippered up her jacket. The earlier glimpse outside the vision showed that the rain had picked up, and a prom dress was poor protection against the chill air.

What were her options? Fleeing wouldn't bring her any ideas of what to do. And as the night stretched on, other terrors no doubt awaited. She didn't look forward to what the demon had in store.

Her situation was bleak. Because of her connection to the Veil, she was trapped in a vision crafted from her nightmares, and lost in the woods on top of it. Daphne shivered, feeling contaminated again.

She wiped the ash on her ruined dress to no effect and fought tears, longing for Nathan's arm around her shoulders. If only she could be stuck in prom instead. Its memory was as distant as the stifled stars above.

The air trembled with another heart-stopping bang.

Daphne watched the fireball streak across the sky, thinking of the demon's words in the clearing. *I have limited time.*

Did that mean it would be forced to return to Hell soon? Could she defeat it simply by outlasting it?

Perhaps the demon was on a leash and would be pulled back to Hell after a set time. Or else the Veil wasn't large enough to let through its full essence, and so it could only sustain itself on Earth for a short while. She could hardly ask the demon, wherever it was, about its limitations.

The demon had said its goal was to convince her to join its superior's cause before the night was over. Maybe the next few hours until dawn were all the time it had. If that were true, and if she could dodge any other dangers until sunrise...

But avoiding danger was impossible. While running, Daphne had sensed the dyszoons that remained in the woods. Tracking them down was her next priority.

Daphne wiped her nose on the wrist without the decayed corsage, growing calmer with purpose and a plan. She could last a few more hours. The demon wouldn't win.

She closed her eyes and felt outward. The presence was far away, and evil. But evil was what she had to find.

A short time later, though it was hard to tell in the nightmare, Daphne sensed the dyszoon nearby.

The tulle of her dress caught on a young tree. She ripped it free, heart stampeding. But the branch didn't spring to life, content with the bit of fabric it had snagged.

Daphne pursed her dry lips, almost overcome by an urge to cry. Her perfect dress was already dirty, and now it was permanently damaged, but it was the least of her worries. She continued forward with caution, the ground vibrating. The presence was unmoving.

She jumped in shock. A woman wearing a gray blazer and

pants, her dark hair in a neat bun, lay slumped against a tree a few yards away.

So it wasn't a dyszoon after all, but a shade. However, the spirit didn't mist—if it was indeed there at all.

"Hello?" she said, approaching cautiously. "Are you okay?"

The woman's face twitched bizarrely, her closed lips moving back and forth. Eyes bugging, she suddenly opened her mouth wide. A hair-raising shriek pierced the air.

Blood drained from Daphne's face. Only one creature made a sound like that.

A dyszoon.

She stepped back, and a dead twig snapped under her retreating foot. The shrieking stopped. The woman snarled and soared forward, arms outstretched and fingers clawed as if eager to close them over a throat.

Daphne screamed and blocked. The woman crumpled against the shield and then flew off, her arms hanging limply as if broken.

Shock immobilized Daphne, and her breaths were short from panic. It was easy to forget that dyszoons had once been human. To see one of the creatures as the person it used to be...

No, it's just a trick. This was another horror of the nightmare. The dyszoon *looked* human, like the demon, but it had lost its humanity. Its appearance was just an illusion.

Branches crashed in the distance. The woman bounced between the trees, piercing the air with shrieks. *Don't panic.* Trees blurred together in an endless sea of decay. *Breathe.* But it was difficult to inhale stale air, to think straight. The temptation to fall into a heap in the ash was overwhelming.

Part of her recognized that the dyszoon's presence was driving her toward despair, an easy task when she was exhausted. But the other part couldn't muster the energy to care.

The dyszoon was returning. Daphne ignored the terror squeezing her heart. *Breathe.* It wouldn't be long now. She settled into a defensive stance. The woman flew at her shield, snarling and clawing at it in a rage, her dark hair wild.

It felt like a real person was attacking her. Daphne pushed out hard in desperation. The dyszoon flew upward, limbs flailing, and then dropped down. She fended it off with growing hopelessness. *It's over. The only way to end this is to let the demon win.*

"No!" she said aloud, but her despair grew. The dyszoon would overcome her defense. Even if the demon wanted to keep her alive, a dyszoon's instinct was to attack. It would kill her as it did Ethan.

The realization slammed into her like a fireball. *It killed Ethan.* This dyszoon was the reason Daphne had failed in her vow to protect others. The reason Beth's future would be shattered by grief.

A streaking flame of vengeance devoured Daphne, burning up despair. It had only one outlet.

She countered the dyszoon's next attack and struck before it could regroup. With each blow, she stepped toward the woman, who flailed and snarled, and then—

The dyszoon burst into a cloud of red, shredded flesh. It was gone.

Daphne pressed a hand against her mouth. *Don't throw up. Don't throw up.* She gagged a few times and whimpered at the unpleasant reflex. *It's okay. It's over.* Yet the explosion of the woman's body burned into her vision just as much as Ethan's dead face.

The break was short-lived. Other dyszoons were closing in, the final two she sensed in the woods. The ground shivered with distant footfalls.

Daphne closed her eyes in case they also appeared

human. A branch shattered, and within seconds they attacked. She blocked both in succession, turning in place. It was a cruel dance held in darkness instead of beneath glittering lights.

Without thinking, she opened her eyes and regretted it immediately. Two men were soaring around in midair to attack, one of them enormous. Every inch of his wide breadth promised great injury.

She steadied herself as another footfall shook the ground. If she didn't move on soon, her pursuer would catch up at last.

Fear sharpened her focus. Daphne struck blind at the first dyszoon that reached her and was surprised to hear its parting scream. *One down. One to go.*

The final dyszoon attacked, undaunted by her blows. A minute passed with no break. She couldn't match its strength. Weak as she was, it would overpower her. No wonder Ethan had died.

"No!" Daphne rasped in an attempted shout. Her fingers went automatically to her dry throat at the pain and met her necklace chain. They lowered to the silver starburst.

The touch anchored her. She was alone, but also not. There were people who cared about her, who existed on the outside. If she could, Claire would have been at her side fighting. And only one dyszoon was left. Just one more.

Daphne yelled and attacked. The dyszoon let out a final shriek. After a few seconds, she braved looking. Its remnants had faded.

A tree fell behind her, and she turned slowly with dread. It was too late to flee.

Her pursuer had arrived.

A man much smaller than the impact of his footfalls suggested was coming toward her with clumsy steps. He stopped, clutching his stomach. A fireball burst overhead, lighting the forest and the features of the man, who looked as though he'd escaped the very depths of Hell.

"Dad," she croaked.

He was straight out of her worst nightmare, the one that had tortured her for years after his death. In the dream, her dad was always burning up and she could only watch, powerless to help him.

This appearance was worse in its realness. He was dirtied by soot and crumbling into ash. A brimmed hat covered burned hair. Small fires sprung up where his feet had touched, devouring any part of the woods that was not already burned.

He coughed, billowing out ash. The fit consumed him. Daphne was rigid, unable to take advantage of his weakness to run.

Finally, he finished coughing and straightened. His blistered face contemplated her.

"Daph-ne," he rasped. "Help me!"

Terror pierced her. She was a small child again, too afraid of nighttime monsters to retrieve the kicked-off bedcovers until the bedroom light turned on and her dad scooped her up with muscled arms. His presence could fend off anything that wanted to harm her.

Now he was the monster.

"Daph-ne." He coughed. "Daphne! Help me!"

Her right foot inched back, cutting a trembling path through the ash.

"Please! Help me! Make it stop!" her dad sobbed, wrenching a leg forward. His cry of pain pierced her heart.

"Stop," she whispered, moving her left foot. She was steadily regaining the use of her muscles, but it wouldn't outpace his shuffle. They were within just a few feet of each other, and his roasted skin was all too real.

"Help me!" His eyeless gaze cut into her. How she had

longed for her dad to see her in her prom dress, but it was torn and dirtied, damaged beyond repair. Like him.

Daphne closed her eyes to block out the monster.

"I'm sorry," she whispered, and then bolted through the trees as if flames were beneath her feet.

"DAPHNE! *DAPHNE!*" Her name was a blistered scream that, if it were a knife, would have rent the sky.

35

CASUALTIES

Daphne stumbled through the woods in a blur, exhausted.

Her dad's screams echoed long after the ground had stopped shaking. *Help me! Help me!* But she couldn't. She never could.

Everywhere was death. She tripped over a root and didn't bother to stop her fall. What was the point?

Daphne lay in the ash and watched, transfixed, as the air exploded with sound and light. A dozen streaks of angry gold cut through the crimson sky. They fell to the ground and faded.

Stale air pushed in and out of her lungs, and she closed her eyes, exhausted.

A cold breeze drifted across her face. She flinched at the tiny drops of water tapping her eyelids. It was raining, a light drizzle that had already drenched her coat and hair. Her eyes opened. If it was raining, that meant—

The sky was black. Daphne sat up stiffly, shivering. Wet leaves had replaced the ash, and her sparkling prom dress was wet and muddy.

It was disorienting, the change. She breathed deeply and

blinked at the sky, which was lighter than her last glimpse long ago. Even if morning was near, her location was unknown. Her car was probably miles away.

The air grew warm, and Daphne braced herself as the nightmare closed in, as real as the scene she had just left. She hugged her legs and rocked. They were heavy from being forced to move for hours through a night that would never end, not until she gave in to the demon.

Her situation was bleak. She was alone, Ethan was dead, and she desperately wanted to talk to her mom, who was probably beside herself with worry...

Daphne stopped rocking. Eyes pressed on her skin. She looked up, and her breath caught.

A large white owl with brown markings was perched in a dead tree, glowing like fresh snow underneath a full moon. Black eyes stared at her, but they were eyes of soul, not death like the demon's.

It was the most beautiful thing she had ever seen.

The owl flapped its wings, prepared to fly. "Wait, don't go —" she rasped, standing as fast as her dress allowed.

With silent grace, it soared to a distant branch. Daphne hurried to follow, her exhaustion and despair forgotten. The owl was the first living creature she had met in the nightmare. It was like stumbling upon a perfect flower blooming in the midst of death and ruin.

As soon as she came near, the bird took off. "No, wait!" Daphne called in dismay, following it to its next perch. Again, it flew away.

"Wait!" she cried, but her foot connected with something hard, and she fell.

The owl was no longer in sight, if it had been real at all. The small hope it had brought was gone. Daphne crawled to the rock she'd tripped over. Frowning, she swept a layer of ash from the flat stone.

Her stomach dropped. It was a gravestone. And it had Ethan's name.

Another was next to it. With a sense of foreboding, Daphne dragged herself to the gravestone and read the name in horror. *Beth*. No—she *couldn't* be dead. She was alive.

But for how long? came the thought. Who knew when the nightmare would end? Maybe the demon was distracting her as it carried out a wave of destruction, and these were the victims.

Tombstones large and small stretched endlessly through the woods in all directions. The number of plots overwhelmed her, so full of death. Daphne visited one after the next. There were Jessica and Zeke. Taylor. Maria. Names of her classmates, teachers, and even friends who had moved long ago. Her mother. Claire.

She crawled to a large gray stone and touched trembling fingers to the name. *Nathan Grey*. Daphne turned and clamped a hand to her mouth, again fighting the urge to vomit. All these people. Everyone she knew. Dead.

And it was all her fault.

As if the grave's contents had escaped, Nathan's voice came from behind. Daphne's exhausted mind worked to remember that it was not, in fact, him.

"So many dead. A tragedy, but a preventable one," the demon said. Its gray suit was spotless, unlike her dirtied dress.

She shook with rage and tears. "*You* killed them."

"No, Daphne Cole," it said softly. "This hasn't happened yet."

She turned back to Nathan's gravestone, blinking rapidly. Of course. None of it was real. Just an imagined cemetery of everyone she'd failed to protect that began, in an irrational way, with her father. His was the only grave she hadn't come across, but perhaps that was because his corpse was currently stumbling through the woods.

The demon walked behind the gravestone. "Tell me. What do you think of these graves?"

Daphne read Nathan's name, etched into stone, as unchangeable as death. "It's what happens if I fail," she answered. The ground trembled.

"No, Daphne Cole. This is what happens if you continue," it said, grazing a hand along the top of the gravestone with Nathan's fingers. She shivered. "What you call failure, I call unnecessary casualties."

It placed a foot on the neighboring gravestone and pushed. The stone toppled before Daphne could read the name. "So much death. Do you really think you can prevent its sting by defeating creatures who can barely last in this world? At least, as they are now...

"You see, the real threat..." The demon approached. "The *real* threat..." Daphne was entranced by its words, its soulless black eyes. She wanted to hear it, and also not to. The demon poked a finger at her forehead, stopping just short of touching it. "That's you."

"No." Her parched throat made the word into a hoarse whisper, weak against its accusation. The demon smiled with Nathan's mouth. She loved that smile. Now, it revolted her.

"But it's true, isn't it?" The demon paced behind the gravestone again. "A dam may block the flow of a river, stopping the natural order of things. But where the river is stronger, the dam will give in eventually. It is inevitable."

Daphne had thought of the same analogy once, except she had imagined the greater demon as a river bent on destruction. She could delay its plans by defeating the dyszoons—or so she had believed.

"You think I'm holding back how things should be,"

Daphne rasped. "That the demon will come no matter what I do."

It gripped Nathan's gravestone and leaned over her like a terrible judge. "Humans are doomed to fall ever farther into a grave of their own making. Any progress is merely a mirage that hides their long, slow defeat." She was ensnared by its black eyes. "There is no escaping this fate, Daphne Cole. It began long before you, and you cannot hold it back."

She had thought herself lost in a nightmare, but maybe the decayed surroundings had just stripped away the mirage of hope and laid the situation bare. Reality had revealed itself, and it was darkness.

The demon straightened. "There will be more deaths like these. The boy was the first. The rest will follow."

Second. Ethan was second. Heather was the first person to die, she corrected silently. Out of the shadow of memory and dream, the shade appeared and gripped her arm. *Don't give in. No matter what it tells you.*

Truth filled her lungs like a breath of cold air.

"You're lying," Daphne told it, rising on shaking ground. "The demon would kill everyone. But it won't. I'll make sure of it."

The demon contemplated her, Nathan's features as stony as the grave that separated them.

"Only one choice is left to you, and you will know it before the night is over," it said. "You cannot stop the river. A new order is coming."

"I know you're running out of time," Daphne retorted recklessly, thinking of the lighter sky she'd glimpsed earlier. Surely sunrise was imminent. The ignored footfalls shook the ground —her dad would be upon them soon.

"Perhaps." The demon's smile grew, grotesque on Nathan's face. "But what is time in a dream? We may only have a night together, but I'll tell you this, Daphne Cole: You could be in here forever."

Her insides curdled. "You're lying," she said, trying to sound confident but unable to hide the pitch of uncertainty in her voice.

"Am I?"

Could it be true? Time flowed differently in a dream. An hour could feel like a lifetime. In theory, she could spend years dodging the nightmare version of her dad and gasping the stale air.

A tree fell over nearby.

"I'll see you soon," the demon said, with no trace of doubt. "When you have realized the only path forward, come find me at the door."

Her feet moved without direction. The demon and the footfalls were gone hours ago, or maybe days. There was no way to tell time inside the nightmare. The demon had spoken truth—she could be trapped forever.

Fireballs exploded in succession, each a cannon blast. As she walked, dead branches snaked across each other, inter-twining limbs.

She had long left the graveyard, but each stone was a weight on her conscience. Those deaths would happen if she failed. And she already had. Ethan's face pressed into her eyes no matter how many times she tried to look away.

If she escaped this nightmare, reality was another. Hot tears fell down her face. His death was her fault. All her fault.

Fighting dyszoons wasn't enough. Had never been enough. The lesser demon had paved the path for its superior, and maybe for stronger dyszoons she wouldn't be able to battle. More people would die.

The greater demon's rise was inevitable. If she didn't know how to fight this demon that tormented her, what of the other? Once it arrived, her defeat was sealed.

If she joined it, however, she would be in a position to negotiate lives. The demon would likely oblige. After all, who would it rule over if everyone was dead?

The demon needed her. It had told her on the bridge that she was stronger than Ashley. A worthier candidate for its plans. Ashley was crushed by the weight of them and had grown sickly and weak, but Daphne could bear the burden.

She was playing a lost game. The dyszoons had never been the point. They were merely paving the path for the demon. Daphne's abilities had grown because of the battles, but it wasn't enough. The only way she could protect others from the demon was to play in its inner circle, not on the opposite team.

Daphne cut through the trees, careful even in her exhaustion not to touch any. She was so tired. Tired of running. Tired of carrying a weight she'd never asked for to begin with. What she wouldn't give for the nightmare to be over and to wake up having never heard of dyszoons. She could stop fighting and give in to the inevitable.

Don't give in. No matter what it tells you. But what about listening to her own voice? The demon had only told her what she suspected all along—that it was all pointless. However hard she tried, someone would die. Someone close to her.

It had taken Ethan's death to make her realize her mistake. Fighting dyszoons and bracing for the demon's rise wasn't the answer. It was a *gift*, really, that it had been him who died and not Nathan, or her mom, or Claire.

Underneath her grief was relief. His death was, in the demon's words, *tragic*. But he had existed in the periphery of her life. His was certainly not *as* tragic as other deaths.

A loud *boom* vibrated through Daphne's skull. She stopped

and clutched her head. The sound had broken the strand of her terrible thoughts, but she was in the same helpless position. Fresh grief washed over her.

She looked over her shoulder, feeling for the second time a set of eyes on her neck. The owl gazed down at her from a branch, glowing with light.

In its presence, the claws of despair and hopelessness loosened their grip. Peace wrapped around her like a shield. The owl hopped to a lower branch, close enough to touch.

"Who are you?" The strange question came naturally. It was outside the nightmare, and yet visible. It was real.

And familiar. The presence was the same one she'd met while hunting the dyszoons after the musical. *The musical.* A fragment of its melody reached her ears like the echo of a heavenly choir that had found its way to Hell.

The owl looked at her. She longed to touch it, this majestic creature of hope, and to have it stay with her until sunrise came. For sunrise was coming, and with it, the demon's departure. It had admitted its time was short. The nightmare *would* come to an end.

After that, there would be time. Time to discover what could be done to prevent the greater demon from rising. It *wasn't* inevitable. Already its position was precarious, being entirely dependent on Ashley, who was in poor health and had attempted to run from it. She was the weak link, and so the demon needed Daphne, if it could have her.

And it would go to any lengths to get her.

Daphne reached a trembling hand toward the owl. It was unmoving this time. The back of her fingers stroked its smooth feathers.

The owl and woods vanished. Flames filled her eyes. But they were gentle, confined in an ornate fireplace, cheerful and warm in the otherwise dark room. Familiarity ached inside her, a memory she couldn't place. It was home.

Too soon, the woods returned. Her hand hovered, but the owl was gone. Even so, a small flame of peace remained within her, something she sensed the nightmare couldn't extinguish.

A tree crashed nearby. Perhaps she'd been in the owl's vision longer than she thought, or else the nightmare played by its own rules. It had sensed the change within her and would hurry to throw its worst, to derail her from the right path before she'd begun to walk it.

Her dad forced a heavy leg over the log in front of him, setting it on fire. "Help me!" he cried, ash spilling from his mouth. He wrenched another leg over, a hand pressed against his stomach.

Daphne swallowed, a painful effort for her parched throat. She couldn't help the twisted nightmare version of him. But even as a nightmare, he was still her dad. She would run from him no longer.

"Help me, Daphne!" he yelled.

She lifted her torn dress and forced her feet forward.

"Help me!"

Her mind was blank with terror, but she continued.

"Help me!"

She stopped before him and let the dress go. He was quiet. His skin was blistered and burned, but the face was still her dad's, once handsome and full of life.

"I love you, Dad," she said, and wrapped her arms around his torso.

Her face lay against his chest, and she fully inhaled the scent of smoke and charred flesh. He shook. Daphne clung tighter, but his uniform was crumbling. He was disintegrating beneath her touch, but she held on.

Larger chunks of him fell like burning wood. Daphne opened her eyes. Her dad's arms were gone, and so were his legs. It was only her embrace that kept him upright. She looked up at his eyeless face, which gazed down to consider her in turn.

"Goodbye, Dad," Daphne said.

The rest of him crumbled. She held on until there was nothing to hold on to. No part of him was left, not even the little fires. The forest was still.

Daphne held out her palms. No trace of their encounter showed. He was truly gone.

She wiped her face, knowing the tears were smudging it worse than ever, but it didn't matter. There was no monster to outrun. He had fallen apart in her arms.

The forest, bright when the nightmare began, had noticeably dimmed. The red sky had darkened to the color of old blood, except for a lighter peach in one direction. It was a hellscape moving inescapably toward dawn, the final climax.

Daphne sensed the end of it all with equal parts hope and dread. The demon's time was almost over. It might not be able to touch her, but it wouldn't go quietly.

The worst was yet to come.

36

DEPARTURE

Daphne faced the lighter sky, where a sun would emerge if such a star existed in this place.

Some force was prompting her in that direction like a string tugging at her chest—the Veil, now making itself known.

When you have realized the only path forward, find me at the door.

The demon was waiting for her so it could secure her connection to the Veil. With her and Ashley helping the greater demon, its rise would be all but inevitable.

She would go to the bridge and face whatever came. Her path was clear, but it wasn't the one the demon expected. Having come precariously close to taking the wrong path, Daphne couldn't be certain that her decision was final. The nightmare wasn't over.

Daphne set out, imagining what she would do when they came face-to-face. The answer to defeating the lesser demon had never been in fighting it with straightforward blows. Instead, for hours, the battle had been fought in the mind.

With each nightmare relived, it had driven her toward

despair, toward believing lies. As she reversed the original outcome of each nightmare, she had pushed back those lies and clung to hope.

She wished the owl could have stayed with her, but the hope it gave her lingered somewhere untouchable within, providing the strength to move forward.

Something glowed ahead. The air had grown almost unbearably hot. Though knowing she was likely cold outside the nightmare, Daphne couldn't help but unzip her jacket as she approached the source of the light.

Below, a golden line of lava snaked around rocks that jutted out like needles. It had to be the creek, which meant she was nearly at the bridge. After running for hours through anonymous woods, the sight reoriented her.

Daphne followed the lava flow, drawn by the Veil. Her parched throat was like carpet. The road, bathed eerily in red from the sky's light, was ahead. She walked along it.

The Veil had grown bigger from the demon's arrival. Daphne's resolve slipped. It called her forward like a parent to a lost child, its pull stronger in the nightmare. The demon stood underneath it, looking dressed for the occasion in the formal gray tuxedo, Nathan's hands behind its back.

"Daphne Cole," the demon called, locking its black eyes on her. "You've arrived at last."

She stepped onto the bridge, equally dressed in her prom dress, though the effect was dampened by her jacket. It was a miracle her diamond hair clip was still in place.

"I'm not going to join you," Daphne said, ignoring the Veil's tug. "You can go back to Hell."

The demon smiled, not at all dismayed by this declaration. "I thought you would say that. But the night isn't over."

"I don't care what you tell me anymore. You're a liar," she

shouted with a scratched voice, made braver by the imminent end of the nightmare.

"Am I? Or do I show you truths you would rather not hear? A side of yourself you would rather not see?" the demon stepped closer. "I have seen your mind, Daphne Cole. I know what you fear."

"So what?" Daphne spread out her hands and let them drop. "It doesn't matter. You're almost out of time."

Its eyes narrowed. She had no trouble seeing only the demon. It was nothing like the real Nathan.

"I see," it said, each syllable clipped and dangerous. "If that's the path you have chosen, perhaps there is no need for you after all."

The stones beneath her feet pushed up. Daphne yelped and jumped ahead, but more stones were rising and threatening to pinch her feet between them. In seconds, they drove her farther onto the bridge and against the railing.

She was lifted up and over it. Her hands slid across the stones and stopped at the edge in time to prevent a fall onto the sharp rocks below. She dangled over an archway, kicking empty air.

The demon had drawn her into its final trap.

Daphne tried to lift herself, but the night's ordeal had sapped her strength. There was no way her brittle fingers, which were already losing feeling, could support her for long.

A fireball burst like a rocket from the lava and exploded. The demon's face peered over the railing without sympathy as fiery rain fell in a slow cascade behind its shoulders. Judgment had come.

"You won't last long, Daphne Cole."

"It's not real!" she gasped, straining to hold on. Her feet were practically baking over the lava.

"When you fall into the fire, can you tell that to *this*?" It tapped its forehead. "Even imagined pain can kill you, but you can save yourself. Pledge your service now and be honored, or refuse and die."

Sweat poured freely down her face. "No," Daphne rasped. Danger would pass with the sunrise—if her fingers held on.

"Who will protect your friends when you die? The boy won't be the last," it said, drawing a hand closer to hers, perhaps to pry it off. "His death was your fault."

"No!" she cried. Every word pierced her like the rocks would below.

Your fault, your fault, your fault, your fault.

Would the fall kill her? Even outside the nightmare, it would have been a tricky landing. She might sprain an ankle at the very least, or slip and knock her head.

Half a dozen fireballs burst from the lava and exploded in a succession of cannon blasts. The resulting vibrations nearly undid her grip.

"You won't last much longer, Daphne Cole," the demon said, nodding at the creek. To her horror, the lava was rising, hastening the decision. One way or another, she would lose. It was over.

An owl soared above the demon's shoulders and landed on the stone railing. It hooted at her, its feathers glowing brilliantly. In the light, the demon looked diminished.

"You came," she exhaled.

The demon frowned. "How can you see that?"

The lava stopped rising. Hope, hanging almost literally by a single finger, surged through her. A foreign cold breeze wafted over her sweaty face. She had forgotten what that felt like.

A little strength returned to her fingers. With a yell, Daphne thrust out a hand. It found a groove in the stone and clung there, followed by her other hand. She pulled, rising far enough to grasp the other side.

She twisted herself back onto the bridge, an awkward maneuver in the long dress, and stood.

The demon had backed away until it was underneath the Veil. For the first time, its eyes were widened in fear. Its hour was up, and it would have to report its failure to recruit her to the greater demon.

Daphne limped to the middle of the bridge but closer to the road, keeping her distance from the demon. The owl remained in the corner of her vision, and its presence strengthened her. Even now, the Veil was attempting to draw her in, enticing her to give it everything.

Once before, she'd stood in the same spot as the greater demon spoke to her through Ashley. It had tried to recruit her to its cause with visions and lies, just like the other demon had that night.

Her connection to the Veil had given the demon insight into her weaknesses, and consequently, its tools for trying again were surgical. The nightmare was an operation—cutting open her worst fears, tempting her to give up hope, and redefining what was real.

In more ways than one, she had come perilously close to the edge.

The creek erupted with fireballs. A multitude surged upward and exploded, as if they, too, sensed the end and had unleashed the finale. The demon cocked its head, the air behind it streaked with flame.

"Last chance, Daphne Cole," it said.

She raised both arms.

"Go to Hell."

Daphne pushed against it, no longer afraid of what might happen. The demon winced and clutched its head.

The lines of fire extinguished as the red sky broke into patches of a pale pink sunrise. Trees unfurled leaves from decay, their branches rustling in the cool breeze. The sound of trickling water came from nearby, though lava still flowed in the creek.

Any resemblance to Nathan rapidly faded as the demon's face whitened like ash and flaked away. Its time was up, and it was leaving, helped along by Daphne.

A force crashed into her mind, and she staggered. The demon was distracted and clutching its head, its departure inevitable. But the Veil filled her vision, tugging at her will. A final appeal.

Her connection to it was like an invisible hook she'd secured to herself before throwing the other end of the line into the abyss. While it was more tenuous than Ashley's, the connection was dangerous. It had made the waking nightmare possible and could conjure up something worse. In the uncertain road ahead, the Veil's hold on her was a weakness that could make her stumble when her strength mattered most.

The owl landed by her feet in a flutter of wings. Its presence anchored her as the Veil drew nearer, attempting to drive her to despair over the inevitable victory of the greater demon.

She perceived an invisible line that ran from her chest into the dark depths, the same that had drawn her to the bridge. However, she wouldn't make the mistake of striking the Veil again. Daphne yanked at the line and immediately doubled over. Pain clawed through her skin, but the hook had loosened.

Her knees crashed onto the stones. The owl flapped its wings. Screaming, she pulled at the line with all her might.

The line went slack and fell into the Veil, which wasn't in front of her, but back in its place above the demon. The connection was broken.

Daphne breathed in deeply, and fresh air filled her lungs. The nightmare was nearly over.

A lightness she hadn't felt for months drew her clumsily to

her feet. It was time to rid herself of darkness, at least for the day.

She struck at the demon. It collapsed to its knees, screeching in a voice that was no longer Nathan's. The hopelessness that had hounded her in the night was fading along with the demon's power.

Daphne threw all she had against it. Against the despair that had held her in its grip for so many months. Against the doubt that there could one day be victory.

The last of the nightmare world faded, revealing sky that had just broken with the dawn.

Her scream matched the demon's as the rest of it flaked away. Particles blew upward and were sucked into the void that was the Veil.

It was gone.

37

CONFESSION

Daphne blinked rapidly at the sunrise. The sky was light blue and fading pink, streaked with clouds. Only the Veil marred it, large and terrible.

Water trickled in the creek. The owl was gone, and she wished it had stayed. Maybe her mind had made it up, but she didn't think so.

Her prom dress, like her jacket and hair, was wet and dirty. Daphne walked along the side of the road, hugging herself against a bone-deep chill.

The nightmare, as she might have expected from past dreams, was fading with each step. She clung to the details, knowing Claire would want to hear them. Any small bit of information could help them in the battle ahead—the one that would decide everything.

Claire! Daphne halted, chilled deeper by the final piece of the real world as it set into place. *Mom.*

She removed her phone from her pocket and pressed the power button. Unlike before, the screen lit up, showing it was almost seven. For nearly six hours, though it felt much longer, she had been lost in the nightmare.

There were dozens of missed calls and texts from both women. It seemed Claire, like Daphne, had sensed the demon come out, even from states away. Her mom pleaded for her location, for a response.

Their words passed through Daphne, and she shut them out, unable to deal with the worry. *It's gone,* she texted Claire. *I'm fine* — she began typing, but deleted the message. It would be a long time before she was fine. The quick text would have to be enough.

When the psychic returned, they could discuss what came next and strategize how to handle the stronger dyszoons, as the demon's arrival had grown the Veil further. With her connection to it severed, the creatures would arrive without warning.

Daphne also suspected that any further visions of Ashley would cease. They could speculate whether she was truly back in the demon's service.

But first, her mom. Daphne didn't plan to listen to the voicemails, left as recently as half an hour ago, and hoped her mom hadn't called anyone for help. *I'm on my way home,* she texted. Inadequate, but it shared that she was safe.

Nathan had sent a final message before bed, and her heart twinged as she stuck her phone in her damp pocket. She needed more than a few minutes outside the nightmare to disassociate him from the demon.

Daphne reached her car, parked ahead of Ethan's vehicle. Nausea spun her stomach. His body was lying where she had first spoken to the demon, but she had no strength to find him, or to call the police and explain her suspicious role in discovering him. Soon, his family would report him missing and his car would be found.

And then him.

Daphne collapsed into her car, realizing distantly that the flowers of her corsage were blue, not decayed. She ripped it off and laid her head on the steering wheel, wanting nothing more than to sink into sleep and forget about everything.

One nightmare had ended, but she had stepped into another. Soon, a family's world would be shattered. The news of a death on prom night would spread like wildfire, and only a few would know the truth of how their classmate and friend had died.

She grabbed a water bottle from her back seat and chugged its contents. Her throat called out for more.

Daphne turned the car around, wondering if it was wise to drive, but there was little traffic. Her greatest longing was a hot shower and then to crawl into bed.

But both desires needed to wait. The morning had arrived, but the night wasn't finished yet. Her mom deserved an explanation.

A mile from home, Daphne realized she had no idea what to say. How to even begin. No imagined tale could soothe over the night's worries. Any attempt to make something up would only cause more harm.

Her attempts to shield her mom had only succeeded in distancing them. Daphne knew now that she had been foolish to try to protect her from that burden. Carrying it alone had almost ruined everything.

After a night of lies, she longed for truth. Lies shrouded the death of Heather, and now Ethan. The truth hurt, but it was preferable to false comfort. Her mom deserved that.

The demon's taunting words, which had been the only thing not manufactured in her mind, were slow to fade. It was gone, but she would need to continue untangling truth from lies, hope from despair. And that battle would always be there, thick with bullets at some points and a ceasefire at others.

She pulled into her driveway. The front door opened, and her mom stepped out, her face ragged as if she had also not slept. Her mouth dropped, aghast at her daughter's appearance.

Daphne paused before the porch steps. Despair made it nearly impossible to speak. "Mom, I have to tell you something," she choked out.

Her mom looked her over and gave a short nod, as if to herself. She stood back and held the door open.

Daphne walked up the steps, knowing she would have to explain why she was wet, cold, and splashed head to toe in mud. And also knowing, as she crossed the threshold, that there was no longer a place for lies.

And so Daphne resigned herself to tell her mom of the horrors of the night. To tell her everything.

ABOUT THE AUTHOR

Kaylin Wise was born and raised in Wisconsin. She doesn't believe in ghosts but loves a spine-tingling tale.

[O] instagram.com/kaylin.wise

www.ingramcontent.com/pod-product-compliance
Lightning Source LLC
Chambersburg PA
CBHW020349220726
48290CB00014B/1387